KIRINS
THE SPELL OF NO'AN

■ ■ ■

KIRINS
THE SPELL OF NOAN
Book One of a Trilogy

JAMES D. PRIEST

YELLOWSTONE PRESS
Shorewood, Minnesota

KIRINS:
The Spell of No'an

Published in the United States by Yellowstone Press.

Cover illustrations by Jim Rownd
Interior illustrations by Marc Johnson
Cover and book design by Marlene Maloney

Cataloging-in-Publication Data:
Priest, James D., 1938—
Kirins: The spell of no'an.
(Kirins, Book One)
1. Fantasy I. Series

Library of Congress Catalog Card Number: 90-90174

ISBN: 0-9626225-4-0

First Edition: September 1990

For information regarding the second book of this trilogy, write:
Yellowstone Press,
24020 Yellowstone Trail, Shorewood, MN 55331

DEDICATION

To my kind and courageous mother,
Gertrude Patterson Priest,
my first reader and my best listener.

ACKNOWLEDGMENTS

This series of novels was written with the help of many people and many books. I want to thank the Hennepin County Library, especially the Excelsior Branch. I have used volumes on subjects ranging from domestic hunting to prehistoric monuments to folklore. Many works on birds were consulted, but I would particularly like to acknowledge Hickman and Guy for *Care of the Wild Feathered and Furred.*

My son, Eric, was my primary consultant in every aspect of this project. Doug Benson was my private editor, and Elaine Smith was the final reviewer. Special thanks to Pauline Pennell for design, and Ed Ramaley and Laurie Grimm for preparation.

I have had numerous early readers, and all of them have contributed. This book belongs to them as much as it does to me.

J.D.P.
August, 1990

GLOSSARY OF
NAMES AND TERMS

Aassa (ah´ sa): squirrel ilon of Blinda

Alsinam (all´ si nahm): raven ilon of Ruggum Chamter

Aris (air´ iss): magical spirit burning within each living kirin

Barwood: tree with both life-giving and life-threatening capabilities

Berin (bear´ in): young boy of the Yorl clan

Biros (by´ ros): son of Silarude of the Grygla tribe

Blinda (blin´ da): girl of the Yorl clan, sister of Hutsin

Boros (bor´ os): member of the Grygla tribe

Bradley, Patrick: friend of Nathan Perry

Broms (broms´): member of the Grygla tribe

Bynaran (bin´ a ran): male of the Shillitoe tribe, father of Runagar

Calamar (cal´ a mar): shiny circular instrument with magical powers

Curlace (cur´ lace): ancient magical language and bond between kirins and their animal and bird partners

Diliani (dee lee on´ ee): female of the Yorl clan

Duan (du on´): magician to the Moger clan

Fairinin (fair´ in in): healing area in the Shillitoe cave

Fairinor (fair´ in or): healer of the Shillitoe tribe

Faralan (far´ a lon): raven ilon of Talli

Footling: name kirins apply to themselves in English-speaking lands

Fuadru Vez (fu ahd´ ru vez´): magician to the Zota clan

Gilin (gi´ lin): youth of the Moger clan, cousin of Hutsin

Glinivar (glin´ i var): sandhill crane ilon, donated by the Shilliron tribe for the use of Runagar

Golin (go´ lin): magician to the Stunfin clan

Gronom (grah´ num): relentless, earth-bound tracking and destroying creature

Grygla (grig´ la): tribe of underground creatures living in the environs of the Shillitoe cave

Gunvir (gun´ vir): helper to the fairinor of the Shillitoe tribe

Halsit (hal´ sit): young male of the Yorl clan

Hodorvon (ho´ dor von): formerly magician to the Shillitoe tribe, now dead; brother of Lanara, grandfather of Runagar

Hutsin (hut´ sin): youth of the Yorl clan (Hut), cousin of Gilin

Ilon (eye´ lon): animal or bird under magical control of kirins

Issar (iss´ ar): elder male of the Shillitoe tribe

Jarod (jar´ od): youth of the Moger clan, brother of Gilin

Kalas (ka´ las): plant from which kirins make rope and twine

Kirin (ki´ rin): intelligent being, one foot tall

Lanara (lan ar´ a): ancient queen of the Shillitoe tribe

Lidor (lie´ dor): magician, healer, and fairinor to the Shillitoe tribe

Lindor (lin´ dor): young boy of the Shillitoe tribe, grandson of Lidor

Lisam (lee´ sahm): raven ilon of Hutsin

Loana (lo ah´ na): raven ilon of Gilin

Loos (loos´): senior curlace practitioner of the Shilliron tribe

Lugor (lu´ gor): senior curlace practitioner of the Moger clan

Manay (man ay´): raven ilon of Diliani

Moger (mo´ ger): kirin clan occupying Rogustin; clan of Gilin, Talli, and Reydel

No'an (no´ ahn): ancient magical spell making kirins invisible to human beings

Ocelam (oh´ si lahm): raven ilon of Speckarin

Olamin (oh´ la min): magician from the north who passed secret knowledge to Talli, Gilin, and Reydel before his death

Orann (or an´): magical word of greeting from kirins to their ilon

Perry, Christopher: twelve-year-old human boy

Perry, Nathan: fourteen-year-old human boy who discovers Gilin

Rana (rah´ na): female of the Shillitoe tribe, mother of Runagar

Reydel (ray del´): girl of the Moger clan

Rogalinon (ro gal´ in on): home tree of the Yorl clan, meaning "Sublime Guardian" in Ruvon

Rogustin (ro gus´ tin): home tree of the Moger clan, meaning "Anchorage" in Ruvon

Ruggum Chamter (rug´ um cham´ ter): overseer of the Yorl clan

Runagar (run´ a gar): youth of the Shillitoe tribe, blessed with a voice of magic

Ruvon (ru´ von): ancient kirin dialect, common to clans the world over, the only language in which kirins read and write

Shilliron (shil´ i ron): kirin tribe neighboring the Shillitoes

Shillitoe (shil´ i toe): cave-dwelling tribe of kirins

Silarude (sil´ a rude): leader of the Grygla tribe

Speckarin (spek´ a rin): magician to the Yorl clan

Stala (stah´ la): squirrel ilon of Hutsin

Stopal (sto´ pul): squirrel ilon of Hutsin's grandfather

Strika (strik´ a): young boy of the Yorl clan

Stunfin (stun´ fin): kirin clan neighboring the Yorl and Moger trees

Tallis (ta´ lis): girl of the Moger clan (Talli)

Tominyeto (tom in yet´ o): herb used by kirins to prevent inflammation and infection

Tomlin, Michael: friend of Nathan Perry

Valtar (vahl´ tar): tree architect to the Yorls and surrounding clans

Versteeg, John: grandfather of Christopher and Nathan Perry

Volodon (vo´ lo don): relentless, airborne tracking and destroying creature

Xorin (zor´ in): magician to the Yorl clan before Speckarin

Yorl (yor´ l): kirin clan occupying Rogalinon; clan of Speckarin, Ruggum Chamter, Diliani, and Hutsin

Zota (zo´ ta): kirin clan neighboring the Yorl and Moger trees

P R O L O G U E

HAVE YOU EVER
wondered whether leprechauns, gnomes, or elves truly exist?
How could the notion of such a shrewd and undersized
creature have originated? The fact is that a substantial
number of these beings have coexisted with humanity since
our inception on Earth.

Furthermore, have you ever had the feeling that you were
able to predict the future, envision a remote occurrence at the
moment it was happening, or in some intangible way
interpret the world surrounding you, as if through a sixth
sense? If you have experienced this, as nearly everyone has,
you have been touched by the intriguing race that inhabits
this planet with us.

In English-speaking lands they whimsically call
themselves "footlings," and for two reasons: Their height is
the length of a man's foot, and their feet are by far the most
outstanding features of their bodies. A race with humanlike
intelligence, they have long maintained a surveillance of
human beings. Yet for eons they have steadfastly preserved
the secrecy of their existence from humankind. Since the
beginnings of recorded history, few men and women have

had the opportunity to communicate with them. But the many legends and stories regarding small, precocious beings have arisen from these infrequent encounters.

No matter where they live the world over, they sustain a familiarity with the local human language. But they communicate among themselves in regional dialects and in an ancient tongue known only to them, and in this they call themselves kirins. While they may live anywhere on Earth, they tend to dwell in areas sparsely inhabited by human beings, a practice they developed to protect themselves over this long period of coexistence.

As long as they live, within each of these creatures burns a flame of magic. This spiritual core, known as aris, was powerful in the distant past. But it has become more fragile over their many thousands of years of subsistence, making life itself more tenuous now than ever before. Even worse, in recent times a new peril has arisen in the kirin world, and this account begins under circumstances never before experienced in the history of kirin life.

PART ONE

■ ■ ■

C H A P T E R   1

THE TERRIFIED KIRINS raced through the forest faster than they ever had before. Talli finally glanced behind and saw no trace of their dreaded pursuer. They were too fast for the brutal gronom, to Talli's profound relief.

She could not see it, but she knew it was tracking them in its unforgiving and relentless fashion. Tiring, she slowed, believing that at least for the moment they were out of its reach.

Gilin slackened his pace also, and eventually he and Talli stopped for a rest.

"Farith kir lucolan?" panted Gilin in the kirin tongue, questioning what they could possibly do next.

"We cannot return to the clan!" answered Talli, trying to catch her breath.

Her long hair was blond, and her eyes were a vibrant green. Gilin's hair was dark, his glimmering eyes black. Both wore the pale yellow tunic and trousers of the Moger clan; on their long feet were hiking moccasins.

Gilin nodded, swallowing hard. The youths knew only too well that they could not retreat to the home tree, and it was just beginning to dawn on them how alone they really were. Olamin, the ailing magician, had warned them that the gronom would stalk only kirins who carried the secrets Olamin had unveiled to the two of them and to Reydel. He said it would stop at nothing to obtain access to its prey, and that it would destroy any defender of the victim in its path, or be destroyed itself. And worse, through keen telepathic senses, other gronoms would know when one of their kind had been slain. They would desist from whatever gruesome tasks they might be undertaking and descend in numbers upon the scene. They would persist mercilessly until they captured the victim their dead counterpart had been seeking. Should the youths return home, the magician had warned, their entire clan would be in grave jeopardy. It was common knowledge that, even though seldom necessary, a kirin clan would defend one of its members to the death.

A slight tremor of the ground signaled the approach of the methodical creature and brought the thoughts of the young kirins back to their imminent danger. Through the low brush and grass they could begin to see, still at a distance, the astonishing appearance and stealthy oncoming movement of the gronom. The creature had two arms and two legs and a hairless body. Its head was stark and bare, and where its face should have been, it was blank. It had no ears, no eyes, no nose, and no mouth, only a smooth and featureless visage.

The shaken youths realized they had no time to waste. Deeply reluctant to make mention of it, Talli forced herself to repeat an admonition Olamin had pronounced before his recent demise, sound in principle, but onerous to put into practice. The knowledge he had imparted to them must be preserved, the old magician had stressed, and it was more acceptable that its survival be in the memory of one kirin than in none at all. Talli knew what they had to do, as did Gilin.

After slight hesitation it was the dark-eyed Gilin who spoke. "We must . . . separate, Talli."

Their right feet touched in the time-honored gesture of greeting, parting, joy, and sorrow. They were fully aware that they might never see each other again, nor any of their clan, and that if one of them escaped the other might not. And both had witnessed what occurs when a gronom seizes its prey.

Their antagonist was now so close they could hear it pushing steadily through the undergrowth. They looked grimly at each other a last time, and then turned and started off in different directions. The gronom, taking any advantage possible to secure its quarry, intuitively gauged the ages of the youths, and then in its mechanical fashion began stalking Gilin, the younger of the two. Neither kirin knew which of them was being followed. But Talli hoped it was her, and Gilin hoped it was him, so that the other might escape.

Talli's course was at first eastward. She moved along at a steady pace through the woods, with the loping gait found nowhere in the world but among kirins. Her only discomforts were the pain of separation from Gilin and her memories of Reydel. Realizing that she could not run on forever ahead of the tireless creature, she began to wonder where she could possibly go. Despite a deep desire to return to the shelter of her home, she knew that she could not do so because of the destruction this would bring upon family and clan.

As she continued to run, now tiring, she longed to be traveling in the manner customary for kirins of her clan, on the back of a raven, in serene flight high above the trees and out of reach of the gronom, rather than traversing the forest floor. Then gradually a plan began to formulate in her mind: Could she possibly summon her raven and at the same time not alert her clansmen of her presence? She would then be able to escape the gronom! But, she realized, she would still be alone. Nonetheless, her alternatives were few, and none appeared as viable as this. She decided that she must take the chance. Aware that she would be imperiling her clan, she altered her course northward and headed toward the home tree.

As she ran onward her thoughts drifted back to Olamin. In the past few enlightening days with the old magician before his death, he had taught the three innocent youths many things about their race, things of which they and their clansmen were completely unaware. He told them about occurrences in the dim past, unfathomable events of the present day, and what the somber future would bring for all kirins should certain influences remain unchecked. By making them receptacles of his knowledge, he had unwillingly but knowingly forced them into the arena of battle, into unheard-of hostilities, not only with deadly creatures such as gronoms, but with the abominable forces behind them. The saddened magician had profoundly regretted the necessity of informing the youngsters because of the dire consequences of their knowing. But he had also realized he was going to die. He knew the knowledge was vital for the survival of the kirin race, and in the end he unburdened himself of his deepest secrets. And thus the unwitting youths, who had come to know the dying magician purely by chance, were adopted as his only disciples.

But now each of us is alone, thought Talli, bringing herself back to grim reality. Then, realizing that it would do no good to dwell on this, she redirected her thoughts to something more hopeful—her raven—and she pictured the two of them together, flying unencumbered through the skies. But even as she did so, she felt a new fear. The old magician had, of course, warned them about gronoms. But he had only vaguely alluded to other repugnant creatures that also sought kirins with the secret knowledge, creatures even more potent and dangerous than the gronom. Olamin had known little of them, had never encountered one himself, and had only heard of them through other magicians. However, what he did know and had imparted to Gilin, Talli, and Reydel was the most important way in which the other beings differed from the gronom. They could fly, while gronoms were strictly creatures of the earth. Olamin had been relatively certain that none of these had been sighted as far north and west as they were now. Nonetheless, the idea of such a flying beast, if it were anything like the gronom, began to distress Talli deeply as she continued onward.

It was a considerable trek for the young kirin, but she ran

as much of the time as she could. The closer she came to home, the greater became her pangs of loneliness and helplessness. She slowed to a walk when she was near enough to almost see Rogustin, the home tree, but she remained careful to avoid any of her compatriots who might be out at this time in the woods. Deciding she might be near enough for the bird to hear her call, she glanced about to be certain no other kirins were in proximity. She moved cautiously into a position from which she could see the uppermost branches of the tree. She cupped her hands to her mouth and was about to make a familiar sound, when she suddenly noticed two other kirins coming through the underbrush only a short distance away.

"My favorite food is the acorn from the chestnut oak," one of them was saying. "Too bad we must wait for them until fall!"

Talli stepped quickly behind the trunk of a tree, and she caught her breath when she recognized who they were. Gilin's father and older brother were making their way toward the clan tree.

"I was sure Gilin was exploring there with his friends," said Jarod, passing but a short distance from Talli. "Otherwise, I would never have taken you all that way. I wonder where he could be? He's been gone into the forest so much lately! Today he was gone all day!"

"No matter," replied the father. "We had a fine walk. But you're absolutely right. We haven't seen much of him recently, and nothing of him today."

Talli nearly called out to tell them why, to tell them about Gilin and herself, and Reydel, and where they had been, and about the dangers of which local kirins knew nothing, dangers rampant in the woods in which they so serenely and precariously existed, about the vulnerability of the entire kirin race, and of her tiredness and loneliness. Instead, she shuddered, waiting until they climbed the tree and were out of sight.

She collected herself and again prepared to summon her

raven. She raised her hands to her mouth, and looking upward uttered a series of four muted sounds. She lowered her hands, raised them again, and repeated the same sequence. Within moments she detected movement high in the tree, and then saw her raven, Faralan. He flapped his sable wings, rose into the air from a towering branch, and glided imperturbably downward, alighting upon the ground next to her. Talli could only hope that no one else had witnessed it.

"Orann," she said softly to the giant bird, a word of greeting customary between a kirin and an ilon, a word imbued with ancient magic. The raven stood alertly and resolutely as the young kirin mounted and entwined her long feet beneath his neck. Talli spoke another phrase. The black bird unfolded his great wings and lifted off the ground. They moved gracefully upward through branches and past the tops of the trees, and then leveled off and continued onward, the raven awaiting further instruction.

As they flew, Talli looked back at Rogustin, the home tree of the Moger clan. She even caught a glimpse of the door of her own family's dwelling. But then the tree slowly receded and began to blend into the forest as they moved higher and farther away. Torn by emotion and yet aware of what must be done, she forced herself to turn away from the scene. Gazing forward, she gave commands to the raven to initiate an easterly course, not knowing whether she would ever see her forest again.

C H A P T E R   2

FLYING HAD ALWAYS
been Talli's greatest pleasure. Her overview of the scenery as
it passed continuously below, the rush of air over her face and
around her body, and the oneness of herself with her raven
combined to give sheer delight. Even now, as Faralan
climbed to a higher altitude and Talli's blond hair flowed
behind, her spirits began to rise as she had anticipated they
would. But on this occasion the enjoyment was tempered by
the painful awareness that they were coursing ever farther
from the home tree.

Nonetheless, the atmosphere was clean and clear and it
seemed as if she could see for several clan dominions in all
directions. As she searched the skies she could find nothing
approaching through the air, no flying monsters, no
creatures of doom, only the usual complement of wood
thrushes, blue jays, and other birds fluttering to and fro on a
sunny and peaceful afternoon, intent upon their daily
business. The contrast between the picture before her now
and the trouble and worry she had left below struck her as
almost inconceivable. Here, flying through the air, she
began to have the sensation that she might be above it all.

At least for the moment she might have a respite and be out of imminent danger.

Not wishing to alter this newly found feeling of safety, she continued onward for a considerable period of time. She would not allow herself to dwell on what had transpired or what was ahead, except that she had a mission to fulfill. She leaned forward and spoke encouraging words to Faralan, intended as much for herself as for the raven.

But as she flew on, it became obvious that she was exhausted, and she started to become aware of hunger, which, because of the strain she had been suffering, she had not felt for some time. Soon she perceived a stream of silver curling through a lush thicket of dark green. A grove of oaks, she surmised, and she spoke to her raven, instructing that he descend. Sailing effortlessly to earth, they landed near the moving water and Talli dismounted. She released the bird to find sustenance, and after enjoying a cool drink of water herself, she collected and ate enough of nature's offerings in the form of fruits and mushrooms to be satisfied and packed the excess away in her back and belt sacks.

Reclining beside the stream, she closed her eyes, hoping to rest; but instead all-too-familiar images of the recent past re-entered her consciousness, and she thought of Gilin. What had become of him? She desperately wished to know. Had he evaded the onslaught of the nightmarish gronom? Wondering whether she would ever see him again, she remembered the toe ring.

She sat up and looked down at her right foot. The ring was on the third toe. It had been Olamin's. Before he died he removed it and gave it to her, at the same time he gave his calamar to Gilin. To Reydel, a younger girl than Talli, he had given a parchment with mysterious writings from the past, from many years before Olamin was born, but Talli had witnessed its unhappy fate at the hands of the gronom. All three of the objects were magical and had properties Olamin had tried to explain. But the three youths' exposure to him was brief, and by the time he chose to pass on to them both his knowledge and his unique possessions, his years of learning and experience were by necessity compressed and abbreviated, and were presented to the youths in a short but precious period of time.

As Talli removed the ring from her toe, she began to review what little Olamin had been able to express regarding it. Made of silver, and with no markings, it was large enough for the third toe of a mature kirin. Talli had been told that she must hold the ring in her hands and look through it, and that if all of the necessary elements were in harmony, and her mental processes operating appropriately, images would become visible in the hollow space within the ring. As she recalled, a vapor would first appear, and then obscure outlines, but eventually true pictures might be seen, and even sounds heard, and actual communication would take place.

She had never seen this happen in the presence of Olamin. But the old magician had explained that when conditions were precisely right, and when she was in dire need of what the ring was capable of doing, she would find a way to employ it. Olamin had gone on briefly, giving her a few ideas on how to initiate the ring's powers. But the old magician was failing and had little time. He did say that the ring might behave differently in the possession of another owner, and that Talli would discover her own methods for bringing it to life. But how? thought Talli. I need it now! She sat gazing at the open circle, nothing appearing within its confines but her natural surroundings—the earth, the trees, and the sky—which she could see through it.

Then her thoughts returned to Gilin, and to the calamar that had been bestowed upon him, a round gleaming piece that seemed more powerful even than the ring. Olamin had suggested that these two objects, the toe ring and the calamar, both of which had been possessed by him for so long a time, could even communicate with each other. An idea suddenly came to Talli. Perhaps she could locate Gilin with the ring.

Now, as she sat and looked through the ring, her enthusiasm was bolstered and she began thinking on a higher level. She had been instructed that the ring would work in concert with her mind, or her consciousness, in rendering its magical imagery and communication. But she was uncertain how to activate it. Olamin had said that one must concentrate in order for it to begin to function. In fact, as Talli thought back on it, one factor the magician emphasized was that the user must clear her mind of all else, and be concentrating upon a single idea or concept in order for the ring to become active.

Talli closed her eyes and began to allow a variety of thoughts to pass through her mind. Vaguely recalling that it should be something desirable, all of the images she conjured up were at first pleasurable: climbing to the top of a brilliantly colored maple in early fall, the smell of wood smoke from the gathering fire, a cloudless blue sky, hiking with good friends in the home woods, warm honey mushrooms for breakfast, and a spectacular flight upon her raven. After concentrating on each of these she opened her eyes and looked, but to her chagrin, nothing was happening in the ring. Nevertheless she persevered, picturing numerous other scenes in her mind's eye, enticing, enchanting, and beautiful ones, but nothing changed.

She decided to alter her approach entirely, and to conceive of things unpleasant and unsavory, which were not difficult for her to imagine after recent events. Yet still nothing happened. After a multitude of thoughts, ideas, and concepts had gone through her mind, she gave up, frustrated, and placed the ring back on her toe.

She glanced about, her green eyes glistening. She had effectively been removed from the world around her for a substantial length of time. Shadows were now lengthening, the sun was waning, and dusk was not far off. She would be spending the night alone, and she shuddered as she thought about gronoms and even more appalling creatures.

Refreshed with food and drink, Faralan had waited all the while nearby for a command. His young mistress, however, was perplexed and undecided about what to do. She could not return home because of dangers to the clan should she do so.

The idea of traveling onward to the east so frightened her that she was almost overwhelmed, even though the revelations of Olamin had clearly dictated that eventually she must go. But, she reasoned, it was never intended that I go by myself! The journey would be unbearably long and perilous even for a traveling party! But my chances of attaining the goal alone are minuscule! And what could I possibly accomplish by myself, should I be fortunate or perhaps unfortunate enough to arrive at the destination?

Distraught and confused, Talli stood up and began to walk by the stream. To make matters worse, she suddenly remembered that a gronom or some other gruesome being might close in on her at any time, and might be doing so even at that moment! She stopped and looked in every direction, and even searched the skies for any sign of an attacker, but saw none. She knew that she was being hunted and that it was only a matter of time before she would be found. But she had no way of knowing when it might happen.

If only I could contact Gilin, she thought with anguish. Could he also have escaped the gronom? Is he still alive? The two of us appear now to be the only ones left with the information that Olamin imparted. I must find Gilin! Could I possibly go back with Faralan and search for him? But I have no idea where to look, and the forest is vast!

Bewildered, the young kirin sat down forlornly by the stream, her head in her hands. As the light of day continued to decline and darkness took sway, she finally raised her eyes and made a startling discovery: The ring on her toe was giving off a dim light. With excitement she recalled something Olamin had said almost casually while attempting to explain all he could to his three young charges. For some, he suggested, the ring might operate better at night than during the daytime. This had not been the case for him, however. He had been able to use it only in the light of day.

"That's it!" cried Talli out loud, removing the ring from her toe. "It will work for me at night!"

Faralan turned and looked inquisitively at his mistress.

But then, recognizing that these were not commands, he returned to his relaxed and obedient posture.

Talli took the ring in both hands. It was, of course, a toe ring, and as kirins' feet are far larger than their hands, the diameter of the ring was the same as the width of her palm. The polished silver glittered under the full moon, reflecting its light. As she studied the ring she noticed that the glow seemed to wax and wane in concordance with the moonlight, fading perceptibly when the moon disappeared behind a cloud and intensifying when it shone fully once again.

She stared impatiently at the ring, puzzled over what to do next. She rubbed it, put it back onto her toe, took it off, dipped it in the stream, buffed it with her tunic, and concentrated on good things and bad things as she looked through it. But nothing seemed to help. Except for the pale glowing, it appeared completely inert. It would do nothing more.

Fatigued and frustrated, she gave up again and slipped the ring back onto her toe. She realized she must find a place to spend the night, and, as was characteristic for a kirin of this region, she wished to be in a tree. Having earlier seen a healthy-looking oak but a short distance away, she summoned the raven, climbed aboard, and spoke a few words of instruction. The giant bird flapped into the air and headed for the tree by the light of the moon. It alighted upon one of the lower boughs and Talli dismounted. With little difficulty she located a comfortable hole in which to rest, and then settled herself for what she knew would be an uneasy stay. Her ilon remained on a branch close to her, alert and patient.

Talli's sleep was indeed restless, but the night passed without incident. A short time before sunrise, while dreaming of a delightful foraging expedition into the woods near home, she awoke and all of the misery of her predicament abruptly returned. Sitting up, she saw that the ring was still producing a perceptible glow. She reached down and once again slid it off her toe. I will try once more, she thought, but with little hope of success. As she reclined on her back, part way out of the hole, she held the ring upward with both hands as directed by Olamin, and looked through it, moving it left and right, upward and downward. By chance as she guided the ring about at arm's length, she angled it into the direction of the waning moon and stopped to sight the orb through the circle. The glow of the ring intensified immediately and a mist began to cloud her view of the moon. Looking quickly about, she could see no morning fog elsewhere, and she looked back into the ring. The thickening vapor was confined within the circumference of the illuminated circle.

She sat up excitedly, careful to continue holding the ring in the direction of the full moon. I have something now, she told herself! It is working, but what should I do next? I won't have much time before the moon has faded into the forthcoming daylight! Again she concentrated, this time frantically, attempting to recall Olamin's explanations. She remembered once more what he had said about what one desired, or what one wanted to see most of all. Of course, she had attempted all sorts of thoughts of this kind the day before and nothing had happened. But now the ring was active! What did she want most to see? Without question it was Gilin, and she fixed her attention upon him.

Instantly the cloudiness within the ring began to clear. An image gradually became visible, blurred at first and then more defined, almost as though the ring were homing in on its subject. Finally, to her great delight, she could clearly see Gilin. By the earliest light of day he was bending over to awaken another kirin, sleeping beside a squirrel in a tree hole. And then to her astonishment she could hear Gilin's voice. "We must move on," he was saying to his companion.

C H A P T E R   3

T HE SMELL of cooked
morel mushrooms was waning as the sweet smoke of the
central fire began to drift across the gathering place. It was a
circular wooden platform securely fit between the boughs of
a giant oak—a considerable climb even for a kirin—above
the forest floor. While kirins can and do live almost
anywhere, they have a tendency to make their homes above
ground, high overhead if possible, out of harm's reach. In
many areas of the world their preferred residence is in trees,
and their natural allies in their lofty homes are the birds and
tree-dwelling animals of the region.

Since time immemorial kirins have had a special kinship
with animals and birds. Many species have become
associated with the small beings, or have come under their
influence, in various reaches of the Earth. It is not surprising
then that the gathering on this evening was shared by beast
and kirin alike.

The fire, small by human standards but memorable to two
young kirins on this occasion, burned brightly at the center of
the gathering place. Flames and embers on a flat stone
fireplace were contained by a border of larger stones. The

blaze projected enough light for the two of them to dimly visualize undulating shapes and outlines at the periphery of the circle, the creatures of their clan, maintaining a patient vigil at the outer edge of the platform.

Kirins have had sufficient experience with the human race to recognize when their undertakings are detectable by human beings, and thus treacherous for themselves, and when they are not. A clan gathering, even with a fire, has proven to be a safe activity. The circular wooden structure, central to the life of the clan, is always purposefully positioned at such a height, and in such a location, that it is camouflaged neatly by the boughs of the tree. Should a human happen to pass by and glance upward, the flames would be impossible to see. And the smoke drifts silently away through the branches and dissipates harmlessly into the air.

The two youngsters involved in that day's encounter stood restlessly near the fire, slightly apart from their families, awaiting the start of the meeting. Behind them, both on the smooth wooden surface and in nearby branches of the tree, the remainder of the clan waited also, each member clad in garments of light brown.

On this chilly spring evening, the two boys were to be recognized; their part in events of the day would be discussed before the entire clan. The others wore foot coverings, but because they were to be acknowledged, the boys' prominent feet were bare, and were becoming cold. They were uneasy as they waited, and anxious for the gathering to begin.

All at once heads turned and conversations ceased when a small door at the edge of the gathering place slowly opened. Inside the portal, carved into one of the largest branches of the oak, was a darkened chamber. Presently a light began to glimmer within the dim space, and as it grew in strength it emerged from the darkness, carried chest high by a hooded kirin and illuminating his grave countenance. The light was not fire, but a glowing greenish-white luminescence, and anyone who had ever been near it had marveled that it was not warm, that its lucent container was actually cool to the touch.

The elderly kirin stepped methodically toward the center of the gathering, toward the fire, his dark green eyes glittering in its light. His moustache and beard were blond but graying, his full-length gown was yellow, and his long feet, bare like those of the two boys, projected far beyond its hem.

He stopped before the fireplace, and across the flames he surveyed the assemblage and the two youths. The birds and animals that surrounded the clan, normally calmer and quieter than any human could expect to see them, were now completely motionless as the kirins waited for their magician to speak. He placed his light upon a standard to his left, indicating to all that he was ready.

"Two young members of our family of kirins, the Yorl clan, encountered certain phenomena today for the first time," began Speckarin in Ruvon, the ceremonious language reserved for spiritual or solemn occasions and known to kirins the world over. "First, they experienced their initial contact with human beings, and second, they perceived the powers of the spell of no'an."

As he spoke, both the luster of his orb and the blaze of the gathering fire appeared to gain in intensity, to work in synergy to brighten the surrounding scene. All of the members of his clan were present, sixty-four in number.

"Will the two in question and their witnesses step forward?" said the magician.

Strika first, and then Berin, moved slowly away from their families and closer to the fire. From two other areas of the crowd Ruggum Chamter, a bearded clan elder, and Diliani, a tall young woman, also came forward. The four stopped before the fire opposite the magician, light flickering on their faces.

Continuing in Ruvon, Speckarin addressed the two youths. "An encounter with humans resurrects old questions and fears, and occasionally leads to serious confrontation," he said. Then, looking over their heads toward the crowd, he went on. "After the recounting of today's events, I will attempt to answer inquiries, in hopes of avoiding future disaster. In addition, I will endeavor to explain something about the history of kirin magic.

"Now," said the magician, turning back to the youths, "the clan would like to hear every detail of your experience."

Hesitantly at first, the younger Berin began, and with Strika's help the two youngsters began to unfold, partly in the formal Ruvon but mostly in the common tongue of the clan, the following version of events that day.

■ ■ ■

The lads had marveled at their find. Even at their ages they were aware that morel mushrooms, a delicacy among kirins, appear only in early spring at about the time lilacs blossom. They had been dispatched to forage for mushrooms for the first time by themselves, and had seen many clusters of other varieties as they walked through the woods on this bright cool morning. But as they happened into an area of small ash and maple trees, sunlight beaming through the branches to create a patchwork of light and dark on the moist forest floor, they were amazed. It was a veritable garden of the coveted fungi, with their unmistakable ridges and hollows.

Could you have seen the lads as they surveyed their discovery, no greater in height than the tallest morel, you would have noticed one feature: their feet.

In general form, except for overall size, kirins resemble human beings. But one difference, and by far the greatest, is their feet. Born with feet of the same relative size as humans, the feet of these beings grow at an enormous rate during their first few years of life. At adolescence they reach complete dimension: between one third and one half the length of their bodies. Not unusually wide, at maturity their feet are long and narrow. One might surmise that pedal extremities of this magnitude would be cumbersome, detrimental to dextrous movement. On the contrary, the feet of kirins are capable of propelling them to lengths, heights, and velocities that would otherwise be unattainable for beings of their stature. In fact, the larger the foot, the more agile the kirin seems to be.

They traditionally prefer to wear nothing on their feet. But for protection against terrain and weather they don foot coverings, and for this excursion into the woods the two young lads were in light moccasins.

Kirins have vision of extreme acuity. But a second difference from human beings is the coloration of their eyes. Their irises range from bright green to dark green to black.

Their amazement at the morels dissipating, the lads went right to work. Out came pruning knives, with which even youths of their age were trusted, and they began incising the hollow stems of the morels. They worked separately and without conversation until each had severed the caps of about twenty mushrooms from their stems. Then they worked together, half carrying, half dragging the furrowed caps to a central location. In a fashion in which kirins have hunted prized mushrooms for centuries, their task had been to find the morels, cut them apart, and stack the edible caps in a place where they would remain safe and intact until the clan could aid in removing them. The youths were tiring, and yet elated at their find, envisioning the accolades they would receive from family and clan.

The sudden cracking of a branch, followed by the unmistakable shuffling sounds of huge feet coming through leaves and brush, stopped the lads in their tracks. Making no attempt to flee, they quietly backed a short distance away, and then stood stock-still.

The oncoming pair of humans were a long way from home, also out foraging, also for morel mushrooms. They came toward the kirins, their eyes searching one side of the pathway and then the other, when the woman suddenly caught sight of the leveled mushrooms. She stopped and surveyed them as the man went around her, continuing to explore.

After a few moments she called out. "Barney," she said. "Stop! Come back here! You won't believe this!"

He hurried back.

"Well, look at those!" he said. "Someone's cut them and just left 'em here! I wonder why?"

"They look good, don't they?" she asked. "Do you think there could be anything wrong with them?"

He crouched, picked one up and then stood up, examining it in his large hand.

"No bugs and no worms," he said. "They look just fine to me."

She glanced about the sunlit glade.

The youthful kirins stood but a short distance away, frustrated and worried, not because they might be seen (although uncharacteristically they remained in plain view, making no attempt to hide), but because of their cache of mushrooms. It was about to be removed, and there was nothing whatsoever they could do about it.

"I don't see anyone around," said the woman, squatting down intently, "and there's no reason to waste good morels. In fact *beautiful* morels!"

To the consternation of the young kirins who could only watch, she began picking up the treasured mushrooms and placing them one by one in her bag.

C H A P T E R   4

AT THIS POINT in the lads' rendering of the encounter Speckarin raised his arms. "You may stop," he said. "I would like your two witnesses, Ruggum Chamter and Diliani, to continue the telling from there. But first let us tend to the gathering fire."

The smoldering incandescence, which had gradually diminished during the tale, was restoked. As it blazed brightly once more Speckarin called upon Ruggum Chamter, a respected overseer of the clan, and he related the following account of subsequent happenings.

■ ■ ■

The woman abruptly ceased collecting the mushrooms and stood up quickly when a huge black bird drifted downward from the tree above and landed between her and the morels. There it held its ground, looking up at her. The startled humans began to back away when another sable bird, even larger than the first, alighted next to its counterpart. It remained unmoving also, staring almost defiantly at the man and the woman.

The man called out and waved his arms, trying to frighten the two ravens. "Shoo! Get away!" he cried.

But the giant birds had stationed themselves directly in front of the accumulated morels and reacted like no other wild creatures the humans had ever seen. The birds retained their positions steadfastly, even resolutely, apparently unafraid of the human beings. When the couple later had an opportunity to discuss what had transpired, they agreed that the birds had actually appeared to be protecting the mushrooms.

"There's something wrong with these crows," said the man hoarsely. "I don't want anything to do with them. Just leave the mushrooms and let's get out of here!"

The woman hesitated for a few moments. The larger raven took a step toward her and threw back its head, and from it poured forth a melody more enchanting than any they had ever heard. The humans looked at each other in astonishment and began backing away, only to be pursued by the bird. Astounded by what was happening, they turned and ran, crashing through the woods as fast as they could go.

Indeed, to this day whenever these unfortunate mushroom gatherers recall the incident, they are unable to fathom or explain what they witnessed. It remains totally incomprehensible that a song, and one so beautiful, could have emanated from the throat of the black bird, yet they were both certain it had. Naturally they never mentioned the episode to another person. But had they stayed at the mushroom site and seen what next occurred, it would have been even more impossible for them to understand.

Berin and Strika bounded joyfully toward the birds as two adult kirins dismounted, a female from the raven that had landed first, and a male from the second.

"*Langastacor, tychiam od nona,*" began the aging male gravely. "This was your first encounter with human beings, but it may not be your last, and we must all learn from it."

The speaker was Ruggum Chamter, overseer of the Yorl

clan. A rounded hat covered his balding head. He had a graying brown beard, dark eyes, and a furrowed brow. Cinched snugly to his side was a tarnished and ever-present axe.

"We seldom interfere in the affairs of human beings," he continued, glowering. The young kirins stood quietly by. "But when it came to morel mushrooms, an exception had to be made. As far as your behavior is concerned, you did not do everything correctly. You might have been detected."

"You followed us!" cried Berin. "I'm glad you did! But didn't you trust us to be alone?"

"You must be quieter!" hissed Ruggum. "You must always be quiet when human beings are in the vicinity!"

"In the case of a first mushroom hunt," said Diliani, "it is not a matter of trusting or not trusting." She was tall for a kirin woman and had penetrating black eyes.

"Experience has taught us," she said, "to observe such events. When we saw that humans had found your mushrooms, we were afraid you might be detected also. We had concern for the morels, but even more for you. Even though you are invisible to human beings, you are discernible in other ways. In almost all cases of encounter with humans, kirins should remove themselves from the proximity. That you did not do. But you did remain silent, even as they were removing your booty. That showed poise and good training. Let me ask you something. Did you understand the meaning of their words?"

"I did for the most part," answered Strika, glancing at Berin. "They liked the looks of our mushrooms! But they did not like the looks of your ravens!"

The youths brightened and almost began to laugh, but were met with the stern gaze of Ruggum Chamter. They had been involved in an unexpected meeting with humans, a happening potentially treacherous for kirins, and frivolity was not appropriate.

But Berin wondered about something. His curiosity got the best of him, and he asked about it. "We have always been told," he said, "that we are invisible to human beings. But this is the first time I have experienced it. We have never been told how it works, only that we must be quiet and they will pass us by. At first I thought the humans were trying to frighten you and Diliani away, but then I realized that they couldn't even see you! They were seeing only the ravens! And the way you made your bird posture! And sing! How did you do that? The humans ran away!"

"But if they cannot see us," asked Strika, excited by the experience with the giant beings, "how could it be that they can hear us, and feel us, as we've been taught?"

"And how is it," said Berin, "that animals, birds, insects, and every other creature but humans can see us?"

"Those are very good questions," answered Diliani. "The other species visualize us with their eyes and with their minds. But while a man's gaze might fall directly upon us, his mind is incapable of comprehending that we are present."

The boys gaped at her silently, trying to understand.

The old overseer spoke. "The time has arrived," he said firmly. "You have encountered humans and you are entitled to know as much as clan elders about these matters. However, it is a complex topic, and even we are not as well informed on the subject as magicians. Since contacting human beings is not by any means an everyday occurrence, the clan will be keenly interested in your observations.

"But this is hardly the time or place to discuss it," he continued, staring about at the woods in which they stood. "We must finish collecting the mushrooms and see to it that they arrive home safely. I will ask Speckarin to call for a clan gathering tonight. There he will impart to you and to all of the clan, I believe, what he knows about the spell of invisibility. But perhaps even he, a magician, does not have full knowledge of it. And," he concluded, taking a provocative step toward the boys, "be prepared to comment on what you have seen!"

"I will bring others from the clan to transport the mushrooms," said Diliani.

She climbed onto her raven and entwined her long feet

beneath his neck as only a kirin can do. Then, after she had spoken a few soft words to the giant bird, he lifted off, cleared the tops of the trees, and headed the short distance home, his rider securely upon his back.

C H A P T E R 5

THOSE MORELS WERE, of course, the very ones you enjoyed for supper," added Diliani at the conclusion of Ruggum's narration. Nodding to Speckarin, she backed away from the gathering fire and resumed her place in the crowd. Ruggum Chamter did the same.

Enthralled and silent throughout the telling, the gathered kirins began to relax and converse quietly among themselves when the elder's account came to an end. A few older members of the clan had also encountered human beings, and memories of their own experiences once again became vivid as they listened. Many, however, had never seen a human, and to them these stories were of exceeding interest. They had strained to hear every word spoken by the magician, the two youths, and the overseer.

Speckarin stood observing the clan for a short while as the crowd's murmurings grew louder and more excited. Finally he raised his arms to call for silence, and the attention of the throng was drawn to him. The old magician cleared his throat and prepared to begin an oration, as promised, on the history of kirin magic.

He spoke first to Berin and Strika, and then to the gathering. "You witnessed two forms of kirin magic today. You were saved from detection by no'an, the spell that makes us invisible to human beings, and your mushrooms were rescued indirectly by curlace, the ancient bond between kirins and our animal and bird friends. You have asked about these powers and I will tell you what I can, even though I know not all there is to know. You have also witnessed humans and human speech for the first time in your lives. Tell me something. Were you able to comprehend what they said?"

Berin and Strika responded. They were able to grasp the majority of what the humans uttered.

"Good," said Speckarin. "I think that for the first time you understand the necessity of training in human language and culture, and during my discussion I will bring up another ancient form of magic that deals with communication."

Next he looked into the eyes of the crowd surrounding him. "Nearly twelve years have elapsed," he began in Ruvon, raising his voice to be heard by all, "since an encounter has occurred between a member of this clan and these giant beings."

Adults and older adolescents had heard this before, the elder ones several times, but they never tired of it and never seemed to learn enough about it.

"In the dim past," said the magician, "long forgotten by humankind and well before recorded history, in an era when magic was abundantly practiced by human and kirin alike, our two races lived together in peace and harmony. We communicated and cooperated for many thousands of years. But as human beings grew more confident and independent, they became aloof and more competitive and unfriendly with our ancestors. As time went by our kind gradually came to learn, sometimes through harsh experience, that humans could no longer tolerate living side by side with kirins. Perhaps we were too much alike as species. Perhaps we became a threat because we persevered in the practice of magic, while humanity, as I will explain in a moment, forsook this pathway and went off in another direction. The true reasons for the division between humans and kirins are not known today, and possibly were not even recognized at the time. What is known, and vividly remembered by kirins, is that we were unceremoniously and unmercifully abused by men and women, whenever and wherever they learned of our existence. We were at times enslaved, and, most regrettably and unspeakably of all, we were occasionally prepared and consumed as a delicacy."

A shiver ran through the gathered kirins. Even though most had heard it before, they looked at one another disbelievingly as Speckarin began again.

"As I mentioned, at that point in history a major divergence occurred in the inclinations of our two races: While kirins continued in the pursuit of magic, humans began to lose their capabilities and even their interest in conjury. Those skills have now long been forgotten by human beings, whose minds have embraced the physical and social sciences, religion, law, and war, but no longer truly have the capacities for the practice and the art of magic.

"Even though many of you do not realize it because it does not enter into your daily lives, at times it is through magic that kirins are able to communicate with one another with or without the spoken word, sometimes over great distances. When conditions are ideal we can even see into the past and the future. This faculty was far more pronounced in the early days of our race, when our magic was more powerful. Today we require instruments, imbued with ancient magic, to accomplish these things. Nonetheless, as a race we maintain the ability to see things and to transmit images and information in this fashion. But humans, once our equal in almost all forms of conjury, have lost this capability almost completely. The only vestige of it in their lives today is an occasional revelation. They foresee something that will occur in the future, or have inexplicable knowledge of an event occurring a long distance away, as if, in their own words, discovering it through a sixth sense. We know a great deal about people. We have observed them for centuries. Their capacity for conjury is now but a fraction of ours since we practice and maintain the old magic, only a remnant of what abilities they had in the distant past when the magic of both kirin and human was robust and forceful."

The magician paused, looking above the heads of the crowd momentarily, and then went on. "Although they have no recollection or knowledge of it, when a human does occasionally have one of these experiences, he is not only having a momentary encounter with his own distant ancestors, but also with ours. The one great gift from our race to theirs was an ability kirins discovered and mastered through magic: the power to communicate over distance and time. This capacity we bequeathed upon humans gladly, when we existed together and were very much alike. But this gift, along with all of their other faculties in conjury, has faded over the centuries.

"Some of their kind, however," he continued, "are still more adept at this sort of information-gathering than others. These individuals are capable of harking back to their origins and bringing to the forefront the latent energies of their race. They are considered prophets, seers, and oracles. Usually they are scoffed at and not taken seriously by their fellows, for the power to obtain information through any means other than the five senses all but eludes humankind today. Of course, there are men and women who claim to have the power of clairvoyance and pretend to predict the future when they have no such ability at all. Labeled as quacks and charlatans, they provide even greater reason for human beings to doubt the existence of such capacities.

"As you are well aware," the magician went on, "kirins the world over maintain a working knowledge of the dialect spoken by humans of the region in which they live. Within this clan you have had lessons from the time you were very young in the tongue humans refer to as 'English.' It is the language spoken by men and women in this part of the Earth. Many of you have found this teaching boring, a waste of valuable time that could be spent on more enjoyable endeavors, such as climbing, exploring, or even searching for morel mushrooms. But the purpose for this training is vital: self-protection and self-preservation. In the case of a chance encounter with a human, should he happen to be with another of his kind, you will be able to understand what they are expressing to one another, as our two youths found out today. You will be capable of comprehending their intentions and plans. And, although hopefully it will never be necessary, you could actually communicate with the beings should an extreme situation arise, even though your knowledge of their language might be rudimentary.

"A few moments ago, I mentioned instruments with which we are able to transmit information to one another. Implements such as these are rare, and are possessed almost exclusively by magicians. Through these tools we are also capable of communicating with humans in their native tongue. When employing them, our skills in the comprehension and pronouncement of their dialect rise far above the primitive renderings you have practiced within the clan, allowing us to speak and understand it as though it were our primary language. Occasions for the use of this technique have been uncommon throughout the centuries. This capability exists nonetheless, and has existed for thousands of years for a single reason: so that we will be able to communicate with humanity when the time of reconciliation arrives."

Should it *ever* arrive, remarked Speckarin inwardly, as the idea of reuniting with humankind sent a shudder through the crowd. The magician paused for a few moments before continuing.

"Following the fragmentation between our two races," he said, "our ancestors deemed it necessary to cast a spell on humanity, the spell of no'an, in order to protect themselves. The effect of it was witnessed by our two young members today. With the institution of this spell, human beings were no longer capable of detecting kirins by vision, although we were, and still are, discoverable by all other senses—taste, touch, smell, and hearing. And we can still be seen by all other creatures. The spell influences only the larger, more developed and intellectual brain of the human being."

Here the magician stopped for a moment, searching for the precise words. "The effect of no'an is a fogging or clouding of an area of the human mind vital to the visualization of kirins. It results in a blind spot in their perception. They simply do not register our presence visually. They quite literally look through us. In this manner no'an has protected our race from destruction for many thousands of years."

At this point, for the first time during the oration, one of his listeners shifted his position and raised a hand. Halsit, a young male who had been seated near the fireplace, arose and faced the magician. Speckarin signaled with a nod that Halsit could speak.

"We know we are invisible to human beings," said the young kirin respectfully, "and we know why we are invisible. What we have never been told is exactly how we became invisible, how no'an actually works upon a human being, and whether the spell can be broken. Many of us, or perhaps all of us, would like to have answers to these questions. That information has stayed apart from us and in the custody of the magician class over many centuries."

He had finished his remarks but he remained standing, as if awaiting a complete answer, which he and everyone else in the crowd knew he would not receive. The old magician allowed himself a half smile, even a slight chuckle, at the raising of such an old issue. But he prevented the crowd from noting his amusement as he coughed and cleared his throat. Then he proceeded to give the customary explanation.

"As I have stated," said Speckarin, "we are protected by the spell of our ancestors, the spell of no'an. To allow its machinations to be widely known among kirins would be to invite disaster, and in more ways than one. Misuse or fragmented use of this power could lead to our discovery by human beings. As a result they might learn more about no'an itself. If not capable of utilizing it for their own purposes, through a more intimate acquaintance with it humans might be able to dull or negate our employment of it, and therefore endanger our species."

What he did not mention, nor had he mentioned at any gathering, was something known only to magicians and a very few clan elders. It was the single means by which the ancient spell could be overridden, by which a kirin might actually become visible to a human being. If, for some reason, a kirin was so attracted to a human that he desired to be seen, he could will himself visible. He could momentarily overcome the spell and actually be perceived by a human being. It was the only flaw in the fabric of no'an.

Why any kirin would wish to do this Speckarin had never been able to understand. Such events were extraordinarily rare, but were known to have happened. Over the centuries they had resulted in sightings of kirins by human beings, and Speckarin had no intention of revealing that such a thing was possible.

Men and women who have seen kirins have subsequently discussed the encounters with others of their kind, referring to little creatures the world over as elves, gremlins, fairies, brownies, dwarfs, kobolds, reina, leprechauns, trolls, menehune, tomte, and gnomes. From these infrequent experiences prodigious legends surrounding small beings have arisen among humans.

It is good, thought Speckarin, for our clan and for the kirin race, that this method of becoming visible has remained secreted within the magician class. I shudder to think what might happen if it were otherwise.

Then, unnoticed by the crowd, his green eyes darkened as he was reminded of another disaster that might all too soon befall the kirin race.

C H A P T E R   6

YOUNG Halsit, unsatisfied
but also not surprised by the magician's responses, settled
back into his place on the floor. He and other clan members
were aware that the ultimate responsibility for kirin magic
fell to a Guardian Magician and his Council. It was they who
had complete control over the spell of invisibility. No'an
required continual monitoring to remain intact and in effect,
something the Council had attended to for eons. This was not
a permanent spell, and was never intended to be, nor was it
designed to perpetuate itself. Since its inception, kirins have
held out the hope that humankind and kirinkind might again
be able to live together in harmony. The exile that kirins had
imposed upon themselves and that had isolated them from
virtually all human contact—invisibility—might someday be
revoked. The time would come, some kirins believed, when
humans would attain enough maturity and self-confidence to
be able to accept them amicably, without malice or jealousy.
But kirins also perceived, through continuing observations of
humanity, that such a day had not yet arrived.

There were those within this clan, Halsit among them,
who had heard inklings in recent times that all was not well

with the High Council of Magicians, or with the Guardian Magician himself. Rumor had it that consequently the magic of no'an might have been neglected, or perhaps, unthinkably, even diminished. Common kirins normally have little knowledge of the Council, its whereabouts, or its workings. But somehow the rumors had started, and if they were accurate, Halsit and others worried that kirins the world over might be facing grave ramifications, the greatest of which would be the loss of invisibility.

Speckarin had been consulted regarding this. He was, after all, clan magician, and he should have greater knowledge of it than anyone else. But the old magician had been tightlipped any time the topic had been raised, and for what he considered a very good reason. He himself had begun to suspect several years before that something was wrong at the highest level of kirin magic. He had discussed this with other magicians of local clans. But his views were not met with universal agreement and in fact were frequently scoffed at, most notably by Duan of the neighboring Moger clan. In spite of the fact that his suspicions were actually in accord with those of Halsit, Speckarin felt that it was his duty to allay the apprehensions of his clansmen, and certainly not to reveal anything that would give their fears more substance. Therefore, while he argued about it freely with fellow magicians, he refused to discuss the subject with members of his clan until he was more certain about it.

Halsit's unpleasant train of thought was broken as the light of the magician began to pale. The crowd again became hushed. Speckarin lifted the globe from the stand, signaling the end of the gathering. Then, holding the dimming instrument before him, he began walking slowly toward the dark portal from which he had come. He disappeared within its obscure confines, the door closing behind him.

Many of the kirins began to move toward their dwellings. One small lad named Hutsin, or Hut, slipped away from his family and headed toward the birds and animals, just now beginning to stretch and relax at the edge of the gathering place.

Prior to flying on the backs of birds, children of this and surrounding clans enjoyed a learning period of playing and practicing with squirrels, preparing for the time they were old enough to fly. One of these animals recognized the lad as he approached, and became immediately quiet and attentive.

Hut had bright green eyes and was short in stature. In fact, he was the smallest for his age in the clan. He made up for it, however, with energy, determination, and daring. He was always interested in something adventurous in the forest, even if it was perilous, and sometimes he had to be discouraged by his parents or elders.

Hut greeted Stala with a touch, a hand upon the animal's ear, and with a single word. *"Orann,"* he said.

It was an ancient salutation from kirins to their animal partners, but also a charmed word, a curlace word, imbued with the magic that kirins have employed for eons in controlling beasts. The animal moved not a muscle, but stood waiting alertly for a command. The lad was tempted to take his old chum for a ride, but realized that within a short time he was to begin training upon a raven, and that he was nearly too old to be riding the squirrel.

"I'll be out early in the morning to greet you," he said in the common tongue, relieved to be using it again after the formal language of the gathering.

"Perhaps we'll go out with Blinda and Aassa," he said, hoping his younger sister would be in a mood to ride in the morning. As he departed he knew that Stala would observe him until he was out of sight, and then would return to his own place in the upper branches of the oak.

Hut started homeward with the gait of a kirin happy and in a hurry. His long feet and strong tendons gave him the capacity to propel himself with results that would be astonishing to an observer not acquainted with kirins. Moving quickly up the trunk, he climbed the giant oak with ease until he reached his family's dwelling.

Kirins of this clan may live in tree holes, but the comfort and warmth of their homes are far above what one might imagine. Being small, Hut did not have to stoop to get through the doorway. His father and grandfather were sitting by the fireplace in the entryway and turned to greet him, knowing intuitively where he had been.

The entry room was carved into the trunk of the tree, as were other rooms of the apartment. In fashioning their homes, however, great care has always been taken by tree-dwelling kirins to preserve the life functions of the tree. Construction is planned and closely supervised by a tree architect with long experience, almost always from another clan. The chiseling and sculpting is performed by tree carvers, and chosen trees are damaged as little as possible. Some rooms are built adjacent to the trunk and branches, but not directly within them. These chambers, for the most part outside of the tree itself, are carefully camouflaged to appear as natural protuberances, the lumpy outgrowths one can see on older trees.

The room, brightly lighted by the fire, was cheery. Hut's father and grandfather were engaged in a practice commonly enjoyed by kirins of the region, especially after a meeting in the chilly night air. They were warming their bare feet by the fireplace.

"Stala was a fine, strong animal for you, Hut," his father said, "and you were a worthy young master. Now you will have plenty of time, perhaps more than you want, to practice with your bird ilon, your new means of transportation."

"My squirrel was Stopal," reminisced his grandfather, "a long time ago. I could think of nothing else the first season we were together. Your first ilon is always special. The others all blend together, but you always remember the first. I can understand, and I can still recall, the kind of excitement you must be feeling now. But when I think it over, I believe I loved Stopal more than any of the birds I was ever in contact with. Yorl kirins, in my opinion, have never been as adept at flying as other clans, nor is it in our blood, the way it seems to be with others."

"A few in our clan have both the skills and the love for

flying," interrupted Hut's father. "Ruggum Chamter and Diliani are experts in curlace magic, as good as any for several clan dominions around, and both employ ravens."

"True," conceded the grandfather. "A few of us have become adept at flying—I myself was at one time. But now I, for one, prefer hiking, especially at my age. As a matter of fact, I must tell you something. I was never truly comfortable flying. Perhaps Hut will be. But it is a shame that we outgrow our squirrel ilon. To me they are still the best."

Hut sat down on the floor before the fire. It was not excitement alone that he was feeling. Having to leave an old friend like Stala saddened him, and hearing what his grandfather had to say made him feel no better. The responsibility of acquiring a raven of his own made him apprehensive, even though the prospect of flying stirred and fascinated him.

He had long known, of course, that kirins have special ties with birds—ravens in the case of his clan—and he knew that the time would come when he might control such a creature and be free to come and go as he pleased upon an airborne ilon. Perhaps I will be one of the Yorls who truly takes to flying, he thought. The change from squirrel to raven, however, signaled a milestone in his young life for which he was not certain he was ready, and it was his anxiety about this that led him into further conversation with his father and grandfather.

"I know it started long ago," he said, "and I have heard the legend recounted many times, but I want to be sure that I fully understand curlace magic between beast and kirin."

"As you heard tonight from the magician," said his grandfather, "the spell of no'an protects us from human beings. Curlace began as a means of shielding us from other creatures, because while our wits were greater than theirs, our stature was not. In very early times, long, long ago, methods were divided into magical and non-magical. Among the primitive, non-magical means were simple prods, sharp objects, hurled items, loud sounds, and even noxious odors, all designed to deter beasts and keep them at a distance. But even more effective ways of protection were discovered through conjury, such as a sudden brightness resembling a flame, fear-inducing charms and spells, and even the transformation of animals into other species—all of which, crude as they were in early days, were found to be successful in shielding kirins from undesirable animals. This variety of magic, however, did not affect human beings, whose brains were more developed and had a greater capacity for reasoning than those of beasts. Eventually no'an, a separate category of magic, was developed and utilized for humanity."

"Over the centuries," interjected his father, "we learned that certain animals and birds could be tamed by our spells and be regulated and directed for our purposes, but without detriment to them. In fact, the ilon, the creature under our control, enjoys a useful and contented existence. One might even use the word happy for the life it leads, if one can consider an animal or a bird to have such a capacity."

"You have been taught many words and phrases to guide an animal and place it under your control, and you will learn still more," said his grandfather. "Sounds are our principle means of controlling the ilon, but we have others also, such as gestures. The 's' sound stimulates him, the 'm' quiets him, and numerous other inflections of voice and speech have varying effects."

"But at one time in the dim past," his father said, "the bond between animal and kirin was purely magical, when the practice of conjury was more prevalent and more powerful among kirins. The conjuring powers of our race have faded gradually over many thousands of years. They have lost some of their potency since those ancient times when magic was utilized by both humans and kirins. In the case of curlace, while we once relied upon conjury alone, it is now a combination of magic and training that regulates the beast."

"That is true," said his grandfather, "and we must begin the teaching early in the animal's life. As you know, it is a revered occupation among kirins to cultivate whatever species are available in a given territory. They happen to be squirrels and ravens in our homeland, but other varieties of bird and beast are utilized in different parts of the world. Some of them are captured, and some are born into the ilon families already under our direction. They enjoy a charmed life, Hut, and usually do not die until they have lived eight or ten times longer than their untamed counterparts in the wild. When you consider it, both we and our ilon live a remarkable life."

Hut was reminded of something curious he had heard earlier that evening, and he asked about it. "At the gathering tonight Strika told of the song of Ruggum Chamter's raven, a beautiful song that seemed to frighten the humans away. I have not heard of that kind of music coming from birds or animals. What made that happen, and could it truly have chased the humans away?"

His father answered. "Ruggum is one of the finest practitioners of curlace magic among kirins in our region. His raven, Alsinam, has been with him for almost twenty years. He has trained the bird to do many unique things. Having the bird sing melodically is one of his favorite contrivances."

"As for the humans," interjected his grandfather with a chuckle, "I am certain they were shocked by the experience. They would never have encountered anything like it before. And I'll wager they'll not be telling another human about it, for fear of being laughed out of the territory!"

Hut's mind turned back to Stala. He thought of the next morning, and what might be one of his last excursions aboard his old comrade. But again he remembered that within a short time he would be flying, and he controlled a slight feeling of exhilaration.

He bid his elders good night, and departed through the doorway leading to his room. Even in the dark he knew the passageway well, partly ramp and partly stairs. When he entered the room he lit the small taper by his bed. Then he undressed and climbed into his long, warm nightgown, with its voluminous distal pouch for his feet.

His was one of the rooms constructed outside the trunk of

the tree. But being well insulated, it was surprisingly cozy and comfortable. He got into bed and pulled up the covers. As he drifted off to sleep, he began to enjoy visions of himself soaring high above the trees, clinging to the back of an eagle, never suspecting that before the light of morning his life would be changed forever.

C H A P T E R   7

GILIN ENTERED through the front door. Kirins have never had a need to lock doors. He made his way stealthily through the warm entryway, coals still glowing in the small fireplace, and to the corridor for the room he sought. He was careful as he traversed the passageway in the darkness, not knowing the way as intimately as his cousin did. He opened the door slowly, stepped into the room dimly lit by the taper, and moved quickly to the bedside.

"Hut! Wake up!" he whispered huskily. "I must talk with you!"

He nudged the shoulder of his cousin, who faced the wall as he slept. "Wake up! I must talk with you now!" repeated Gilin, with urgency in his voice.

Hut stirred and turned toward the intruder. He was surprised but pleased when awake enough to realize it was his cousin and best friend. Gilin was from the Moger clan, whose home tree was one clan dominion away. Hut had not seen him for several days.

"What are you doing here at this time of the night?" whispered Hut. "You didn't waken anyone on your way in, did you?"

"I was quiet," whispered Gilin. "No one heard me."

"Well, what are you doing here?" Hut repeated, rubbing the sleep from his eyes.

"I need help," said Gilin. "I am in serious trouble—nothing that I have created, but a predicament I simply find myself in. I am being followed, and I am in grave danger."

Hut threw his long feet over the edge of the bed and sat up, now almost fully awake. "What kind of trouble could that be, that you didn't start but that you find yourself in?" he asked, his heart beating faster as his green eyes glimmered in the pale light. His cousin appeared genuinely frightened and exhausted.

"This will be difficult to understand," answered Gilin, "but . . . I cannot tell you what it is. For your own good and for the safety of your family and your clan, I cannot tell you the full history. If I did, it would place you in as much jeopardy as I find myself in."

"Why can't you tell me?" questioned Hut, becoming more agitated. "How can that make any difference? Did you take something that was not yours, or . . . or argue with an elder, or interfere with someone's ilon, or what?"

"None of those," said Gilin. "I have done nothing wrong. I would tell you immediately if it were anything like that. It is something totally different, much more important and much more dangerous. It could be a threat to us all."

Hut was now awake, standing in his nightgown beside the bed and staring at Gilin. They had been close friends since childhood. Hut was younger and smaller. Gilin was black-haired, handsome, and sturdy in build. His dark eyes had depth, and he was often said to be the best-looking lad of either clan.

"What do you mean by 'a threat to us all'?" asked Hut, suddenly speaking in a loud voice.

"Quiet!" whispered Gilin, glancing back toward the door. "I wish I could tell you more! I wish I could tell you everything! But I have told you that I cannot, and I simply cannot! At this point, Hut, you have no choice but to believe me!"

Gilin continued with gravity in his voice. "Hut, I must have your help. I would like you to go with me tonight."

"Go with you?" asked Hut. "Tonight? Where? What are you talking about?"

"I am not certain where," answered the beleaguered Gilin. "But I simply must get away and I must hurry. I am being followed by . . . a thing, something that you have never heard of, nor had I until very recently."

Becoming more desperate by the moment, Gilin decided that he must tell some of his secret in order to secure aid from his cousin. "Something is tracking me," he said. "It is very dangerous."

"What?" questioned Hut incredulously. "Is this a game, like we played as children?"

"It is no game," replied Gilin with utter seriousness. He paused. "Hut, I cannot reveal more or you would be tracked also. I haven't told anyone else! Even my family knows nothing about it! My parents, my sister, and even Jarod—none of them know anything about it!"

"Well, I don't know what to say or what to do," said the bewildered Hut. "I've never been much farther from home than your tree!"

"What I need is an ilon," said Gilin. "A raven would be ideal, but I know that your clan has only a few of them. Your sister's squirrel, Aassa, would do. You are acquainted with her, and at first you could help me command her."

"What would Blinda think about waking up in the morning and finding Aassa gone?" replied Hut, less enamored than ever with the ridiculous plan his cousin seemed to have in mind. He was not eager in the least to leave his comfortable, warm bedroom to go out into the dark at this time of night. Nonetheless, his cousin did seem truly in trouble.

A chill entered Hut's body and he gasped as he suddenly became aware of a scraping, grating sensation just beneath the level of hearing. It was distinct and intense and seemed to be shaking the very fiber of the room in which they stood.

Gilin spoke quickly. "It is the gronom! It has followed me

and has located me here! We must leave now! In a short time
it will arrive: If I remain here any longer I will endanger your
clan! When I depart and it senses I am gone, it will search
this place no longer and will not bother your family or your
home tree! It will move onward in its grim quest for me! But
now, Hut, we must leave!"

Not in the least happy, Hut quickly removed his
nightgown and began putting on his underwear, convinced
now that something indeed was very wrong. "May I ask what
a gronom is?" he said, the vibrations and gratings becoming
ever stronger.

"We have no time to talk!" responded Gilin. "We must
summon the ilon! Without an ilon, I know I would be
captured by the creature! It is relentless!" He paused for a
moment and shuddered. "I have witnessed what happens to
someone who is captured!"

"Who was captured?" rasped an increasingly excited Hut,
but his cousin simply shook his head and gave no answer.

"Well, why is it following you?" asked Hut, searching
frantically for his shirt.

"I have done nothing wrong!" replied Gilin. "It is what I
have learned, what I now know, that attracts the deadly beast!"

"What do you know?" exclaimed Hut. "Tell me
something about it! How can I go if I know nothing?"

Gilin's right foot touched Hut's in the traditional gesture
of kirins on serious occasions, and he looked his cousin
squarely in the eye. "You must trust me," he said calmly. "I
am in danger, one that grows by the moment. If I told you my
secrets, you would become one of the hunted. As it is now,
you will not be its target. It wants only me, or anyone like me
who has the knowledge. It cannot see or sense you in any
way, unless you have this knowledge, or unless you threaten
its existence or its seizure of me."

The gratings were becoming ever more palpable. It was
almost as though an earthquake was shaking the small room.
Hut was fumbling with the laces of his pants, wishing he
could awaken his father and his grandfather, but he knew

they did not have time, and it was obvious that Gilin would not tell them anything anyway. Gilin was apparently in imminent peril, and in great need of an ilon. But Hut could sense that he needed something else just as deeply: a companion, an ally.

"How long would we be gone?" asked Hut, placing his hiking cap on his head, still not totally convinced he was going anywhere.

"A few days, perhaps," said Gilin, "or in all sincerity, from everything I have learned, it is possible that we might not return."

At last, this was too much for Hut. "I will call the ilon for you Gilin," he stated, "but I am afraid you will be going alone!"

They hurried down the corridor, through the warm entryway, and out the front door.

As Hut closed the door behind him, his mother turned over in her sleep. She was only half-awake, but felt a sense of sadness and loss deep within her heart. It must have been a dream, she concluded, and she fell back into a fretful slumber until dawn. And, while she could not know it at the time, with each awakening for unnumbered mornings to come, the emptiness and melancholy would return to her anew.

C H A P T E R   8

HUT AND GILIN stepped into the cool night air.

"How far away do you think the gronom is?" whispered Hut, the awful grating having disappeared entirely as soon as they left his room.

"It could be as close as the foot of your tree," said Gilin aloud. "So we must hurry. Call Aassa for me, and Stala for yourself if you want to go. You needn't be quiet now. The gronom does not hear, as we know it. It senses in a way foreign to us, through a form of telepathy or perception we do not understand."

Hut had not been sure of what he was doing up to now, and was even less certain out here in the dark, on a branch of the oak tree. Without the horrifying sensation from the gronom, the need for departure seemed less urgent. Nonetheless, he did not wish to tarry and increase the risk for his cousin, and once again he sensed the desire within Gilin for a companion.

Hut placed his hands to his mouth and made two whistling sounds, the first high and the second low. They were softer than one would think audible to animals some

distance away. Then he repeated the call. In a few moments
Stala scurried down the tree from his sleeping place high
above. He stopped on the branch in front of Hut and sat up on
his hind legs, forelegs together. He waited calmly by the light
of a full moon.

Hut whistled again, this time sounding four tones in
repetition, and Aassa hurried down the tree. She came to rest
next to Stala, where she stood motionless on all four feet. She
tilted her head as she eyed the young kirins, apparently
curious why Blinda was not there. Hut felt a pang of guilt
when he thought of his sister. He had observed her
summoning Aassa on many occasions, but this was the first
time he had done so himself.

Unacquainted with Gilin, Aassa shied away from the
stranger when he approached. The youth was exceedingly
anxious to escape before the gronom arrived on the scene,
however, and he was well acquainted with curlace magic.
Together with Hut, who was familiar with the animal, he
calmed her with relaxing words and phrases. Then, gently
stroking and speaking to the squirrel, Gilin pulled himself
onto her back, and intertwined his long feet beneath her neck.

With a kirin aboard, squirrel ilon are taught to move more
smoothly than in the wild, to protect the rider from being
injured or even becoming disengaged. While they still travel
swiftly, the bouncing, jostling, and long leaps of such animals
are curtailed.

Below they heard a noise. Hut glanced down and saw it
for the first time. Halfway up the trunk, ascending diligently
and easily visible by the light of the moon was the gronom.
The creature had two upper and two lower extremities, a
naked and hairless torso, and feet that were miniature in
comparison to those of kirins. But the most astonishing thing
about its appearance was its face, or more accurately the
absence of one. It had no features whatsoever, no eyes, ears,
nose, or mouth, only a smooth and vacant countenance.

The being's startling form, coupled with the industry and
enthusiasm with which it ascended, forced a quick decision

upon Hut, who had been wavering until this very instant. Climbing onto Stala, he looked down once more at the eagerly approaching thing and gave the command for immediate departure.

Stala jumped quickly to the next higher bough. Gilin and Aassa followed closely. Hutsin and his cousin were not children; they were at the upper size limit for transportation by squirrel ilon. Nonetheless, the two animals bore them with little difficulty at first. They moved along the bough to its outward reaches. There the ilon leapt with some effort to the upper branches of a neighboring oak, the young kirins clinging to their backs. Here Gilin and Aassa took the lead.

They traversed this tree and another in the same fashion, the splendor of the full moon showing the way. It is uncommon for squirrels to travel by night, a fact known to both kirin youths. But urged on by the words of their masters, the ilon, though slowed by the burden of their riders, were cautious and surefooted in their progress. A while later they were many trees away from Hut's home, and he began to wonder whether they should stop. But Gilin showed no sign of abating.

After a considerable period of steady travel Gilin raised an arm, signaling for a halt. Both youths spoke commands to their fatigued animals. Stopping in the branches of a towering maple, the ilon breathed laboriously. With their long feet the riders could palpate the rapid heartbeats of the animals. Traveling in this concerted fashion was taxing not only to the animal, but to the rider as well, and the two kirins were glad for a rest also.

As he looked around, Hut had little idea where they were. He had simply followed his cousin as they negotiated the trees. He had tried to study the moon and stars overhead, as he had been taught in curlace orientation. But with their rapid movement through the forest, and with leaves and branches frequently above, he had found it difficult to keep even the heavenly objects in sight, and he was not certain how to use what little information he had gleaned. During ilon training far more time is spent on daytime than on nighttime travel. But unless they had been going in circles, he judged, he was farther from home than he had ever been in his life. And the uncanny appearance of the gronom still haunted his thoughts.

"We have come far enough," stated Gilin, taking a deep breath.

"I should hope so!" declared his cousin. "I wouldn't think that . . . whatever it was could follow us this far!"

"It is following us," said Gilin. "But we can rest here. It will take it awhile to get here. By the first light of day we will look for food and drink, for us and for the animals. But we must be cautious. We are only out of danger from the single gronom you saw. Others of its kind exist and are tracking me at this moment. And even they are not the only things to be feared."

At this point, thankfully, Hut was too weary to fully comprehend Gilin's last remark, and was beginning to search for a place to rest. He located a dry tree hole and spoke to Stala, who joined him in the small cavity. They curled up next to each other, the animal to keep his master warm. Within a short time Hut had begun to relax. Exhausted as he was, he soon became drowsy. Shortly, he rejoined the sleep from which he had been so abruptly awakened earlier that night in his comfortable bed. But this time, as he drifted off, he did not dream of soaring upon an eagle. Instead, he envisioned himself alone with Stala, entrapped in an obscure dark place, confronting the merciless onslaught of a horde of hideous and faceless things.

C H A P T E R   9

AT THE FIRST LIGHT of dawn, Hut was awakened by Gilin.

"We must move on," said Gilin.

Hut sat up next to Stala, and for the second time that night rubbed sleep from his eyes. He looked out of the tree hole onto a portion of the forest he had never seen, and all at once the astonishing events of the recent past came back to him: stealing out of his home, fleeing the gronom, and riding Stala through the night.

Just as the words escaped him, Gilin became aware of the polished object he carried in his belt satchel. It was not as if he did not know it was there. Of course, he knew where the calamar was; he had employed it throughout their journey during the night. But his attention, for some unknown reason, was now all at once drawn to it. Reaching into the sack he felt for the object, and when he found it, to his surprise, it was slightly warm. It had always been cool to the touch before. He began to wonder whether it had somehow been altered or activated.

Unaware of Gilin's quandary, Hut stepped out of the tree hole onto a branch. He looked downward. Where were they, he

wondered? He knew, of course, that they were farther from
home than he had ever been. Or were they? What if they had
been going in circles? He admitted to himself that he had no
idea of their location, and that made him very uncomfortable.

Stala was nearby, and by the dim light of early day Hut
climbed atop his ilon and gave brief instructions. Still tired
from the long trek, the faithful squirrel descended the tall tree
headfirst, using his tail for delicate balance. Upon reaching
the ground Hut dismounted and again looked about. He was
joined momentarily by his cousin, who had followed
immediately after him upon Aassa.

"I trust you know where we are," said Hut cooly. "How
far did we travel, and where are the home trees from here?"

Hut was aware that the ilon could find the tree of their
clan, even if their masters were somehow incapacitated.
Since this species of animal did not naturally possess a
homing capacity, the squirrels were endowed with such an
instinct during curlace training. Nonetheless, Hut was
bothered by not knowing where they were. Lost is another
term for it, he thought with displeasure.

"We are thirty-one clan dominions to the south of your
tree," said Gilin, climbing down from Aassa.

Hut hesitated for a moment, stunned at the precise nature
of Gilin's response. "How do you know that?" he asked. "We
rode together last night, and I haven't a clue as to where we
are! Except," he continued, extending an arm toward the
surrounding trees, "that we are somewhere deep in the forest!"

"I know through two means," answered Gilin
imperturbably. "First, I have been taught reckoning, by the
moon and stars at night, and by other indicators during the
day. My method has a far greater accuracy than any we were
given as children during our training with ilon. It was one of
the first things we were taught by . . ."

Here Gilin stopped, undecided as to whether he should go
on further about who had been teaching him, or the plight in
which he so inextricably found himself. He was not anxious
to involve Hut any more deeply in the entanglement. And

yet, here they were, together in the forest, far from home, and both in danger. To Gilin's regret, his cousin was already unmistakably enmeshed in the plot.

"I can teach you this method of reckoning," continued Gilin after a few moments, "but it will take time. The second means by which I know our location," he said, removing the warming object from his belt sack and holding it out to his cousin, "is this."

Hut took the smooth and shiny thing in his hand, immediately noting its warmth. It was the size of his palm, and he turned it over and examined it. Disc-like in shape, it was round in one dimension and flat in another. It had a mild concavity in one of its flatter surfaces and a convexity on the other.

"It is called a calamar," said Gilin. "It is magical, and no one can employ it but myself. It has many capabilities, one of which is to indicate location and direction. I used it last night throughout our trek. My learning period with it was brief, however, and I have not mastered all of its powers. But hopefully with time, its other functions will become apparent, perhaps even soon. Something may be happening to it right now. I have never known it to change temperature before."

Hut stared at the object and tried to sort out what he was hearing. He could sense nothing about it, nor within it, no matter how hard he examined it, except that it was smooth and circular and that it was indeed warm. In fact, warming further, he thought, even as he held it. He did not understand what was going on, and he began to feel more uncomfortable than ever about his circumstances.

To make matters worse, as the first rays of the morning sun splashed over leaves of the surrounding trees, he began to feel hunger, and his thoughts turned to home. Perhaps his mother was preparing breakfast, of which he would not be there to partake.

Absent-mindedly fingering the object, he became vaguely aware of an image shaping itself in his thoughts. It rapidly took a more palpable form, and finally crowded everything else out of his consciousness: It was a picture of his mother preparing breakfast at the same moment he was thinking about her. Somehow he knew that she was unaware of his absence, having awakened early in the morning with a heavy heart, explaining it to herself as the result of a bad dream she could not recall.

Struck precipitously with fear, Hut dropped the object to the ground and the image vanished immediately.

What happened, he wondered? What was it? How could I have known that? And yet it seemed so real! It was my mother! I knew what she was doing and thinking at that very moment, all that distance away! It was her! I knew what she was thinking! Becoming more confused and agitated by the moment, Hut glared at Gilin and pointed down at the gleaming piece.

"Where did you obtain this . . . this thing?" he asked incredulously.

Then a sudden realization came to Hut as he recalled Speckarin's words at the gathering the evening before. Kirins retain the capacity to see things far away, and even into the past and the future, but now usually with magical instruments. This must be one of those devices the magician was referring to! Through it, or because of it, I was able to see something a great distance away and at the moment it was occurring! But Speckarin also said that these were almost exclusively the property of magicians! He stared in unabashed wonder at the mysterious object on the ground, then looked up inquiringly at his cousin.

"How did you obtain something like this?" he asked. "And tell me something else. How did you become involved in matters such as these?"

Gilin tried to remain calm, at least outwardly, and attempted to answer. "Not by choice," he said. He bent down, retrieved the calamar, and slid it back into his satchel.

"Well," asked Hut, "how did you get into all of this . . . trouble, or intrigue, or whatever you wish to call it?" And you've dragged me into it too, he thought.

Gilin did not directly respond to the question. "Even though it was in your hands," said Gilin, "the calamar was working through my mind and through me. I saw the same thing you did, your mother at home. It somehow sensed that you wished to see her, and it provided the images for both of us. I could feel her sadness also. I could sense it working through me, but I do not know how it happens."

Hut stared at him, dumbfounded.

Gilin glanced about, his dark eyes alert. He realized that they must not linger in their present location. Gronoms somewhere, be they near or far away, were homing in on him even as they stood in conversation. It was vital that they move on. Nevertheless, he recognized also that he was obligated to reveal more to his cousin than he already had, and that the time had come to do so. I will tell only what is necessary, he concluded, to help him understand. To tell everything would be to place him in the same peril I am in.

"I would feel more comfortable if we were in the tree," said Gilin, carefully retaining his composure.

Hut nodded. They moved to the trunk of the large maple in which they had spent the night, instructing the two ilon to follow. They climbed to a considerable height and then out onto one of the boughs. In an area where the sun was shining brightly, and with the ilon waiting patiently nearby, the two young kirins sat down, and Gilin recounted a portion of what had transpired in recent days.

"It happened purely by chance," he began. "Some days ago, two of my friends and I were foraging in the woods. We encountered, or I should say almost stepped upon, an ancient kirin, hiding alone in the forest. As it turned out, he was dying. I am sure that you know my two companions, Talli and Reydel from my clan."

"Of course I remember Talli," replied Hut, "from meetings our clans have had together, especially when we visited your tree last summer. She's older than you, isn't she? I remember her blond hair. And Reydel is about three years younger. Her feet were just beginning to develop the last time

I saw her!" he joked.

"Reydel is younger, but Talli and I are the same age," answered Gilin, and he returned to his story. "The elder we found was a magician. His name was Olamin. He came from so far to the north that we were obliged to use the formal language in order to converse with him, as he did not understand our dialect, nor we his. He refused to allow us to remove him from his hiding place and escort him to our clan tree, insisting that to do so would endanger the clan. At first we could not comprehend why. Later, of course, we understood. Even though we did not know all of his motives, the three of us were greatly attracted to him, for reasons we could not verbalize nor totally identify. For several days we fed and cared for him as best we could in the forest, and stayed with him as much as possible. At his earnest request, we did so without informing our families or anyone else what we were doing. The elderly magician was exhausted and was near death."

Gilin paused, uncertain how much to tell, but then he went on.

"Olamin carried much information, and found us to be eager listeners and pupils. Much of it was harmless, and designed only to make our lives more useful and more fulfilling. These things he taught us as we passed our first day or two with him. Among them was the capacity to orient one's self by the moon and stars, which I referred to earlier and utilized last night during our trip. But much of what he knew was deeply secret, and hazardous to anyone knowing it. It was this knowledge he felt impelled to pass on to someone before he died.

"His energies had been depleted by the relentless pursuit of gronoms," said Gilin, bathed in warm sunlight, "but, partly due to his magical powers, he had been able to stave them off. Knowing that he was going to die, he was grateful we had chanced to find him, and that he had someone to whom he could impart his secrets. He was also distressed, however, and greatly hesitant to reveal that information, and for good reason: The knowledge places its possessor in imminent danger. As he weakened further, he recognized that he would have no choice but to tell us, or the knowledge would perish along with him. He finally decided that the three of us, Talli, Reydel, and I, should all know. He could see that we were young and strong, and while he fully realized that the information would imperil us, telling all three would diminish the chances of the knowledge being lost. His final period of time was passed in revealing as much as he could. He taught us about the world, opening our eyes to matters totally unknown and foreign to all unsuspecting kirins, unknown to our clansmen, almost certainly unknown even to our magicians. At this moment, Hut, the three of us . . . or perhaps the two of us, Talli and I, are the recipients of Olamin's knowledge. But it is not only we who are in jeopardy—our danger is constant, from gronoms and other heinous creatures. The entire kirin race is endangered. Olamin first wanted us to know that, and then he revealed what might be done to counteract it. He told us how to alter and combat the impending shape of things to come, the harsh and chaotic future of the kirin race, even though any attempt to challenge it would involve extreme peril. All of this, Hut," said Gilin, "is included in the knowledge I now possess."

Hut was dazzled. For a few moments he was unable to speak. Finally he asked a simple question. "What happened to Talli and Reydel?"

Gilin shuddered, and then continued the tale. "After Olamin died, in accordance with the customs of his homeland, we buried him in the ground, and not in a tree as is customary for us. As we were covering his body with earth, the ground began to move suddenly and violently, and to vibrate, and the grave site heaved and shook even as we stood burying him, much as your room did last night. We were terrified, naturally, but we finished the burial out of respect for our mentor, our dear friend. All at once we caught sight of something nearby, approaching the grave."

Gilin's lips quivered and his face paled, but he forced

himself to carry on. "It was a gronom that had finally caught up with its old prey, Olamin. But it was not Olamin it now cared about. The knowledge was no longer alive in him, but it was within us. The creature could sense this, and it began its deadly chase anew. The three of us turned and fled. Reydel was the youngest and the slowest afoot. She tripped and fell attempting to escape, and before we could help her the monster attacked. Talli and I stopped and looked back in horror but could do nothing to rescue her. Once the merciless creature had finished with her, it turned toward the two of us. We were unprepared to confront the fiend. We had no way to combat it. Again we ran, and of course it pursued us. As we fled we made a decision to separate. I know nothing of what has become of Talli, but I hope intensely that she was able to escape. As I moved away I soon realized that traveling on foot would be too tiring and slow to insure evasion of the gronom for very long. I knew I was not far from your tree, and I desperately needed help, especially in the form of an ilon. I thought of you, Hut. I knew you would help me, and here we are.

"You may go home if you like," said Gilin softly. "You need not become involved. Stala will take you and you will not be harmed."

C H A P T E R   1 0

HUT WAS STUNNED.
Just yesterday he had been saddened by the thought of riding through the woods upon his squirrel, perhaps for the last time. He had been exhilarated by the thought of piloting his new raven. He had enjoyed morel mushrooms at the gathering, where he listened to tales of encounters with human beings. But all of these now seemed unimportant and mundane. Overnight his world had changed completely. Reality, he now recognized, was that his cousin and others, perhaps many others, were in acute danger, and that the shadow of some dark and undefined menace was being cast over all of kirin life.

Gilin suggested he might go home. Hut admitted to himself that earlier in the morning he had thought of doing so. But now he wondered just how well his cousin would get along without him. Gilin had come looking for help, and not just in the form of an ilon. He was alone, isolated from other kirins because of the secrets he held. He can tell no one what he knows, thought Hut, nor what he has been directed to accomplish with this mysterious knowledge. He needs a companion desperately.

"I will stay," said Hut.

He had not come to this decision lightly. Many ideas flashed through his mind. He had, of course, considered Gilin's unenviable predicament. But a recollection from childhood days had also come to him. Have not I always been the one looking for adventure, he asked himself? I have taken delight in every fresh and exciting undertaking, trying something new in the woods, anything, no matter how hazardous, and then daring friends to do the same. This happened many times with Gilin. He met all my challenges. But now Gilin is the one in danger. And true danger, not childish play. How could I possibly back out now? Would Gilin run away if I were threatened? Besides, this is a chance for actual adventure! Almost certainly perilous, but nevertheless real, something I have always longed for! The prospect occupied his consciousness, and his doubts subsided.

Gilin touched Hut's right foot with his own in the age-old gesture of camaraderie and gratitude.

"Then we must move on," said Gilin.

"I understand," said Hut. But in spite of the morning's anxieties and decision making, something important still nagged at him.

"Would we have time to look for something to eat?" asked Hut.

Gilin was famished also, having not eaten for a very long time. He acquiesced, and they descended the tree with their ilon.

They were not accustomed to searching for food in strange territory. At home, the clans knew where to look for food throughout all seasons of the year, either in the field or in storage, and good things were nearly always plentiful. But the youths were well trained in foraging, and here managed to gather enough mushrooms, nuts, and wild berries to satisfy their morning hunger, and even a surplus to store in their knapsacks and belt satchels.

Upon finishing their meal, and with the ilon nearby, the two spent a brief time relaxing in the warmth of the morning sunshine, their backs against a small log. Gilin was apprehensive about being on the ground rather than in a tree. But he was aware that the approach of a gronom would be signaled by the undulations they had experienced the night before in Hut's room, and he allowed himself a few precious moments of rest.

Early rays of sunlight filtered obliquely through the trees. Maples, less common in the home region, dominated this portion of the forest, and their multilobed leaves, radiant with varying shades of green, particularly attracted Hut. The forest here is very different from ours, he thought, gazing about, and yet just as lovely. Surrounded by tranquility and beauty, as he had been all his young life, he began to question how and why something so evil as the gronom, and the more deplorable forces that must drive it, had ever come to exist in the world. For a moment he wished he knew what Gilin did. Then, remembering the consequences of that, he hoped he would never find out.

Hut then spoke to his cousin, who rested uneasily next to him, eyes closed. "Gilin, is there any way in which I can particularly aid you, aside from merely being your companion? Is there a special way in which I can help?" Except for his brief encounter with the gronom, and Gilin's superficial rendering of his experiences, Hut knew nothing about what they would be facing or where they might be going.

Olamin had taught his three young charges as much as he possibly could about gronoms. He knew little about volodons, but he was painfully well informed about their earth-bound counterparts. He told them of the stalking habits of gronoms, of the pace at which they moved, about their climbing capabilities, and about many additional tendencies that might aid the youths in evading the relentless creatures.

Among other things, he revealed that human beings had no greater capacity to see gronoms and volodons than they had to see kirins. What a tragedy, said the old magician, that kirins all over the Earth were being tracked, assaulted, captured, and killed, that kirins were striking back to protect their clans and themselves, and yet human beings were oblivious to any of the struggle whatsoever. What an irony, he said, that what had begun in the world of kirins was nothing other than an invisible war, totally unrecognizable and unknown to humanity, kirins' most ancient of allies.

Gilin had been mulling over all of these matters. He now drew on information he had gleaned from Olamin to answer Hut's question. He opened his dark eyes halfway, and responded, measuring his words.

"There might be something you can do to help, regarding the gronom," he said. "Olamin alluded to it the day before he died. A kirin with the knowledge is, of course, the ultimate prey of the creature. In its grim quest it ignores all else, expending energy on nothing else, except protecting itself from assault or dealing with anyone defending its quarry. Normally, when it senses a nearby assailant, its foul attentions are diverted toward this enemy until the challenge is subdued. However, when the creature comes into very close proximity with the victim it is seeking, it may become frenzied in its fervor for capture and ignore an aggressor even close at hand. At that moment, another kirin might be capable of surprising the monster, especially from behind. It would be a perilous undertaking, both for the prey and for the challenger. If the gronom were not destroyed, it would turn on its attacker and dispatch him mercilessly, and then quickly be upon the heels of its unaided prey."

Gilin opened his eyes and looked at Hut. "It is the only method Olamin knew to harm, or perhaps even to kill, a gronom," he said. "The fiend was created with dark magic and lives but to carry out a single inglorious purpose: to destroy kirins with the knowledge. Its body is compact and dense and has a hard exterior that is, for all practical purposes, impenetrable to attack. However, the wretched creature appears to have one flaw. Its featureless head has no shell or skull, as we know it, but has a pliable and yielding outer covering. This may relate to its uncanny telepathic capabilities, but it also leaves the thing open to incursion and vulnerable to assault. Should a skillful attacker maneuver into close enough range, he might make a strike upon the vile head, dealing it either a heavy blow with a blunt instrument, or a stabbing wound with a sharp one."

Hut swallowed hard at the thought. Then, looking through his belt satchel, he found the pruning knife he always carried into the woods. He used it for cutting berries, mushrooms, and the like. It had not been used as a weapon, and had never been involved in killing. Because of their association with animals and birds, with only a few exceptions kirins the world over are vegetarians. The slaying of birds and beasts is not part of their lives. Hut unsheathed the blade, examined its cutting edge, and tested its sharpness upon a fallen leaf. It cut smoothly and with precision.

Kirins carefully maintain equipment they employ frequently. Hut's blade was exceedingly sharp. It was difficult for him to conceive, however, that this knife might be used for the purpose Gilin described. Never would I have dreamed of such a possibility, he thought. Nonetheless, he had seen the gronom for himself, and he had listened to Gilin's commentary. How, he wondered, continuing to examine the knife, would I react to such a crisis?

Sliding the instrument back into its sheath, he turned and faced his cousin. "I will follow you, Gilin," he declared. "You have said that we must move on. I will accompany you, and aid in any way I can." But only if I can, he thought uneasily.

Just then a shadow passed over the ground on which they rested. Something momentarily blotted the rays of the sun. The startled youths looked upward to see a giant winged creature, darkly outlined in the glare, descending through the trees and moving unmistakably in their direction.

C H A P T E R   1 1

I FOUND YOU!" was the cry the astonished Hut and Gilin heard, as a large raven alighted near them. Off leapt the blond-haired Talli, silver toe ring in hand.

"I found you at long last!" she cried once again, striding breathlessly up to them as they scrambled to their feet. Her green eyes sparkled in the sunlight.

She reached out eagerly to touch Gilin's right foot with her own. "I was afraid I might never see you or any of the clan again!" she exclaimed.

The amazed Gilin clutched his friend's toes with his own. "Talli! How did you find us? What happened after we separated yesterday? How could you possibly have located us here in the woods, so far from home?"

Then remembering Hut, Gilin introduced him. "Talli, this is my cousin, Hut, from the Yorl clan. I'm sure you've seen him when our clan meets with theirs."

"Yes, of course I have," replied Talli. She touched Hut's foot.

"In attempting to escape the gronom after you and I parted, I'm afraid I involved Hut in all of this," said Gilin. "He supplied me with his sister's ilon, and used his own in accompanying me." Gilin indicated the two squirrels nearby. "But, Talli, what about you? Where have you been? Where did you go? And how could you possibly have found us here?"

Talli proceeded with an animated narration of her experiences over the past day and night. She told of the long run homeward, of hiding from Gilin's father and brother, of summoning her raven, of their flight to the stream, and of her loneliness and misery overnight. Then she told of her discoveries about the magic ring.

"Just as the moon was beginning to fade and the sun was about to rise," she related excitedly, "I saw you and another kirin—it must have been Hut—and even heard you talking! The picture did not last long, however, only a very short time. But I am certain the moon activated the ring! Then, with the onset of daylight, your images blurred, and the mist reappeared and then gradually dissipated. Again the space within the ring was clear, as it is now."

She showed them the ring. As usual, they could see directly through it.

"I was overjoyed to see you, alive and unharmed," she said. "Somehow I knew it was truly you, that what I was visualizing was exactly what you were doing at that moment, even though I had no idea where or how far away you were. After seeing and hearing you, my desire to find you was strong! Because of that, I think, the ring kept operating even after the moon disappeared! The ring seemed to know what I wanted, and it began to tug at my hands, and to actually move away from me, so that I had to hold on to it in order to keep it from leaving my grasp. At first I could not understand why, but the ring continued its surprising behavior—pulling, and always in one distinct direction, as though it were being drawn by something or it was trying to draw me! I wondered whether it was attempting to take me in tow and lead me somewhere, but of course I knew nothing about where! I considered the possibility that something treacherous might have taken control, and might be trying to lure me into ambush—something related to the fiendish gronoms or the depraved power behind them. But I also realized that this had been Olamin's ring, and as such I questioned that it would lead me any place where I might come to harm. Could it be, I began to wonder, that it knew where you were, and that it was trying to guide me to you?

"I called Faralan," she said. "I mounted him and we took off. The ring continued pulling even as we flew, as if inviting me onward to an unknown destination. My commands to Faralan kept him moving the way it seemed to be taking us, westward, back in the direction of our clan tree. But we were going south of the course I had taken the previous day, into an area of the forest I had never been. After flying for some time, and when we were almost directly above the place we now stand, the ring seemed to increase curiously in weight. Then it became extraordinarily heavy, as if it had entered a shaft of enhanced gravity or magnetism, but one that affected only the ring. It suddenly had such a downward drag that it was all I could do to keep it within my grasp, and I quickly instructed Faralan to descend. We followed the momentum of the ring downward through the trees and arrived at this very glade. As you saw, we landed there, just a short distance away! And look! Now that we have found you, the ring has returned to normal! It has no pull whatsoever!"

She held it out toward her companions. Gilin took the ring, and turned it in his hands, examining it and shaking his head. "These pieces Olamin entrusted to us have powers beyond our comprehension," he said.

"Gilin," said Talli, "it is my feeling that the ring was in communication with your calamar, or I would not have been able to locate you even after seeing you!"

"You are probably correct," answered Gilin, handing the ring back to its owner. "Instead of the ring knowing where I was, and leading you to me, it must have known how to find its old companion, the calamar."

Gilin then recounted how his attention had been suddenly and mysteriously drawn to the calamar, just as he was awakening Hut, and also how the magical instrument had, for the first time in his possession, been warm to the touch. "That must have occurred precisely while you were viewing us," he said.

"Olamin told us," said Talli, as she slid the ring back onto her toe, "that the two objects had been in his possession so long that they were able to communicate with each other."

Gilin removed the glimmering calamar from his belt sack to re-examine it. Its normal coolness had returned.

Hut had been deep in thought throughout all of this, and was currently in a quandary about what to do. His cousin now had a companion, one who knew considerably more about what was happening than he did. Might he now, he wondered, be able to slip away and go home? And yet he realized that even the two of them together would need the greatest of support for whatever quest they were about to embark upon. He had seen a gronom, and had heard about as much as he wished to regarding its abhorrent capabilities. His companions appeared to be imperiled to such a degree that he seriously doubted whether, unaided, they could accomplish their mission. In the end he decided that his friends needed help, but far more than just he could provide. Knowing that they would not ask for aid themselves, he decided that, regardless of whether they accepted or rejected the idea, he would seek assistance on their behalf, even without their blessing. He broke his conclusions to them gently, to see how they would respond.

"I have told Gilin I will help in any way I can," said Hut. "But I am not certain that the three of us alone can be successful. I must assume, from what Gilin has told me, that we have a mission to fulfill, or a destination. He said that a dark menace threatens the world of kirins, and that Olamin told you how to confront it. Can you reveal anything more about what this might entail?"

Talli turned quickly to Gilin. "How much does he know?" she asked with concern.

"He knows of our situation only superficially," said Gilin.

"I have told him a small portion of it. He will not attract the gruesome enemy as we do. His only danger is being with us."

Gilin and Talli looked at each other silently, uncertain how to answer Hut and how much to disclose.

"We will be obliged to travel," said Gilin finally.

"Where, and how far?" asked Hut.

Again the two hesitated, and then Talli spoke. "Many thousands of clan dominions upon land, and perhaps even farther over the sea."

Hut's mouth gaped in astonishment.

"Thousands of clan dominions over land . . . and perhaps farther over the sea?" he repeated. "How could the three of us accomplish that? Except for Talli last night, none of us has been further from home than we are now! How could we possibly undertake that kind of a journey?"

"We have not asked you to do this, Hut," answered Gilin resolutely. "We do not mean to involve you."

Nonetheless, the keepers of Olamin's knowledge admitted inwardly that they would welcome any sort of assistance.

"But you did involve me!" responded Hut. "Last night, when you walked into my room! I find myself included in a plot so freakish and far-fetched that nobody would believe it! I would not have believed you, had not the effects of the gronom been felt in my room, and had I not seen the wretched thing for myself!"

He was absolutely right, of course, and Talli and Gilin knew it. Hut had been unceremoniously brought into it, and was now definitely a part of it.

Hut was chafing. "Well, we can't just stand here!" he said impatiently. "Personally, I'm going back to the clan. My being there will not attract danger, and Stala knows the way."

Hut was about to climb onto his squirrel when another consideration struck him, and he stopped to voice a new concern. "To embark upon an expedition of that magnitude we would all need bird ilon! Animals would certainly not do! And yet I have had no training with ravens! No bird has even been assigned to me! Both of you already have them! But where would I obtain one, and do so without alerting the clans? Perhaps it is not such a good idea that I join you after all!"

Talli and Gilin, of course, had no answers, and again both were silent. The quest had been outlined by the failing Olamin just before he died. But since he had so little time, details were, by necessity, left to them. They were in as much a quandary of how to accomplish the mission as Hut was. They knew that they would require support, but had no idea how to obtain it.

Finally Gilin spoke. "If Talli agrees, Hut, we will accompany you. But we will remain some distance from your tree, so as not to invite danger to the clan. We might even be safer there, at least for a short time. Gronoms could be closing in on us here. You might want to secure a raven, if you are able, or ask for help, if you are so inclined."

Talli nodded, and with little further discussion the three mounted their ilon. With Talli aboard, Faralan took flight and moved gracefully upward through bright shafts of morning sunshine. They climbed above the tops of the trees, leveled off, and adopted a northerly course.

Still not recovered from their exhausting overnight trek, the squirrels moved stiffly to the trunk of the nearest maple. With Hut and Gilin gently urging them on, they climbed slowly to the top and out along a thin branch overhanging an adjacent tree. There the animals hesitated, measuring their next moves carefully. Then one by one they jumped, landing heavily in the boughs of the neighboring tree as their two young riders held on tenaciously.

The kirins recognized at once that their animals were in no state to traverse the forest in the upper branches of the trees, in the manner in which they had come. To entreat them to do so would be foolhardy and perilous, for ilon and rider alike. The trek had taken more out of them than their discerning masters had realized. Despite the kirins' natural penchant for being in trees, especially in a forest that might be teeming with gronoms, the squirrels were forthwith instructed to descend, and to travel on the ground for now.

Meanwhile, Talli had not gone far, because when she glanced back to locate the others, she discovered they were not in the tree tops at all, where she expected to see them. Suddenly feeling very much alone again, she quickly circled back, descended through the branches, and flew low enough to search the ground cover. To her relief, she found them moving along the forest floor. Drifting in close and hovering above their heads, she sensed what had transpired.

"I will watch for danger!" she called. "Follow me!"

Once more she ascended to a level above the trees, and with spoken instruction caused the raven to go no higher. She ordered Faralan to tarry in flight, allowing the animals and their riders to maintain visual contact with them, so at least for the present, as they progressed northward through the forest, the three young kirins would not be separated again.

C H A P T E R   1 2

THE magician's quarters were more elaborate than those of others in the clan. Throughout the history of the kirin race, it has been a tradition for magicians to live and work in places that are more generous in size, and more comfortable, than those of the average family. Speckarin required space enough to store materials dealing with the teachings and maintenance of curlace magic and for documents pertaining to the spell of no'an. He needed an area for the preservation of the magical instruments kirins have employed through the centuries. It was necessary to have a place for communication with other magicians, even with the High Council, when that was possible. In summation, he required room for all the trappings of a kirin magician.

Speckarin stood in the cooking area preparing an herbal tea, one of his own invention, to soothe himself after a long and trying day. Perplexing enough was the fact that one member of his clan, young Hutsin, had disappeared from Rogalinon without a clue. According to the history given by his parents, and by the looks of his room, which was examined carefully by clan elders and Speckarin himself, the lad had dressed and departed hurriedly sometime during the night. More baffling still was the fact that two of the squirrel ilon were missing as well. Not just one, thought Speckarin, not just the lad's, but two, both his and his sister's!

These unnerving occurrences are unexpected and highly irregular, he thought as he stirred his tea, and for two reasons. First, Hut was nearly too old and too large for Stala, his long-time animal ilon. He was preparing himself for a bird ilon. Unless Hut had decided to embark upon a last trek with his trusted friend, it was unclear why, or even whether, he had taken the squirrel with him. If he had, why did they depart in the middle of the night? Secondly, it was unheard of for an ilon to go off unaccompanied by a master, except in dire emergency, which was certainly not known to have occurred here. Yet Aassa had disappeared as well.

This puzzling series of circumstances had troubled everyone in the clan. As they discussed it throughout the day, no one was able to put forth a logical explanation of what might have taken place. Finally, the confused and fatigued magician had returned to his quarters to contemplate and to wait.

At this moment, during his ruminations, he stood on the elevated cooking platform overlooking the large open area of his dwelling. While the usual kirin apartment consists of several small and interconnecting rooms, the lodging of a magician is usually a single space, larger than most apartments, cut skillfully into trunk or branch where it is unlikely to harm the tree. Speckarin looked out over the beloved old chamber, his long-time home. Weary of contemplating the untoward events of the day, he allowed himself to reflect for a few moments upon the room itself, and his many years of residence within it.

To his immediate left was the wooden door, a detailed rendering of a raven in flight carved into its inward surface. It was the only entrance to his quarters, and it opened directly onto the gathering place of the clan. On the far side of the room was the stone fireplace, the largest in the clan, and its gentle fire illuminated the space surrounding it. He glanced toward the working area between the doorway and the fireplace, the tall magician's chair before a long and cluttered workbench. Shelves above were stuffed with objects and documents concerning the varieties of magic he managed. Above everything, hanging alone upon the wall, was the circular emblem of the Guardian Magician.

As his eyes fell upon this insignia, he was again reminded, uncomfortably so, that communication between himself and the High Council of kirin magic had been dwindling for many years. For reasons he could only speculate about, no communication whatsoever had occurred in recent times. He had occasionally admonished himself for this breakdown in the exchange of information. Perhaps it is partially my fault, he told himself. He had not attempted to initiate contact for a long time, partly because communication had almost always originated from the Council itself. But he found himself shying away from contact for another, more disturbing reason. The last messages, it seemed, had become somehow unsatisfactory, mildly distasteful, or even distorted. It was as if something untoward, which he could not identify, had imposed itself upon the normally forthright relationships between the Council and the magicians of outlying territories.

Yet in recent times, things had been going exceedingly well, not only for his clan but for all surrounding clans, and the need to be in touch with the source of kirin magic had simply not been pressing. He reassured himself that the same was true for all the local magicians of his acquaintance. None of them had heard from the Council recently either. Some were distressed by that fact, while others appeared not bothered by it at all. Some had sensed the same undertones that he had, while others had not. Perhaps, he conjectured, the messages various magicians had received were different. Speckarin had engaged in numerous discussions about these matters with his closest friend, the magician Duan of the Moger clan, and the two of them could not agree why it might be happening.

He frowned and turned away from the insignia on the wall. He had pondered too long in recent days the powers behind the symbol, and the problems that might be associated with them. His gaze fell upon the living area to his right, and the furnishings for entertaining his too infrequent guests.

I have lived here a long, long time, he mused. He had been magician to the Yorl clan for forty-one years. He thought back to the first time he saw these quarters, when he was about to assume the position of clan magician from Xorin, who was retiring from the post after nearly thirty years. He could remember standing in the doorway of this recently created chamber, carved for him before the clan moved into the tree, sensing the similarities between himself and his new quarters. How fresh and raw the wood had smelled, and how utterly young and untried he had felt. Nonetheless, throughout the years since, he had managed to guide the clan and to shepherd his charges through whatever trials and misfortunes they met in their sylvan existence. No crisis, however, had arisen like the one he feared was upon the horizon in the realm of kirin magic . . .

Here he stopped, shook his head, and altered his train of thought, realizing that he was beginning to ruminate again upon another problem he was momentarily trying to forget. He looked once more about the familiar room and smiled to himself. Both of us are aging now, he thought. He sipped his tea and began to wonder about the longevity of the tree.

How much longer will the clan be able to remain in this old oak, he asked himself? He recalled the traditional relocation procedures among tree-dwelling kirins. Home trees are, of course, under the constant surveillance of all of their kirin inhabitants, but especially those of a special class: the tree architects. What exceptional lives they must lead, thought Speckarin. Kirins of this respected vocation are comparatively rare and greatly valued by clans of the territories in which they work. While nearly all other individuals live out comfortable lives within the clan to which they are born, those of this unique calling depart from their families, and by necessity relinquish the luxury of living at home. Due to the nature of the profession, throughout their careers tree architects move constantly between clans, existing as the welcome guests of the kirins with whom they work.

The tired magician continued to allow his mind to wander, recalling fond memories of his tree and its cherished history. Responsibility for a currently inhabited tree falls to the architect, who supervises its maintenance as long as the tree is sound. When he finally determines that an old tree is failing, or is otherwise unsuitable or unsafe as a residence, it is his duty to locate an appropriate new tree and to make plans for its occupancy. Predicting the demise of an inhabited tree is frequently difficult, and in this matter the experience, wisdom, and judgment of the architect is of ultimate importance. However, the finding of a new tree is usually not difficult, and in this task he always receives more help and opinion than he requires. Neighboring trees are so familiar to kirins that those suitable for housing are widely recognized. Because of the delicacy of these affairs, a triad of esteemed kirins—the architect, an elder, and the clan magician—is finally responsible for the condemnation of an inhabited tree and the selection of a new one.

An ancillary and yet equally vital function is also fulfilled by tree architects: that of communication among clans. In their travels and stays with kirin families, they glean masses of information that they subsequently transmit to others. In this traditional manner they allow clans that otherwise would not be in touch with one another to communicate on a wide variety of matters: food supplies, births, deaths, marriages, clan relocations, social trends, and, of course, ordinary gossip. And thus, throughout the realm of tree-dwelling kirins, an elaborate network is provided for the continual exchange of information.

In fact, recalled Speckarin, it was from Valtar, the architect serving the Yorl clan, that rumblings of impending disaster were first heard. He could still remember the scene. It was some years ago. Both he and the visiting architect were at the supper table of a family in Speckarin's clan when Valtar revealed startling news. Magicians of neighboring clans had expressed dissatisfaction, or, more accurately, distress, at the type and the lack of communication between themselves and those in the hierarchy of magicians. He suggested that something might be wrong, perhaps even with the ultimate authority of kirin magic. Just as I have been suspecting, thought Speckarin, but he mentioned nothing to the others, and the matter had not been discussed further.

Irritated with himself for continuing to think in this vein, the old magician shook his head and steered his mind away from these affairs, forcing his attention on something else. Again his thoughts returned to the history and development of his tree. Upon several occasions during his lifetime, Speckarin had witnessed the ceremonious selection and naming of a new tree, always for a neighboring clan, but not yet, he thought with a certain amount of apprehension, for his own. Moving out of a revered old tree and into a new and unfamiliar one is a stressful undertaking for any clan. But when the time comes, it is mandatory that it be accomplished, and without unwarranted delay. According to kirin tradition, once it is determined that an occupied tree is degenerating, the clan must be moved out within three years.

Upon selection of a new tree, the call the goes out to tree carvers and carpenters of nearby clans. This group is made up of two kinds of individuals: young kirins aspiring to someday become tree architects, and older ones who at one time had an interest in the vocation but did not fully qualify, or who became disenchanted with the lifestyle of the trade. They discovered that they prefer the comfort of living with their families. Nonetheless, they enjoy maintaining contact with the profession and its attendant satisfactions.

When the word goes out, carvers from many clan dominions around come to work the new tree. Some from close by commute daily, while others from farther away remain on the site for long periods of time. Preparation of a fresh tree takes two to three years. It involves both internal sculpting and external construction, including the camouflaging of structures exterior to trunk and branches. The architect supervises every activity, and the work must be done to his satisfaction. This important kirin must become acquainted with the families of a condemned tree and be sensitive to their needs within the new tree, as well as to the requirements of the clan magician.

So as not to unduly harm trees, careful consideration is given to the location of all dwellings. This is especially true for that of the magician, due to its configuration and size, and because it must be contiguous to the gathering place. In the case of the Yorl clan, whose tree had been investigated and chiseled more than forty years earlier, a branching area well above ground was considered the optimum location for the communal place, and an immense branch was chosen at this level for the home of the magician.

Throughout the long period required for carving and preparing the tree, members of the clan who feel the need to be involved, and yet have neither the experience nor the skills for building, scour the local terrain for boughs, fallen or otherwise, with a special and desirable configuration. They must be as long and undeviating as possible, and their diameter must be within prescribed limits. Once harvested and collected at a single location, these branches are shaped, milled, and honed by a team of carpenters into flat and straight pieces, suitable for incorporation into a unique structure. Next, through an age-old process, the wood is treated for protection against weather: Pitch is procured from nearby pines and combined with other natural elements to make a viscous oil. This is heated and thinned, and the warm admixture is applied to the wood and rubbed lovingly into its porous surfaces. The resultant boards are both smooth and durable, capable of serving the needs of the clan for many years to come.

Construction of the gathering platform is the final project before a clan moves into its new home. Under the supervision of the architect, wooden beams of an understructure are hoisted through an elaborate pulley and windlass system to the desired level. Once properly positioned, the timbers are lashed together with an almost indestructible twine fabricated from the stalks and leaves of a plant that kirins call kalas. With the scaffolding in place, the last procedure is the fitting and fastening of the carefully prepared planking. It is an operation performed with the utmost exactness, a single piece at a time, so that the floor will be uniform and comfortable for the many kirin feet it will bear during the lifetime of the tree. Work is traditionally halted, however, before placement of the final piece. Its installation is a ritual overseen by the magician and witnessed by the entire clan. This was the last official act of Xorin, recalled Speckarin. It was performed, in fact, on the very day he retired. With the structure finally complete, a celebration of thanksgiving is held in the new sanctuary, a function attended by all concerned with the massive accomplishment of fashioning the tree: the clan about to move in, selected individuals of neighboring clans, the carvers and carpenters, and, of course, the architect himself. The following day is reserved for the naming rite, and in the case of this tree, Speckarin could remember it well.

Another duty of the esteemed council of three is to select a title for the new tree, a matter of great import to all tree-dwelling kirins. The structure upon which and within which they reside is a living, breathing organism, a fact never forgotten by its inhabitants. It is granted a degree of respect unknown for any domicile outside of the kirin world. The relationship between a kirin clan and its tree might even be described as symbiotic, the tree providing a haven for the clan and the kirins in turn offering protection for the tree. Kirins expend much effort in nurturing, repairing, and grooming a tree, doing whatever is necessary to perpetuate the life of their home. Many a clan tree has been protected from blight, breakage, and attack, by the diminutive creatures in occupancy. The invasion of parasite and disease is rigorously assailed. Even animals and birds foreign to the clan are closely observed and are discouraged from harming the tree in any way.

A name, therefore, is not arrived at without a great deal of deliberation by the magician, the elder, and the architect in the months before moving in. Although it is an affair of great interest to the clan, in this official task the committee solicits and receives no help. When the tree is ready for occupancy, a naming ceremony is performed that few kirins, other than magicians, have witnessed more than once or twice in their lifetimes. The name finally selected is not announced until that occasion.

In the ancient dialect, Ruvon, the term for tree is "ro." For a tree in which kirins choose to live, the appellation invariably begins with this syllable. The remainder of the title is what is so carefully considered, so that it reflects both the essence of the tree and the character of the clan soon to reside within it.

For the Yorl clan, those forty years ago, the move had been more traumatic than usual. The previous tree had failed early, the clan being forced out far sooner than expected, not long after they moved in. Even more unsettling, the old magician Xorin was retiring at the same time because of age and ill health.

The newly selected oak was large by any standards, and majestic in posture. It was almost domineering, seeming to rule the portion of the forest in which it had grown. It was a tree well known for clan domains around, and the Yorls, to a kirin, were gratified to be able to relocate into such a desirable structure. In the end, the ancient term "galinon," meaning "Sublime Guardian," was chosen for the new tree.

Again, as he looked back, Speckarin recalled how large this room had seemed when he first laid eyes upon it, so new and so empty, those many years before. It was the day of the naming rite, before the clan moved into the tree. As though it were yesterday, he remembered donning the long yellow gown, departing the empty chamber alone, and descending the tree to perform his initial act as clan magician, that of conducting the naming ceremony. Since that time he had attended several of these occasions for other trees, and had always been struck by the similarity between this rite and the sacrament of marriage, because of the intimate relationship between clan and tree, of which this signaled the beginning.

The entire clan was gathered at the foot of the great tree, grateful for its new home and immensely proud that it was theirs. He could still recall with pleasure the murmurs and nods of approval when, during the ceremony, he as new magician first pronounced the title, "Rogalinon." He had heard it repeated over and over, in hushed tones, as members of the clan intoned "Rogalinon," analyzing and relishing the name of their new home.

Lost all these moments in thought, it was within that same tree and the same chamber that the old magician now shuffled, tea flagon in hand, from the cooking area toward the fireplace. There he sat down in his chair next to the fire. He positioned his long bare feet on a stool in front of the hearth to warm them and relaxed with his tea, still reflecting upon the old tree.

His reverie was suddenly interrupted by a familiar sound. The great toe of a kirin's foot was tapping on a hollow portion at the base of his door. The resonance carried throughout his chamber. It was as easily recognizable to him as the sound of a door knocker is to a human being.

His mind returned immediately to present concerns, the disappearance of Hut and the two ilon. But, again, why were two of them missing, he asked himself? Hut could only have ridden one, yet his sister's was also gone. The burden of fatigue and worry returned to him, and he chose not to rise. He knew every clan member well. Even though he was concerned about the missing youth, he was confident that harm was not at his doorstep. He called out for the visitor to enter, and the always-unlocked door opened.

At first, as he blinked and looked toward the doorway, he could not identify the kirin who entered, his chamber being illuminated only by the fire. "Who is it?" he asked earnestly.

"Speckarin," responded the visitor as he stepped inside, "I

have come for help."

"Hut! Is it you?" asked the magician, straining to see.

"Yes," came the answer from the young kirin as he moved toward the fire. "And I am in great need of assistance."

The magician studied the troubled youngster, and found himself doubly perplexed—both by the sudden reappearance of the missing lad and by his sincere appeal for aid. He managed to conceal his surprise, however, remaining resolute and cautious. He continued to observe the youth, whose form was outlined by the fire as he faced the magician.

"Sit down, little one, and tell me where you have been," said Speckarin gently, though a bit shakily.

"I am glad to tell someone," answered a relieved Hut, as he sat down opposite Speckarin, his green eyes glimmering in the fire light. "I have not even gone home yet. We felt you were the only one we could approach."

"And who are . . . we?" asked the puzzled magician.

Then, as Speckarin listened intently, Hut proceeded to pour out the amazing history of the past day, from the arrival of his cousin in his room to their reunion with Talli, and finally to the journey home, the lad leaving out not a single detail. Of most compelling interest to Speckarin was the part about Olamin, the special knowledge he had transmitted to the three unwitting youths, and the quest upon which they must now embark.

"I left Gilin and Talli half a clan dominion to the south," said Hut, "but with only one ilon, Talli's raven. I brought Aassa home. My cousin and Talli are in imminent danger, sir. They will soon be departing on a hazardous journey to a destination known only to them, but one that is far away, very far away! Whether they receive aid from anyone or not, they must obey the admonitions of Olamin, and they will go! They will not ask for help, nor am I certain they would accept if it were offered. If no one is inclined to support them, they will be forced to go alone on a mission so dangerous that, in my opinion, there is little likelihood they could accomplish it! And," concluded the youth with intensity, "our clan must help them!"

Speckarin had concentrated upon the account with such rapt attention that he barely moved a muscle during the time it took to tell. Now he shifted in his chair, took a deep breath, and arose slowly. Without uttering a word, he walked stiffly past Hut toward the working area of his room. In front of the cluttered bench, he slid open a drawer, extracted a small wooden box, and placed it on the bench. Opening the container, he removed something, and then turned and moved slowly back toward his visitor, examining an object that gleamed in the light of the fire.

"I have clearly not used this as much as I should have," said Speckarin. "That is obvious now."

As he neared the fire, Hut suddenly recognized the bright object as a calamar, identical to Gilin's.

"But then if I had," continued the old magician, "it might have been me the three youths found in the woods, rather than Olamin."

He sat down heavily in his chair and stared silently at the calamar in his lap. After a few moments he said, "Yes, we will aid your friends, Hut. We must do so. We will help them so that they can help the rest of us, the entire kirin race. I have feared the coming of this day for a very long time."

"What should we do next?" asked Hut.

Speckarin looked up at him. "Both of your companions are of the Moger clan. We must at once, tonight, call for a gathering of the two clans, Yorl and Moger, and together formulate a plan."

As he rose and ushered Hut to the door, he wondered precisely what the two youngsters knew that made things so desperate for them, and at the same time he suspected that the answer was in the calamar in his hand.

C H A P T E R   1 3

AT THE PERIPHERY of
the gathering place, among the startled animals and birds
encircling the meeting, Speckarin and Duan were in heated
discussion.

At Speckarin's request, earlier that evening messengers
had left the Yorl tree and sped upon ilon to Rogustin, home of
the Mogers. There they entreated their neighbors to join them
for a meeting of the two clans, even at this late time, and to
come as quickly as possible. Although it was nearly
midnight, and the purpose of the unusual gathering was not
disclosed, the Moger magician and his clansmen responded
without hesitation. The entire clan, save sentries, soon arrived
at Rogalinon.

The discussion in which Speckarin and Duan were
embroiled centered on far more than protocol, a matter not
inconsequential in kirin life and occasionally posing
problems between magicians at joint clan gatherings.

Members of the two clans intermingled uneasily around a
freshly rejuvenated fire at the center of the wooden platform.
They exchanged nervous greetings in the cool night air. They
glanced frequently at the two magicians, anxiously waiting to

learn why this unexpected meeting had been hastily arranged. Those of the Moger clan asked the host Yorls whether they had any information regarding Talli, Gilin and Reydel. The Yorls could only respond that Hut, too, had been missing since early morning, but that he had suddenly turned up and was here this evening. They conjectured that the gathering had something to do with these unexplained disappearances and the still-absent Moger youths. The bird and animal ilon of the two clans, more crowded now than usual, waited quietly at the outer border and in nearby branches of the tree, as poised and well behaved as ever.

Duan had actually welcomed the invitation to the Yorl tree. Had it not come, in fact, he would have made the trek to Rogalinon, or to some other neighboring clan, the next morning on his own. He had discovered something which appalled him and troubled him deeply, and he gravely required the consultation of another magician.

The discussion between the two magicians was about an old topic. Speckarin was trying to convince his friend that the time had finally arrived that some of the magician class, and even common kirins, had feared for a very long time.

Duan was simply thankful to be in the company of a fellow magician. In part because of the flow of Speckarin's rhetoric, and partly due to his reluctance to bring up the worrisome subject, he at first chose to stand his ground and resist the age-old contention rather than discuss the matter concerning him.

For years two factions had existed among magicians, one that held that all was well within the world of kirin magic and its High Council, and one that suspected that problems existed within that body, and perhaps even with the Guardian Magician himself. Duan was of the former faction and Speckarin the latter. As Speckarin related Hut's astonishing story to his confrere, it was becoming almost too much for Duan to combat, especially in the light of his own discovery that day.

"What else could possibly explain the ghastly thing

trailing the youths?" asked Speckarin. "Duan! Those are youngsters of your clan! You must begin to recognize that something desperate is happening! The time has come to face facts, my friend! Wishful thinking will do us no good now! It is no longer acceptable within the ranks of kirin magicians!"

Those recent events relayed by Hut, thought Duan, have made Speckarin more adamant than ever, and now he is almost thoroughly convinced that something irregular is occurring in kirin magic. It would mean so much discomfort, so much misery, to accept that he is right, that these ideas might be true! Our lives have been comfortable and serene for so many years, so many hundreds of years! It seems impossible that something truly serious could go wrong! Is there not some other explanation? Kirin magic has functioned flawlessly for thousands of years!

But as the discussion continued, Duan's resistance weakened and eventually wore down. The troubling revelation made earlier that day, along with Speckarin's rendering of Hut's experiences and the host magician's pummeling logic, combined to give Duan doubts about the state of kirin magic. Vainly, at first, he attempted to interrupt the Yorl magician, whose words continued unabated.

"Stop for a moment!" declared Duan finally. "Let me say something!" But it was to no avail.

In recent times, the state of kirin magic had ceased being a frequent topic of discussion between the two magicians. Their beliefs were dissimilar, each was inflexible in his position, and mention of it merely brought on argument, one unpleasant to them both and in which neither made headway. Speckarin had learned not to broach the subject with his friend, to simply to keep his opinions to himself. Due to the seriousness of the matter, and the possibility of untoward consequences for kirins in general, he had felt it improper to discuss the topic with any member of his clan, including elders. Left to mull it over by himself, he had usually chosen not to think about it. Perhaps I am wrong, he told himself many times over. And for the good of kirins everywhere, he deeply hoped that he was.

Nonetheless, as time went on, doubts remained in Speckarin's mind. Thus, when the question was suddenly reopened, and new evidence was available, a veritable stream of arguments came from Speckarin as he ventilated suppressed opinions and fears.

"I have something to tell you that may prove you are right!" the battered Duan declared, and finally he attracted Speckarin's attention. The Yorl magician was silent.

While walking through the woods earlier that day, said Duan, he had happened upon the girl, Reydel, in a state that he was not prepared to discuss with anyone except another magician. Shaken by the bewildering discovery, and not knowing what to make of it, he did not tell anyone of his clan, including the girl's parents, waiting until he was able to discuss it with Speckarin or another magician. Throughout the day as he meditated on the matter, he began to admit reluctantly that something worrisome and unpleasant might be creeping into their lives and imposing itself upon the sylvan existence of the clan.

Duan's finding of Reydel in her astonishing condition only confirmed Speckarin's dreaded suspicion. While it lent proof to his argument, he was now not intent upon pressing the Moger magician further. His compatriot was in a state of mild confusion, his traditional beliefs dissolving before his eyes. After all the years of denial, his old cohort was beginning to realize that something might be wrong indeed.

After brief further discussion, the magicians determined that the clans must be informed. Something must be done, they agreed, but neither of them knew what.

"I suspect," said Speckarin, "that only Reydel, Talli and Gilin know that."

Duan had begun to recover his composure. He was relieved to have talked to another magician about Reydel, and now he spoke again.

"All three are members of my clan," he said. "I am not certain what dangers their presence might bring, what assaults might have to be fended off, but I have a deep sense that inaction on our part would bring shame upon our clans, and upon the kirin race! We must not leave them frightened and alone any longer! It matters little what they have done or what problems they might have created! They are kirins of the Moger clan! They must be retrieved from self-imposed exile and accepted without delay!"

My sentiments exactly, thought Speckarin, gazing at the Moger magician. And so movingly expressed, my misguided old friend! Well, Duan! You leapt out of your shell in a hurry! And just when I needed you and your old flair and energy! You have mellowed and softened over the years. I haven't seen you so stirred up for a long time.

He reached his foot out to touch Duan's. "I agree with you wholeheartedly," he said. "We must act! Not to do so would be the far greater miscalculation!"

"Now," Speckarin went on urgently, "I need your help. We must inform our clans!"

Without further ado, the Yorl magician went to the center of the gathering place. He was closely followed by Duan. Kirins of both clans hushed. The moment they had been waiting for had arrived. The Yorl magician raised his arms for silence, and when he began to speak the audience listened to every word with great attention.

"While it will be difficult for many of you to accept in these tranquil surroundings," said Speckarin, "there are those among us who suspect, and have for a long time, that all is not what it seems. Something is wrong, very wrong indeed, and it goes far deeper than the disappearance of four youths and three ilon! I am among those who believe that something untoward is at work in our world, and recent happenings only confirm it!"

A shiver ran through the crowd as the magician continued. "The full scope of the difficulty is not known to any of us. It may be, however, to the youths who are missing. We have knowledge of where all three of the Yorl youngsters are, and we could summon them at any moment. But to do so would place each of us in jeopardy, the full extent of which is not known. We do know that peril would exist for all of us!

"Through no fault of their own," he said with urgency, "these youths find themselves in deeper peril than we will ever be, whether they are among us or not! They have remained apart to protect us, to face the danger by themselves! If they can make such a choice, what other decision might we make than to bring them back into our midst, and protect them with every means at our disposal? What I expect to transpire upon their return, however, will be anything but pleasant, and might prove catastrophic! Nevertheless, we have little time to waste if we wish to retrieve them! I would tell you all of what I know if we had more time, but I fear we may be too late already! Do I hear any dissent in this matter?"

Speckarin's question was answered by a virtual chorus.

"No, bring them back!" shouted some.

"Where are they?" called others.

While most of them were bewildered by the astounding turn of events, to a kirin they wanted Gilin, Talli and Reydel returned to the clans, no matter what danger it might impose.

Recognizing the ultimatum, Speckarin turned quickly to Ruggum Chamter. He instructed the overseer to accompany Hut to the hiding place of Gilin and Talli.

"Take an ilon along for Gilin," said Speckarin. "He has none."

Another group, led by Duan, was asked to bring Reydel to Rogalinon.

As the rescue parties were hurriedly departing, a cry of sorrow suddenly pierced the air. It came from a small grouping of Moger clansmen near the edge of the gathering platform. Duan had imparted the grave news to the mother and father of Reydel.

C H A P T E R   14

IN AN ATTACK MODE unknown to the kirins, three gronoms were stalking and surrounding Gilin and Talli in the dark of night. Since the youths had evaded the relentless creatures more than once, an alteration had occurred in the actions of the three gronoms nearest them.

Information on the behavior of these beings had come from the dying magician Olamin. He had known only what personal experience taught him, and what he gleaned from other magicians. None of them were aware that under certain circumstances a gronom could subjugate its incessant and single-minded drive and shift to a different and more subtle style of aggression: cooperation with fellow gronoms. Acting individually, and in the proximity of a prey, they often become frantic, and dispatch an involuntary wave of excitement, palpable to imminent victims. Hut and Gilin had sensed it in Hut's room. Reydel, Talli and Gilin had experienced it at Olamin's grave. One advantage a more restrained and collaborative effort gives gronoms is that, when working in concert, no vibratory warning of impending attack is released.

The exhausted youths were sleeping in a tree hole. Two of the gronoms sat patiently on the ground some distance from the tree, featureless heads erect, transmitting information silently to each other. A third gronom was half a clan dominion away, approaching from the south. It was in constant communication with its two comrades. It moved in the stiff, determined fashion of its kind, pushing tirelessly through leaves and underbrush toward its companions and their goal.

Transmissions of gronoms to one another, could they be intercepted, would be as foreign to kirins as to human beings. Through remarkable telepathic capabilities, they are able to communicate in an unrestricted fashion. But the messages consist only of plans for tracking and confronting an enemy and arrangements for conducting an ensuing battle. They have no concept of victory, no thought of defeat, no idea of morality, and no understanding of emotion. They are, quite simply, merciless and fearless creatures. They were created for the purpose of stalking and destroying, and for none other.

The two near the foot of the tree had ascertained that their prey were in a resting state, and that a single bird accompanied them. The only reason they took notice of the raven at all was that, through telepathic probing, they had discovered it had a special relationship with one of their victims. Their concern was that the bird, alert and watching, would warn its masters of their approach, and the two kirins would escape once again.

But the foreign creatures expected that the bird would eventually assume a resting attitude like its masters, at which time they would advance and attack the somnolent party with relish. The gronoms were not aware, however, of an unusual capacity of the ilon. It would remain awake to protect the kirins while they slept.

Talli and Gilin possessed the only thing that would attract gronoms, the knowledge Olamin had imparted. The creatures were only peripherally aware of other kirins, becoming concerned about them if they were aiding their victims, or if the gronoms were under direct attack themselves.

Thus it was that the gronoms showed no interest when Stala and Aassa jumped from the high branches of a neighboring tree to the oak providing haven for Talli and Gilin. They showed no reaction as Hut and the ilon moved swiftly down the tree toward the hole where the fugitives slept. They paid no attention to the graceful landing of Ruggum Chamter's raven on a nearby branch. But as soon as it became apparent that the newcomers were here to help their victims, the gronoms reacted immediately. They were on their feet and moving silently toward the tree. Reaching its base, they began an industrious ascent of the trunk. They were but a short distance away when the rescue party, unaware of their presence, departed swiftly upon ilon, leaving their zealous pursuers behind, empty-handed once more. Incapable of sensing frustration, the tireless creatures descended to the ground, and resumed the relentless stalking of their quarry.

When Hut arrived, Gilin and Talli had not resisted. They were too exhausted to refuse to go to Rogalinon. The prospect of being in the bosom of their clan, no matter what danger it might attract, was overwhelming.

The journey to the Yorl tree took but a short time for the squirrels, and even less for the raven, kirin masters on their backs. Upon arrival at the gathering place, salutations and outpourings of relief abounded from both clans for the missing youngsters. Their feet were touched by friends, clutched by their fathers, and caressed by their mothers. Talli's mother noted for the first time something she was certain she had never seen before: a ring on her daughter's right third toe. She was starting to question Talli about it when Speckarin's voice rang out, calling for an end to the celebrating. He appealed for quiet and asked the throng to resume their places for continuation of the meeting. It had been a long night, he told them, and all was far from settled.

"We must decide what to do next!" he said earnestly.

The fire was restoked, and as soon as everyone was positioned comfortably, Speckarin began anew. "We wish to welcome our lost youths home," he said, extending a hand in their direction. "It behooves us now to formulate a plan, based upon what information we now possess, both to protect all of us and to strike out, if necessary, against our inscrutable enemies."

Looking toward Talli and Gilin, the magician chose his next words carefully. "I understand that you cannot reveal everything, but we need some information before we can take any kind of action. Hut has told me all he knows. Some of it was confusing, both to him and to me. My good friends, please come forward and tell us what you feel you can. Start from the beginning."

Talli and Gilin stepped away from their families toward Speckarin and the gathering fire. By now the clans were aware of the fate of Reydel, and realized that something unprecedented and serious was happening in their midst, in their normally peaceful forest. They listened eagerly as the two youths began their tale.

Talli started. Her hair was radiant and her green eyes sparkled in the scintillating light of the fire. She told of the three accidentally finding Olamin in the forest, and of their lengthy sessions with the elderly magician. But she referred only superficially to their communications, revealing nothing of their content. Gilin entered in when the history was at the point where they separated.

"Thankfully," said the striking, dark-haired lad, "I was able to convince my cousin Hut to come with me. We used his ilon and that of his sister . . ."

Interrupted by a rustling sound, and by agitation of the ravens in one area of the periphery, Gilin and Talli froze when the first gronom hoisted itself over the edge of the platform. It pushed its way through the ring of alarmed ilon, and started without hesitation toward them. The crowd parted before the heinous creature as it advanced, shocked by its faceless appearance and foreign demeanor. When it was halfway to its victims, the brave Halsit of the Yorl clan, sensing that the thing meant to inflict harm, stepped squarely into its path and attempted to deter it.

"What manner of beast are you?" he asked, unsheathing his blade. "What business have you here?"

The monster stopped momentarily and reached out two upper extremities, grasping him by the shoulders. It raised the helpless kirin overhead and hurled him to the side so powerfully that when he struck a group of observers both he and a bystander were rendered unconscious in the collision, his knife clattering harmlessly to the floor. The monster started again for Gilin and Talli, and as it closed in it seemed to move more rapidly, extending its extremities in the direction of its prey.

"Hut!" called Gilin loudly.

Hut was nearby in the crowd. The moment the creature passed him his action was rapid and accurate. He sprang toward the back of the gronom, pruning knife glinting above his head in both hands. A stabbing stroke into the back of the featureless head arrested the creature's progress. It turned toward its attacker, a dark, bilious fluid pouring from the wound. It lunged toward Hut, and in the process collapsed heavily to the floor, the foul wound still seeping.

The second gronom was close behind and heading toward Gilin and Talli. Another courageous kirin, the female Diliani, stepped from the crowd as the creature moved past, attacking it from the side. Her knife blow grazed its neck. The monster neglected its prey momentarily and turned toward its unfortunate aggressor.

"Strike it from behind!" called Hut, too far away to do so himself, but it was already too late for Diliani.

The gronom reacted quickly. It extended its arms, gripped her by the torso, and with a force never before witnessed by the kirins propelled her through the air to the edge of the gathering area. She landed on the hard surface and lay stunned among the frightened animals and birds.

The gronom turned to pursue its victims, the nearest of whom was Gilin. Ruggum Chamter, however, had learned from events of the previous moments. He stepped quickly behind the single-minded creature. With his wood cutting axe he rained down such a blow to the back of its rude head that the wound gushed a dark, putrid fluid. The fiend fell in its tracks, never to stalk again.

The panic-stricken kirins searched about in all directions, but no other attackers were in sight. Horror was on their faces as they attended to their fallen and injured fellows. In their wildest nightmares none could have foreseen such dreadful events occurring on their peaceful gathering place.

"What manner of creatures were these?" a shaken clan member asked of Speckarin.

"I am not certain myself," he answered unsteadily, "but I believe they are called gronoms."

He glanced toward Gilin and Talli for confirmation. The pale youths looked at each other. Shocked and uncertain how much to divulge, they made no response.

But Hut answered. "Those are the creatures I told you of, sir! They stalked Gilin and Talli and Reydel in the forest! I saw one of them last night, here on our tree, in pursuit of Gilin!"

"I thought as much, little one," said the magician, starting to recuperate and to collect himself. The horror of the unprecedented ordeal was slowly beginning to dissipate.

"My good kirins!" he called shakily to the crowd. "Bring the wounded closer to the fire, so that they might better be examined and attended to!"

The injured were carried or helped to the center. Speckarin and Duan inspected them carefully, and were thankful to find that none were mortally wounded.

For a time, the confused and beleaguered throng circulated, discussing animatedly the awful events, their implications, and the possible reasons behind them. But all stayed well clear of the two gruesome carcasses that defiled the surface of their sanctuary, uncertain whether it was advisable to approach them again.

Eventually, as no further disturbance occurred, or appeared to be forthcoming, their tensions were alleviated, and a semblance of order returned to the crowd. Mention was even made of plans to house the neighboring Mogers for what little remained of the night.

A few of the host kirins were beginning to leave for their homes when the scream of a small girl shattered the quiet. All faces turned toward her. She was pointing toward a tree branch above, just as the third gronom leapt from it and landed next to Gilin.

C H A P T E R   1 5

E VENTS OF the next few moments occurred so quickly that to this day they are discussed and debated among kirins who were there, as well as by many who were not. Those present agree that the third gronom jumped from an overhanging branch, alighting on the platform close to Gilin. What happened next is where disagreement exists, and the truth may never be known.

Witnesses, of course, observed the attack from a variety of vantage points. Some who saw it state with utter certainty that Gilin froze in terror, others that he tried to fight the monster, and still others, just as assuredly, that he attempted to retreat. A second point of contention is what the creature did when it seized him. Some say the gronom reached out one of its extremities and touched him on the shoulder, some think on the head. Others contend that it was not a touch at all, that the creature never came into contact with Gilin, and that it merely pointed a grisly finger in his direction. In any case, it is widely agreed that the gronom did not deal the young kirin any kind of blow. It did not demonstrate the type of violence toward him that the other two gronoms had toward the interfering kirins.

And, while none of the witnesses grasped what was occurring at the time, all agreed later that at the precise moment of attack Gilin disappeared, suddenly and completely, from the view of everyone present. He vanished altogether, leaving not a single trace.

Furthermore, nearly all who were present concur that his disappearance took place almost simultaneously with the piercing thrust of Hut's knife into the back of the monster's head. Like one of its counterparts, the creature still had enough power to turn on its assailant, extending vulgar arms in his direction. But it fell to the floor before taking a step, foul fluid staining the surface upon which it rested.

■ ■ ■

The third gronom lay at Hut's feet. Observing that it was not moving, he glanced about for Gilin. The stunned crowd also looked for Gilin, and then in astonishment at one another. Everyone looked for Gilin, but in vain. Only Speckarin, who was close at hand and had seen it all occur, suspected immediately what had taken place.

"What has happened to Gilin? Where is he?" were the outcries of the bewildered kirins as they searched the area, calling his name and conversing among themselves in total disbelief. Speckarin moved to the center of the assemblage and raised his arms, asking for silence.

"My friends, please! Listen to me!" he shouted, attempting to achieve some measure of order. "Try to sit down and be quiet! Please, be seated and listen to me!"

Eventually they became still, and then one of them shouted back at him. "What has become of Gilin? We cannot find him!"

"Nor can I at the moment," answered Speckarin in a subdued voice, trying to control the throng as well as himself. "But *see* him, rather than *find* him, may be a better way to phrase it now."

The crowd hushed further as they strained to listen.

"I think Gilin may still be among us," said Speckarin.

The magician took a few steps toward the site of the youth's disappearance, near the place where the third gronom lay. "Gilin! Are you there?" he said. "Can you hear the sound of my voice?"

"Yes I can, Speckarin," came the clear response.

It came from the magician's right, and he turned quickly in that direction. It was unmistakably the voice of Gilin.

"Of course I am here! But I . . . I am confused, even though I . . . suspect what might have happened. In all the furor since Hut struck the last gronom, I have tried to talk with several of you! All have ignored me as though I were not there! Speckarin, something has happened to me!"

Silence reigned as the astonished kirins searched for the source of the voice.

The old magician was quiet for a few moments. Then he cleared his throat. "I thought as much," he said.

He took another step in the direction from which the voice was emanating. "Gilin," he said. "I fear that, through some form of unspeakable magic, this ghastly creature has cast a spell over you. The effect is making you . . . invisible. You are not visible to us, though we are to you. How long it will last I do not know."

"Gilin!" exclaimed Talli, his companion in knowledge, who had listened to this exchange with growing excitement. "But . . . then . . . all that has happened to you is that you are invisible! You are still here! You are still with us!"

She stepped forward gleefully, and moved toward the source of his voice.

"Yes, that must be what has happened," answered Gilin blankly, hardly as relieved as his friend. "Talli," he said numbly, as if in a trance. "You and I and Reydel learned from Olamin that something horrible would occur should a gronom ever capture one of us. We saw one seize Reydel. Remember? One moment she was there, the creature attacking. The next moment she was not. Yet the creature remained. We did not know where she had gone, nor what had happened to her, only that she had vanished."

"Of course I remember," said Talli, hanging her head.

After a silence Gilin began again, now with life in his intonations. "But . . . Talli!" he said. "That means something! It means that Reydel may not have been destroyed as we thought! She may be safe! Does anyone know what has become of her? Is it possible she was only rendered invisible by the attack? Has anyone found her? And is she . . . is she still all right otherwise?"

"Duan has been dispatched to bring Reydel to this gathering place," answered Speckarin. "They have not yet arrived. But it is my understanding that, except for being in the same . . . condition as you, she is unharmed."

Talli looked at Speckarin, and now she spoke animatedly. "After we saw the gronom apprehend Reydel," she said, "we had no idea whether she was dead or alive, only that she was gone! Now I think Gilin is right, that she is alive!"

Then, turning toward Gilin's voice, she went on. "I am sorry the monster touched you this time. I can only wish it had been me."

She looked back at Speckarin. "Olamin told us that the fate of any of the three us caught by a gronom would be one of several possibilities. He said that it might vary for each one of us: immediate death, a maiming injury, loss of memory and orientation, or even something different, of which he was not completely certain. Thank goodness it is the latter for both Reydel and Gilin! I am glad of that, for they are both still with us!"

The crowd of befuddled kirins was astounded by the entire conversation, to say nothing of the events of the unbelievable night. Two of their young ones were now invisible! What kind of creatures could these attackers have been, whose behavior was solely aggression and violence until they set upon their prey? Then their culminating acts, it seemed, were to render victims invisible! And yet from what

Talli had stated, it could have been worse: They could have been maimed or killed by the beasts! As they gradually came to grips with the situation, the incredulous kirins were thankful that their two youths had not been dealt a worse fate.

Soon many of them collected around the area from which Gilin's voice was coming. They spoke to him and consoled him, and reached out to find his body and to touch his foot. They tried to comfort and encourage him, even though they could see nothing of him whatsoever, neither his foot nor any other part of him. Eventually they moved away, one by one, leaving only his bewildered family nearby.

"He was the handsomest lad in either clan," mumbled a kirin in the crowd. "What a shame it should have happened to him."

To all of them, to every kirin in the assemblage, the affair was so incredible, so incomprehensible, that they were completely at a loss. They knew not what to think. What were they to do now, they began to ask themselves, and then to ask one another. Finally one of them asked the clan magicians.

"Speckarin and Duan, what has happened here?" called Halsit from the crowd. This brave kirin had been injured trying to intercede when the gronoms attacked. As he arose painfully from the floor, he spoke with more authority and credibility than before, and all listened.

Addressing the magicians, he again implored, "Why is this happening? These rude creatures descended upon us, apparently with the sole purpose of damaging our youths! We know not why, nor when, nor whether another assault might occur, nor how many more there might be! Who can be dispatching these fiends, and controlling them, and for what purpose?"

The crowd shouted out in accord. They wanted an answer, demanded an answer, to why these dreadful and unfathomable things were occurring.

Speckarin looked at Duan, who seemed almost in a state of shock. Then the Yorl magician raised his arms to quiet the throng.

"You ask something of which we have little knowledge," said Speckarin, "but I will attempt to tell you what I know! On the one hand I wish to know more about these affairs, as you do! But on the other, it is my understanding from young Hut that simply possessing the knowledge places one in jeopardy! You saw the results of it a short while ago! I can only speculate on what has transpired! But it is my suspicion, which I expressed earlier tonight at our gathering of Yorls, that something has gone horribly wrong in the realm of kirin magic!"

The crowd was dead quiet as he went on. "I have only the information supplied by Hutsin, related to him earlier by Gilin and Talli. And of course we know what happened to Reydel. The ghastly creatures who attacked tonight, gronoms as they are called, apparently have but a single function in life: to pursue and capture any kirin with a certain category of knowledge. Three youths of the Moger clan, Gilin, Talli and Reydel, have just such knowledge! It was imparted to them by a magician named Olamin, who came from afar and has since died. From the time they received this . . . this information, whatever it may consist of, the three of them have been hunted, day and night. Both Reydel and Gilin have now been apprehended."

At this point the magician's account ceased abruptly, and the attention of the crowd was drawn away from him. For at that moment, the party headed by Duan arrived at the gathering, the invisible Reydel among them. They were welcomed, and the girl was led to her family. Other kirins tried not to stare, but she was received awkwardly by her parents and her brothers and sisters, the only indications of her presence being her voice and her touch.

Then, as the astonished Speckarin watched, an unparalleled scene took place in front of his eyes.

Apparently having waited until she was certain the other girl was present, Talli now walked slowly toward the family of Reydel, her right hand clutching what appeared to be nothing. All at once the magician recognized what was happening. Talli was escorting Gilin to greet the young Reydel, their long lost friend. Both of Talli's companions were invisible.

When Talli arrived before the family, she asked to speak with Reydel.

A cry of "Talli!" rang out, Reydel having presumably seen her for the first time. Then she must have touched Talli's foot with her own. The blonde girl glanced downward, and then looked up, smiling, and greeting her.

Reydel told Talli how dreadful it had been to be alone in the forest after being caught by the gronom. Talli expressed relief that her friend was well and back among her clanspeople.

"But, where is Gilin?" Reydel was heard to ask.

"He is here," responded Talli. Then, not knowing how well Reydel would receive the news, but realizing that eventually she must know, Talli explained that what had happened to her had just happened to Gilin. A cry of surprise and distress escaped the younger girl. Talli reassured her, saying how thankful she was that they were both still alive and finally under the protection of the clans. Then she told her that Gilin was with them.

"But where?" asked Reydel, startled and obviously upset.

"I am here," answered Gilin calmly.

Then he apparently touched Reydel, sensing where she was by her voice and by the manner in which Talli was addressing her, because the younger girl suddenly called out excitedly.

"Gilin! Is that you?" she said. "Are you all right?"

"I am well," came the reply, "except that I am in the same . . . condition as you."

The three youths with the knowledge of Olamin were together for the first time since Reydel's seizure by a gronom, and what was happening was almost more than the old magician could bear.

The two invisible ones were conversing actively with each other, relating what they had been through since they were last together. Each of them expressed grief at the other's disheartening condition, and gratitude that they were both still alive. Talli had stationed herself between the two voices, looking first to one side and then to the other, arms extended, a hand apparently on the shoulder of each unseen compatriot.

The girl appears to be mediating between shadows, thought Speckarin unhappily, shadows that talk and think, and have emotions, and are kirin youths of our clans! He looked away, shaking his troubled head, knowing not what to do next, but unable to tolerate the unthinkable scene any longer.

Things have happened all too rapidly and have gone too far, Speckarin told himself, distressed to the core. I must retire and confer with Duan regarding everything that has occurred. I must find out what he is thinking! My mind is swirling!

He quickly made his desire known to the Moger magician, who now seemed to be recovering his composure. Before they left, however, Speckarin collected himself and made one last announcement to the throng.

"All of you who are able-bodied!" he called out. "Carry away from our gathering area the carcasses of these dead mongers of evil! And remove the stains of their vile blood, if it can possibly be called that! These foul remains defile the revered surface our forefathers constructed so many years ago with dedication and affection! They must be eliminated forever from this peaceful place!"

The magicians then departed the circle for Speckarin's apartment. Several of the kirins set about the gruesome task of moving the bodies and eradicating the abominable blemishes on the floor. They soon found, however, that the remains of the noxious fluid could not be removed completely. It had seeped and soaked its malevolent way into the very grain and substance of their cherished wood. From that day forward, and for the long life of Rogalinon, this onerous disfigurement endured as a reminder of this unspeakable night.

"Tell me more about Reydel!" Speckarin implored as soon as the magicians were sequestered within his quarters. "Tell me again about how you found her, and about her present condition!"

Duan cleared his dry throat and began in earnest. "While I

was walking through the woods early this morning, someone called my name. I looked about but could see no one. Nonetheless, the voice of a young girl persisted, explaining that she was Reydel, and that she had discovered her invisibility. She was frightened but otherwise all right. She had not returned to our clan, but she refused to tell me why, or anything about how she had become invisible. Now, of course, we know the answers to those questions. She would tell me nothing, but she did promise, at my request, to stay in the vicinity in which we spoke. I have since, of course, been sent to persuade her to rejoin us, regardless of the consequences. She had little choice, nor did we," he concluded, "and finally she came."

"Now that you have had a chance to be with her," said Speckarin, "have you found her to be harmed or changed in any other way?"

"To the best of my ability to assess that," answered Duan, "no. Her only damage seems to be invisibility."

"Good!" said Speckarin. "Hopefully the same is true of Gilin! Now, tell me something else, and in doing so draw upon the deepest of your wisdom and knowledge, for it may be the most important advice you ever give! In your judgment, what must we do next, you and I, and our clans?"

Duan spoke without hesitation. "After what we have seen tonight, the most important thing we can do is protect and support the youths with the vital knowledge! We should do whatever we can to help them! If that requires making sacrifices for the good of the youths, we must do it! If it means embarking upon a dangerous quest, we must find the courage and stamina to do so! And if it demands defending them to the death, that also must be done!"

"My sentiments precisely, my old friend," said Speckarin. "But I am afraid it might mean all of those things, and perhaps more! Nonetheless, we have no time to spare! We have seen what havoc those vulgar beasts of prey can wreak upon us all!"

Their discussion went on a short while longer, and then

the two magicians reappeared on the platform, Speckarin with luminescent globe in hand. As they walked toward the fire, he thought fleetingly of the unique piece he carried. He was fond of it and wondered how much longer he would be able to use it. One of his prized instruments of magic, it was the one he had utilized with most frequency during his tenure as magician. It was brought forth for clan meetings, of which there were many, and momentous occasions, of which this was tragically one. Whether it was actually true or not, in his mind the light showed the way to proper answers and correct decisions. It gave him a sense of confidence and direction. And in this distressing time, he thought as he approached the fire, guidance is sorely needed by all of us.

Arriving at the center of the gathering place, Speckarin placed the globe upon a standard to his left. It began to grow in brightness, illuminating the scene as the light of the fire dwindled. Drawing himself up to full height, the old magician took a deep breath and delivered a message that everyone present would remember for the remainder of their lives.

"My good kirins!" he said. "We have been a fortunate group, having lived peaceful and sheltered lives here in our verdant and plentiful forest! But, as you have witnessed, something reprehensible has come alive to challenge all of this! Something deeply wrong threatens to take control over everything! The evil has begun to affect us all, as you have seen at this gathering tonight, with dark magic, violence, and killing!

"We are but common folk," he continued. "But someone must begin to fight back against this iniquity and suppress it before it is too late! Duan and I have discussed the matter, and we believe that nothing will stop the madness if we do not ourselves intercede! It appears that the only means by which we can do this is to aid the three chosen youths! We know not whence this menace emanates! Nor do we have a notion about what, if anything, can be done to combat it! But it is our supposition that the three youths possess just such information! Therefore we must help them! They have special knowledge that seems so important and so compelling that any possessor of it is under perpetual attack!

"Gilin and Talli have revealed to Hut," he went on, lowering his voice, "that they must embark upon a mission, and travel a great distance in order to accomplish whatever task it is. After due consideration, it is the estimation of Duan and myself that our two clans must select a group to support them. It will undoubtedly be a dangerous expedition, but hopefully a rewarding one. We have been told nothing directly about this matter, and know no specifics, because such information places its owner in jeopardy. The purpose of the mission, we presume, is to arrest the mysterious and indecent changes that have taken hold in the very fabric of our civilization, of our kirin world! In conclusion," he said, his voice becoming even quieter, "we think that a means of halting this evil was at the crux of Olamin's teachings before he died."

Talli was standing nearby. Speckarin stopped to glance at her for confirmation.

"We will not reveal the knowledge entrusted to us," the girl answered solemnly. "But the three of us have conferred. We have concluded that to succeed we will require support."

Speckarin looked back at the crowd. "Then," he said firmly, "we have no choice. We must select a traveling party to be at the command of the young kirins who are the repositories of Olamin's teachings! If we tarry, I fear our chances to right the wrongs will worsen!"

Here the old magician paused and glanced to the east, where the earliest glint of daylight touched low-hanging clouds. Then, pointing a finger toward this first evidence of dawn, he continued. "This much the chosen youths have revealed: The expedition must be in the direction in which the sun rises, eastward, and thousands of clan domains over land and sea! Something lurks beyond the horizon that must be assailed, and dismantled, and finally destroyed! I know not what it is, nor what land it inhabits! But this is both a duty and a mandate that none of us can ignore!" And here his voice again became hushed. "To do so, in my humble estimation, would be to sound a certain death knell for the kirin race as we know it."

Cries of disbelief escaped the crowd as the magician went on.

"We shall form such a party from our two clans," he declared, "to journey this great distance, and to do our part and our bidding to rid the kirin world of the derangement that threatens it!"

Even though, he reminded himself disquietingly, we know not where it is, nor what it is, nor what we can possibly do when we arrive.

Now, slowly, he turned once more toward the early glow of daylight. Then he looked back into the faces of the stimulated kirins around him. "This horrendous night is finally coming to an end," he said. "But from this moment onward we may not relax our vigil. For we know not when, nor from what direction, the next assault might come. The only thing we can be assured of is that eventually it *will* come.

"Duan and I have conferred about the composition of this traveling party," continued Speckarin. "We feel that a workable and an appropriate number of participants would be five. An inordinate number would not thereby be removed from the clans, but enough would be included to help one another should the need arise. Beyond this we have few preconceived notions about who should go.

"But now," he concluded, looking at the kirins about him one by one, "I will ask each one of you to do something, and to do so at this very moment. Please, take a short time to search your souls. Then tell me something. Which of you would like to be part of such a mission? Then look into the eyes of those around you, and tell me something else. Which of those among you would be best suited and best equipped for such duty?"

C H A P T E R   1 6

RUGGUM CHAMTER of
the Yorls was the first to step forward, tarnished axe in hand.
He strode from his place in the crowd toward the luminescent
globe of the magician. The circle of light was still spreading
from Speckarin's instrument, but was dimming gradually as
the early light of day gathered in the sky. The stern elder
turned to face the throng.

"I would hope to be among those to go," he began. "I am
not accustomed to boasting, nor electing myself for hazardous
duty without adequate reason. But it would hold that my
experience in the forest is as broad, my handling of ilon is as
competent, and my understanding of occurrences in the realm
of kirin magic is as encompassing as any from either clan."

Whispers of agreement were heard running throughout the
crowd as he went on. "Exceptions, of course, are the young
ones, so deeply involved in the plot, and the clan magicians,
who rightfully understand the machinations of magic better
than the rest of us. Whatever other candidates come forward, I
would hope you will keep my qualifications in mind."

He bowed, first to the two magicians and then to the
audience, and walked back to his station in the crowd.

"We will do so," responded Speckarin, nodding toward Duan. "Are there further brave volunteers?" he asked, looking out over the crowd.

Another murmur ran through the gathering as the young Talli stepped forward. The first rays of morning sun were tinging the upper branches of Rogalinon, and Speckarin's globe continued to pale in comparison to their light.

The brave girl turned toward the crowd and began to speak softly, so softly at first that those seated farthest away were unable to hear or understand her. But as she went on, her voice strengthened along with her resolve, and when she began to relate her ideas about the party of adventurers, the gathered kirins were mesmerized.

"No debate should exist whether Gilin and I must go," she said. "We two and Reydel are the only ones with the required knowledge. At least one of us is obligated to go, and both Gilin and I wish to go. We desire to satisfy the spirit of Olamin, and to seek an end to the problems that began far away, but now touch not only us, but kirins in many other lands, perhaps the world over. We are not braver, nor more adventurous, nor more desirous of facing danger than any of you. Nonetheless, through no fault of ours or anyone else's, we were chosen to do this thing, and now we must do it."

She paused briefly and then continued. "We are undecided about Reydel. The three of us with the knowledge are, or at least were, all attractions for gronoms and other monstrous inventions of our enemies. Both of my friends have been accosted by the brutes, and rendered into the state you have observed. Whether they are still alluring is not known; it may prove that they are now free from . . . this curse."

Here Talli stopped again. Everyone realized that she was now the only one with the secret knowledge who had not been captured, and it began to dawn on them that it was possible that only she remained attractive to the creatures. She recognized it more acutely than anyone, and the burden of this liability was preoccupying her, for at this point in her speech she faltered. After a few moments, she recovered.

"Should Gilin and I depart upon this journey," she said, debating the alternatives aloud, "gronoms and their counterparts would surely follow. Should Reydel accompany us, it might intensify the appetites of the foul beings in our pursuit. Again, we do not know whether all three of us are still prey or whether I am now the only one. If Reydel were to stay among you, her clansmen, it might partially divide the persuasions of the deadly creatures. That situation, however, could place each member of the clan in jeopardy, as you have already witnessed. The beings might stop at nothing to apprehend her again, creating a danger for the clan that, in essence, Gilin and I are not prepared to permit."

Talli continued, presenting her beliefs regarding the expedition and its possible participants. Speckarin listened intently to the girl's courageous words, and marveled at their insight and maturity. What these youths have seen and endured, he thought, and how they have responded! He was proud of them, and because of them he felt pride in the entire kirin race.

He had heard enough, however, to know that it was time to intervene. The matters Talli was discussing were too far-reaching, and had too many ramifications, to be left to two or possibly three troubled youths. Whether their encounter with Olamin could be interpreted as their being chosen was beside the point. Too much of the decision making for both clans was being assumed by the brave youths. This was in addition to the burden of their knowledge, the threats to their lives, and the specter of their own invisibility. It was time, thought Speckarin, to relieve them as much as possible. At least the choosing of members of this expedition should not have to fall to them. The travelers should be chosen by the conjoined clans.

Speckarin raised his arms in the usual gesture. "I will interrupt you at this point," he said, "and be a spokesman for thoughts that must be running through the minds of our clansmen as they listen. You three have the hindrance of this knowledge, which someday may change the kirin world but at present merely places its caretakers in peril. I suggest that the combined clans be the ones to select those who accompany you. The burden of choosing should be upon us, not you. You carry enough already."

Talli hesitated, but then relief showed in her face, and she retired slowly to her place in the crowd. There she began to speak in a whisper to no one, or so it appeared. But of course it was to the invisible Gilin, who had waited for his companion.

Speckarin stood beside his dulling orb, now little brighter than a candle, as beams of sunlight washed over the unprecedented scene. He began to catalogue the candidates for such a quest.

"It is our opinion," he said, nodding toward Duan, "that Talli and Gilin must both go. They are young and strong, and of course both have the essential knowledge. Although we earnestly hope nothing like this will occur, should harm chance to befall one of them, the other could carry on. Do I hear any opposition to this?"

The crowd was silent, many of them numbed by the unfathomable events of the night. But no one seemed to disagree.

"As for Reydel," continued Speckarin, "I have conferred with Duan. He knows her well, and we agree that she would be too young and too inexperienced to participate in an undertaking such as this. We must find a way of protecting her and keep her in our midst, despite the potential dangers of such action. We simply feel that she should remain at home. We must work out a methodology that would encompass both her defense and the safeguarding of those around her. None of us have had any experience in enterprises such as these. But at the present time we have very few choices, and things that have never been done, nor even thought about before, must now be accomplished."

Reydel did not come forward herself, nor did anyone argue that she be included in the mission.

"Now," the magician said, "we need three responsible and resolute kirins. They will accompany the two youths on an expedition—and here I will not mince words—from which none may return, but that may contribute to the preservation of the kirin race. We have heard from our overseer, Ruggum Chamter. Who else would volunteer or qualify for this adventure?"

To the front strode Diliani, and she turned to face the crowd. She was striking in appearance, tall for a kirin woman, and had penetrating black eyes. She had been attacked earlier by a gronom, being hurled aside in the process. But she appeared fully recovered now.

The Yorls knew her to be self-reliant and particularly adept in the training of ilon. She was the most accomplished in the clan at communication with birds and animals, appearing at times to have an almost inexplicable link with them. She was also a proficient student of animal lore from around the world, knowing not only about creatures of the home forest, but about those from far and wide as well.

"I volunteer to join the quest," she began. "The travelers will be in need of ilon along the way. I have talents in this area, and feel I would be of special value to the party. I hope you will consider me when you choose," she concluded. Then she returned to her place in the crowd.

"We thank you," said Speckarin. "We thank both Diliani and Ruggum for their willingness to join the entourage. Do others among you have an interest in going?"

He looked to his left. He thought he had seen the movement of yet another youth. Indeed, Hut stood up and came forward, stopping by the magician.

"I was wondering how you felt, Master Hutsin," said Speckarin. He nodded toward the young kirin's family. "Especially after being home for a while. You were adamant about the clans helping when you were in my chamber. How do you feel about things now?"

"I know more about the background of this problem," said the small youth, "and the reasons for such a quest than any except my three friends. I promised Gilin I would help him, and I will. I have thought about it, sir. I have talked it over with my family. I would like to volunteer. I have always wished for a true adventure. How could I stay at home, with my cousin and my friend going on such a trip?"

"Do not allow youthful desire to color your reasoning," answered the magician gravely. "You might find adventure enough to satisfy you forever, should you be fortunate enough to survive."

From the crowd to Speckarin's left came the voice of Hutsin's mother. "We have discussed it within our family," she said. "In a way, Hut too has been chosen, not by an encounter with a dying magician, but by his cousin Gilin, who is in great need of support. They are not only cousins, but best friends. Our son would like to help Gilin and the others and ultimately, it would seem, each one of us. We are not eager for him to depart on a dangerous mission. He is young and he can be impetuous. But we feel he is mature enough do what he desires. We will miss him and worry about him every day. But if he wishes to go he has his family's blessing."

Speckarin turned to the place in the crowd where he knew Gilin to be, and then he spoke. "Do you desire your cousin to go?"

"I would like it . . . very much," came the invisible lad's response. "We know each other well. He would help me. He has already helped by coming to you on our behalf."

"So be it, little one," said Speckarin, nodding to Hut. "The party might need some youthful spirit."

Hut smiled. "I will attempt to supply it," he said. Then he returned to his family.

Duan had been observing the gathering with great interest from a position near his fellow magician. Now he stepped forward and spoke. He was usually a magician of few words, and here he went directly to the point.

"This crusade," he said, "would be deficient if it did not include a certain kind of individual, one knowledgeable in magic. It must be Speckarin or myself. For reasons he and I have discussed privately, I will nominate Speckarin."

The Yorl magician was not altogether surprised at this turn

of events. Of the two magicians, he had been the one suspicious of the hierarchy of kirin magic for years, while Duan had supported the status quo. Both clans were now deeply embroiled. One magician certainly had to stay at home, and it was apparent that one should accompany the party.

"I will go," responded Speckarin without hesitation. "In so doing I will turn over to my compatriot Duan the overseeing of all matters pertaining to magic within my clan. It will not be an easy task, remaining at home in times such as these. It might be easier, and safer, to go."

Speckarin looked over the crowd again. "We now have four members, Talli, Gilin, Hut and myself," he said. "Do I hear opposition to any of the four?"

None was offered and he went on. "In that case the next and last choice is between Diliani and Ruggum Chamter, who have both volunteered. They are knowledgeable and valued members of the Yorl clan. It is my opinion, as magician, that one of them should be included and one should stay at home. We must remember that those who stay, as in the case of Duan, may have as much responsibility as those who go. None of us knows where a quest such as this will lead, if anywhere at all."

Speckarin turned away from the crowd and spent a short time conferring with Duan. Again he faced the throng. "It is our recommendation that members of the Yorl clan cast votes for these two, one vote per member over twelve years of age, and that we abide by the decision. If no one opposes this plan we shall proceed."

No dissent was voiced. The Yorls prepared themselves for an election in the customary manner, covering their eyes with both hands. The names were called out by Speckarin. He and Duan counted the votes cast by the raising of a right foot by each eligible individual.

"The balloting is over," announced Speckarin, and all eyes were again upon him. "Diliani has been elected."

A disturbance caused Speckarin to glance to his right. Someone was rising from the floor. "How can it be?"

questioned a gruff voice, and then to the forefront strode Ruggum Chamter.

"How can it be?" asked the chafing overseer. "Does my experience in the forest, and with ilon, and with travel, command no respect within this clan? I am appalled and unable to comprehend what you have done!"

"The vote was not close, my old friend," answered Speckarin gently. "And I must tell you that I agree with the clan. It is my feeling that this was more an election of who should remain than of who should go. Of course you are experienced and capable, and you have wisdom. The clan needs an individual of your stability and stature to be with them in this unparalleled time of unrest."

The chagrined Ruggum shook his head and growled, but said nothing further, returning to his place in the crowd. But at that moment a plan began to formulate in his mind that not even Speckarin, his intimate friend and long-time associate, could possibly have imagined.

C H A P T E R   17

WHEN THE momentous meeting was over, the kirins rested. Sentries were left on duty to oversee Rogalinon, but most of the Yorls retired to their homes. Mogers were asked to remain and were provided hospitality, so that they would not need to make an immediate journey to their tree. The two clans felt a certain security in being together after the horrifying events of the night. For the first time in a long while, during these early daylight hours, the three youngsters with the knowledge were protected in the bosoms of their families, and they slept soundly.

Noon was chosen as the time for departure for the elected party and the visiting clan. The morning passed uneventfully and quietly.

Before the appointed time, mothers of the Yorl clan arose to make ready a meal for families and friends, as they had arisen to prepare breakfast from time immemorial. But it was without joy on this day, for they knew in their hearts that their peaceful and bucolic existence had been changed, probably forever.

Hut's mother, deep in thought about her son's impending departure, was almost mechanically preparing his favorite meal of spring berries and nuts, and she glanced up when he entered the small kitchen. Moments later his father followed quietly through the door. Gilin and his family rested in the small entryway, warmed by the dying coals of the fireplace.

Hut and his father sat down in the breakfast nook in a corner of the kitchen. The table and benches, indeed the room itself, had been sculpted from the wood of Rogalinon, carved by woodworkers who had labored those many years before to shape this into a habitable tree. Above the table was a small window to the outside. Through it shined bright rays of the late morning sun. The two sat silently as Hut's mother served breakfast. No words were exchanged as they began to eat.

Eventually Hut spoke. "We must leave shortly for the Moger tree to select bird ilon."

"We know," answered his father. He glanced up at the sunlit opening. "It will be a good day for travel."

He paused. "Hut, whatever happens on this crusade, remember something at all times, especially when things become difficult: Your family, your clan, and your race are already proud of you, for what you have done and for what you must do."

"Thank you, father," said Hut. "I hope I can live up to the responsibility placed upon me. I hope all of us can." He paused. "I am excited. But I explore my heart, and I find no fear."

"I will send spring fruits and nuts with you," said his mother, aware of the despondency each morning's awakening would bring until her son's return.

■ ■ ■

Speckarin and Duan had not slept. They spent what was left of the morning collecting implements of necromancy in Speckarin's apartment. Realizing that magic might be the only means by which the traveling party could combat certain forces, the two worked diligently at the cluttered bench, sorting through what equipment and materials the Yorl magician had

collected over the years. Toward noon, after examining and
testing the supply of magical paraphernalia as thoroughly as
possible, and after selecting what would be most useful and
reliable, they still had a little time to rest. Both fell fast asleep,
Duan in a chair by the fireplace and Speckarin, perhaps for the
last time, he thought, upon his old bed.

■ ■ ■

The gathering place had begun to fill and bustle with
kirins of both clans before the announced time for departure.
Yorls were alert and prepared for activity, and Mogers were
eager to leave for Rogustin. As yet no sign of danger or
recurrent attack had been encountered, and everyone was
grateful for that. Of the traveling party, Talli and Gilin of the
Moger clan, and Hut and Diliani of the Yorls, were ready and
awaiting departure. When it became apparent, however, that
the two magicians were not present, a slight tremor of anxiety
ran through the crowd. Halsit was dispatched to Speckarin's
apartment at the edge of the meeting place.

The tapping of his great toe upon the door immediately
brought the exhausted magicians to life. And after all too
brief a slumber, thought Speckarin, as he struggled to his feet.
Gathering the instruments into a manageable pack took only
a short time, and then the magicians appeared, moderately
disheveled, on the wooden deck outside.

Speckarin raised both arms, slowly this time and wearily.
Then he cleared his throat and made a final pronouncement to
the clans.

"To those of you who stay at home," he said, "be safe and
of good health. To us taking leave, may thoughts of home and
clan be with us wherever we journey. And whatever should
befall us, may those thoughts remind us why we roam."

It was not such a bad speech, he thought later, for a very
old and tired magician.

The chosen party and the members of the Moger clan then set off, a few on foot and many upon bird ilon. And, for the last time, Hut rode his long-time friend Stala.

■ ■ ■

Earlier that morning, at the conclusion of the long meeting, Speckarin had sent messengers to two of the neighboring clans, inviting the magicians to a conclave at Rogustin. Already present when Speckarin and Duan reached the Moger tree were Fuadru Vez from the Zota clan and Golin of the Stunfin clan.

They, along with Duan and Speckarin, retired immediately to the Moger magician's quarters for a private discussion. Speckarin described in graphic fashion the recent astounding and disturbing events and the intentions of the traveling team. Although the neighboring magicians had heard inklings of trouble, nothing similar had occurred within their clans. Both of these leaders were of the persuasion Duan had formerly espoused—it was unclear to them how anything major could have gone wrong within the hierarchy of kirin magic. Therefore, even after considerable discourse, they were still unwilling to volunteer their clansmen to support an entourage for anything as unsubstantial and risky as this quest.

"Just as I suspected," said Speckarin after the other two had departed. "Very, very shortsighted of them. Duan, we are on our own."

■ ■ ■

Hut, Speckarin and Diliani stood together on the gathering place of Rogustin. The name of the Moger tree was hardly appropriate for those about to depart on the journey: It means "Anchorage" in the ancient tongue of Ruvon.

The communal area was smaller but otherwise not unlike that of the Yorl tree. They waited in anticipation, for each of them was about to be given control of a raven. For reasons that were not completely clear, except for Ruggum Chamter, Diliani, and a few others, Yorl kirins were not as proficient in training and utilizing bird ilon as members of the Moger clan. The Mogers' expertise in this area was widely recognized and appreciated among kirins of the region. Gilin was already an expert master of Loana, a strong and reliable bird, while Hut had never ridden upon a raven. Talli had flown upon Faralan for several years.

Diliani's current raven was in an early instructional phase. Because of the bird's youth and inexperience, he was considered unqualified for the distances they expected to be traveling and the trials they would doubtless encounter. It was decided that her bird should be left at home. And, surprising as it may seem, although few within his clan even knew it, the magician Speckarin had, like young Hut, never flown upon a raven.

Neither the occasion nor the requirement to learn to fly had truly arisen, the old magician had rationalized over the years. Nearly every day he had seen one or more members of his clan arrive or depart upon one of the sable winged creatures, and he had often wondered what it would be like to fly. But his duties were almost always close to home. Learning to take control over a wild creature such as a raven was a lengthy procedure, and he had never expended the effort to do so. He had traveled occasionally—to the tree-naming ceremony of a neighboring clan, for instance. But he had merely taken a little longer than customary and hiked the distance, pleased to have time to himself in the woods. However, on occasion, when he closely scrutinized his feelings, he realized that he had, in actuality, an aversion to flight.

Tree-dwelling kirins almost never have a distaste for heights, and in climbing trees Speckarin was as fearless and confident as any. But that meant bark and branches solidly against his hands and feet. Sailing through thin air, however, upon nothing more substantial than a bird allegedly under his control, was quite a different affair. While the occasion to learn flying had never come up directly, he had also not actively sought it out. And yet now, not only the opportunity to fly but the absolute necessity to do so was just as imminently upon him as it was upon the other members of the traveling group. Thus, as he stood gazing across the gathering area at three giant birds, he was more than a little anxious.

After the momentous meeting of the two clans, but prior to departure from the Yorl tree, elders of the Moger clan had met. They recognized the ultimate importance of this mission. Therefore, in case they were needed, the elders had selected three of the most seasoned and dependable ravens of their clan. Later, when informed by Duan that the party would receive no help from other clans, they made a decision to part with all three.

One of the elders now approached the Yorl visitors and informed them that they would be introduced to their new ilon by Lugor, senior practitioner of curlace magic. He then began escorting them to the opposite side of the gathering area, where a group of Mogers stood by the ravens.

As they were starting to go, Hut caught sight of Stala. His animal was being led away, to be returned to the Yorl tree. Hut stopped to watch his long-time companion. At the same moment, the squirrel turned to look at him, unsure why he was being removed from the master he had served these many years. Hut nodded toward his old chum, and then called to him.

"Tonica, alcia nim bontar!" he said in curlace. "Go home! I will return as quickly as I can! Wait for me!"

Reassured, Stala turned and continued on his way.

When that might be I know not, thought Hut uncomfortably. According to Gilin and Talli, not until we have traveled countless clan dominions to the east.

Hut had little concept of what that meant. He had never been farther from home than he was two nights ago with

Gilin. He only knew that it was a long distance and that it would probably take a long time.

He watched until his squirrel was out of sight. He was not just sad at the parting. He was aware of the finality it signified. Stala had been a playmate, a friend, a confidant throughout much of his lifetime. This parting meant the end of an era, the end, in fact, of childhood itself. It was not a child's problem that was threatening the clans. It was not a child's mission he was undertaking.

Hut forced himself to turn back toward the other kirins. They were stationed around three ravens on the opposite side of the platform. For a few moments he stood by himself and watched. A ceremony of curlace magic was commencing, unlike any he had witnessed. As he observed, the realization that he would imminently be graduating to a bird ilon began to filter into his thoughts, and to mingle with his misgivings.

Slowly he approached the conclave, Diliani and Speckarin already there. Each ilon, Lugor was explaining, was a mature and fully trained raven, graciously loaned by the bird's owner for the upcoming journey. Upon this occasion the current master accompanied his ilon. Through the lovingly soft words of curlace, and with touches and caresses, control of these winged creatures, whose entire existences were spent serving their kirin masters, was deliberately being transferred from the owner to the curlace elder. At a point when a bird was completely under Lugor's direction, the previous master literally backed away from his beloved ilon and faded into the crowd. When all three were within Lugor's power, he turned toward those observing. By now Hut had joined the others. Lugor called the names of the three Yorls, and asked that they come forward.

During the portion of the ceremony that followed, neither the birds nor the kirins, save Lugor, made a move. Until they were called upon, no one other than the elder spoke. The procedure of transmission was carried out entirely by the senior practitioner, and in the language of curlace. Beginning with Speckarin, and proceeding to Diliani, the new masters were requested to select a bird. Speckarin hesitated briefly, and then with conscious effort to quell his trepidation, indicated the oldest and largest of the three ravens. The bird's name was Ocelam, which means "Enchanted Flight" in Ruvon, and control of the sable bird was transferred to the magician. Next, Diliani chose Manay, or "Protector," and stewardship of this bird was given to her. The remaining one, Lisam, "Seeker of the Skies," was placed under Hut's guidance.

Hut had often dreamed of soaring upon the back of an eagle, or upon any bird for that matter, the dream of many a kirin youth. But now, as the ceremony ended and he approached Lisam, he was surprised at his lack of excitement that this was his bird, that his dream was actually coming true. He found he still yearned for Stala.

His ruminations were interrupted by Lugor. Hut felt later that the curlace elder had been reading his mind, because he made a statement startlingly similar to one his grandfather had recently made.

"The first one is forever special," said Lugor. "You will miss Stala. But he must be left behind, even as we all must separate from squirrel ilon, and from many things of childhood. Even though we may not outgrow those ilon in spirit, we all outgrow them in size. But now, my young friend, you have much to learn about this fine and faithful creature Lisam, and little time to do it. Diliani and Speckarin must have had a great deal more experience with bird ilon than you, and even they will require as much practice as can be afforded."

Speckarin was lingering nearby. He overheard Lugor's commentary. His statement is clearly true for Diliani, he thought, but I have as much to learn as my young compatriot.

He moved in closer to watch Hut and the elder.

"Bring your bird and follow me," Lugor said.

The lad spoke to the bird and patted her sable chest, using some of the words he had learned for Stala. The giant creature did not move.

"The phrase to use is this," instructed Lugor. *"Ovonn, momeysum tiosico."*

Hut repeated the words and the great bird moved toward him. As Hut began to walk the ilon followed him.

"Come," said Lugor. "We will go to the upper branches, and within a reasonable time you will be flying."

"Oh!" called Speckarin, starting toward Lugor. "May I join you? I must admit something! I have not had as much experience flying as I should have had!"

"Yes, of course," replied the elder, puzzled at this.

Hut and Speckarin spent the remainder of the day with the curlace practitioner, learning how to control and care for their new ilon. It did not take the venerable tutor long to recognize that Speckarin was as much of a neophyte in these activities as Hut, and that he had some old fears to overcome. Diliani, meanwhile, became acquainted with Manay on her own, leaving more time for Lugor to be with the other two.

That night Hut rested as well as could be expected under the circumstances. He had slept little the past two nights, and he fell into a deep slumber in the security of Gilin's dwelling. Arising early in the morning, he again met with Speckarin and Lugor. The elder related that since their arrival on the Moger tree, no attack or evidence of gronoms had been encountered by either clan.

This news circulated throughout the Moger clan and relieved most of the kirins, at least temporarily. It did little, however, to allay the apprehension of the five members of the chosen party, and throughout the days in which they solemnly prepared for departure, they were never fully at ease.

Lugor had devoted a lifetime to the study and practice of curlace magic, and his two pupils could not possibly be expected to absorb everything he knew. In the little time available, however, they were able to learn enough to fly capably, and to comprehend how much more skill and knowledge they must accumulate in the days to come. Hut rapidly became comfortable upon the beautiful and graceful Lisam, and because of this Lugor was able to spend more time with the old magician, whose anxieties dissipated gradually. Nonetheless, even by the time they were ready for departure, the magician did not relish the idea of flying. He viewed it purely as a necessity, a means of transportation, and not pleasurable by any stretch of the imagination.

Speckarin passed the evenings in Duan's apartment, in deep discussion on matters pertaining to the two clans as well as the upcoming expedition.

Talli and Gilin remained with their families. Each of them already possessed a bird ilon, both of which were considered healthy and resilient enough for a long journey. Talli's raven was Faralan, meaning "Shimmering Ebony" in Ruvon; Gilin's was Loana, which means "Timeless Fortitude."

Gilin's last two days at home were most unusual and difficult due to his condition. Nonetheless, despite his invisibility, his family demonstrated their deepest affection for him and encouraged him with utmost sincerity. They were uncertain what was truly best for him. They were torn between advising him to go forth on the quest and encouraging him to remain at home. They finally concluded, despite the dangers involved, that his best opportunity for recovery was to journey with the others, in the hope that something might occur or be discovered that would reinstate his visibility.

Although she had never said it, his mother knew in her heart that he was the handsomest youth in either clan. She could only hope that somehow he would recover and return home, and that she would be able to see her beloved lad again.

On the third day after their arrival at Rogustin, the traveling party, the entire Moger clan, and visitors from the Yorl clan came together early in the morning for the departure of the chosen few. The spring sun was warm upon the gathering area as final good-byes were spoken. Then the group of five mounted their ilon, and at a signal from Speckarin they lifted off together. They climbed through the air to the tops of the trees, and in moments they were gone.

PART TWO

■ ■ ■

C H A P T E R   1

THE FIVE KIRINS flew
eastward in formation, Talli at the lead, her blond hair
flowing behind. Of the two acquainted with the nature of
their mission and destination, she was the only one the others
could see. Speckarin was slightly behind and to her right,
Gilin to her left. Diliani flew to the rear of Gilin in order to
keep his raven in sight, and Hut filled out the "V" formation
behind Speckarin.

The kirins did not speak, although they could easily have
conversed from the backs of their ilon in flight. They were
deeply into thoughts and emotions of their own, ranging
from exhilaration to melancholy. Talli recalled her short
expedition in this direction four days ago, and after they had
flown for a while she actually sighted the stream by which
she had spent the night.

Turning to her left she called to her friend. "Look below,
Gilin! There is the stream I slept by the other night! And on
that very bank I saw you and Hut through the toe ring!"

Gilin looked down and could see the area Talli pointed
out. He felt for his calamar, knowing it was in his belt
satchel, and was relieved just to touch it.

"I am glad you discovered the ring's abilities and found us," he answered, trying to seem cheerful and optimistic. But because of his condition, he was the most depressed of all.

They flew steadily throughout the sunny morning with little further conversation. Hut had never strayed from home. But the anxiety he felt was tempered by the enjoyment he was having flying upon the back of an ilon. He had dreamed of this, and had taken training runs upon Lisam during the past two days. But to be in full flight for the first time, to feel warm air rushing by, to see blue sky above, and to view the forest, lakes, and fields moving continually beneath was an experience he would never forget.

The ravens were large and strong, and Hut was struck by the power of these great creatures as their wings undulated upward and downward. He became accustomed to the oscillating upward thrust of the bird's head and neck on the down stroke of the wings, followed by a downward movement on the up stroke. He found the gentle motion pleasing and almost soothing. But much of the time, as is characteristic for a raven, and not for its smaller counterpart, the crow, the giant birds simply glided and soared, resting their wing muscles in flight, allowing their masters both a smooth ride and an incomparable view of the scenery.

It was a long morning for Speckarin. He had known it would be. He could only hope that things would get better as time wore on. Not enjoying either the flight or the view, he expended most of his energy simply gripping the raven, and with grim tenacity maintaining both his carriage and his composure.

When the morning was nearly spent and the sun was almost directly overhead, Diliani called ahead to Talli. "We must look for a resting place for the ilon," she said.

Within a short time they saw a small lake. Diliani signaled that this would be a suitable area. The kirins spoke gently to the birds, stroking their necks, and with Talli in the lead they descended and touched down next to the water.

The riders dismounted, took a few moments to stretch and

regain their earth legs, and dismissed the ilon to search for food. Then they sat silently by the glimmering blue water and ate a lunch packed earlier that morning.

Speckarin glanced about at the small party of his fellows. A woman, he thought, a girl, and two lads, one of whom I cannot even see, upon a mission more treacherous than any of them can fathom. I fear that our success or failure will somehow depend upon me, my decisions and abilities. Upon me! The one least suited for flying, and perhaps for the mission itself! He shuddered and tried to think of something else.

"This will be our last home meal," said Diliani, "for a long time to come. Let us hope along the way we have others we can enjoy as much."

"This is not a bad trip so far," said Hut encouragingly. "We have a long way to go, but I love flying! I could do it forever!"

It may indeed seem like forever before we are finished, thought Speckarin glumly. These youths have little concept of what they are getting into.

The old magician stood up and brushed off his gown. "Summon the ilon," he said to Diliani.

She whistled and called aloud. Within moments the five birds returned.

"Off we go, then," said Speckarin wearily, as the kirins remounted their ravens.

Talli departing first, the five lifted off. They slanted upward to their previous altitude and continued in an easterly direction, moving ever farther from home.

By late afternoon all were ready for a rest. They had made a few stops during the day, but now both bird and kirin required a longer respite. Sighting a wooded area adjacent to a small stream, Diliani indicated that they could spend the night there, and they glided slowly to a landing. The kirins climbed off and began to explore.

Their preference, of course, was to sleep above the ground in trees, as they always did at home. They searched a few of the trees, mostly oaks, and selected several clean, dry holes. Recognizing that under the circumstances this was the best they could hope to do, they settled apprehensively into sleeping locations in various trees after a supper of berries, mushrooms, and tender greens. Gradually they relaxed and watched as the sun set in the direction of home.

Several red squirrels had been observing them and now cautiously approached their locations, but then withdrew after their curiosity had been satisfied. Later the call of a horned owl awakened some of the kirins from an uneasy sleep. Otherwise the night passed without incident.

In the early morning Speckarin arose first. He climbed down the tree he had slept in and began to search for breakfast. The weather was beautiful, sunny and cool, with a promise of warmth in the clear air. The others soon joined him, and they ate together, partaking again of the regional fruits and fungi. Then they summoned the ilon, who had rested above them in the trees, and departed their first campsite.

As they continued their flight eastward, they began to note an occasional long, narrow line traversing the terrain below. These were usually straight, and sometimes they intersected another one going in a different direction. Curious, and wondering whether they could be related to human beings, Hut called to the magician, ahead of him in formation.

"Speckarin, have you seen the strips or channels that have been passing below us?" he said. "Do you know what they are, or where they came from?"

The magician was somewhat more at ease aboard Ocelam on this second day than he had been on the first. He had been observing the features of the earth as it slowly passed beneath, and had identified the paths as passageways for travel, produced and utilized by human beings. Even he had never been this far from home before, and he had personally never seen such a creation. But in his training as a magician he had learned to recognize these as manifestations of human civilization.

"They are called 'roads'," he answered, turning cautiously toward Hut while gripping his ilon tightly. "Humans construct them, carve them through forests and into the sides of mountains, lay them out through fields, even over marshes and rivers, so that they may travel the countryside uninhibited. It is a concept unfamiliar to us, to roam far and wide and to require a smooth course. We kirins normally embark upon no long journeys. And, thanks to our ilon, we have no need for roads. Except for our present venture, our wanderings are by comparison exceedingly close to home. That is our custom. We know it that way and enjoy it."

At least I do, he said to himself, strengthening his grasp on the raven's neck.

"Then," asked Hut, "are we likely to see human beings on these roads?"

"Our home trees are comparatively close to human settlements," said Speckarin. "We have flown only a day and are already beginning to observe signs of human population. I suspect that not many live in this vicinity, but we may be entering a more populous region, and evidence of their inhabitance may become more frequent. Yes, I think we will observe human beings on these roads, and perhaps even in other contexts. As you may know, they generally live in freestanding structures, instead of in homes carved into a tree, as is our practice."

"They would be rather too large for that, wouldn't they?" chuckled Hut. "And they would fall out!" he added with a laugh. He pictured the hulking creatures lounging about in the boughs of trees, attempting to sleep, eat, and carry on daily lives in that strange environment.

"You are correct!" said Speckarin. "In the local human dialect their dwelling place is called a 'house.' I have not personally seen such a thing, but I have studied kirin documents describing their many shapes and sizes. Throughout history, as you know, our species has kept a close and careful watch upon its human neighbors."

"Speckarin," called the invisible Gilin from across the formation. "What, may I ask, does a house look like?"

"They vary widely around the world, as I understand it," came the magician's reply. "But in this land and in this region, they usually have upright walls and a roof that comes to a point—but not to a single point as one might imagine. It is as though two walls are placed together and form a peak where they meet, a design that theoretically allows rainwater to be shed from the building."

"Then, is that a house there?" came the voice from the back of Loana. The others had been engrossed in the conversation, and had uncharacteristically not taken notice of the structure they were approaching.

Gilin pointed toward the dwelling ahead, but, of course, none of them could see him. Realizing that, he described the location from their vantage point. Then they all saw the mustard-colored house, tiny from the altitude at which they cruised. All watched with a sense of moderate uneasiness but keen interest as it passed beneath them. They continued watching, heads and necks craned rearward, until it became small and far away as they flew onward.

No sign of human life had been detected. Nonetheless, this was the first time any of them had seen an edifice erected by human beings. To a kirin they were affected by the proximity to the giant race that this sighting signified. Hut felt a mixture of both curiosity and revulsion when he considered the prospect of actually seeing the creatures themselves.

When evening came, Talli led them again to a landing in a suitable glade of trees near a lively and bubbling stream. They released the ilon to find nourishment, collected food for their own supper, and selected uninhabited tree holes for the night. Luckily, they thought, this time they had found a single tree to accommodate all of them. As darkness began to fall for the second time upon the small group, they relaxed and readied themselves for sleep.

But they were entirely unaware that another party, whose interest in them was paramount, had arrived and settled itself in the top of their tree.

C H A P T E R   2

A STEADY RAIN had begun to fall during the night, but the kirins remained dry and comfortable in their carefully selected tree holes. The early light of day revealed a misty, humid forest as Speckarin stretched and looked down. Then he climbed out of the orifice and onto a branch of the tree. The rain had ceased for the moment, but heavy clouds hanging low overhead showed promise of more to come. This morning, for the first time since their expedition began, he missed the comforts of his apartment, his bed, his kitchen, and his old fireplace.

"It is too early to think thoughts like that," he told himself aloud. "You have a very long way to go before seeing those things—if you ever should see them again!" The real question, he thought, is just how long? How far must we go, and where are we going?

He had his suspicions. He had speculated for years that something was not right, perhaps even deeply wrong, in the realm of kirin magic. During his forty years in practice, communication between clan magicians and the upper echelons of the magician class had diminished to nothing. He had argued about his beliefs with fellow magicians such as

Golin, Fuadru Vez, and, of course, the unflappable Duan, but
to little avail. He had referred to something being wrong with
kirin magic at the combined clan gathering. He was not
certain this quest was related to that matter, but he strongly
suspected it was.

He had no distinct idea where the Guardian Magician and
his court might be located. None of the local magicians had
ever known. Messages and teachings had always arrived via
magical means and devices such as his calamar. It was
impossible to tell where they originated.

In reality, he recognized as he stood in the morning mist,
he had no means of knowing whether his old uncertainties
had anything to do with their present mission.

And not knowing was beginning to wear on him. He
could not know the particulars of Olamin's secrets. If their
small party had any chance of succeeding, he must not know
more than he already did. But to succeed at what? he asked
himself. Where might our final destination be? What might
we be forced to do once there? What will we be capable of
doing, if anything?

Suddenly he realized that with his right hand he was
fingering the calamar in his belt satchel. He pulled it away
quickly. He knew why his hand had searched it out. The
instrument, with its ability to see past, present and future,
could tell him the answers to all his questions. This must be
why Olamin had been pressed and beleaguered by gronoms.
Through a calamar, or similar device, he had obtained the
knowledge that made him consummate bait for the deadly
creatures.

Speckarin's ruminations were interrupted as a gentle rain
started to fall again. He climbed down the tree to the damp
ground and began to forage for food. He was soon joined by
Diliani, while the younger kirins rested in the tree.

The two gathered enough sustenance for all, and called
the three youths for breakfast. They found a dry area near the
trunk and quietly consumed a morning meal. They knew they
would soon be departing. They had nowhere to go except

onward, further into the unknown. On this dark morning, however, each of them thought of home.

We are but two days from the home tree, thought Talli, and yet how much farther it seems than that. It feels as though we have been gone for a week, perhaps two. But we cannot go home. For the sake of the clans, and for all kirins, we must continue.

She knew this. But, she admitted to herself, she did not like it, especially since she was, very possibly, the only prey of their adversaries.

"We must prepare for departure," said Diliani. She called the ilon. The five birds landed on the ground and stood resolutely as the kirins gathered the leftover food and stored it in their satchels for a mid-morning snack.

"You will need rain coverings," Diliani instructed. Each had a lightweight, waterproof jacket and hood. These were removed from their back sacks and donned. Then they mounted the ilon and took off, Talli first, and flew upward through the trees.

On this dank morning the early light of day had intermingled gradually with the darkness of night, causing a dim illumination in the forest. But the direction of the sunlight could not be ascertained. Fog and clouds had made siting the sunrise impossible. Their course was determined by recollections of their path the evening before, and they embarked correctly in a due easterly fashion.

As they flew on, however, and the rain continued to fall, they found it not only difficult to plot an accurate course, but uncomfortable to keep their eyes open. They were not accustomed to tolerating this sort of weather. At home when it rained and the rain was bothersome, they simply desisted from their work or recreation until it was over. They never felt pressure to continue, as they did now. In their present circumstances they felt they had to go on.

As the morning wore slowly on, the waterproof cloaks grew less and less impenetrable, less successful at keeping them dry. Rainwater leaked in at the ends of sleeves, seeped in at collars and around the edges of hoods, and eventually got through the tightly woven fabric of the garments.

Speckarin was no more comfortable than anyone else. He realized, as did the others, that they were flying without a distinct point of reckoning. He sensed that they were traveling eastward, but in this kind of weather he had no way of confirming this. He looked toward Talli and wondered how long she wished to persevere.

All at once the wind rose and began to buffet them from side to side. The kirins clung ever more tightly to the saturated necks of their ilon. These brave birds, which in the wild would have long before abandoned flight under such conditions, struggled onward at the behest of their small masters. The bright flash of a lightning bolt, followed closely by a jolt of thunder, caused even these ravens, with lifelong instruction and discipline, to shudder, to falter for an instant, and then to accelerate as they beat their wings wildly.

The kirins held on grimly. Through desperate entreaties and the influence of curlace magic, they were able to quell the fears of the birds, to regain control, and to direct the unsettled creatures back into formation. More flashes electrified the sky, and the ensuing thunder shook the atmosphere. The beleaguered ilon lurched and wavered in the rising wind and the now torrential rain. It was all their riders could do to prevail over them once again, as primordial instincts all but overruled the ravens' many years of training.

Throughout, as the storm raged unabated, the kirins miraculously managed to stay together, and even in a semblance of formation. Talli remained at the head position. However, even though she and Gilin had been given command of the expedition because of their unique knowledge, this party of kirins had only one truly experienced leader. When the weather turned from a source of discomfort into one of palpable danger, the other four instinctively, and without a spoken word, looked to the old magician for direction.

Speckarin had known this would happen eventually, but was surprised it had occurred this early in the journey. Nonetheless, as quickly as he sensed their need for guidance, he flew forward to take over the lead, and Talli dropped back. He immediately signaled for descent, in hopes that they could find a decent place to land and gain shelter from the storm.

Because of the drenching rain and low-hanging clouds, however, they could see little of the terrain as they glided downward. Communication between the kirins was made extremely difficult by these conditions. The majority of their efforts were expended in directing their ilon to stay close to those ahead and to follow in formation. Finally, with difficulty, they could see a wet landscape beneath. It was marsh land, with no solid area to light upon. They sailed onward for some time above the marshy territory, soaked to the skin. Eventually the wetlands ended, and they were coursing over firmer ground. But they still could not locate a place protected from wind and rain, a satisfactory place to settle down. Then, as if they were struggling through a bad dream, they entered a dense and impenetrable fog.

Suddenly, through a break in the clouds, Diliani caught sight of a copse of trees some distance to the south. She tried to call Speckarin's attention to it, and just as he saw what she was pointing to, it disappeared again into the haze. Nonetheless, he gave signals for a change of course. They turned their ilon to the right and flew blindly for a while longer. All at once the area of foliage reappeared through the haze, and they landed under trees and upon a relatively dry patch of ground. The shivering kirins slid heavily from the backs of their ravens, relieved indeed to be down. But they were exhausted by the harrowing morning, and were anxious for warmth.

"We must locate dry wood, if possible," said Speckarin, "and start a fire."

The weary band spread out among the shrubs, and under a particularly dense formation of foliage they located twigs and sticks dry enough, they hoped, to kindle a fire. One of the items the magician had collected and included in his baggage was a fire-starting device. He retrieved the short, narrow instrument from his kit, which was just as soaked as everything else. After several vain tries at bringing the moist instrument to life, a flame suddenly burst from its end, to the relief and delight of all. Speckarin touched it to the wood and it ignited immediately. A fire was soon burning readily, and more wood was brought to stoke it. Before long they had quite a satisfactory blaze, especially under the circumstances. They began to strip off saturated outer clothing to dry it next to the flames.

"Gilin, are you starting to warm up?" asked Talli. But she received no answer. "Gilin? Where are you?" she asked apprehensively, glancing about for the invisible lad.

Quickly Speckarin counted the ilon standing around the bonfire. To his dismay they were only four in number, and for the first time he realized that Gilin was no longer among them.

C H A P T E R   3

NO ONE IS TO BLAME,"
said Speckarin.

He was attempting to stay calm and unemotional in order to think clearly. But one of his charges was gone, unaccounted for, and the very thought of it was like a cold wind blowing through his heart.

Diliani had been flying behind Gilin. Since the lad was invisible, she had considered it part of her responsibilities to keep Loana, his ilon, under observation.

"It would have been when I sighted these trees," said the distraught Diliani, "and began indicating them to you. My attention was drawn away from usual activities. I cannot recall seeing Loana from that time onward."

Shaken, the four kirins stood staring silently into the flames of the fire, wondering where their companion might be, and what could conceivably be done to find him.

Raindrops spattered Speckarin's face as he gazed upward into a dark sky. He looked back into the fire and eventually spoke. "It would be folly to send out a search party under conditions such as these," he said. "We would not know where to go."

"Being on the left side of the formation," said Diliani, "he may have lost sight of us when we veered to the right. Perhaps in the storm he did not see the signals for landing and flew straight onward."

Hut echoed the feelings of all. "Whatever happened to him, we must find him!" he said.

"He might begin looking for us," said Speckarin, "and our bonfire might lead him here." Then, with a fragment of optimism, he stepped toward the fire and threw a log on top. "We must keep this blaze stoked," he said sternly. "It may be our best hope."

Realizing that at least for the moment they could do no more than this to be reunited with their friend, they spread out again into the surrounding shrubs and trees to locate flammable wood. They gathered enough to keep the fire going throughout the remainder of the day and the night.

The distracted Speckarin sat down a short distance from the fire in a relatively protected area. At last with some time alone, he began to contemplate alternatives to recover Gilin. Until the weather cleared, he thought, searching for him would be senseless, and undoubtedly dangerous. Keeping the bonfire aflame was the one thing they could do, and hope for improved conditions in the morning. But what would they do then to locate him? Send one or two of the party to search, the others waiting at the site of the fire? And what were the searchers to do? Call out his name from aboard their ilon, or seek out Loana, since Gilin was invisible? Could Talli possibly use her toe ring to find him again? The old magician simply did not know.

And then there was the calamar. He shuddered as he thought of it. Should he employ it now, after ignoring it all these years? Would he even be able to use it? Would he uncover something he would wish he had not found? He did not know the answer to this, nor to any of these questions. He did not know much of anything at this point, he thought uncomfortably, and his head was beginning to whirl. He arose unsteadily, stood quietly for a moment to recover his composure, and then walked slowly back toward the fire.

Standing by the bonfire was Talli, staring blankly into the flames. The ring on the third toe of her foot glimmered in the light. A beleaguered Speckarin approached her.

"On one occasion a few days ago," the magician said, "you contacted Gilin through your ring. Is it possible . . ."

"I have been thinking of just that," interrupted Talli. "And . . . I think not. I will try, but I believe the moon was responsible for activating the ring." She peered upward into the murky sky, rain against her face. Her blond hair was saturated. "There is no moon at this time of day," she continued, "nor would we see it if there were. Nevertheless, I will try."

She sat down by the fire and removed the ring. Then she proceeded through much of the routine she had employed by the stream some days before. But it was to no avail in this setting, to the disappointment of the others, who had all been observing, and to herself. After a while she gave up and despondently slipped the ring onto her toe.

Before dusk the rains ceased for the first time since morning. Sadly, as what little light was left faded from the sky, the small party gathered close to the blazing fire to rest and to wait, some sitting, some lying down. The four ilon stood at the outer boundary, between the open area and the surrounding woods. Within a short while the kirins drifted off to sleep, one by one. But Speckarin, who had concluded that all of this was ultimately his responsibility, sat gazing into the flames and stayed awake. He stoked the blaze periodically when it dwindled, and he waited. But no sign of Gilin came.

Throughout the night the magician watched the skies. He saw the clouds gradually diminish. Stars began to shine through faintly. But he did not catch sight of the moon, which remained shrouded by the covering. At one point in his sleep, Hut cried out the name of his cousin, but Speckarin was the only one to hear. As the remainder of the night passed, a scheme for searching for Gilin became outlined in his mind, and eventually he relaxed. At least we have the semblance of a plan, he told himself.

Toward morning the overcast began to part, and stars filled portions of the sky. Suddenly the moon shined brightly through, and Speckarin was moving to awaken Talli when the orb was obscured again, just as rapidly as it had appeared, behind an opaque bank of gloom. The old magician settled heavily back into his place to wait out what little was left of the night.

The first light of day finally brought promise in the rosy glow of a sunrise and clear skies overhead. It was not surprising to Speckarin that the sunrise was spectacular. But he took no pleasure in it. His thoughts were only of the missing Gilin. Where might he be as the sun rises on this sparkling morning, he asked himself? What might he possibly be feeling? Will we ever lay eyes upon him again?

C H A P T E R   4

SPECKARIN AROUSED
the others shortly after daybreak, and they sat up, leaving
dreams behind, to again face the reality of their situation:
Gilin had not reappeared.

Responding to the unspoken question in each of their
minds, Speckarin spoke solemnly. "No sign of Gilin came
during the night. However, I have devised a plan for finding
him. Arise and gather your breakfasts, and while we consume
the morning meal I will explain it to you."

Diliani allowed the ilon to depart to hunt for their own
food. Hut and Talli entered the damp woods to do the same
for the kirins. With the two youngsters so occupied,
Speckarin discussed some of his scheme with Diliani, and
she concurred with the substance of his ideas. Not wishing to
risk disagreement, however, he did not tell her everything.
When Hut and Talli returned, all sat near the fire as Speckarin
began anew.

His voice was grave indeed as he presented a surprising
proposal. "Before attempting any other method of locating
Gilin," he said, "I wish to try the calamar." With tremulous
fingers he withdrew it from his pack.

The others, including Diliani, looked quizzically at one another. This was a possibility Speckarin had never previously disclosed, even to her. They all knew Gilin had a calamar, and Hut had seen the one before them briefly in the magician's apartment, on the occasion of his return to the clan. But none of them had been aware that the instrument was present, accompanying Speckarin on this journey.

"But," blurted Hut, "if you brought it along, why did you not use it earlier?"

Speckarin had known this was coming, and attempted to answer without revealing all of his fears. "A calamar," he said, after clearing his throat, "is a very capricious device, and I must admit that I have been loath to employ it, probably to a fault. I have not utilized it for many years, and I am not certain I retain the knowledge or power to bring it to life, to say nothing of discovering what we want to know. Nonetheless, I have decided that I must try. But in order to do this I will require privacy. For reasons that only I may know, I must be alone when I attempt to enliven it. Therefore, I am going to ask that all of you depart."

The others reluctantly yielded to his wishes. After brief preparations they lifted off upon their ilon, leaving only Speckarin, Ocelam, and the calamar by the fire. Their instructions were to fly a short distance away and to return as the sun first appeared above the tops of the trees to the east.

As soon as they departed, Speckarin sat down by the waning fire and took the calamar into both hands. They shook slightly as he began to gaze into the magical instrument. I have neglected this calamar, he thought, and Gilin does not know much about the one given to him by Olamin. Nevertheless, perhaps we can make contact.

Of course Speckarin recalled how to make it work. With chagrin he admitted that he had used his lack of experience purely as an excuse to help persuade the others to leave. The real reason he wished to be alone was that he was afraid of what might happen when it began to function. His lack of recent exposure to the calamar, coupled with the frightful and radical changes occurring in the kirin world, made him very uncertain what, if anything, would come through when he unleashed the complex capabilities of the device. It could result in his finding and communicating with Gilin, it might bring no success whatsoever, or it was indeed possible, the magician remarked somberly to himself, that it would lead to something unpredictably damaging. Because of this, as difficult as it was to be separated from the others, he sent them away. And quite on purpose, he had not suggested where they go, nor had he observed the direction of their flight upon departure. If anyone is to be harmed by the unchecked powers of this device, he thought, it will be me and none other.

Now he concentrated upon the gleaming instrument, and after a brief time he looked up and into the glowing fire. *"Tabaylan vay norsulo,"* he said in a low voice. Shortly the calamar began to warm, and when he looked down again the opacity within it had begun to clear. He wished to see Gilin, and his thoughts turned exclusively to the lost companion. The central portion of the device soon became transparent. Then all at once it began to flicker, and vague images appeared fleetingly, but nothing came that he could identify. Multiple scenes and objects took shape within the warming instrument, coming into focus for an instant, only to be replaced by yet another. Nothing was familiar, the picture changing over and over as he stared, still with trepidation, into the heart of the calamar.

All at once the dizzying succession of images ceased, and a raven standing resolutely in the forest came unmistakably into view. This picture was present long enough for him to study it. Loana, he thought excitedly! Living so closely with the ilon during their trek, he had grown to recognize each of them individually. But he saw no sign of Gilin. He is of course invisible, Speckarin told himself, and even this amazing device may not be capable of unshrouding him.

Suddenly the heartening image of the bird began to waver, and to lose clarity, and finally it became blurred. Then superimposed over it another likeness appeared, as if trying to take precedence over what was being seen in the apparatus, and eventually the raven was blotted out as the new image took over completely. To Speckarin's horror, now occupying the center of the calamar was the smooth and unmistakable outline of a gronom.

■ ■ ■

Unknown to the kirins, either to Speckarin or to the party of three, a gronom was in the vicinity where the three had landed and were now waiting. The thing had been stalking Talli from afar, and was gratified to sense that its prey had suddenly been delivered nearer at hand. The victim was still not close enough, however, for the beast to become frenzied and to release its involuntary wave of warning. After it noted the change in position of its quarry, it persisted once again in its methodical tracking.

Then, all at once, through uncanny telepathic abilities, the gronom became aware of something else: Yet another kirin, somewhere nearby, was attempting to communicate with an individual already affected by a gronom, a discovery that attracted its interest immediately. It stopped in its tracks, to listen and to interpret. The transmission was coming through a magical means, but was one which the creature could readily intercept, and was now deciphering and comprehending. As it sifted through the information, not only could it understand what the message was about and to whom it was intended, but the preternatural creature could also grasp intimate and vital details regarding the sender. Ascertaining that the transmitting kirin was wholly endeared to the one the beast had been seeking, it homed in upon Speckarin in an attempt to extract and learn everything it could about its prey, a still uncaptured kirin with the alluring knowledge.

■ ■ ■

An amorphous menace flowed into Speckarin's mind. Before he could resist, it was probing him deeply. He could feel it delving, and searching, as though seeking a specific area of his brain or a particular kind or piece of information. He was alarmed and far from certain what precisely was happening. But he found that, strangely enough, he could still carry on the process of thinking. He deduced that something foul had intruded itself through the calamar, as if his bringing the device to life had somehow cleared a telepathic channel to him, and then had opened a window to his consciousness, and to his memory, and to his entire mind. He also sensed that, through no desire of his own, his hands were now gripping the calamar ever more tightly.

In the beginning he felt utterly defenseless and naked, as though his very core and self were being violated by an evil force, and were under a scrutiny against which he had no power or protection. Then he sensed an alteration. The initial probing had proven unproductive. The desired purpose had not been achieved, and the assault took a different turn. The presence within him seemed to have become patient and quiet, as if willing to wait. He could sense it lurking near the center of his consciousness. Then it began to prod him, gently at first, with hints and inducements, into initiating a train of thought about a fellow kirin, one very close to him, a traveling companion who possessed a special knowledge.

Suddenly recognizing its vile purpose, the besieged magician reacted instinctively to oppose the insidious invader. Consciously avoiding any thoughts of Talli, realizing that this is what the fiend coveted and was awaiting, he began to labor against the will and intent of the unyielding thing, and he found himself locked in deadly confrontation. The magician resisted all the urges and impulses created by the monster to reveal anything about his companion, and in fact purposefully led the creature into memories and emotional sensations regarding other friends and acquaintances.

The relentless intruder was not to be fooled and was not to be denied. This tactic resulted only in arousing it, and soon its patience wore thin. It became more overtly persuasive, then aggressive, and eventually loud, as its requests for information were denied over and over again. It began demanding the desired information, and raised such a clamor and a din within his mind that Speckarin felt his head would split open. He knew that he could not combat the overwhelming will of the creature very much longer, and that eventually it would gain sway. He knew not, to his great despair, how he could possibly continue to resist.

All at once, through the increasing uproar, he somehow remembered the calamar. It was through this device that the thing was invading! His only defense would be to break contact with the malevolent creature!

Through ultimate effort and with every fiber of his being, the defiant magician began to force his grip to loosen on the instrument. The creature sensed this immediately, and the burgeoning noise abated suddenly and completely, as its foul attention was attracted to a new cerebral arena.

The mute battle was now being waged in the motor portion of Speckarin's mind, the area controlling the movement of his body, the nerves, muscles, and tendons of his extremities. Here as Speckarin strove to extend the fingers of both hands and to release the calamar from his grasp, the monster sought grimly to counter this action, and fought to make his grip ever tighter. For a time a silent standoff existed, neither one yielding. But ever so gradually Speckarin gained a slight measure of control over the beast, and as a result his digits began to loosen their hold. It became apparent to the magician that in this area he might be stronger than his opponent. His confidence built, and as it did, he seemed to attain even further dominance over his adversary. Against a last burst of will from the intruder he forced his clenched hands open and apart. The calamar, so heated that it was beginning to burn his skin, dropped harmlessly to the ground and the conflict ceased abruptly.

Breathless, Speckarin reeled backward to the earth, shocked and stunned. Vainly he attempted to collect his scattered thoughts, but at first to no avail. After a brief time, however, things began to fall into place: He remembered who he was, and where he was, and the dreadful assault he had just endured. He attempted to concentrate and to comprehend what had transpired.

He had known that the relentless creatures possessed unfathomable telepathic capabilities. But he never suspected that initiating communication through the calamar might somehow alert and even enhance these abilities, and that the creatures might home in upon him and assault him. Yet it appeared that this was precisely what had happened. I knew this would be a hazardous business, he thought. I was fearful that something like this might occur. But it was far worse than I ever anticipated.

Throughout the engagement he had not been aware of Talli's location, and now he was deeply thankful for that. Had I known, he thought with a shudder, I am certain the initial probing would have revealed it.

"I must never use that wretched instrument again!" he said aloud, struggling to a sitting position. He looked down at the calamar, once again opaque and inactive.

The old magician stayed by the fire, recovering his composure. He was finally becoming himself again when Diliani, Hut and Talli landed.

"What happened?" called Diliani as she ran to him. She kneeled down at his side and noted his strained expression. "Have you been harmed in any way?" she asked.

"I think not—and I hope not," said Speckarin, as she helped him to his feet. He had taken time to rest, and by now had recovered his faculties almost fully. Dignified as always, he brushed off his yellow gown and cleared his throat.

"Communication with the calamar," he announced summarily, "was wholly unsatisfactory." But he stopped there, and despite inquiries would reveal nothing more. He was unwilling to cause further concern for any of them, especially Talli, about whom the creature had been searching for data. But he felt, and he hoped, that he had resisted and interrupted the inquisition before any significant information had been gleaned. And, he told himself again, I am gratified the others were gone. Sending them away meant that Talli was not nearby during the attack. Had she been present the fiend might have sensed it, and very possibly, through the calamar, could have aimed its vile intent toward her.

Diliani could tell that something had gone gravely wrong. She said nothing about it, but resolved in her own mind that, if she possibly could, she would prevent him from using the calamar again.

"We must ready ourselves immediately," the magician said in earnest, knowing that a gronom was somewhere in the vicinity. Then he explained his second plan to locate Gilin. The first strategy failed miserably, he told himself, and nearly ended in disaster. I hope the second is better.

"We can no longer stay here and wait for Gilin to locate us," he said. "He is alone, and he may be injured or bewildered. But even if he is perfectly unharmed he doubtless has no idea where to find us. We must search for him. However, because of yesterday's tragedy, I am opposed to any of us being apart from the others." And after today's experience, he told himself, I hope we will never be separated again.

"We must depart," he went on. "We will head toward the location where Diliani thinks Gilin may have lost us, where we turned southward and headed for these woods. Once we are at that point, assuming we can still locate it—things may look very different on a sunny day than on a stormy one—we will begin flying a circular route, gradually widening our pattern. We will stay close to the ground and search for Loana, as we are unable to see Gilin. We have eight sharp eyes among us, and unless she is hidden we should be able to discover her. If I know Gilin, he will adhere to the woodsmanship teachings of

kirin elders. This is especially true for children, but I think also
for Gilin in this situation: When alone, remain close to the
point where you discovered you were lost. He will know that
should he wander far from that position, our chances of finding
him will diminish with time."

"What if he decides to look for us," asked Hut, "and he
succeeds in locating this fire and campsite and no one is
here? Should we not leave some kind of sign?"

"A good point, little one," answered the magician. "I think
we have time to leave a message. It will be in Ruvon, and it
will signify that he remain here until our return. If he should
happen upon this place, he will not mistake the meaning."

Kirins use the verbal form of the old tongue at special and
ceremonial gatherings, while the written language of Ruvon is
usually known only to the magician class. But a more primitive
form is learned by all kirins in their training. It is a simple,
symbolic rendering of ancient words and phrases, and can be
formulated with natural objects found virtually everywhere. It
is employed by kirins for communication when not in each
other's presence, for leaving directions or warnings, or for
pointing out special features of the terrain or locale.

"Make yourselves ready," said Speckarin. "I will create a
sign for Gilin."

But first he bent over and looked once more at the
calamar, still opaque and gleaming at his feet. He reached
down and touched it with one digit. It was cool. He gradually
forced himself to finger the object, then to grasp it, and
finally to pick it up off the ground. Then he stood up and slid
it unceremoniously into his pack.

The ilon were summoned and the kirins prepared quickly
for travel. Speckarin spent a brief time examining the twigs
and sticks near the now-spent fire. He ventured into the
nearby brush, found some suitable stones, and broke off
several small branches with leaves still attached. Upon a
mossy, open area near the fire he began arranging the objects
into a pattern. Using triangles, crosses, and other shapes, he
skillfully prepared the communication. Then he stood back to

review his handiwork. The three others, anxious to be leaving and glad they were finally doing something to find their missing friend, also came to view the message.

"*Gilin, nedsam rutwanym ut ilon serpodin,*" read the old magician under his breath. "That will suffice," he said aloud. "Let us depart and carefully mark our way as we go. We must be certain we can find this place again."

Diliani checked the fire. It had smouldered its last and was out. The kirins mounted their ilon and departed northward, no sign of the gronom having appeared.

With Speckarin in the lead, they flew for what seemed only a brief time before Diliani indicated they were over the location where Gilin might have lost contact. There they began their search. They drifted in low over the terrain, each of them painstakingly observing bushes, trees, and open areas for any sign of Loana, or possibly even of the invisible Gilin. After a time they began to enlarge their pattern, circling gradually away and outward from the central focal point.

They had flown in this fashion for quite a long while, and had found nothing, when all at once Faralan began to quake and shudder so furiously that he nearly threw Talli off in midair. The girl's long feet clenched more tenaciously beneath the neck of the giant bird, and it was only through intense effort that she was able to remain astride the shaking creature. The flying capabilities of the bird seemed totally disrupted, and to the consternation of all he began to lose altitude precipitously. Talli held on unyieldingly until, just as suddenly as the violent activity had started, it ceased completely. Except for signs of fatigue, the raven returned to a normal pattern of flight.

Having observed the entire aberration, the other three kirins were stunned. With the apparent recovery of the bird, they flew quickly down to Talli's side, questioning what might have transpired and asking whether she was harmed.

"Could it have been a seizure in mid-flight?" Speckarin asked Diliani, as they coursed next to Talli and Faralan.

It was Talli who answered. "No!" responded the shaken

girl as she began searching the skies. "But I believe I know what it was! I have encountered that sensation before, at the moment we were discovered by the gronom in the forest! The ground shook just as violently, and I had the same feeling of being naked and exposed!"

She gazed in every direction for something she hoped never to see. The others, sensing what she was referring to, also began looking about frantically.

"There!" cried Diliani, pointing.

They all stared. To the kirins' abhorrence, there they were, on the northern horizon. Still at a distance but approaching wildly were two foreign creatures with an erratic pattern of flight they had never before envisioned.

Upon each creature they could make out two pairs of stubby wings, one at the front of the torso and one toward the rear. The four wings beat in no unified fashion, each one apparently autonomous, and yet somehow the creatures not only remained aloft but were moving in the kirins' direction at an astonishing rate of speed.

"Volodons!" exclaimed the terrified Talli.

"We must hasten!" said Speckarin as he turned his ilon to the south and commanded that it attain the greatest velocity possible. The others followed, and in moments the four ravens were gaining altitude and fleeing the approaching menace at top speed.

Speckarin glanced rearward, the sable wings of Ocelam undulating at a rate he had never before witnessed. He estimated that the creatures were no longer closing in. The kirins were maintaining a uniform distance between themselves and the volodons. This separation was sustained, to his satisfaction, for a considerable length of time, but despite every effort they could not increase their lead.

These are the winged counterparts of gronoms, the old magician recalled as they flew onward ahead of their unyielding pursuers. *They must be behaving in a similar fashion, with the notable exception that they have the ability to fly. Gilin is gone and they are seeking Talli, the only one* here with the precious knowledge.

Finally, on one occasion when he glanced back, it became apparent that the monsters were gaining. Diliani pulled her ilon over to his. She also had estimated that the pursuers were closing the gap. Should the creatures continue to advance, she suggested, as seemed inevitable, the others might have to defend Talli.

None of us has seen a volodon before, thought Speckarin. Even the dead Olamin had not. In challenging them we will have nothing to go on but courage and intuition. But he hoped a little luck would be thrown in as well.

In a short time the chasing fiends were beginning to overtake the fatiguing ravens. Like gronoms, they were single-minded, tireless, and totally without pity in approaching a quarry. The lead volodon, several moments ahead of its companion, was now near enough for them to make out the same face and head, smooth and featureless, as possessed by gronoms.

Talli was pale as the trackers came ever closer, holding grimly to the neck of her raven, knowing that she alone was their victim. In her agony she had nearly given up hope. But the other three kirins had not, their minds working more rapidly as the beasts of prey neared their final goal. All at once Hut flew to the rear of Talli, hoping to decoy the creatures and to attract some of their vile attention. But like gronoms they ignored him completely, as they did the other kirins and their ilon, homing in only upon the alluring one.

The first was almost within striking distance of the petrified Talli when Diliani suddenly swerved her ilon toward the creature. With a burst of speed from her bird she flew adjacent to the volodon for a few moments. Leaning toward it and taking aim, she thrust her knife ferociously into the back of the creature's head. To her great satisfaction, a crude darkness exuded as it turned toward her. The beast began to descend, and it clutched at Diliani with primitive claws, dragging the brave kirin and her ilon downward.

The second volodon was nearly upon Talli. Speckarin had

dropped back, finding it impossible to gain further acceleration from his exhausted raven. But he had witnessed the courageous actions of Diliani, and he recognized that the cranium of the volodon must be susceptible to assault, just as it was with gronoms.

Talli veered to the side, trying to evade her attacker, giving the magician a few vital moments. From his bag he quickly withdrew a long silver instrument. It came from the days of ancient kirin magic, and he had never before employed it, but he immediately held it high above his head.

"Tay lassis obilan!" he cried.

A narrow bolt of energy instantaneously spanned the distance between the tip of the gleaming device and the rear of the beast's head. Within a claw's breadth of its victim, the creature stiffened and rotated in the air as its wings ceased to beat. Then it plummeted toward the earth, motionless as it fell.

Diliani had wrested herself from the desperate grasp of the other volodon and watched it too fall toward the ground below. Flying to the magician's side, she found that he was unharmed, and she hurried toward Talli. Hut was already beside her, reassuring her that the attackers were gone and that she was indeed safe.

"For the moment," uttered the girl, quaking. "Perhaps for now."

As their anxieties subsided and the group slowed in flight, Speckarin examined the landscape below, and a sickening realization struck him. In trying to escape the volodons, they had flown madly for he knew not how far nor how long. He was not even aware of the direction in which they had come. Perhaps, he thought, they had gone in circles!

He quickly searched the terrain for recognizable landmarks and found none. He had no idea where the campsite was nor where they thought they had separated from Gilin. To his great dismay, he realized that now he had no notion where the missing youth might be.

C H A P T E R   5

AT THE HEIGHT of the storm Gilin fought desperately to maintain visual contact with the lead ilon, but he found it increasingly difficult to do so. Through the foul weather and trying conditions, he continually encouraged his ilon forward with words in curlace and Ruvon.

"Onward we must go!" he exhorted. "We will stay with the others! On Loana! Your name is "Timeless Fortitude" in the old tongue! You are a strong and courageous one!"

Drenched and exhausted, Gilin remained in formation throughout the descent and the flight above the marshes. Stroking Loana and imploring her to persist through the downpour, he suddenly realized he could no longer see the other members of the party. Looking frantically in every direction through rain and murky atmosphere, to his consternation, he could find no one. He did not know whether they had pulled ahead or had turned in one direction or another, and he slowed the flight of his ilon to consider what to do. Alone, and after moments of apprehension and indecision, he concluded that he must land. When he eventually found a grassy area with leafy coverage above, he made his approach and touched down upon moist ground.

"The others must be nearby!" he said hopefully to the ilon, at the same time trying to reassure himself. "For the time being we must stay here! We have no other choice! We have no idea where the others went! They will notice very soon that we are not with them!"

To his surprise, within moments another raven, kirin aboard, flapped downward through the wind and raindrops, and alighted but a short distance away. To his amazement it was a soaked Ruggum Chamter who jumped off.

"Gilin! Are you here?" called the bearded elder.

"Yes!" replied the lad excitedly. "I am!"

"Where?" questioned the overseer, glaring about.

"Next to Loana!" said Gilin.

Ruggum began stalking through wet grass toward Loana, staring about as he came, obviously unable to see the lad.

"What are you doing here, so far from home?" asked an astounded Gilin. "And how in the world did you find me?"

"It is a very long story!" said Ruggum as he neared Loana. "Let me touch you!"

"I am here!" said the youth. He approached the overseer and reached out to grasp a saturated shoulder with his hand.

The startled Ruggum drew back momentarily, and then placed his hand upon Gilin's. "I am very glad I found you!" he said.

"How could you have found me? What can you possibly be doing here?" questioned Gilin, bewildered and yet deeply grateful for the astonishing appearance of the elder.

"We haven't much time if we wish to find the others!" said Ruggum.

Gilin eyed the overseer. "What do you know about the others?" he asked. Then suddenly he knew. "You have been following us!" he declared.

"It is a very long story indeed," said Ruggum. "We haven't time right now for me to tell it, unless . . ."

The elder looked up at dark, low-hanging clouds moving

rapidly to the east, and at sheets of rain, showing no sign of abatement.

"Let us find shelter where we can talk," said Ruggum.

They released their ilon who, needing sustenance, went to search for it in the dank surrounding woods. Then, so that he would not lose Gilin, Ruggum gripped him by the wrist and led him deeper into the forest. They located a small patch of ground covered thickly with overhanging foliage, and there they sat down upon damp rocks.

"Though I do not like it," said Ruggum, "I think we must wait for the weather to clear, at least partially." And then, staring at the place where he knew the youth to be, he spoke in earnest. "Gilin! The five of you were flying together a short while ago! When the other four swerved away, to the right, you went straight onward! Why did you do so? Did you not see them change direction?"

"No!" answered the astonished youth. "I did not see them at all!"

"It is terribly unfortunate this has happened," said the elder, shaking his head. "And, yes, I was following you. I have been behind you since you left the Moger tree, three days ago! But I have done it skillfully and secretly. I kept just enough distance that you would be unlikely to detect me. I was there. I was constantly able to keep you in sight, and you have all been so busy that you never did discover me. But I had to come much closer to your party in the kind of weather we endured today than in the clear conditions of the past two days."

"I am glad you were following us," said Gilin, "for whatever reason. Loana and I would otherwise be alone."

"I saw what was happening!" said Ruggum. "You were continuing straight ahead on your own! I had to make a quick decision whether to follow you or the group of four. I surmised that you might have missed a signal, or some indication that they were turning. If I did not pursue you, I concluded, you would become completely and perhaps irrevocably severed from the party."

"I might have indeed!" said Gilin. After a pause, he

continued. "But, sir, if I may ask, why were you trailing us?"

The old overseer looked silently at the ground, trying to compose his thoughts and words. "I made a decision at the gathering," he said solemnly, "after the vote had taken place, that I would be a part of this expedition. I would not be prohibited from participating in it! I respect the members of the clan, and hold nothing against them for the manner in which the voting took place, nor against Diliani for gaining a position in the entourage. But I knew that this quest would be vital, and that more experience would be required than existed in the chosen group! I determined that I would track you, and keep you in sight, and at the proper moment reveal myself, in hopes that I would be included in the entourage. I must admit that I had not expected the occasion to arise so early! I had hoped it would be later, and farther from home, so that it would be more difficult for you to refuse me and turn me away!

"I will tell you something else," continued Ruggum with a slight chuckle. "Once I came very close to losing you entirely! Do you remember that first night, when the party broke up and slept in several different trees? Well, that evening, to stay undetected, I decided to station myself some distance away, and I did so. But because of it I missed your departure when morning came! I was finding breakfast, and somehow, before I knew it, you were gone! But I got off the ground quickly, and knowing the easterly course you had been pursuing, I was soon able to catch up with you! I decided I would never let this happen again! Therefore, last evening, in order not to miss your parting a second time, I nestled in with Alsinam within the uppermost branches of your tree. Unbeknownst to you, we lodged there overnight. When the mists and rain moved in, and visibility became reduced, I was very thankful I had done so, or you might have gotten away from me again!"

"I am most grateful that you tracked us," said Gilin, "and that you chose to follow me today!" He continued, apprehension in his voice. "But what should we do now?

How will we locate the others?"

Ruggum rose to his feet and poked his head out of the sheltered area. Rain drops spattercd his face and moistened his beard, and he could see no break in the storm. His eyes darkened, and he was glowering as he turned back to face Gilin. When he sat down he was pensive for a few moments. Then he spoke.

"We must wait here," he said, "probably through the night. Let us make ourselves as comfortable as possible. In the morning, when the weather has changed for the better, we will depart and find the others."

His grave concern, which was not shared with Gilin, was whether, rain or shine, they would ever find the other party again.

C H A P T E R   6

WITH NO instruments of magic at their disposal, Ruggum Chamter and Gilin used the age-old implements of flint and steel from the overseer's pack to start their fire. Far smaller than that of their compatriots, it was nevertheless enough to warm them through the night, and to dry their clothing. When they awoke in the morning the weather had cleared, and they extinguished the fire and prepared for travel.

Their plan was to return to the site where Ruggum had observed Gilin becoming separated from the others, a brief flight to the west. Upward they flew, and after yesterday's foul conditions they were taking pleasure in the early morning sunlight, when all at once Gilin caught sight of two ghastly creatures, appearing out of nowhere and hurtling through the air precisely in their direction.

As the things closed in upon them, Gilin identified their featureless countenances immediately. Filled with terror, he plunged downward toward the earth.

Ruggum saw them also. Recognizing the visage as identical to that of a gronom, he followed his companion closely. To their amazement, the creatures did not give chase at all, but flew by at breakneck speed. Hovering near the ground, the kirins watched the incredible flying beings until they were out of sight.

After landing, it was some time before Gilin recovered his composure. "They were volodons," he said, his voice quavering. "I am sure they were. Olamin had never seen one, but he was aware of their existence and he described them in what detail he could."

He stopped for a moment as if struck by a sudden realization. "But I still carry Olamin's teachings, his knowledge, and they did not pursue me!"

And they both suspected the reason. They surmised that Gilin, having already been attacked by a gronom, was no longer attractive to the beasts.

"If we are right in that assumption," said Gilin, "it would mean that we need not worry about Reydel, nor the clans, with regard to gronoms and volodons." He paused again, and then finished numbly. "Nor about me. Talli would be the only one still in danger."

Ruggum was far from certain that their supposition was correct, and he searched the skies long and hard before recommending departure a second time. When they did take off it was with caution, but they ascended and headed to the west. After a short while, with no further sightings of the monsters, Ruggum began to search the terrain below, and eventually he thought he saw the area they were seeking.

"I believe this is where they left you and went that way," he said, pointing to the south. Gazing in that direction he spied a grouping of trees, some distance away but easily discernible. Around it was an open area and then more forest. Sensing that the party might have landed there for a respite from the storm, he turned Alsinam and flew toward it, and Gilin followed. As they neared the copse, they saw something they had hoped for, evidence that someone had recently been there: remnants of a fire.

They descended swiftly, alighting next to the charred wood and ashes, and immediately saw Speckarin's sign.

Quickly dismounting, they approached the Ruvon figures, and as they deciphered their meaning, their doubts and fears were laid to rest. As Ruggum read the message, he recognized the work of his old friend.

Gilin placed a hand upon Ruggum's shoulder, knowing that the overseer could not otherwise be certain where he was. Then he touched the elder's foot.

"All we have to do is wait," said the relieved Ruggum. "They are gone, searching for you. They will return if they do not find you."

He paused, greatly cheered by the discovery. "In the meantime," he said, stroking his stomach, "do you realize something? We have not eaten! Neither last night nor this morning! Let's see what we can find for breakfast!"

They collected food and ate, and rested in the sun for the remainder of the morning. After lunch, they whiled away the afternoon, as alleviated of tension as they had been in many a day. When evening drew near they began to expect their compatriots' arrival. They glanced frequently at the sky, and toward the horizon in every direction. At one point Gilin mounted Loana and flew upward just to look about. He hoped he would see his friends approaching, thinking that he would fly to them, and surprise them by greeting them in the air. But he saw nothing, and descended once again to earth.

As darkness fell, Ruggum re-ignited the fire, both to help the others relocate their campsite and for warmth against the cooling air. The evening wore slowly on, and the two waited, stoking the fire and rationalizing the tardiness of the party. The moon rose, and the sky filled with stars.

Gilin fell asleep, and eventually Ruggum did also. But he was startled awake by an owl hooting nearby, and it took him some time to get to sleep again. The owl reminded him of one living near the home tree, and as he drifted off he envisioned a merry clan gathering, which he had enjoyed upon Rogalinon not long ago, with Speckarin and all of his friends, and he recalled the sylvan life they led before all the trouble began.

They awoke to another clear morning, but their compatriots had not returned. They passed a second day of waiting, quietly and in contemplation. By mid-afternoon Ruggum was becoming agitated by the situation, and he began to wonder out loud whether they should start searching for Speckarin and the others. Deciding it was too late in the day to do so, the disgruntled kirins simply waited, and after dark they rekindled the fire.

Before lying down to sleep, Gilin removed the calamar from his belt sack and handed it to Ruggum. "It was given to me by Olamin," he said. "Only I can use it. But I know very little about how it works. It was activated only once, some days ago. Talli and I were being followed by a gronom and we separated. She used her toe ring, also given to her by Olamin, to find me while I was with Hut in the forest. She thinks the ring was brought to life by the moon. After she visualized us within it, the ring led her to us. During the time the ring was active, this calamar also came alive. It became warm to the touch. Later, after we were reunited, the warmth disappeared."

Ruggum examined the object, just as Hut had in the forest. Untrained in magic, the overseer could make nothing of it.

"I hope Talli will use the ring again," said Gilin. It was the first time either one of them had hinted that the others might not be returning after all.

"I will wait for the calamar to warm again," said Gilin. "If only I knew how to activate it myself! I am certain Olamin would have taught me, had he lived even a short while longer!"

Gilin reclined by the fire, calamar in hand. The overseer rested under a nearby tree. They passed another restless night. A cloud cover moved across the sky before dawn, and when they awoke, with still no sign of the party and the calamar remaining cool, almost all hope of a reunion at this site was gone.

It was Ruggum who verbalized a severe question, one that had been formulating in their minds as the waiting had become longer and more intolerable. It had been unspoken, however, until now.

"Gilin," he began, "we have a grave decision to make. We have two choices. We can return to the clans, or the two of us can continue the quest alone."

After a pause, he went on. "You have Olamin's knowledge, and can lead us to our destination. You also wear the pall of invisibility. It may be that your only hope of regaining visibility is to go on."

Gilin was silent only briefly, fingering the calamar. He had been thinking about it even this morning, and it did not take him long to answer. "The two of us can make it," he said. "I have the knowledge, and you have experience. And perhaps we will find the others along the way."

"So be it," replied the elder. "We must collect food and prepare to leave."

When they were ready, Ruggum stood for several moments staring down at the Ruvon sign of Speckarin. Without touching it or altering it in any way, he turned and boarded Alsinam. Then they departed.

They headed eastward under a sunless sky. The flight was uneventful, and they had time to sort out their thoughts about Speckarin and the rest of the party. Some of it they discussed aloud, and some they kept to themselves. During the two days of waiting, they had gradually come to a realization. Something must have befallen their friends. Now they might be alone. At times, as they flew onward, they were almost in a state of mourning for their lost compatriots. Yet at other moments they realized that their friends might be perfectly unharmed, that the party might merely be dislocated temporarily. They could run across them at any point. In any case, they reassured themselves, the two of them had a mission and they were on their way to accomplishing it.

They traveled eastward for two days, sleeping overnight in trees. In the late afternoon of the third day, while looking for a place to spend the night, they spied an idyllic pond, surrounded on one side by a grove of tall and shining spruce trees and on the other by waves of swamp grass and reeds. Without hesitation they descended. They landed among the evergreens and dismounted.

They had not even had time to release the ilon when they became aware of an unusual rustling nearby. To their astonishment two human beings, an adult male and a young female, came out from behind a tree and walked by within a short distance of them, moving through the woods toward the pond.

The man had a fishing pole and tackle in hand. Intent upon his destination, he took no notice of the kirins or their ravens. But the girl, half the man's height, happened to glance in their direction, and she stopped.

"Come on! We're almost there!" said the man, continuing toward the water.

The kirins froze in their tracks. For their entire lives they had known that if they were confronted by humans they should become still and quiet, and the giant beings would pass them by.

The girl stared for a few moments at the two great birds and moved a little nearer. Her gaze then appeared to leave the ilon and to fall upon Gilin, and she moved even closer.

Paying no attention whatever to Ruggum Chamter, she looked down inquiringly at Gilin.

"Who are you?" she said.

C H A P T E R   7

E MUST FIND the
campsite," said Speckarin. "Gilin may be waiting for us now."

They were in flight high above the ground. Beneath was a
vast and striking landscape of greens and browns with an
occasional blue, and above was a vacant azure sky, not a
cloud in any direction. No familiar landmarks could be seen
in the terrain below, and none of them could recall in which
direction they had fled, even in relation to the sun.

The calamar might be useful for locating the camp, thought
Speckarin, but he had no intention of using it. The ilon were
flagging after the punishing volodon chase, and all of the kirins
knew they would soon be obliged to land. They could only
hope that they would descend in the direction of the campsite.

Perfect conditions for flying, mused Speckarin, but not for
retracing our route from the camp. Floating above the earth
will not reunite us with Gilin. Realizing that they were
compelled to make a decision, and thinking that perhaps he
recognized a small strip of landscape to the south, the
magician spoke.

"We may have been driven northward," he said. "Perhaps
we should go back to the south."

No one argued. No one knew for certain. But they turned in the direction he suggested and gradually glided downward, landing in a wooded area near a brook. There the spent ravens were released. It was their masters' wish that the faithful birds be forced to fly no more the rest of this day, the fourth of the expedition. Yet they knew that further exertion would be required from each member of the party, including the ilon, since every moment counted in the search for Gilin.

They replenished their supplies, and after only a short respite lifted off and proceeded southward again. For the remainder of the afternoon they flew on, scrutinizing the terrain to their right and to their left, but saw nothing familiar—and no sign of Gilin and Loana. Nor did they relocate the campsite. At dusk they halted and found trees to sleep in. Exhausted, but greatly disappointed at the results of their search, all except Talli took a well-deserved rest.

Talli spent the better part of the night endeavoring to once more communicate with Gilin. Recalling precisely how she had accomplished it before, she held the toe ring at arm's length, viewing the moon through it and concentrating on Gilin. She thought long and hard about her friend, about their times together at home, about where he might be now, and about everything she could think of regarding Gilin. But to her dismay, no matter how she tried, nothing happened. Nothing appeared within the circle, and she could not sense a tugging or pulling of the ring in any direction. Drained and dejected, she eventually fell into a fitful slumber.

A clear morning greeted the kirins. At breakfast Speckarin voiced what had been on all of their minds. "I believe we have taken a wrong direction," he said solemnly. "We should have discovered the campsite by now. We must try again today, but if we have not located Gilin by evening, I am afraid our chances of finding him will grow small. Now, together, we must decide upon the bearing we choose today."

They discussed their situation, and everyone but Talli expressed an opinion. The distracted girl had been deeply troubled by the encounter with the volodons, and after spending a fruitless night attempting to communicate with her lost friend, was hardly herself this morning. She had no idea in which direction they should go and did not want to risk a wrong guess in the search for Gilin. The direction that finally seemed most promising, and in which they eventually must go in any case, was to the east, and off they started.

They flew all day at a steady pace under a bright and sunny sky, but again found no sign of Gilin. They stopped to rest overnight, and the next morning awoke to an ominous sky, dark and overcast.

Speckarin gathered the others around him, and he was grave. "We cannot continue to retrace our steps," he said. "We have not found Gilin. But somehow we must carry on ourselves. As you all know, Gilin is a resourceful youth, skilled in woodsmanship, and he has a strong ilon in Loana. He is undoubtedly all right, and since he is only a few days from home he may already have elected to return to the clan. He might well be on his way right now. But we, as the surviving party, must continue eastward in pursuit of our quest."

They all knew this had been coming. No one dissented, and they soon departed. Little was said as they traveled that day. They were becoming resigned to the prospect that they would not be reunited with Gilin during this journey. And yet all, including Speckarin, wondered what his fate had truly been. They could only hope that he was safely on his way home, as the magician suggested. In his heart, as he tried to rest that night, Hut wished that he was on his way home with his cousin. But he realized, as did all of them, that the mission must go on.

The small party made its way eastward for four more uneventful days, stopping at night for rest and traveling during the day. Talli became increasingly unsettled as they progressed, and for several reasons, only some of which the others were aware of. At home, Gilin had been closer to Talli than to anyone in the party except his cousin Hut. Gilin and Talli were, of course, the only members of the Moger clan who had joined the quest. But of even more significance, they were the only ones with the knowledge of Olamin, and now that Gilin was gone Talli bore that burden alone. The attack by the volodons had underscored that fact convincingly, and had shaken her to the core. Her sleep at night was also disturbed by repeated efforts at communication with her lost friend through the ring. Lastly, she was attempting to utilize the ring for an entirely new purpose, but her endeavors continued to meet with no success.

One reason for Talli's discomfiture was a fact that none of the others were aware of. It was a matter she would not discuss with them because it verged on the boundaries of the secret knowledge. Yet it was what troubled her most deeply of all. Olamin had instructed the youths that it would be Gilin's calamar that would eventually direct them across the giant body of water, and then carry them on to their ultimate destination upon land. How, wondered Talli ruefully, will we locate our final place of reckoning with Gilin and his calamar missing?

Her only hope, as she considered the alternatives, was that she could discover a method of employing her ring for the same purpose. If that did not work, she knew that the entire mission would be doomed to failure. It was the burden of this worry that weighed on her most heavily and kept her sleepless. In addition to her attempts to contact Gilin, she was endeavoring to become more proficient with the ring.

The others were cognizant of Talli's distraction, yet they were powerless to help. She had long since been displaced from the lead flight position by Speckarin. Now she flew in Gilin's old place, behind the magician and in front of Diliani, so that someone could keep watch over her.

During their fifth day of travel without Gilin, six days after leaving the campsite, something happened that would alter the mission completely. The day was hot and muggy, typical of late spring. Talli, fatigued and distraught, rode astride Faralan in the hazy midday sun. As the warm afternoon wore on, even as she tried to concentrate on the flight, her eyes began to blur and her head to swim. The grip of her long feet beneath the neck of the ilon began to slacken.

The sole means by which kirins remain upon ilon is grasping the necks or torsos of the creatures with their strong feet. In rare instances, loss of grip has been known to occur, and has led to disaster. What is remarkable, however, is that more kirins have not fallen from their ilon.

Diliani first noticed that Faralan had broken rank and was heading downward, and then that he was riderless. As she gazed down, to her horror she saw Talli tumbling earthward.

C H A P T E R   8

"T ALLI!" screamed Diliani
as she plunged her ilon downward. Seeing what was
happening, the others dove directly after her. Faralan chased
his mistress as fast as he could, but within moments Talli
struck the ground.

Diliani landed next to her. She leaped from Manay, and
kneeled down by her side. "Talli!" she cried, but the girl
made no movement or sound.

Speckarin touched down, and then Hut, and they were
immediately at Talli's side. "Is she breathing?" asked Hut
earnestly. "Will she be all right?"

"She is breathing," said the magician after observing her
for a few moments. "But whether she will be all right I do not
know. She was fortunate. We were flying lower than usual,
and she landed on a soft area of ground." He indicated the
grassy plot upon which Talli had fallen. A short distance in
one direction, he pointed out, was bare, hard earth, and in
another were gravel and rocks.

"She could have been more severely hurt," said Speckarin
intently. "But even as it is, I cannot be certain how serious
her injuries are. She is unconscious; she must have received

an injury to her head or neck."

Moving closer, the old magician began to gently palpate her motionless body—the limbs, the torso, the skull, the neck and the spine. He could discover no skeletal disruptions, and no obvious internal injuries. Her companions were all relieved.

"I should have known it was going to happen," said Diliani. "It is the second time for me. I was behind Gilin when we lost him."

"We all knew Talli was exhausted," said Speckarin reassuringly. "It probably happened so quickly that no one could have stopped it."

That did not console Diliani. Courageous as this kirin was, tears of contrition welled within her eyes. But her feelings of guilt were interrupted by the old magician's voice and supplanted by concern over what to do next with the prostrate youngster.

She was lying directly in the heat of the sun. Glancing about the site, Speckarin gave instructions. "We must move her into the coolness of the shade. There, under those boughs," he said, pointing toward the low-hanging branches of a large hemlock tree.

With the utmost of care, the three kirins lifted their limp compatriot off the ground and carried her to the shelter of the tree. They laid her down upon a dry sheet of cloth carried by Diliani in her pack.

Then they waited.

In his hasty preparations with Duan the morning they departed Rogalinon, Speckarin had included in his baggage many of the magical instruments he had collected over the years. But he had a limited amount of room, and choices had to be made. Now, to his consternation as he searched through his baggage, he had only a few of the balms, potions, and antidotes customarily employed by a magician in serving his clan. He found to his dismay that he was nearly impotent in trying to minister to the recumbent Talli.

Hut discovered water nearby. The magician applied a cool, moist compress to Talli's forehead, and elevated her long feet so that the circulation would travel to her head. He uttered magical incantations, and paced back and forth next to the youngster. But in the depths of his heart he knew that alone, without aid from someone or something else, he could do nothing further for the reclining lass.

Had Talli been human, or from any of a number of species on Earth, nursing her and waiting for recovery would be all that an attendant could do. If the trauma proved not to be severe, the injured being would in time recuperate; should the injury have been great, however, death would probably be the end result. With kirins, as the old magician knew well, the pattern was different.

Unlike humans, this race of beings has retained, from time immemorial, a semblance of the magic of their ancestors. It is not only essential for continuation of the race-wide spells of no'an and curlace, but vital to the normal functioning of each individual. A fraction of magical spirit is alive, and burns like a flame within the soul of every kirin. This essence, called aris in Ruvon, enables the individual to participate in the spells and the magic of the race. But, like a candle, it can be snuffed out.

As Speckarin was also aware, the conjuring powers of his race have declined throughout its lengthy subsistence on Earth. The spell of no'an is still sufficient to maintain invisibility, but it is not as powerful as it once was. For perpetuation it requires the constant attention of the Guardian Magician. Curlace, which at one time was a purely magical bond between kirin and beast, is now a mixture of magic and the lifelong training of ilon. And, most significantly to Speckarin at this moment, the critical core of magic, dwelling within each kirin, has grown more fragile over time. Consequently, the survival of every individual has become more tenuous than in the past.

Bodily trauma is something feared by kirins, not only because of the possibility of structural injury—Speckarin had already searched for this in Talli—but more important because of the frailty of the indwelling core. Physical or psychological injury can lead to a decline in this aris—indispensable for life—and damage inflicted upon it can be irreversible. It is known that the flame becomes steadily weaker after injury, and that if revival does not occur early, the chances for recovery shrink with each ensuing day.

Even prior to the fall, Speckarin had been concerned about Talli's aris. The psychological pressures and punishment she was enduring were profound. The magician had worried that their effects would result in a diminution of her internal flame. The fact that physical trauma had been added concerned the magician deeply, and it led him to action.

Speckarin knew, as did every kirin magician, that one thing could be done to sustain this magic spirit, even within an unconscious kirin. A few rare and precious substances had been discovered in nature that, if skillfully administered, could fuel and possibly rekindle the quintessential flame. They could keep it burning even in the face of severe damage, aiding incalculably in recovery.

As evening drew near and Talli showed no sign of improvement, Speckarin came to an agonizing decision. Wishing Diliani to stay close by to help nurse the girl, he dispatched Hut to find a barwood tree.

This mysterious tree was known to possess a sap and leaves with the quality Speckarin was looking for. The products of this tree could be lifesaving to a fallen kirin, but also, if inappropriately administered, could render irreparable harm. Searching his memory and his experience for anything that might aid the fallen girl, the magician had decided to risk the capricious powers of this tree. With incredible fortune, Speckarin had noted a grove of the darkly hued trees before Talli's fall, some distance back, to the west of their present location.

Desiring to go back himself, Speckarin was torn about what to do, and for two reasons he finally selected Hut for the task. The old magician was exhausted. But Speckarin also found that, in her time of great need, he was unwilling to leave Talli.

With trepidation Speckarin called Hut to his side, and began to describe the appearance and the properties of the tree. Easily recognizable because of its characteristic leaves and covering, the barwood tree, though rare in their home forest, was known to kirins of the Moger and Yorl clans. The young kirin listened only briefly before confirming his acquaintance with the tree.

The unique bark consists of what appear to be a series of tubular rings encircling the trunk horizontally. But in fact, if following them around the tree carefully, one would find that what seem to be many are but a single cylindrical structure, spiraling the trunk many times over in the manner of a corkscrew. With the largest of the rings at the base, the hollow structure gradually narrows as it circles upward, and then bifurcates as it spreads to cover the branches.

No tree is difficult for a kirin to negotiate. But the barwood is the easiest of all for them to climb because of the ladderlike configuration of the bark. In addition, the deep, enticingly colored leaves attract youthful kirins, and almost beckon them upward. Not a single kirin of the home clans, however, has ever touched a barwood tree, and certainly not climbed one, having been instructed from childhood that they can be highly dangerous.

The old magician reviewed the precautions to be taken against these perils, and Hut listened with interest. It is known, he told the lad, that sap is contained within the circumferential structures of the bark. While the leaves have potent qualities of their own, it is the sap of the barwood tree, running through the giant veins, that has both life-giving and life-threatening capabilities.

Speckarin spoke quickly but with utter gravity as he explained what Hut was obliged to do. "You must climb the tree, gather several small leaves, and place them directly in this container." He removed a small silver box from his bag. "Then climb back down to earth!

"Do not tarry in the tree, little one!" he cautioned, his brow furrowing. "Stay there only long enough to collect the leaves! When you are back on the ground, pierce one of the circular vessels of the trunk. Carefully extract a few drops of the liquid and sequester them within this," he said, producing a silver vial.

The magician spoke in earnest as he went on. "Throughout the procedure you will wear a mask to protect yourself! Here is a cloth to cover your face, leaving only your eyes exposed! It is to be tied tightly behind your head! This garment will have to do! We have nothing else! Under no circumstances must you allow the leaves of the tree, or the sap, or the fumes of the sap, to come near your face! Your senses of taste and smell must be shielded from the vapors of this tree! In the wild, or in a magician's laboratory, the slightest ingestion or inhalation of the essence of barwood can be disastrous!"

Taking no time to explain further, he hurried on. "Hasten back to us with your harvest! After its modification we will attempt administration of the product to our fallen friend!"

Speckarin was aware that a method for taming barwood sap, there in the woods and with precious little equipment, was yet be determined. He did know, however, that first he must obtain the substance.

The magician told the youth where he had sighted the barwood grove, due westward. Diliani called Lisam, and Hut was quickly off. Having flown for but a short while, he spied the grouping of unmistakable trees, fully laden with leaves of a rust-brown hue. Setting Lisam down in the midst of the grove, Hut dismounted and chose a large one. He strode up to the tree and examined it briefly. There was no doubt whatsoever that this was a barwood tree, with the characteristic circular ridging of the bark and the unique coloration of the leaves. Out came the cloth, and he tied it in back of his head. Then, stepping up to the tree without hesitation, he placed a long foot upon one of the lower protuberances and began to climb.

Kirins of the Yorl clan feel very much at home in trees, and demonstrate the greatest of dexterity when climbing. On this clear evening, after all they had been through, and despite the warnings of Speckarin, the tree was a pleasure for the youngster to be ascending. Reaching a branch well above the ground, he began to cautiously move outward toward the coveted leaves. He tarried but a few moments in making his selection, beginning to notice, even through the cloth, a pleasing and delicate scent. He chose several leaves, each a perfect specimen, he thought, and placed them in the silver box. After applying its top securely, he returned it to his belt satchel.

Then, whether due to youth, inexperience, curiosity, fatigue, the charm of the barwood grove, the insidious infiltration of its essence, or a combination of everything, Hut found himself aware only of the beauty and the solitude surrounding him. He sat down quietly on the branch to enjoy a sunset of gold and dusky purple. He wondered what the evils of the barwood tree could be, and even thought fleetingly of removing the mask. The party had been through such a tiresome time. He simply wished to enjoy an interim of peace and quietude.

After a brief time he realized that he must be getting on about his business and got to his feet. He was starting to move back toward the trunk of the tree when he noticed that the branch ahead appeared fuzzy and out of focus. The sensation cleared, but within moments returned, and this time more intensely. He found himself barely able to edge his way back toward the trunk. But he finally made it, and upon reaching it he clung to it, because his balance was becoming impaired and his vision steadily more blurred. Had it not been for the barlike striations of the tree, he might not have been able to descend to the bottom. As it was, he felt his way slowly downward to the ground. By then he was able to perceive little more than darkness and light.

As he clutched the giant veins at the base, he could recall only vaguely what his mission was to have been. Removing the pruning knife unsteadily from his belt and the silver vial from his satchel, he forced himself to make an incision through the wall of a great channel, and felt a warm liquor exude therefrom.

With considerable effort he maneuvered the vial into position. He managed to capture a small amount of the fragrant fluid and cap the container, before collapsing motionless at the foot of the tree. His final recollection, before losing all awareness, was of thick sap oozing from the hole, running down the trunk, and forming a dark, aromatic pool next to him.

C H A P T E R   9

SPECKARIN and Diliani
hovered over the unmoving Talli throughout the night, one
made far longer by the fact that Hut had not returned. They
took turns watching over the girl, for there was nothing else
they could do with what little they had. Many concerns ran
through the old magician's mind as the night wore slowly on,
not the least of which were the perils young Hut might be
facing at that very moment. When the earliest light of day
finally arrived, there was still no change in Talli's condition,
and no sign of Hut.

The magician was frustrated, fatigued, and close to
desperation. "Now one of us must be off in search of Hut!"
he told Diliani. "Will our fortunes never change for the
better? This quest has been grossly unkind to our youths! All
three of them are either lost or frightfully injured! The
barwood tree may be what has smitten the most recent one,
but I fear that any number of other evils might have befallen
him! Diliani! I must now go myself! I know where the grove
is! I wish you to remain with Talli! Call Ocelam while I
gather the few things I might need!"

Shortly, the magician was in the air, moving hastily

westward, yellow robe flying in the early morning breeze. He soon sighted the grove of darkly colored trees. He descended among them and dismounted. Looking quickly about, he could see no one, nothing, save the mysterious and alluring trees.

"Hut!" he called loudly. "Hut! Are you here? Are you anywhere where you can hear me?"

He called many times aloud, and strode through the trees as swiftly as he could. Suddenly he sensed the aroma of barwood essence in the air, an unearthly and unforgettable fragrance, one he had experienced only once before in his lifetime. At almost the same moment he saw a collection of sap at the foot of a nearby tree and its source, an oozing wound in the trunk.

That must be where Hut made his cut, he told himself. But he dared not venture closer because of the intoxicating liquid. What could have happened to him after that? he wondered apprehensively. If he is not here, where could he possibly have gone? Why did he not return to us with the sap and the leaves? He and his ilon seem to have disappeared without a trace!

Now nearly at his wits' end, and with no idea where to search for Hut, the old magician remounted Ocelam dejectedly and flew slowly away from the barwood grove. Searching the terrain methodically as he traveled eastward, he could see no sign of Hut. Eventually he found his way back to the hemlock tree and landed next to it. Distraught, he related to the awaiting Diliani what had happened, that he could find nothing of Hut save the laceration in the tree and the exudate upon the ground, and that he was at a loss what to do next.

"The exotic powers of the barwood may have overcome our young friend," murmured a disconcerted Speckarin. "But if that were the case, why was he not still by the tree? And what of his ilon? If he were still capable of directing her, and they left the grove under his command, where else would they have gone but here? And should he be dead, Lisam would have sensed that she no longer had a kirin master, and with her curlace teachings she would have immediately

returned to us, alone, to lead us back to his body! I know not
what is happening nor what to do! Our party has been broken
tragically asunder!"

The old magician, confused and exhausted, slumped upon
a log next to Talli, his head in his hands. Diliani was about to
sit down next to him, to offer what consolation she could,
when out of the corner of her eye she caught sight of a great
figure gliding toward them through the air. Turning quickly
she saw the raven, Lisam, alighting adjacent to the hemlock,
no rider aboard.

"Speckarin!" she cried. She leapt to her feet and ran to the
side of the bird. "Lisam is here! But Hut is not with her! She
has returned alone!"

The dazed magician arose unsteadily and moved as rapidly
as he could to examine Lisam, and found no evidence of her
young master. He knew what this meant. Every kirin did.

"It must have been the barwood tree after all," he said
disconsolately, turning away. "The ilon has returned alone,"
he repeated several times over, knowing full well what it
signified. He looked at Diliani, his chin quivering, and his
next words came with great difficulty.

"She has returned alone," he said. "If he were alive she
would have stayed with him. Ilon are trained to do that. Hut
. . . must be dead. Lisam would never have returned without
him . . . unless he were . . . such."

He sat down wearily. He said nothing further, and did
nothing for some time except to stare at Lisam. Diliani tried
vainly to comfort him.

"We must allow Lisam to lead us to him," he said finally.
Then he went on, his voice breaking. "I fear this exploration
is at an end! It has failed! I was simply unable to hold it
together! The forces against us were too great! The party has
disintegrated, has been decimated, I am afraid, beyond repair!
And it all occurred so quickly and so early in our journey!"

Speckarin was unable to go on. It was the lowest he had
ever been in his life. Now, deep within his heart, what was
significant to him and to the party began to change in

priority: The survival of those who remained was more important than the success of the mission, whatever that might have been. Gilin was gone and Reydel was exceedingly far away. Unless Talli awoke, they had no one with the knowledge to lead them to their final destination. The mission was over. For the first time since the quest had started he considered going home, and even how they would transport Talli on the way.

His ruminations were interrupted rudely by a shrill voice coming from behind, saying in Ruvon, "I see you already have one dead lad! Behold! I bear his brother to your hemlock tree!"

C H A P T E R   1 0

GILIN STARED back at
the human girl, not knowing what was happening. She cannot
be looking at me! he thought. She must be looking at
something nearby, but certainly not at me! She cannot see
me! I am invisible!

He did not move a muscle, afraid he might make a sound
or cause a leaf or a flower to move, and she would
somehow detect him. But he was absolutely certain she
could not see him.

Nonetheless, she continued to gaze directly at him, and
after a few more moments, she knelt down as if to have even
a better look.

Because of lifelong training, the bewildered Gilin stood
motionless and uttered not a sound.

Ruggum, but a short distance away, was unable to see his
friend and therefore could not discern precisely what was
happening. The human girl, however, at first appeared to be
eyeing the area in which he assumed Gilin to be, which
disturbed him greatly. But there was nothing he could do
about it. He became even more alarmed when she moved
closer to whatever she was looking at, and especially when

she kneeled down and appeared to be scrutinizing it. If only I could see him, thought Ruggum, becoming more agitated by the moment. If only I knew exactly where he was!

If Gilin is there, anywhere nearby, thought Ruggum, he must realize that he cannot make a move, or take a deep breath, even though she is blind to him! What could she be doing? She must be looking at a flower, or a rock, or a root, or an insect near him, perhaps something behind him, in which case she would be looking through him! That, he consoled himself, is the function of no'an magic! Gilin knows he must not do anything to reveal himself! But what an agonizing experience for the poor lad, to have a human being so extremely close! Why doesn't she just go away? Perhaps Gilin is not there after all, where I thought he was! In any case, he reminded himself, I can do nothing but stay calm and quiet.

"Who are you?" said the human girl.

Ruggum realized now that Gilin might indeed be in trouble. He was no expert in languages. But he was acquainted enough with English to know the meaning of what had been said, and that it had been spoken to someone in Gilin's vicinity.

Could it possibly be Gilin after all? wondered the overseer. Of course not! he answered summarily. She cannot see him! She must be looking at something near him, and Gilin is trapped in the immediate area! I must do something to extricate him from this incredible situation: a human who cannot perceive him, and yet is, astonishingly, examining something in his location! What can I do, he wondered frantically, without giving myself away?

His mind was in a whirl, but suddenly an idea surfaced. I must divert her, he thought, take her attention off whatever she is eyeing!

He recalled the trick he had played with Alsinam, some days before, when humans had threatened to remove the morel mushrooms of Berin and Strika. Making movement in the presence of a human went against all of his instincts. But

Ruggum determined that in this predicament he must gamble. He would summon his ilon.

He started cautiously, signaling to the bird with subtle head and hand motions. The intelligent old raven, who had kept Ruggum under constant surveillance throughout, now cocked his head, and at first simply observed the gestures. After slight hesitation and with head still tilted, the ilon began to walk slowly toward his master.

The movement of the giant bird caught the girl's attention. She stood up, her glance, at least for the moment, away from Gilin.

Further visual commands were given as the bird approached. The raven stopped, watching his master closely.

Alsinam turned and faced the girl. Then he opened his beak and began to sing a song as lovely as she had ever heard.

Unlike the humans at the morel site, this young one did not flee. Instead, filled with wonder and curiosity, she took a few steps closer, and while the raven continued to sing she listened with rapt attention.

Gilin, still questioning why she had been looking so intently at his position, why she even had seemed to be examining him, had not noted the signals from Ruggum to his ilon. He did recognize the song, nonetheless, as a stratagem to draw her concentration away from him. When she looked away, Gilin gladly seized the opportunity and slipped behind the trunk of the nearest spruce tree. Within moments of the song's ending, however, her eyes darted back to where he had been.

"Where are you?" she said, moving back through the grass toward the place she had been. She bent over and began searching the area. "I saw you! I know I did! Where did you go? You must still be here somewhere! I won't hurt you! I just want to see you again, and talk to you!"

"Sandra!" came the call from her father. He was climbing up the bank from the lake and looking about. "There you are!" he said as he caught sight of her. "What are you doing, Sandra? Come down here, to the lake! You want to go fishing, don't you?"

"I'm over here!" she cried. But she did not turn her head nor take her eyes off the place Gilin had been. "I saw something! A little person with big feet! And then I heard that bird singing!" She turned to point at Alsinam.

By now the father was approaching the scene. "What bird?" he said. "Oh, that big black one? That's just a crow, honey. You know that! They don't sing! They just croak and caw! Come on! You do want to go fishing, don't you?"

"No!" she insisted. "I saw a little man right there, and I want to see him again!"

But the mortified Gilin had no intention of reappearing. After more discussion the man led his daughter away by the hand, moving toward the lake. Until she was out of sight, however, her head remained turned and she continued to gaze in the direction of the kirins.

When Ruggum was finally certain they had left, he peered toward the location where he thought his companion to be. "Gilin!" he whispered. "They seem to be gone! Where are you? Are you still there?"

Frightened by the inexplicable confrontation, Gilin cautiously left his hiding place and walked unsteadily toward Ruggum. The overseer stood anxiously between the two ravens, awaiting either a return of the humans or a word from his invisible friend.

As he approached, Gilin answered tremulously, "I am here."

Ruggum began to move toward the sound. "I am happy to hear your voice!" he said. "Are you all right?"

"I am unharmed," said Gilin.

Confused by the event, however, Gilin described what had occurred, how she had gotten very close, how she had seemed to be looking directly at him, even though he knew it was impossible for her to see him.

"She could not . . . have . . . actually seen me, could she?" he asked.

"Of course not!" the overseer answered vigorously. "Never! Kirins have been invisible for thousands of generations! She was looking at something near you, perhaps behind you! They look directly through us! Still, it must have been horribly disconcerting to be so near a human being, and even more so to have one staring at you! It will never happen again! It was purely coincidence that you were where she was looking!"

"But then," asked Gilin, "what did she mean by little man and big feet?"

"She was looking at . . . a bird," said Ruggum, "or an animal, possibly a frog, which has large feet. Or she might have been playing some kind of game with her father, because she did not wish to go with him! But, my young friend, you must remember and be assured of one thing! You are a kirin! As a kirin, she could never have seen you!"

Unless, thought the overseer suddenly, Gilin had employed the only means by which a kirin can become visible, that single flaw in the spell of no'an known to only a few kirins. But how could he possibly have done so, the overseer asked himself? He would not have known what to do, and it would be repugnant to virtually any kirin to do it! Certainly any average kirin!

And yet, Ruggum was reminded with a jolt, Gilin is hardly an average kirin! He has been severely traumatized, is even invisible to his own kind! Perhaps, thought Ruggum, the isolation and suffering caused by carrying the secret knowledge, the attack and seizure by the gronom, his separation from the traveling party, and his invisibility among family, friends, and race finally combined to bring him to a breaking point, and he did something rash and out of character. After a few moments of contemplation Ruggum decided to question Gilin further, even if it meant revealing the secret defect in the spell of no'an.

"It may seem strange that I ask," he began, choosing his words carefully, "but when the human came close to you, did you sense, within yourself, any sort of . . . if you will pardon the word, and I am truly sorry to ask . . . any sort of enjoyment . . . or . . . pleasure in her presence?"

Gilin was shocked by the words of the elder. He responded quickly and angrily. "Of course not! I was deeply concerned and frightened by her nearness. How could you conceive such an idea?"

The overseer wished to assuage his young friend. He also knew that they were alone in the woods far from home, and that the knowledge he might now impart would go no further. Ruggum decided to reveal the secret.

"I ask because of this," said the elder in earnest. "To explain why I questioned you in such a manner, I must tell you something only magicians and selected elders know. The only occasion upon which a kirin has been seen by a human, since the inception of no'an, has been when the kirin chooses to be seen, desires to be seen, for whatever reason. Under those circumstances the spell temporarily recedes. The kirin materializes, so to speak, and is visible for whatever length of time he wishes. Then he fades once more from view. But such cases are so infrequent that they are almost unheard of. It has not happened in my lifetime. Oh, it may have occurred somewhere in the world. But I have not heard about it, and you were certainly not wishing or willing that this human see you!"

"Of course not!" repeated the lad, exasperated by Ruggum's suggestion. "What kind of kirin would have such a desire, to be seen by humans after their despicable treatment of our race so many centuries ago?"

"You are correct, naturally," answered the overseer, chagrined at having asked and hoping it would not alter his relationship with his young companion. "But unbelievable as it may seem, it has happened!"

Neither of them wished to discuss the matter further, nor did they desire to linger in this territory. Therefore, with little conversation, they mounted their ilon and departed.

The sun was setting behind them as they headed, almost by instinct, in an easterly direction. As they flew on, searching for a place to spend the night, Gilin was haunted by what had transpired, unable to get the picture of the young girl out of his mind.

At the same time, further questions about what had occurred crept into the overseer's thoughts. He did not know why, but as they progressed he found himself becoming more uneasy about the confrontation.

Is it possible, he wondered, that somehow the human actually could have . . . perceived Gilin? Absolutely not, he reassured himself, almost rhetorically. It would have been impossible, unless he willed that it happen! I am certain that is something he did not do! And yet she was looking precisely at him! And she described him! If only I could see him! I could do a better job of protecting him! If only the reprehensible gronom had not captured him!

And then an onerous idea shook Ruggum. The gronom had made Gilin invisible to kirins, indeed. Could it be that the sting of the beast had at the same time altered Gilin's visibility to human beings? Is it possible that the sting caused a gruesome reversal: At the moment he was rendered invisible to kirins, he was shorn of the cloak of invisibility provided by no'an, allowing humans to see him?

Ruggum shuddered at the thought. But he retained his composure and stayed outwardly calm so as not to show his concern. The last thing he wanted to do was alarm his young friend further, give him more of a burden than he already had. He kept it to himself, but he continued to worry. Visible to human beings, and without willing it! Could it possibly be true? We will not know the answer to that question, he thought, unless we encounter another one, an unlikely happenstance under any conditions!

Deep in their own thoughts, neither of them uttered a word as they flew onward. Ruggum's ominous meditations were eventually intruded upon, however, by their overbearing need to find a place for the night. It was past dusk. The stars were now visible in a clear sky above. As he searched the terrain for a suitable landing site, he saw something at a great distance ahead, and at first did not know what it was. Blinking through the atmosphere, and scattered across the landscape, were pinpoint dots of light, single and in clusters.

A sickening realization dawned upon the old kirin. The humans they had encountered today were, of course, not an isolated pair. As a race, humanity was of a social and societal nature. The appearance of those two had only signaled the proximity of others, possibly many others, and what they were rapidly approaching was nothing other than a sizeable settlement of human beings.

C H A P T E R   1 1

DILIANI turned quickly toward the startling voice. She was astonished to see something she had never before perceived. Two kirins, some distance away, sat astride animals larger than she had ever known to be used as ilon. An expert in animal and bird ilon, and in curlace magic, she at first almost ignored the foreign kirins. Her rapt attention was drawn to the two sleek animals with shining silver backs, rust-trimmed legs, and white underbellies. Having encountered them occasionally in the home forest, she recognized them immediately as gray foxes. The animals stood as quietly and attentively as the bird and squirrel ilon she was accustomed to, black eyes sparkling in the early morning sun as they awaited commands from their masters.

"Speckarin," she said quietly to the distracted magician, who was not fully cognizant of what was happening. "We have visitors."

He also turned, and in his exhaustion dimly saw the recently arrived party.

One of the new kirins gave a soft command, and his animal started slowly toward them. The rider was clad in a traveling garment of a light shade of green, similar to those of the Yorl and Moger clans, but of lighter weight for this warm weather. He also wore a forest green hunting hat, but his legs and long feet were bare.

The newcomer halted his ilon. "Which of you is leader?" he asked, continuing in Ruvon, his voice high and piercing.

Diliani was still examining the sizeable and powerful ilon. These animals lived in the home forest also, and they were occasionally discussed among practitioners of curlace magic as having the potential to be ilon. And with good reason, she thought, as she gazed upon the striking creatures: They are beautiful, and they are the only breed of the fox family that climbs trees. They do so undauntedly and with great ease. But because of their size, one problem had never been solved: how to house them in a clan tree. Diliani had never actually known them to be used as ilon. Yet here they were, obviously well trained, and being employed as ilon by foreign kirins. What solution, she wondered, had they found to this problem? The answer would be forthcoming, but not for some time to come.

"The magician, Speckarin, is our leader," answered Diliani, also in Ruvon. She glanced at her demoralized companion. "But he is spent from events of the past several days."

The kirin and his animal started forward again, and the foreigner perused them with unhidden curiosity. As he came closer, Diliani could make out a series of narrow straps with which he seemed to maintain stability aboard the animal. The home clans had no need for harnesses with squirrel and bird ilon, but she could understand the need for such an arrangement with an animal of such magnitude. However, command of the animal was not, she could see, gained by use of the harness, but through the gently spoken sounds of curlace.

The animal stopped a short distance away. The rider climbed down and began walking toward them, but he passed directly by Diliani and Speckarin, his attention obviously drawn to the prostrate Talli. He knelt down next to the blond girl, examined her for a few moments and then spoke in Ruvon.

"She is not a lad after all," he said. "She is a girl. And she was not a victim of the barwood tree." As he stood up he motioned to his companion, and called, "Bring the other one here!"

The second kirin uttered a word and his ilon moved forward. Almost upon them, the animal halted. As the rider climbed down Diliani could for the first time see another kirin, obviously unconscious, strapped to the back of the animal. The kirin unleashed bindings at the flank of the ilon and slid the limp body gently to the ground, where Diliani and Speckarin immediately recognized their lost companion.

"Hutsin!" cried the old magician, coming alive. He rose shakily, and moved as rapidly toward the motionless body as he could, Diliani at his side. Both knelt down next to the reclining youth.

"He is not dead," remarked the first kirin in a strident voice. "Only a victim of the barwood tree. You need not worry about him. He will sleep another day, or possibly two, and when he awakens he will be as healthy and fine as he has ever been, but a little hungrier. He will have had a good sleep, and be far better rested than the two of you seem to be!"

"Thank goodness you found him and bore him here!" exclaimed Speckarin in the dialect of his home region, forgetting in his excitement to use the ancient tongue. Reminded of it by Diliani, he corrected himself, and repeated his acknowledgement in the common language.

The old magician stood up to more clearly see the new kirins. "How can we possibly thank you for what you have done?" he said.

"You have no need," said the stranger. "I am Issar, and this is Runagar," he continued, indicating his younger companion. Then, raising his hands in an obvious gesture of greeting, but one that the travelers were not accustomed to, he declared, "Welcome to the domain of Queen Lanara."

"We thank you," said a moved and relieved Speckarin. "But how did you chance to find us here in the woods?"

"I shall explain," said Issar. "But first, what of your

other?" he continued, turning toward Talli. "She is badly injured. How did it happen?"

"Yesterday afternoon," said the old magician haltingly, "in a moment of distraction, she fell from her ilon to the ground. She has been unconscious since that time. I am deeply worried about her, but I have had almost nothing with which to treat her. In desperation I sent the other youth to collect the sap and leaves of a barwood tree, a task that proved to be his undoing."

"It has been many a kirin's undoing," said Issar. "The charm of the barwood is subtle and almost undetectable until it is too late."

"I was aware of this, and should have taken on the duty myself," answered Speckarin, still struggling internally about the entire affair. "But in that moment of crisis, my imprudent choice was to send the youth."

"No matter," said Issar. "He is safe now, and back with you. I must relate something about his rescue that I am certain you will find of interest. When we found him, the essence of the tree had subdued him, but not completely. It had deprived him of his senses, but not of other functions. He was still breathing, and therefore we know he will recover, slowly perhaps, but fully. Had he remained much longer by the tree he would have perished. Strangely enough, however, we did not find him by the tree.

"Late yesterday afternoon," he continued, "Runagar and I were outside on a mission for our queen. While coming through the woods we became aware of the unmistakable odor of barwood sap in the air, and realized that the vein of a tree must somehow have been ruptured. We immediately searched the grove and located the tree, liquid still seeping from a laceration made quite obviously by a sharp instrument, possibly a kirin knife."

Here he paused, looking pensively into the woods for a few moments. "Violation of a barwood tree is an uncommon and perilous occurrence in our forest. We concluded that the one who performed this deed must have acted out of desperation, or out of total ignorance, and now might be in serious difficulty because of it. But we could see no one, could find not a sign of the one who had cut into the tree, save kirin footprints leading up to the tree, and other tracks, not made by a kirin, which I will mention later. After patching the wound in the tree, a hazardous procedure in itself, we again searched the grove, and eventually came across your friend. He lay almost half the dimension of the grove away from the assaulted tree.

"By him stood that ilon," said Issar, pointing to Lisam. "We think it is this bird to whom he owes his life. Our deduction is that the raven sensed its master was in imminent peril next to the oozing tree, and that it lifted him and transported him from danger. When far enough away, it gently set him down, where we found him. We have no other explanation for how he could have arrived there. And if this is true, the bird acted courageously indeed, for whether the creature was aware of it or not, it was just as susceptible to the essence of barwood as its master. We believe this is what truly occurred, because while we found no kirin footprints leading away from the tree, we did discover the tracks of a giant bird, heading away and disappearing where it must have become airborne."

The recovering Speckarin glanced gratefully at Lisam. "Feats such as this are known in the long association between kirins and ilon," he said. "But in my tenure as magician no incident like this has occurred within our clan. Such acts have been preserved over the centuries in the annals of curlace magic, so that they may be remembered, just as Lisam's brave actions will be transcribed and recalled. For without her bravery it appears that Hut might now be dead."

Throughout the conversation, Diliani had found it interesting, almost amusing, that Issar employed the word "it" when referring to Lisam. A kirin of the home clans would routinely have used the more personal "she" or "her." It might be a cultural difference in the use of language, she conjectured, or perhaps that these new kirins are simply not acquainted with bird ilon and their capabilities. She determined that she would follow their words closely, especially with reference to ilon. Through this, she thought, she might gain insight into their make-up and culture, which was perceptibly different from that of Yorls and Mogers.

Diliani also was gratified at the rescue and return of Hut, but she was still perplexed about one thing. "May I ask," she interjected, "how you were able to locate us in the woods, in order to bring our friend back to us?"

"This was not an easy task," answered Issar. "When we found him it was plain that this youth was foreign to our territories, and we were almost certain that he would not be in this region alone, so far from home. His ilon, of course, had waited close beside him."

"And would have remained so until her master expired," interrupted Speckarin.

"Through our actions," continued Issar, "and through curlace sounds and words, we were able to introduce into the consciousness of the bird the concept that we, too, wished to help the recumbent youth, and even the idea that we would follow, carrying its master, should it lead us to his companions. At one point it appeared that the bird was confused and might attempt to pick up the limp body in its beak in order to fly away with it. But we were able to convince it that this would be more perilous for its master than our bearing him on the ground, and eventually it seemed to understand.

"We strapped the foreign youth to the back of Runagar's ilon," he said, "and departed. As the raven flew ahead, we followed, transporting its master as we had promised. Of course, we traveled much more slowly than the bird could, but it kept us under close observation so as not to fly too far out of our range. Even though our foxes are swift afoot, throughout this trek we kept them at a walk so as not to damage your unconscious friend. We do not travel in the dark. With the onset of night we camped in the forest, seeing to it that your compatriot was comfortable. This morning we started off again, and the raven led us here to you."

"Once again, may I thank you for your gallant efforts," said Speckarin, deeply relieved. The old magician had revived temporarily at the return of Hut, but now he was flagging again and becoming overcome by fatigue. His energy dwindling rapidly, Diliani helped him sit down. Issar noted the magician's condition, and tendered the following invitation.

"If you wish," he said, "we will take you to shelter, to minister to your youths and provide a place for all to recuperate."

Then, turning to Runagar and pointing to the fallen Talli, he said in a shrill voice, "And you, my friend, who have often yearned to soar through the air as your cousin kirins do! Are you not happy now that our tribe does not employ creatures that fly? You see what has happened to this girl!"

The youthful Runagar did not respond. He simply turned his fox ilon into the direction from which they had come. Then he and Issar, with the help of Diliani, carefully lifted Hut's limp body back onto Runagar's animal, and then Talli onto Issar's, and both were gently but securely strapped into place. The new kirins then climbed atop the animals.

"We must go as quickly as we can for Talli's sake," called Speckarin. "I fear that her aris is fading."

"You must follow," Issar instructed. "It is to the west, and it will take a while to travel the distance. We will not tarry, but we will not move so fast as to disturb our passengers."

Diliani summoned the four ravens. She helped the weary Speckarin aboard Ocelam and then mounted Manay. The other kirins departed with their valuable cargo as the four birds took off. Throughout the journey the anxious Lisam and Faralan kept a close watch on their young masters, riding below upon totally strange ilon.

It was a warm and a sunny afternoon as the unusual party progressed through the woods. Diliani realized that it was the first time she had been aware of the weather during the entire day. As she watched the enervated Speckarin gripping the neck of Ocelam, she also recognized that things had changed within the hierarchy of their small group. She was now the strong one, and at least until he recovered, it might be she who would do the difficult deeds and make the troublesome decisions. But she was convinced that the magic of Speckarin would be required before their mission came to an end. She resolved to see the magician through this crisis and to help him become himself once again.

She considered suggesting that Speckarin go down and ride upon one of the animals. But she could sense that he was comfortable in the air with Ocelam, his trusted friend. Little did she know that some days ago the magician would gladly have traveled upon the ground, and shunned transportation in the air. But now she was indeed correct. Speckarin was more at ease upon his raven than he had ever hoped he could be, or thought possible, and in this time of his discontent he was grateful to be with Ocelam.

They passed to the north of the barwood grove and eventually arrived at the foot of a small hillside. The foxes came to a standstill beside a glade of trees and brush. Diliani was flying low overhead, and could see no reason for them to stop. Then, although it was almost imperceptible at first, she saw the leafy branches of a bush separating and continuing to part. After a few moments, a gap in the rocky base of the hill became visible. Issar motioned that Diliani and Speckarin should land, and at the same time the animals started forward again. Issar motioned the two visitors to follow. Then the new kirins, the foxes, and the unconscious youths disappeared into the increasingly gaping opening.

The ravens landed adjacent to the aperture and began eyeing it furtively. Still aboard, the kirins also peered into the black orifice. They could see nothing, but they were fully aware that they must enter. Their two insensible companions had, after all, just gone in, and they needed to be with them. However, despite the ravens' life-long discipline, and much encouragement by Diliani from the back of Manay, the birds were so unnerved by the idea of passing into a dark, enclosed space that they refused to follow the others in. As highly trained and faithful as the ravens were, Diliani realized that they were here encountering a proposition more threatening than the thunder and lightning storm of some days before. She knew that she must act. She dismounted and helped Speckarin down. Then they proceeded on foot, Diliani in the lead. With more than a little trepidation in their own hearts, the two kirins led the apprehensive ilon into the dim cavity.

C H A P T E R   1 2

FTER THEY had all
entered, Diliani turned her head, only to see the gap behind
them closing.

"We must go forward," she said, and they did so slowly,
encountering nothing but darkness. Issar's shrill voice called
from far ahead, instructing them to follow, explaining that
they were in a tunnel, that the passageway would soon
narrow, and that it would take a while for them to arrive at
their destination.

Diliani and the magician soon found that in order for the
party to proceed at all, the four ravens would require constant
encouragement. To an ilon the voice of a kirin master is of
ultimate importance, a source of both support and pleasure.
But even though many loving words of curlace were spoken,
the progress of this party was slow and unorderly. They could
hear and feel the birds, and attempted to keep them close
together so as not to lose contact with any of them in the
dark. Ocelam and Manay gamely followed their masters. The
two lone ilon, Faralan and Lisam, persevered also, because
they could sense that their stricken masters were somewhere
ahead. Throughout, Issar continued to reassure them, his

voice echoing through the darkness from in front, telling them that they were doing well and not to be discouraged. But not one of the trailing party, ilon nor kirin, shared his enthusiasm or confidence.

The tunnel at first seemed to curve to the left, then to incline upward, then turn to the right, and then to slope downward. It continued to wind and change its path as they proceeded onward. The black passageway became smaller, to a height just greater than an adult kirin and to a width of equal extent. The two visitors, who could see nothing, found themselves brushing or bumping against the sides and the low ceiling.

"I think that we have found where the tunnel narrows," suggested the irritated magician.

The ravens, larger than their masters, had an even worse time as they wound their restricted way through the gloom, abrading heads and bodies against rough walls and ceiling. Even more difficult than the scraping was the confinement the tunnel forced upon these creatures, whose normal habitats were tree tops and sky. Unaccustomed to hearing any sound from the throats of the ilon, the kirins sympathized when gravelly moans emanated from the beleaguered birds. Then, finally, ahead at a distance, Diliani could make out a small circle of light and surmised that they were nearing the end of the tunnel, and perhaps their destination, whatever that might prove to be. The area of luster grew wider and brighter as they approached, and within a few more moments the kirins passed through an arched entrance, and were dumbfounded.

All at once in a large, brightly illuminated chamber, Diliani and the magician stopped to gaze in wonder and were nearly bowled over from behind by four anxious ravens, pushing their way eagerly through the doorway, overjoyed to be out of the cramped darkness.

The room was incredibly large by kirin standards, by far the largest enclosed space Diliani and Speckarin had ever entered. As tree-dwelling kirins, their existence was primarily in the out-of-doors, in the forest. Their rooms in the home trees were always modest in size. None of their kind could have dreamed of an indoor space of this magnitude.

Buoyed by the astonishing configuration of his surroundings, the reviving Speckarin explored the space visually. He gazed about with keen interest, and recognized that they were a cave, a huge one indeed. So, he thought to himself, cave-dwelling kirins came to our rescue! I have never encountered them before, but I have always been aware of their existence!

The next thing he saw was the moving water. Flowing through the cave, halfway between where he stood and the opposite wall, ran a lively underground stream. The water issued from an aperture high in the wall to his right, descending vertically in a cascading waterfall and forming a clear pool at the foot. From there the stream coursed to his left and departed the cave under a shelf of rock. Over it had been built three bridges, a large one of stone near the center of the cave, and two smaller ones of wood at either end.

Illumination of the space came from a great number of torches hung from the rough stone walls and the ceiling. The floor of the cave was flat, and from the floor the wall went up almost vertically to the outer border of a dome-shaped ceiling. But from left to right the wall was rounded, and as he followed the sheer wall completely around, Speckarin realized that it was a single curved surface, enclosing the entire cave. This space was, then, cylindrical in shape, with a rounded roof overhead.

Looking upward, Speckarin estimated that the immense cave, from the floor to the uppermost reaches of the spherical ceiling, was equal to one and one-half times the height of a fully mature maple tree, and that its side-to-side dimension was nearly three quarters its altitude. The stone wall was honeycombed all the way around, numerous corridors and passageways opening onto the cave like balconies or terraces at random elevations above the floor. How much of this architecture had been natural, and how much had been created by its inhabitants, Speckarin had no way of knowing.

Something that had clearly been excavated by kirins was an elaborate network of ramps, stairways, and ladders hewn into the surface of the rocky wall, which sccmcd to connect all of the orifices and lead at some points down to the floor itself. Kirins dressed like Issar and Runagar now appeared in many of the entrances and looked down with interest upon the visitors and their unusual ilon. Some of them raised their arms in the gesture of greeting Issar had used in the forest.

Radiating outward from the floor were several larger tunnels, and within these the travelers could see numbers of the sleek gray foxes this tribe used as ilon.

So this is how they have solved the problem of housing their animals, thought Diliani! They do not live in trees at all, neither kirin nor fox! Here there is plenty of room to spare! Living in a cave, she thought, smiling inwardly, is not a solution a kirin of the home clans would consider!

Issar had dismounted and was walking back toward Speckarin and Diliani. His arrival interrupted their thoughts and their inspection of the great interior.

"Your sanctuary is truly astounding!" exclaimed Speckarin. "I could never have imagined anything like it! How long has your tribe been privileged to live here?"

"Many hundreds of years," replied Issar. "But I must allow our queen to answer your questions. In the meantime, may I welcome you to our home, where it is indeed our hope that you will find rest, healing, and recuperation."

Then, indicating one of the tunnels to their left off the floor of the cave, he said, "Your birds may stay in that place." Diliani noted that this one was devoid of animals.

"They will be well cared for," said Issar, "and be given food and drink. After you have conveyed them there I will present you to Queen Lanara."

Speckarin remained, conversing animatedly with his host near the arched entry, while Diliani led the four ravens away. As they moved along parallel to the stream, they passed by the fox ilon of Issar and Runagar. Diliani stopped and observed as several kirins carefully untied the bindings of Talli and Hut, and gently lowered them to pallets on the floor. To her relief they appeared unharmed by the trek. She then went on to the place indicated by Issar, and after pronouncing loving and encouraging phrases to each of the ilon, she left the faithful birds in their cool and roomy shelter, hopeful that they would soon be attended to.

Just as Diliani was returning, the host kirins were lifting the pallets off the ground, four to a unit, and were bearing Talli and Hut toward the far wall of the cave. The portable surfaces upon which they had been placed were rigid enough to easily support a kirin.

She decided that she would follow. They crossed the large central bridge, and upon reaching the opposite wall, ropes were slipped through perforations in the four corners of the pallets.

As she watched, Diliani caught her breath, for within moments the two supine youths were being hoisted off the ground and drawn rapidly upward along the face of the sheer wall. Try as she might, she could not discern by what mechanism this was being accomplished. Backing away and looking upward, she could see her compatriots reaching an altitude she estimated to be three quarters the height of the cave. There they were swung, one by one, into the mouth of a passageway, and they disappeared.

By now Issar and Speckarin had joined her. Noting her concern, Issar spoke reassuringly. "That is our fairinin," he explained, "our place of healing. Therein we have many of the medicinal substances you lacked in the woods. The kirins who will handle your friends now are especially trained and skilled in the curing arts. One of our magicians, Lidor, is a healer, a fairinor. He has been informed about your youths: One was overcome by the barwood tree, while the other fell and was injured, and her aris must be sustained. In fact, there he is right now, attending to one of your friends," concluded Issar, pointing toward the terrace of the healing place high overhead.

Certainly Issar was more accustomed to the cave than

Diliani and Speckarin, and perhaps he had sharper eyes. But from this distance and vantage point neither of the visitors could see the healer, or their two recumbent friends.

The old magician felt uneasy at relinquishing control of his young charges. At home, he thought, where we have no fairinor and where I am the healer, I would be caring for the two youths myself. Here, however, we have little alternative but to trust these newly found kirins. Without them we would doubtless still be in the woods, and helpless, while here we have a far greater chance of aiding Talli.

"Now you must meet our queen," said Issar.

He started toward the wall of the cave. There he began climbing what they could see was a long series of ramps and steep stairways. He motioned for them to follow and they did.

Even in his depleted state, Speckarin could still do something all kirins can do with facility: climb to heights. This climb, in fact, turned out to be a great pleasure for him, for the higher he ascended the more of the space could he see, or so it seemed. As they scaled the wall he gazed down upon the floor of the cave and its stream, and across at the opposing wall, and into many of the passageways and openings, and he viewed everything with great interest and from a continually changing perspective.

Upon reaching a level slightly above the healing area, Issar entered a tunnel larger than the others. Speckarin and Diliani followed, and there, upon a throne carved of stone, was an ancient kirin woman. She wore a garment of a pale green hue, as did everyone they had encountered in this tribe, and she was surrounded by several attendants.

Kirins are never stout beings. As a race, due to their largely vegetarian diet and high level of activity, they are invariably slender. But the travelers looked with wonder upon this woman. She was the thinnest and most wizened kirin they had ever seen. But the eyes on her wrinkled face sparkled, and seemed to dance with curiosity as she inspected the two strange and foreign individuals brought before her.

In Ruvon, and showing the deepest respect for the elderly woman, Issar made an announcement. "May I introduce Lanara, Queen of the Shillitoe tribe."

Then, addressing the queen, he said. "I bring you the voyagers, whose two youthful compatriots rest within our fairinin."

"Welcome to the cave of the Shillitoe kirins," rasped the old woman in Ruvon. "Few kirins travel as far as you must have, and very few pass through this region. Where did your journey begin, and where are you going?"

Diliani marveled at her voice. She was only the second Shillitoe kirin they had actually heard talk. Runagar had hardly spoken a word. Issar's voice, she had noted, was high-pitched and piercing, totally unlike any she had ever heard. She did not know whether this was peculiar to him, or whether it was characteristic of how these beings spoke. But this old woman's voice was entirely different. Hers was slightly coarse and gravelly. Somehow, however, its tone was not harsh, as Issar's was. The queen's voice seemed old, very old, just as ancient, in fact, as she looked, and yet at the same time it was gentle. Diliani began to wonder whether all the kirins of this tribe possessed voices unlike those of kirins at home. Her thoughts, however, were interrupted by Speckarin, who stepped forward to respond to the old woman's questions.

The venerable queen listened with rapt attention as he told of the home clans, of their sylvan existence in the woods, and of their revered trees. But when he began to relate the nature of their quest, the brightness left her eyes and what little color had been present seemed to drain from her face. She raised a shriveled hand to stop him, but offered no further commentary, nor any explanation why she was so affected. Her reaction, however, left Speckarin's curiosity keenly aroused.

"Rest, and recover your strength," she said, visibly touched, "for I feel that you will require it. When you are refreshed we will talk again. We have a great deal to discuss, and I have many things to ask."

Issar touched her wrinkled right foot with his own. This gesture is the same as ours, noted Diliani.

Issar turned then to lead the travelers back down the wall. They left the ancient queen and her entourage and started to descend, but this time they did not go all the way to the floor. A third of the way down, they began to move horizontally along a ramp leading to a special corridor. Issar entered and the visitors followed. Extending outward from this tunnel were several chambers, hewn out of the stone of the cave. They were reserved for guests, and two were selected for the visiting kirins. Here, it became apparent, they could finally rest. Food was already present in the rooms, and fresh garments to wear, and attendants waited quietly outside in the passageway while their guests prepared for sleep.

The old magician reclined upon a soft bed and closed his tired eyes. However, exhausted as he was, he soon became aware that he could not rest until he had seen the youths in the healing area. He got to his feet and departed his room. Accompanied by Diliani, he was taken to the fairinin by one of the attendants. There he was introduced to Lidor, who wore a long gown similar to his own, but of a light green color. The two magicians proceeded to discuss plans for treating the unconscious youths, now also clad in garments of the host tribe. Hut, they knew, would awaken unharmed. But it was Talli and her aris they shared concern for, as she continued to show little sign of recovery.

Lidor, the fairinor, spoke in a voice somewhat similar to that of Issar, higher in tone than Diliani was accustomed to. But it was far less shrill and irritating than Issar's, and in fact when compared to kirins at home, it had a pleasingly different and almost enchanting quality. It must indeed be the case, thought Diliani, that these kirins speak in a fashion different from ours. As time went on she found this to be true, for every Shillitoe they encountered spoke in a voice not unlike that of Lidor, and the sound became so commonplace that after a while she took almost no notice of it. The queen's was the only one with rasping intonations, undoubtedly, reasoned Diliani, because of her markedly advanced age. And the Yorl woman came across no other Shillitoe who possessed a voice like that of Issar.

As Diliani listened to Lidor, she wondered fleetingly what her voice sounded like to them. But her attention was once more drawn to the fairinor, who was speaking. She focused her concentration on the substance of his words and attempted to ignore the sound, so unusual and yet so soothing was it to her ears. And indeed, with all of her other concerns, soon the almost indescribable uniqueness of its quality was all but forgotten.

"For feeding the flame of aris," Lidor was saying, "we have no more potent drug than the essence of barwood. However, we have found that after its extraction from the tree, its powers decay rapidly. Within a few days it is ineffective in inducing either harm or good, and therefore we make no attempt to preserve it."

Then he revealed a fact of which Speckarin was totally unaware. "The roots of all of the trees in a barwood grove are intertwined and interconnected," he said. "When one tree has been injured, as happened yesterday, all the trees respond, almost as if every one of them had been violated. Blossoms of a golden hue, latent, and apparently awaiting such an incident, come forth within a day, or even half a day, to cover the branches of every tree. It is a stunningly beautiful but deadly occurrence. The flowers perfuse the air with such a saturation of essence that it is impossible to enter the grove for weeks without the risk of serious consequences. In our grove this process is already under way. Issar reports that the flowers were just beginning to appear as he was leaving. Your young friend has already learned of the pitfalls of procuring barwood sap, even under normal conditions. But now it will be many weeks before the grove can be re-entered. Unfortunately, however, the essence might be the only medicine in this part of the world capable of maintaining the aris of the young girl and, ultimately, of saving her life."

As Lidor spoke of Hut's procurement of the liquor, a question suddenly entered Speckarin's mind. Could it possibly be that the lad secured the sap after all? Throughout the trials of the past day, no one had thought to see whether he might have succeeded at the barwood tree.

"Did you find anything among the belongings of this youth," asked the old magician earnestly, "such as a silver box or a small vial?"

"It is the long-standing custom of our tribe," answered the fairinor, "to cast into the stream below all of the clothing and belongings of one struck down by the barwood tree, to be rid of all traces of the essence, which will be detrimental for several days. As you know, the sap must be altered from its raw state before it can be employed medicinally, or it will cause only harm. It is well known how to modify the potent liquor in liquid form. But we have no means of altering slight traces of barwood in garments, cloth, or other personal items, and therefore they are destroyed."

"Who cast them in, and where?" asked Speckarin, growing more agitated by the moment.

"Into the water," came Lidor's reply, and he seemed surprised by Speckarin's inquiries. "One of my helpers did it," he said. "We can find out precisely where."

"Instruct him to lead me to the place now!" commanded the old magician.

The attendant was found quickly, and he led Speckarin, Diliani and Lidor hurriedly down the wall, across the floor of the cave, and to the edge of the running water.

"I threw them in right there," he said, pointing to a place in the stream. Holding up his gown, Speckarin waded out intently into the current and explored the area. Joined by Diliani, the two searched the rocky bottom diligently for some time, but unfortunately to no avail. Nothing could be found. Reluctantly, they climbed back out and rejoined the others.

As they were beginning to make their way back to the wall, Speckarin caught sight of something to his left. A short distance downstream a young Shillitoe boy was sitting on the bank next to the moving water. He was examining a small, silver object in his lap, and before the old magician could react, his inquiring little hands were starting to remove the cap.

C H A P T E R   1 3

O!" CRIED Speckarin.
"Stop!"

The silver vial tumbled to the ground from the startled
child's hands. The lad froze in fear as the group led by the old
magician hurried in his direction. Arriving at the boy's side,
Speckarin reached down, picked up the vial, and examined it
carefully. It had remained unopened, but nonetheless he gave
the cap a prophylactic turn, sealing it as tightly as he could.

Then, turning to Lidor he said, "This vial came from my
belongings! I gave it to Hut yesterday to take with him to the
barwood grove! This container must be transported to your
fairinin and opened with utmost precaution, for if Hut did
succeed before he was overcome, it might indeed contain the
liquor necessary to revive Talli!"

Looking back to the child, he asked, "Where did you
find this?"

"I was swimming and saw it glittering at the bottom of the
stream," he answered. "I swam down and picked it up."

"It must have been just heavy enough to fall out of Hut's
clothing," said Speckarin. "Did you find anything else in the
water, such as a box made of silver?"

The boy looked down at his feet for a few moments and did not speak, nor did he move. Then he stood up and walked slowly toward a pile of stones near the water, glancing back furtively at Speckarin and his entourage. Unhappy at the prospect of giving up both his treasures, he hesitated briefly. Then he reached down, and from behind the stones he brought out a small silver box.

"I am afraid you must give that one up too," said the magician. "But you have done extremely well to find these things," he said, taking the box. "You may have saved a young girl's life. What is your name?"

"Lindor," the boy said.

Noting the similarity in names, Speckarin turned toward Lidor, who until now had been silent.

"He is my grandson," said Lidor.

"He must be rewarded," said Speckarin. "Since these objects came from my bag, I will find something else in it for him. But now we must make haste to the fairinin where Talli lies awaiting our help!"

The group, now accompanied by the child, moved quickly to the wall and scaled the incline to the healing area. There they found Hut and Talli attended by Shillitoe kirins, both youths resting on beds near the entrance to the cave, and both still unaware of their surroundings.

"You are more familiar than I with the handling of barwood sap," Speckarin told Lidor, handing him the silver vial. "Would you and your helpers open this, and if sap is found therein prepare it for medicinal use?"

"Indeed, we would be honored to do so," said Lidor, bowing slightly as he took the container.

"This box may have barwood leaves in it," said Speckarin, holding out the small, square object.

"Keep it," replied the fairinor. "The leaves have different properties than the essence. They would probably not help in this situation."

Speckarin placed the box in his bag. I thought the leaves were important also, he told himself. But this fairinor obviously knows more than I do about barwood trees.

Diliani stayed with the two unconscious companions, while Lidor, Speckarin, Lindor, and three youthful fairinin helpers moved toward the rear of the small cavern. There was a long working table, not unlike Speckarin's in the home tree. The area was brightly illuminated by torches overhead. The table was literally covered with a variety of instruments of both the magic and healing arts, as well as with jars, boxes, and other containers of varying colors, sizes, and shapes, many of which were unfamiliar to the visiting magician. Against the rock wall above the bench was a large wooden door, hinged at the bottom. Lidor and his assistants busied themselves removing all of the paraphernalia from the central part of the bench in front of this door, and as they proceeded Speckarin smiled to himself. Lidor's workbench is no neater than mine, he thought, and in fact is a bit more cluttered.

The healer then unlatched the door at the top and swung it down over the table, dust and debris following in its liberation. "We have not had the need to make use of this ventilation shaft for a very long time," he explained apologetically to his fellow magician, brushing bits of stone off the door, then the bench, and finally his gown.

The door now covered the surface that had been cleared. Speckarin could immediately sense a draft moving out of the cave and through the opening, the torches above suddenly burning even more brightly.

"It opens to the outside air," explained Lidor, "the draft removing all of the noxious and hazardous vapors from the fairinin. When working with material from a barwood tree, such ventilation is mandatory. I would not attempt to open the vial anywhere else inside this cave. In fact, I was relieved that Lindor had not succeeded in uncapping it by the stream."

Speckarin recognized a fire starter on the bench, and it was to this object that Lidor next turned his attention. He picked up the instrument and then moved it, along with several other odd-looking pieces, onto the surface of the wooden door, now lying flat and open upon the bench. Then he appeared to be attempting, with some difficulty, to arrange these items, few of which were familiar to Speckarin, into a single apparatus. But somehow he could not fit them all together. After struggling for a short while, he turned toward his assistants, who had been standing quietly by, and enlisted the aid of two of them.

"We have not used this for a very long time either," the fairinor said to Speckarin. Then among the three of them, with whispering and disagreement as they worked, Lidor and his helpers did apparently complete the assembly. When finally satisfied, they stood back to admire their handiwork.

"We are now ready to open the vial," announced the fairinor.

It was handed to him by the third of his assistants, who had been guarding it carefully. The fairinor held the silver container ritually over the bench in front of the open vent. He began methodically turning its cap, and finally he removed it. He peered down inside the tube and then cautiously sniffed the contents.

"We have barwood sap," he said, turning toward his observers, to the immense relief of everyone. "We have the ingredient necessary for treating your girl and her aris. We must begin at once the procedures for taming this frivolous substance."

Turning the vial upside down over the assembled apparatus, the fairinor waited. After what seemed to Speckarin an interminable length of time, a single drop of thick liquid fell into a green, funnel-shaped piece atop the complex device. The first drop was followed by another, and then several more, all directed fastidiously by the fairinor into the funnel, and from there the precious liquor collected in a copper receptacle below. When it was apparent that no more fluid would be forthcoming, he reapplied the cap to the top of vial and placed it upon the bench. He carefully removed the funnel, and Speckarin could see that it was made from the leaf of a tree, folded into the desired configuration. Lidor handed the leaf to an assistant, apparently for disposal. He next placed a tightly fitting lid over the copper receptacle, sealing it well. Finally he turned to the visiting magician.

"The sap will be distilled within this mechanism according to the laws and traditions of our tribe," he said. "It will take time, perhaps as long as a full day, for the procedure to be completed. Unfortunately there is no way to hurry the process."

He picked up the fire starter, and within moments a flame burst from its end. That was quicker than mine worked in the woods! thought Speckarin with a chuckle. But his was not drenched with rainwater!

Lidor touched the flame to an under portion of the machine. Fire jumped immediately from this part of the apparatus to several other areas. Relieved that everything seemed to be operating properly, he stood back ceremoniously. "The time-honored process has begun," he said.

Just as Lidor ended his sentence, Speckarin could hear a low tone emanating from the device. He observed the machine intently and saw that several components of the structure were aflame, and that the metal portions of the instrument appeared to be warming perceptibly. And the sound, he noticed, was gradually becoming louder.

The fairinor moved closer to Speckarin's side, so as to be easily heard. "The distillation must be continuously monitored," he confided. "Mishaps, even catastrophes, have been known to occur in processing the potent sap, as the life-giving essence is extracted from the injurious dregs of the liquor. But as you probably know, it is never proven whether the product will be effective until it is administered."

The noise of the mechanism continued to swell, and Lidor, his mouth quite close to Speckarin's ear, now spoke loudly. "You can do no more good here! Wait until the distillation is completed! You would better serve your compatriots and yourself by returning to your chamber and enjoying a well-deserved rest!"

The mere mention of the word rest made the old magician stop for a moment and allow himself to feel what had been building inside. It was fatigue, so heavy as to be almost a palpable weight. In addition, the growing noise was a painful reminder of the clamor that was in his brain when the gronom intruded through the calamar, and he was now very uncomfortable indeed.

Agreeing with Lidor about the need for rest, Speckarin realized how much he wanted to leave, and nodded. He turned away from the heating engine and the burgeoning whine and moved toward the mouth of the cave. The boy, Lindor, followed.

As they reached the prostrate youths, Diliani, who had remained with them, spoke to the magician. "I think one of our young friends might soon be back among us," she said.

Speckarin stooped over and peered down at the two. At first he saw no change in either one. But Hut was lying on his side, and upon examining him more closely, the magician saw the semblance of a smile on his face. As he watched, the youth's eyes opened slowly, but they appeared blank and unseeing. Then he closed them and he proceeded to stretch and yawn and then to relax, and finally it appeared that he was falling asleep again.

"Hut!" called Speckarin, touching him on the shoulder, trying to be heard above the infernal noise building at the rear of the cavern. "Are you awake, my small one? Can you hear me?"

The youth responded only by turning over onto his other side. With a bit more prodding from the magician, however, he opened his eyes again. Then he sat up, and all at once he swung his long feet over the edge of the bed.

"What a dream that was!" he declared with a playful grin. Then, turning his head toward the energizing distillation machine, he went on. "Where's that awful noise coming from?" Turning back, he stretched and yawned and shook his head as if trying to awaken. "Oh, never mind that," he said, pointing over his shoulder at the machine. "What I really meant to say was—I've never been so hungry in my life! What's for breakfast?"

The two senior members of the traveling party looked at each other. They were so moved at having one of the stricken youths back in their midst that momentarily they found it impossible to speak. Diliani wanted to welcome Hut as if he had been very far away and for a very long time, which in a way he had. She did greet him with a touch of her right foot against his. She also began to sense, deep inside of herself, a feeling of relief, and at first was uncertain precisely why, because she had known all along that Hut would awaken. But it dawned upon her that while they had been told there was every reason to believe he would recover and be no worse for the wear, it was not until he did awaken, and began to respond like his old self, that they could finally relax their vigil. And yet she was also aware that what she sensed was not complete relief, for a second of their youths lay still and senseless, awaiting the results of the capricious distillation process.

A tottering Hut was helped to his feet. After expressing farewells to the unknowing Talli, with the aid of an assistant from the fairinin, Speckarin and Diliani led the recovering youth out of the healing area. The first thing they noted outside was the relative peace and quiet compared to the awful din within.

"What a relief to be outside!" remarked Speckarin, as they descended the stairs of the wall, the boy Lindor trailing behind.

"Yes, but we are not outside at all!" said an astonished Hut, as he glanced about the huge, brightly lighted space. "Where are we?"

From that point on, it was all the three adults could do to keep the amazed youth's attention on the steps and the ramps. With one of them in front of him, and two at his sides where the pathway permitted, the party descended the trail haltingly at best. Lindor also did what he could, but from behind there was little he was able do to help. The unsteady and wide-eyed Hutsin moved at his own pace and in whatever direction he seemed to desire, his gaze ranging throughout the cave, and he seemed to lean and lurch in whatever direction he happened to be looking.

At one point early in the trek, where a tunnel opened to the right and the narrow path proceeded straight ahead, Hut turned in his erratic progress to the left. As he was about to step over the precipice, Diliani flung her arms about his waist, brought him back onto the level surface, and edged him into the tunnel for a brief intermission. He was eventually coerced into proceeding downward on the proper trail, and onward they went. Diliani and Speckarin learned quickly that accompanying their blissful companion down the incline was as harrowing as anything they had experienced on their quest.

The slowly moving party finally arrived at the passageway leading to the guest rooms. They were unscathed and greatly relieved to be there. They pushed Hut unceremoniously through the tunnel's entrance and ushered him to Speckarin's room. After coaxing Hut to remain with them instead of exploring the cave as he wished, they finally had the opportunity to relax. Attendants brought them a meal of honey, wild blueberries, and an unusually delicate mushroom with a very long stem. Speckarin, Diliani and Hut consumed the food together about a small table. The lad ate especially ravenously, having been deprived of sustenance for such a long time.

As the meal progressed Hut appeared to be recovering more fully, and Diliani and Speckarin recounted for him the extraordinary occurrences since his visit to the treacherous grove. Drink was provided in silver goblets. It was designated for Diliani and Speckarin, the attendant explained, and supplied by Lidor. It was an elixir extracted from a local fruit that, by its description, seemed to be unknown in the home woods. Nonetheless, the drink was both delicious and soothing, and within a short time it became apparent that they were ready for sleep.

Hut, on the other hand, who had just slept for two days, was wide awake and more rested than ever. He was ready for action and wanted to explore the cave. He demonstrated to them, prancing confidently and adroitly about the room, that he was fully alert and recovered.

Speckarin finally decided it would be safe for him to go if he was chaperoned by a Shillitoe kirin. The lad, Lindor, had been sitting on the floor beside the table throughout. He had observed and listened to everything. He immediately jumped up and volunteered, and Hut and his new companion cheerfully departed. Diliani was ready for rest and retired to her chamber.

At last alone, Speckarin used the opportunity to take inventory of their small party. He and Diliani, he knew, were spent, but with rest they would be all right. Regarding himself, he thought things had lightened remarkably since they were found by the Shillitoes earlier in the day. Prior to that, he admitted, he had been more dispirited and disillusioned than ever before in his life. Some of the problems that had seemed insurmountable then were being resolved one by one. Thankfully, Hut had returned to them, and seemed his usual self. With the discovery of barwood sap there was new optimism for Talli and her aris, but until it was ready for administration he could do nothing more for her.

He had not had time to think of Gilin for a long while. "That matter is totally out of my hands," he said aloud, to reassure himself. He still had remorse and a hollow feeling within his heart about the entire episode, but there was nothing he could possibly do for the lost companion. "In truth," he continued, trying to buoy himself, "the lad might have started home, as I suggested earlier to the others. He might even be there by now."

When finally assured he had done all he could for his charges and that his duties as leader could be temporarily suspended, he sat down upon the soft bed and then reclined. In the quietude and comfort of his chamber, he allowed himself to begin what he hoped was a well-deserved repose. What he could not know, as he drifted into slumber, is that no kirin before him had ever been entitled to a respite and a rest more richly than he was now.

C H A P T E R   14

W HAT CAN IT BE?"
asked a bewildered Gilin, seeing the points of light ahead.

Ruggum did not bother to answer, but began looking frantically for a place to land. Not being particular at this point, when he saw a stand of trees with no lights nearby he indicated that they should descend. They did so, but somewhat erratically, as their raven ilon were not nocturnal creatures. They could not see the terrain well in the semi-darkness, and were not acquainted with these woods. Nonetheless, they alighted upon the ground, clumsily but safely, and the kirins disembarked. They explored the area briefly, located an oak tree reminding them of ones at home, and settled in nervously for the night.

The overseer never did respond to Gilin's query. After due consideration the youth did not pursue it himself, because with time to think it over he realized what the illumination must represent. Although nothing untoward happened during the night, it was passed restlessly by both kirins. They were aware that they must be in foreign territory, inhabited by human beings, and as kirins they were instinctively apprehensive. In addition, both worried about what had happened with the humans by the lake.

The morning, however, was bright and sunny, and after little preparation they departed. As they gained altitude it became obvious that just to the east was a considerable grouping of buildings occupied by humans, as well as many of the pathways and roads they used for travel. Upon seeing several of the giant beings themselves, moving slowly about on paved areas adjacent to the buildings, both on foot and in vehicles, Ruggum elected to circumvent the town rather than fly directly over it. He motioned to Gilin, and they proceeded quietly, without speaking and without incident, soon leaving the settlement behind as they moved off to the east.

"That's much better," remarked Gilin finally, after glancing back. He breathed a sigh of relief as vestiges of the pocket of human beings faded into the distance.

Ruggum did not respond, his thoughts remaining on their current circumstances and the perplexing occurrences of yesterday. He knew that human settlements were frequently not far apart, and that if one was sighted others might well be in proximity. But he saw no reason to concern Gilin further, and therefore kept his ruminations to himself. As they flew onward, however, he intently searched the landscape ahead for further signs of human life.

As they progressed during the morning, sightings of the gray and black strips that humans use as travel pathways became more commonplace, and eventually so frequent that they crisscrossed the landscape below. The kirins knew, however, that this could not deter them. They had no choice other than to go on. Ruggum considered the idea of flying further to the north, or the south, in an attempt to avoid the area entirely. But he concluded that either of those directions might take them into even more densely inhabited regions, and their destination, after all, was eastward.

They saw an occasional metallic vehicle, with human inhabitants, rolling along the paved thoroughfares. Knowing that all of this existed, since kirins had kept human beings under scrutiny for many generations, Ruggum looked on with both curiosity and a little excitement. He had seen this once before. But Gilin, viewing these phenomena for the first time, found himself mystified and somewhat frightened. Before noon they identified another town and skirted it to the north. For the remainder of the afternoon their progress continued in the same pattern, and by the end of the day they had passed by several human settlements.

Toward dusk Gilin spied something unusual. High in the blue sky ahead was a shining white body with wings and a tail, and it appeared to be moving slowly in their direction. All at once he realized that his calculation of its speed might be wrong at this great a distance, that the thing might be moving very fast indeed. For a moment he was alarmed, fearing it might be a volodon or some other variety of evil creature they had not yet encountered. Olamin had said there might be others. Pointing toward the object, he asked Ruggum anxiously what it could be.

The elder studied it and then answered. "I have seen them before. On an expedition to the south, some years ago, we sighted several of these flying things. Through our surveillance of humankind, we know that what you are seeing, believe it or not, is their means of airborne transportation. Humans are too large and cumbersome to participate in the type of flying we enjoy with our ilon. They have created the gigantic machine you see above to move themselves from one place to another."

Gilin watched and drew in a breath as the object passed directly overhead, far above them. A tail of white mist trailed after it, and all at once the noise from its power source became audible. Its speed must be incredible, thought Gilin, turning his head and following it until it was completely out of sight in the western sky.

"What could the track of smoke possibly mean?" he asked, fascinated by the entire sighting, the cloudlike streak hanging above them in the atmosphere.

"I have seen that before, too," answered the elder, staring upward. "Unfortunately, I have no notion of its significance."

Gilin was hardly satisfied. He asked nothing further about the incredible flying machine as they moved onward, but he continued to think about it.

Not long thereafter, as the sun began to sink into the horizon behind, Ruggum searched for a tree in which to pass the night, one with no signs of human occupation nearby. They had no trouble in finding one and landed. After locating an adequate place to sleep, they passed an uneventful night.

Clouds moved in overnight, and the following day was warm and muggy. They departed early and flew steadily again. It was not until noon that they encountered another human village, and at Ruggum's direction they circumnavigated it. Throughout this day even the highways were seen less frequently, and during the hot afternoon only a few roadways were sighted at all, and these had no vehicles whatsoever.

Late in the afternoon, Gilin was all at once shaken by something. It was an inexplicable feeling of horror and loss. He looked about and nothing appeared wrong. Ruggum was close at hand upon Alsinam, and everything seemed perfectly normal. Then suddenly he knew what it was: Something dreadful had happened to Talli, wherever his friend might be. The lad was deeply disturbed, but he flew on and remained silent, and kept his concern to himself so as not to bother Ruggum. He realized that he could do nothing for Talli, but he knew that something had happened to her. After landing, they spent the evening saying little.

The next morning was clear and pleasant, and as they flew onward, seeing no signs of humans whatsoever, Ruggum was less anxious and more talkative than usual. He and Gilin shared their impressions about their recent sightings of humans and the fragments of their civilization.

"I presume that the large vehicles," said Gilin, "are employed for the same reason we use ilon. But judging by their magnitude they must have been built for four, or five, or even six human occupants, and yet most of the ones we saw carried only one, or two at most. Why would that be?"

"I will probably be wrong should I speculate about human

behavior," answered the elder. "But no matter. I will make a guess. Perhaps the organization of their society is not so advanced, nor so exact, that they know at any given time how many of their kind are moving in one direction or another. Therefore, some of the space in the machines is wasted. I think this is the case, for I have seen the same phenomenon in the past during the one trek I made to the south."

They conversed throughout the morning, and by noon Ruggum had relaxed to the point where he was his old self again. His confidence had risen immeasurably. We have traversed a fair amount of human territory, he thought, and even though one of us might be visible to them, no harm has come to us. We have not had even the slightest of emergencies since the human girl appeared to confront Gilin three days ago. The terrain today has been totally devoid of humans.

The old kirin began to enjoy the sun, the blue sky with its thin white clouds, and the wind against his face. It would appear, he thought, that at least for now we might have a respite.

The party of two flew on restfully for a time before Ruggum noticed something in the distance ahead. Situated beside a lake was a small house, all by itself, with no roads or other buildings around it. As they drew closer it became apparent that it was not so small. It was a larger structure than usual, actually two or three times the size of a normal home. But it was isolated, he reassured himself, and in his relaxed frame of mind he saw no particular reason for them to go out of their way to avoid it. He elected to continue the present course, and they did, flying uneventfully over the structure. Looking back as they passed beyond it, he caught sight of three human figures, one with a metallic instrument raised upward. As he concentrated his attention upon them, a white flash startled him, and then a thunderous discharge shook the atmosphere.

C H A P T E R   1 5

RUGGUM STRUGGLED
to maintain control of the terrified Alsinam in the wake of the
resounding blast, and in the same moment caught sight of
Loana plunging earthward.

"Downward! Follow!" he commanded, and Alsinam dove
in rapid pursuit. In the moments until Loana struck the
ground Ruggum wondered frantically where the invisible
Gilin might be, and whether he was even still with the bird.

The giant bird was in shock, and barely moving, when the
elder landed next to her. He jumped off and ran to her, and
immediately noted an open breakage of her right wing.

"Gilin!" he called. "Gilin! Are you here? Where are you?"

"Yes," came Gilin's voice weakly from the vicinity of his
ilon. "I am here, and I seem to be all right. I don't think I've
been injured."

Gilin had found himself lying next to Loana, having been
thrown off the moment she hit the ground. Slowly he got to
his feet. He reached out and touched the agitated elder so that
Ruggum would know where he was.

"But Loana has been hurt," said Gilin.

"I have seen the wound!" replied Ruggum.

Relieved that Gilin seemed unscathed, the overseer moved quickly to examine the wing more closely. He knelt down, and the stoic creature allowed him to palpate and evaluate the painful extremity. He took only a brief time to do so, because he realized that they now faced adversity of a magnitude they had not before experienced, both because of the damage to the ilon and because of the proximity of the human beings who had inflicted it.

"How did it happen?" asked a stunned Gilin.

"We have little time!" answered the elder. "It must have been a human weapon! We must hide both of the ilon!"

And we must certainly hide ourselves, he thought desperately, recalling the encounter with the humans three days before, where Gilin seemed visible.

He looked intently about the woods in which they found themselves. He spied, but a short distance away, a fallen oak tree beginning to decay. That might be precisely what we need, he thought, and he directed Gilin to follow him with Loana.

"How can we move her?" questioned the frightened youth.

"We have no choice but to do so!" answered Ruggum forcefully, taking little time to explain. "Her attackers may soon be upon us!"

Together Gilin and Ruggum coaxed the courageous bird to her feet. Wing dragging, she moved as resourcefully as she could at her master's side, Ruggum and Alsinam in the lead. Arriving shortly at the dead tree, the overseer studied it for a few moments and then motioned affirmatively to Gilin. The elder stepped into a hole in the side of the trunk and commanded his ilon to follow.

The raven hesitated, instinctively wary of entering a dim, enclosed space, fearing the darkness within and the unknown. But gradually, with Ruggum speaking the enchanting words of curlace, a lifelong history of rapport and trust between the elder and the bird overcame Alsinam's misgivings, and he started forward haltingly. Reaching the aperture, the raven first placed his head inside and looked uneasily about. Then, with further encouragement, he squeezed himself through the hole.

Stepping outside, Ruggum intended to aid Gilin in persuading his ilon to enter. But he found that the deteriorating Loana was more easily influenced than usual, and less aware of her surroundings than Alsinam. Though wounded and in pain, she slithered inside with only a modicum of direction on Gilin's part. The two kirins followed her in, and within moments the unmistakable shuffle of human feet could be heard moving through the glade. With whispers and gestures, the ravens in the dark cavity were quieted. The large creature outside could be heard moving farther away.

Ruggum positioned himself at the edge of the opening so he could peer out. He found that he could view a portion of the surrounding scenery, and he wondered whether he would catch a glimpse of their adversary. He ducked back quickly as the sounds of the human came near again, and he dared not look out until the shuffling was moving away. He was preparing to look out again when suddenly the sounds came so close that he could hear the thing breathing. It sounded as though the searcher was kneeling down very close by, and he dared not breathe himself. Hopefully, he thought, as he leaned further away from the hole, it would never consider that a wounded bird might seek out a hiding place such as this.

Suddenly he thought of something. He looked back toward the injured bird. Blood was on her injured wing. He wondered whether a trail of it had been left on the ground, and he was more apprehensive than ever.

The search outside continued for a considerable length of time, but the human never came near again. Eventually the noises came from farther and farther away, and finally they were gone. The kirins waited patiently, however, for a while longer before the overseer felt comfortable poking his head out to look around. When he finally did so he saw nothing, and cautiously he stepped out of their hiding place. Still nothing threatening could be seen or heard, and he called for the others to follow. Alsinam responded promptly, happy to depart the enclosure. But a worried Gilin saw that Loana was slow to move and appeared to be suffering more from her injuries than before.

"We must examine her wounds more thoroughly in the daylight!" said the overseer, standing in the opening and looking inward. He stepped inside, and together they persuaded the faithful bird to her feet. She struggled painfully out of the hole and staggered a short distance away, but there she collapsed, unable to move further.

They took more time to assess her injuries than they had previously, and what they found made the overseer's heart sink. They discovered two open breaks in the right wing, one at the point where the wing joined the body itself and one between the outer joint and the tip, bone protruding through both wounds.

Ruggum knew through long experience that birds suffer injuries, the fracturing of wing bones among them, both in the wild and even under the control of kirins. Wing breaks, he realized, are uniformly devastating, because the victims are deprived of their primary means of locomotion. Their mobility is so vastly curtailed as to place them in jeopardy. When an ilon becomes impaired, the kirin master also is impaired, shorn of his normal transportation. In the home woods this might merely present an inconvenience. But under the current circumstances, he thought with consternation, it could prove catastrophic indeed.

After working with ilon for many years, he recognized that the combination of injuries Loana had suffered was particularly devastating. The proximal break, through the joint between wing and body, was the most painful of all wing fractures because the entire weight of the extremity hung from the injured region. Penetration of the fractured bones through the skin permitted the loss of blood. Without proper cleansing of these wounds, highly improbable here in the woods, inflammation about the perforations would eventually ensue. He also realized that the mending time for the injuries Loana had suffered would be prolonged, even under the best of circumstances, should sufficient healing occur at all.

As a long-time practitioner of curlace, and through close association with birds and beasts, he had a thorough acquaintance with the methods utilized in caring for ilon. His total experience in this was at home, however, where he and his clan had both the materials and the expertise to handle these occurrences. But, he recognized now, with worry and utmost regret, we are not at home. We are very, very far from home, in foreign and human-infested territory, and moment by moment he was more concerned for the well-being of them all.

Gilin looked on, alarmed and disbelieving that his faithful ilon could be in so grave a condition. "What can we possibly do for her?" he asked.

"Perhaps we should ask the humans to help!" snarled Ruggum sarcastically, ever more desperate as he pondered their situation, and as the number of available options for them and the fallen Loana lessened rapidly in his mind.

So distracted were they by their predicament, and engrossed in the examination of their raven, that they were unaware of the passage of time. Uncharacteristically, they were not watchful for the approach of other creatures. Until this moment, neither one of them had noticed the drawing near of a massive shape. It was Gilin who first glanced upward and saw it, the gigantic presence of a human being, garbed in red, poised but a short distance away and staring directly down at them.

Gilin nudged Ruggum Chamter and he looked upward also. The kirins knew to remain motionless if ever in the proximity of a human. But the disturbing experience with the girl a few days before had concerned Ruggum deeply. It had left him confused about what to do should the occasion arise again, which he was distinctly certain it would not. Now, not only had their raven been gravely assaulted, but they were suddenly confronted with an alarming reality: One of the enormous attackers was glaring down at them.

Ruggum did not know precisely where Gilin was, nor whether he was actually visible to the immense thing. But he made a decision and acted upon it immediately. Even though he knew himself to be invisible, he scurried back to the fallen oak and disappeared unceremoniously into the hole.

Gilin remained exactly where he was, his concern for Loana replaced by completely different feelings. Unlike what had happened to him during his previous encounter, he found that he had no desire to flee or to hide from this creature. A desire to remain beside his ravaged ilon outweighed his natural impetus to be out of sight and undiscoverable. In addition, as he looked up at the huge being, he had no sense of the fear that is normally instinctive for a kirin under such conditions. Indeed, he began to feel a nearly opposite emotion, an intense one, one foreign to kirins before the recent appearance of gronoms and volodons.

Since initiation of the spell of no'an in the far distant past, kirins have been resigned to their circumstances upon Earth. Knowing that historically they have been mistreated and even mutilated by humankind, they have chosen to avoid them and have gone about the business of their daily lives. Over the millennia, they have developed societies and cultures and their own ways of life throughout the world. During their lifetimes they experience many of the same feelings human beings do: frustration, sadness, guilt, fear, happiness and love. But for thousands of years they have seldom had occasion to sense two other emotions, common to both kirins and humans before their schism: hatred and anger.

Now, however, the innocent Loana had been savagely attacked by a human, tragically wounding the innocent bird and endangering the party and its very purpose. As Gilin rose to face the towering being he felt what few kirins had felt for centuries: profound outrage and resentment.

As far as Gilin knew, years had passed since a kirin had spoken to a member of the human race. Prior to his recent trials and distresses, he would have been considered a wholly unlikely candidate for such a role. Yet he had passed through more adversity in a brief period than a thousand kirins could be expected to experience in their lifetimes. Now he and his brave ilon had been mercilessly assaulted, and their circumstances were nearly hopeless. All of his frustrations came suddenly to the fore, into clear focus, and he found himself eminently prepared for confrontation.

Not in the least concerned whether he might be visible, Gilin glared back seethingly at the human. Just as it was turning away, he drew himself to full height and projected his voice upward.

"Stop!" he commanded.

C H A P T E R   16

W E'VE BEEN WAITING a
long time for this day, haven't we Christopher?" said
Grandpa Versteeg.

The old man was negotiating the path with a decided
limp. Shrapnel wounds, incurred during the invasion of
Okinawa more than forty years before, had caused his knee to
become stiff and painful, and it was gradually becoming
worse with age. He could no longer cover the distances he
was accustomed to, to his deep regret, and one of the greatest
pleasures in his life had been curtailed. However, today
marked a special occasion, for he would be passing to his
second grandson some of the knowledge of guns and game
hunting he had acquired over many years. He was enjoying
the event so much that he had almost forgotten about his leg.

"I know I have, and I'm just glad it's finally here!"
answered the twelve-year-old Chris cheerfully.

He was moving along behind the deliberate old man. His
older brother was in the lead. The two boys had been this
way many times before and knew the path well.

Nathan, fourteen, was growing impatient with the pace.
Over his red sweat shirt he wore a blue backpack loaded with

groceries and with today's lunch. Anxious to reach their destination, after holding back for a while, he glanced over his shoulder and hurried on ahead.

During the two-hour drive, they had discussed firearm safety most of the way. Now, after parking the car, they were walking the last half-mile as usual through the woods, the old man wearing khaki hiking clothes. He took this opportunity to recount his most memorable hunting experiences, many of which related to the lake and the lodge they were approaching. He was not only an expert in firearms, and a fine shot himself, but he was also a hunter. It was the thrill of hunting, which he could no longer enjoy the way he did, that he was attempting to convey to Christopher.

Since his days as a captain in the Marine Corps many years ago, John Versteeg had maintained an interest in guns, and he had a sizeable collection. Even though he was in his late seventies, his family considered him competent in the care and handling of weapons. For years Christopher had wanted his grandpa to teach him how to shoot, but his parents had insisted he wait until he was twelve years of age. His birthday had been yesterday. This trip to his grandfather's hunting lodge was a long-awaited birthday present.

His yellow jacket brightened and darkened as they passed through sunshine and shade. Unlike his brother, Chris was content to walk along with the slowly moving old man. The morning was cool and pleasant, and he listened with interest to the tales of his grandfather's past.

Upon reaching the grassy clearing adjacent to the lodge, the grandfather stopped. "And now, I have a surprise for you, young man," he said. "It isn't just the trip out here that I'm giving you for your twelfth birthday!" He handed over one of the two encased guns he was carrying.

The boy's eyes lit up as he reached for the gift. "A gun? For me?" he asked excitedly.

"All your own," answered his grandfather with a smile. "And your mother and father approved of it, as long as I didn't give it to you until you were twelve years old, and as long as I taught you how to use it. That's what we're here for today."

The boy unzipped the case and removed the gleaming piece. He was acquainted enough with guns to recognize this as a brand new twelve-gauge shotgun. Not knowing what to say, he simply gazed at it and fondled it for a while.

"Can I shoot it?" he asked finally.

"Well, of course," answered the grandfather. "But first we have to go through a few steps leading up to that, and then you'll be able to shoot it all right. This is a full-choke shotgun, Chris, which gives a good shot pattern for hunting duck, and I'll have to spend a little time teaching you about it. But it's been a long morning. Let's go inside and have something to eat and talk more about it. Now, where do you think Nathan ran off to with our lunch?"

He unlocked the door at the end of the large building, and they entered the downstairs level. As they traversed the long hallway they passed several bedrooms, and the grandfather switched on the lights and looked into some of them along the way.

"No varmints this time," he said.

Halfway down the hall they turned right and climbed a flight of stairs to the upper level. There the old man walked about, checking the living room, the den, and the kitchen, until he was satisfied that everything was in order. Then he slid open a glass door and stepped out onto a deck that ran the entire length of the lodge and overlooked the lake to the north. Christopher followed him out.

"This is what I have always loved," the old man said, resting his elbows on the railing and gazing out over the surrounding woods and the wide expanse of still water. "This is what I come for now."

Just then Nathan came to the doorway and looked out onto the deck. "Where have you been, Nate, as if I didn't know?" asked his grandfather. The older boy had discovered a family of raccoons on a recent visit and had spent considerable time observing them each time he returned. "Could you see them at all today?"

"They only come out after dark," said Nathan. "I didn't want to get too close to their den. They sleep during the day. But last time they had a litter of four babies."

"Ah, how nice," said the old man. "Now, my young friend, what's happened to our lunch?"

"It's inside," replied Nathan, and the three of them, all hungry, turned and stepped back into the kitchen.

After eating, Christopher was eager for his first shooting lesson. Cradling the new gun, he followed his grandfather down the stairs and outside to the area in front of the lodge, where a grassy clearing, dotted with yellow and white wildflowers, ran all the way down to the lake. Taking the new shotgun from his grandson, the old man checked it to make certain it was not loaded, and then proceeded to demonstrate several aspects of correctly shooting a firearm.

"First of all," he said, taking a proper stance, "your feet must be spread apart like this, and since you're right-handed, your left foot is out in front, both feet planted and solid, so you have good balance. Your hands go here. Your left is down on the fore-end and your right is here by the trigger. Then, when you're ready to shoot, you bring the gun up slowly against your shoulder like this. When you pull the trigger of a rifle you should squeeze it slowly, but with a shotgun you don't have to be so particular. You can pull it as fast as you want."

At this point, Nathan joined them. Never having been as close to his grandfather as his younger brother seemed to be, he had always been a little jealous of Christopher. It appeared to him that Chris and his grandpa had always been the best of buddies, even since his brother was little. He had been told that Christopher was getting a shotgun for his birthday, and it had bothered him. I already know how to shoot, he had said to himself, and I don't have a gun of my own.

"Oh, is this Christopher's gun?" asked Nathan. "Neat! Can I see it?"

Nathan had also been trained by Grandpa Versteeg, and had been shooting for almost two years. All at once his grandfather began to sense what the older boy was feeling. "Sure, you can," he said. He lowered the gun and handed it to him.

"Is it full-choke?" asked Nathan.

"It is indeed," answered the old man.

Placing the shotgun against his shoulder, Nathan pointed it out over the lake and looked down the sights. Then, lowering the gun, he was about to give it back to his grandfather when he caught sight of a pair of birds approaching from the west.

"There's one more thing," the grandfather was explaining to Christopher. "You can learn it only by practice and experience. When you aim a gun at a moving target you must give it a certain amount of lead, or you'll find yourself shooting behind it."

The two black birds, crows, thought Nathan, were now nearly overhead and not flying very high, and they appeared unusually close together. They were much larger than average, he noted, and would be easy targets. He had a few shells in his jacket pocket, and before the others knew what he was doing he had loaded one and was aiming slightly ahead of the birds.

"This is how you lead them," he said.

As the birds passed over a pine-covered ridge to the east, he fired.

C H A P T E R   17

A S NATHAN lowered the shotgun one of the giant birds fell toward the earth like a stone.

"Why did you shoot at those crows with my gun?" cried Christopher, shocked at what had occurred.

The grandfather watched the birds intently, because something was happening that he had never before observed in nature. Moments after the first bird had been hit, its partner, apparently uninjured, had altered its flight path and had made a sweeping turn downward as if to follow its injured companion. The two of them then disappeared, one after the other, just beyond the trees.

John Versteeg had never been fond of crows, nor of ravens, which he knew these to be, but he had a healthy respect for them. Crows had often raided his garden, and he thought of ravens as scavengers. When he was younger, he and his friends had hunted crows, and when they did manage to kill one it was not wasted. It was cooked and eaten. He had found that crows were uncannily wise and cunning, and worthy hunting adversaries. Somehow they always seemed to know when you had a gun in your hand and when you did not, and they usually stayed out of range when you did.

Nonetheless, he had never seen a bird behave as the second one had in this situation. "You had better go and bring back the one you hit, Nathan," he said evenly.

"No, I will!" cried Christopher, angry and frustrated, and for more than one reason. He had wanted to be the first, naturally, to shoot his new shotgun, a birthday present from his grandfather. But something else was bothering him. He was appalled that his older brother had attacked the two innocent creatures.

He had been with Grandpa Versteeg and other hunters on several previous occasions when game birds had been brought down, and it appeared to be a natural phenomenon. The birds, usually ducks, were later cleaned and eaten in pleasant surroundings, just as fish were when caught. But somehow this incident was totally different for Christopher. It might have been the fact that it was his own gun that had been discharged, and therefore he felt some kind of responsibility for what had occurred. Or maybe it was that these were not actually game fowl that had been attacked, but ordinary birds that normally would live out their lives as free creatures, high in the skies, and ones that he would not have considered eating. He was not certain what it was. His emotions and thoughts were confused, and at first he did not know what to do. But he did know one thing: He was outraged at the shooting and he wanted to find the bird that had been assaulted.

The older boy made no move to follow as Christopher darted off in the direction in which the birds had gone down. Near the edge of the lake he crossed the ridge and entered the grove of evergreens and oaks. He was certain that the bird that had been hit was in this vicinity. Moving stealthily through the woods, he searched in all directions and under every tree. Finding nothing, he began looking upward into the trees themselves, and he traversed the region several times, but he saw no sign whatsoever of either bird. Puzzled and disconcerted, he finally gave up, and walked slowly back to the hunting lodge.

By that time his grandfather and his brother had gone inside. Christopher entered and found them in the large living room upstairs, where a deadly silence greeted him. The grandfather had reprimanded the older boy, not so much for shooting down the raven, but for the fashion in which he had done so—with his brother's new shotgun. The two of them sat looking at Christopher when he arrived, and did not say a word.

"I couldn't find anything, Grandpa," said Christopher, standing in the doorway and breaking the silence.

"Well, it must be there. It couldn't be anywhere else," responded the old man. He paused and then said, "Well, no matter."

Realizing that Christopher was disturbed by the event, he looked at the younger boy. "Maybe it was able to fly away after all," he said. Yet at the same time he knew, deep within his heart, from the way the bird had dropped out of the air, that it was either dead or severely damaged. He thought again about the unheard-of behavior of the second raven, diving steeply after the first, an act that still mystified and intrigued him.

Nathan was thankful that his brother had returned and that his grandfather's attention was at least momentarily not focused upon him. He got up, slid past Christopher in the doorway, and ran down the stairs and out the door.

The grandfather was chagrined at the turn of today's events. This day, which both he and Chris had awaited with great anticipation, had not gone at all the way he had planned. As he sat by the empty stone fireplace in his aging leather chair, he searched for something to say to his disillusioned grandson.

He knew that the boy was in no mood for shooting. "Would you like me to go out and help you look for the bird?" he asked.

"No," answered Chris, his head down. "I really don't want to go back there, and I don't think we could find it anyway."

"Then, would you like to go out in the boat and do a little fishing?" asked the grandfather, knowing this to be one of the boy's favorite pastimes.

Christopher realized that his grandpa was also feeling disappointment. "Yeah, that sounds okay," he said.

The old man rose, limped across the room, and put an arm around the youth's shoulder. Tears of frustration began to burn in the boy's eyes, but he wiped them away quickly with his hand. He followed his grandfather down the stairs, and together they went outside and traversed the lawn downhill toward the dock. There they collected their poles and fishing gear and climbed into the small boat. The grandfather started the motor and then handed the helm over to his grandson.

The quiet motor purred behind Chris as he held the throttle. It was only a rowboat with a small outboard motor, but at age twelve, navigating it was still a pleasure for him. With his grandpa in the front of the boat they toured the mirrorlike body of water without much conversation. The sky was clear and the sunshine warm, and there was not a breath of wind to unsettle the water. The scene was one of unspoiled and uncluttered beauty, without another house or sign of human life anywhere. Arriving at one of their favorite fishing spots, Chris stopped the engine and they both dropped lines into the water. As they waited for a bite, Christopher found that he could not forget the episode that had occurred with his brother and his new shotgun. As time went by he resolved that when they docked he would go looking for the fallen bird again.

His thoughts were interrupted suddenly by a faint sound. At first he could not make out what it was, and yet he had the distinct impression that it was something he should listen to, something to be reckoned with. His grandfather, fishing with his back to him, showed no signs of hearing it whatsoever, and the boy realized that at his advanced age he would probably not be able to. He avoided saying anything at the moment, in order to preserve the quiet, and he strained ever more intently to listen.

Coming to him from across the shining surface of water was what seemed now to be a voice, his brother's voice he thought after a few moments. Looking back toward the distant lodge, he could see the building itself, and he thought that he might barely be able to identify the form of his brother standing on the dock, but they were too far away for him to be certain.

At first the syllables were muffled, and he could not put any of the words together. Gradually he understood more, and just before a breeze came up to obliterate the sounds entirely, he believed that he had deciphered at least a portion of a message, but it was fragmented, as he had caught it only in bits and pieces.

"I found the bird!" was the one thing he thought he had heard repeatedly, and which excited him. In addition, he was quite certain he had comprehended other words and phrases as they drifted far across the still water. He turned them over in his mind, trying to make sense of them.

"Grandpa! . . . Come back!" he had made out, and "Christopher! . . . Tiny little being! . . . Both birds! . . . Next to them!"

CHAPTER 18

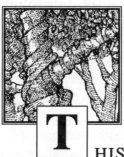

THIS TIME it was the human who wanted to run.

Nathan was dumbfounded when he stumbled upon the small grouping in the evergreen grove: a normal-looking black bird, alert and on its feet, the other one prostrate upon the ground and obviously injured, and a tiny humanlike creature apparently examining the fallen bird's wing. Feeling remorseful during Grandpa Versteeg's lecture, he had gone for a walk. He eventually decided to try to find the bird he had shot down. He headed toward the grove where they had all seen it fall and suddenly ran across the two birds and the little person.

The astonished boy observed them intently for a short while. Then the small being apparently noticed him and stood up, staring directly at him. Nathan was awe-struck and yet fascinated, but as he continued to look on fear began to creep into his consciousness. He thought of running for his grandfather and his brother. He was just turning to do so when the cry of "Stop!" froze him in his tracks.

"What right has your race had to treat ours in such a despicable fashion?" said the small creature, to Nathan's total amazement. And the words were in English!

Having barely comprehended what had been said, the astounded teen-ager managed to blurt out, "Who are you? Where are you from?"

Clasping Olamin's calamar firmly in his hand, Gilin was surprised at the clarity and precision with which he was both speaking and comprehending the human language. The dying magician had told him that communication, even with human beings, was one of the key functions of the magical piece. Confronted by the huge being, he had suddenly recalled this, and had fumbled for the calamar momentarily and withdrawn it from his belt satchel. Uncertain how he had even activated the instrument, he felt a precipitous surge of confidence and energy after his first effort, and was ready to carry on in the foreign tongue. He was inflamed, incensed at what had transpired. He was unafraid for his own safety, yet desperate for that of Loana.

He was about to assail this human for all past and present transgressions, when he began to sense the anxiety and wonder this enormous being was feeling. How he was able to recognize it he did not know. But his attitude toward the creature gradually softened. Slowly realizing that nothing would be gained by berating the creature, and recalling that they might require its assistance, Gilin altered the tone and substance of his speech.

He knew they had nothing to lose. No matter what happened they were in the profoundest of difficulties. To the utter astonishment of Ruggum Chamter, who observed fretfully from the hollow log, comprehending only traces of the conversation, Gilin decided to pursue communication with this human, and even let the truth about their species be known.

"Our race has lived upon Earth as long as yours!" he declared, in impeccable English. "By our choice, for many thousands of years you have been virtually unaware of our existence! We normally have no malice toward you individually. But my ilon has been damaged in an assault by one of . . ."

But before the young kirin could finish, the human

turned and ran away through the trees as fast as his legs would carry him.

The surprised Gilin watched until he was out of sight. Then he turned and looked about for Ruggum and saw him coming out of hiding and then striding toward him.

"You were visible to it," exclaimed the elder, "as you must have been to the other, to the girl! I was right in suspecting that when the sting of the gronom rendered you invisible to us it made you visible to humans at the same time! And you were speaking English! I recognized it! You must have been using the calamar! It worked exactly the way you once mentioned it would!"

Caring little about invisibility or language at the moment, Gilin was preoccupied only by concern for his fallen ilon. "Ruggum!" he entreated. "You must mount Alsinam quickly and follow the human! Without someone or something to help Loana soon, you know as well as I that she will probably perish!"

The overseer hesitated for a moment. He knew all of the repercussions of the injuries to the ilon, far better, in fact, than his young companion. But it went entirely against his upbringing, all of his teachings as an elder, and indeed the very heart of kirin philosophy to consider what Gilin was suggesting: approaching a member of the human race for help. Yet at the same time it was becoming painfully apparent that they might have no other recourse.

"I shall follow it," he said. Ruggum had a deep distrust for humans. He resolved that he would have nothing to do with the being other than to keep it in sight. "I shall be cautious," he said curtly. "They may have further intentions of harming us. I will return as soon as I can." He climbed aboard Alsinam and abruptly flew off.

He controlled the ascent of his raven and hovered close to the tree tops so as not to be detected. Soon he sighted the human and directed his bird to alight upon a branch high in a tree. The being was standing on a wooden platform projecting outwardly from the edge of the lake. It was shouting loudly to the north over the calm surface of water. Ruggum searched both the lake and the surrounding terrain for signs of other humans with whom it might be communicating, but could see none. The human continued calling, however, repeating sounds that Ruggum thought, with his rudimentary knowledge of the language, might be names. It stated that it had seen a bird, and it even described Gilin.

Observing that this time it apparently carried no weapon, Ruggum and Alsinam took off and climbed to a higher altitude, moving northward over the lake. The old kirin continued searching the water and the land below and soon spied a small vessel afloat some distance away. Flying toward it, he came close enough to identify that it was occupied by two human beings, one wearing clothing of a dark hue, and a second in bright yellow. He purposefully kept his distance as he observed them working in the rear of the craft. All at once he heard a burring noise, followed by a deep humming, and the vessel started to move slowly to the south toward the building over which Loana had been attacked. He flew along above them until they landed, disembarked, and joined the one on the platform. Then to his surprise the two smaller ones began to run in the direction of Gilin and Loana, while the largest of the three trailed slowly behind.

Immediately concerned for his young compatriot, Ruggum descended hurriedly through the trees to Gilin's location. Not knowing precisely where his companion was, he touched down next to Loana just before the first two humans burst unceremoniously upon the scene and stopped a short distance away.

"See what I mean? It's right there!" exclaimed the taller of the boys, attired in red. He stared unabashedly down at Gilin.

Although Ruggum could not see his companion, the young kirin referred to was standing resolutely next to the unmoving Loana.

"There, Grandpa! See? I was right, wasn't I?" continued Nathan, pointing at Gilin when the largest of the three humans arrived, puffing heavily.

"Well, I'll be . . . darned!" breathed the old man as he stared. "And both the ravens are here too!" he wheezed, the picture of the second raven diving after the first running once again through his mind.

Ruggum Chamter was totally unnerved by the proximity of the humans and instinctively hid himself once again in the hollow log. Gilin's courage, however, was not diminished and he would not be deterred. Calamar in hand, he elected once again to speak, this time to an audience of three astounded human beings.

"Whether you choose to believe it or not, as I related earlier to the one of you in red, a species of beings like myself and like Ruggum Chamter . . ."

He paused, and nodded toward the place where the overseer had been standing. He stopped, because the elder was no longer in sight.

For an instant Gilin too lost his nerve, as he looked back up at the giant creatures. Then, seeming to derive strength and courage from the calamar, he recovered his composure. Almost before he knew it he was going on, hardly missing a syllable.

"Our species has existed upon Earth as long as yours!" he said. "But we have chosen to live a life sequestered from your race, and thus you have not been aware of our existence!"

As the small creature held forth about things that John Versteeg could not begin to comprehend, the astonished old man blinked, removed his glasses, and rubbed his eyes before putting them on again. Beads of sweat were beginning to stand on his forehead, both from the running, which he was unaccustomed to, and from the unearthly experience unfolding in front of him.

What, he wondered, could he possibly be witnessing? Something supernatural? Extrasensory? Or extraterrestrial? What kind of incredible phenomenon could this be? And yet the tiny being, except for its size and its feet, did look similar to humans! And it appeared to be intelligent! As he watched and listened in amazement, the diminutive creature chronicled its existence in trees, its habit of flying on the back of a bird, the long history of its ancestors upon the Earth, and how its bird had been mortally wounded.

Finally, outrageous as it seemed, John Versteeg wondered whether there might be some truth to what it was saying. After all, he told himself, Nathan had shot one of the ravens down. Here was the injured bird, lying on the ground in front of them, and beside it stood a small being that knew all about the shooting and even claimed to have been riding it at the time!

"Who's rug . . . rugger . . . or whatever you said?" asked Nathan, interrupting the small creature.

"Are you a leprechaun?" asked Christopher.

"How come you can speak English?" asked Nathan.

"There is much to tell and to discuss," answered Gilin, "but at this moment we have a serious and pressing problem. We desperately need your help. My raven has been assaulted by one of your kind and lies in front of you severely wounded. Left alone with us here in the woods, she would almost certainly die!"

Ruggum, observing everything from his hiding place, was able to grasp fragments of the speech of both Gilin and the human beings. His fear for himself had subsided shortly after he had become hidden. His concern now was for Gilin, whom he knew to be visible and in direct confrontation with three of the huge and unpredictable creatures. I can do nothing for him from here, he thought despairingly, and yet I can do little, if anything, for him out there!

Then, as he watched, Ruggum was struck by a realization: His young confrere was performing an act of unprecedented courage. What he was doing was unheard of in the long history of the kirin race. There he was, facing and holding conversation with three human beings, totally alone, and in a state of visibility that he had no means of controlling or reversing!

Nothing like this had occurred since the inception of no'an, and Ruggum knew it. In the light of Gilin's fortitude, the overseer was chagrined at his own reflex to hide, and he determined that he must do something to aid his young companion. Perhaps it will not be of much help, he thought, but there is one thing I can do. It is the very least I can do. I can leave this log and stand beside him! I know not exactly where he is, but I can follow his voice, and I can move into the gaze of the three human beings! Then I will be close to him!

Without further hesitation, Ruggum stepped out of the hole and strode toward the incredible conclave between kirin and human. Approaching, he glanced up furtively at the humans. When he neared the fallen Loana, Gilin's voice ceased abruptly. The overseer stopped also, momentarily uncertain what to do.

Gilin stopped speaking as soon as he caught sight of the elder. He immediately recognized what the presence of his compatriot signified, and what bravery it had taken for him to come out.

"I am here," said Gilin to the old overseer, to indicate his location. He spoke in the familiar dialect of the home clans. "And," he continued, "it inspires me that you are here also."

Ruggum made no reply, but stationed himself near the place from which the voice was emanating. For only the second time in his life he was deliberately allowing himself to be a short distance from human beings, and he found the experience distinctly uncomfortable. He could not force himself to look up at the creatures, now so close at hand. Keeping a steady gaze ahead, he crossed his arms resolutely in front of him and waited.

Gilin, on the other hand, turned his attention back to the humans. They had been confused momentarily by the pause in his recitation, and then by his foreign words, apparently being directed at someone or something nearby, but they were unable to perceive who or what it was. When he looked back at them and spoke again in English, they listened once more with rapt attention.

Not knowing what might come of it, but recognizing that they had few alternatives, Gilin made an impassioned plea. "In the far distant past," he said, "humanity and our species were friendly, at times even synergistic. I am imploring you to give us a modicum of the cooperation that once was commonplace between our races! Our bird has been grievously injured! We are a great distance from home, and we have nowhere else to turn! We are drastically in need of help!"

Christopher glared accusingly at his older brother, and Nathan looked guiltily at the ground. John Versteeg was still far from certain what this little creature represented, but one fact was irrefutable: A wounded raven, undoubtedly the one his grandson had shot, was lying in front of them. Becoming more curious about its injuries, he began to cautiously move forward.

Then, barely able to believe that he was talking to a being less than a foot tall, he said, "May I have a look at your bird?"

Gilin indicated that he could, and the old man knelt down beside the raven to examine its wing. "Does it have any other wounds?" he asked gently.

"No," answered Gilin. "Just the right wing."

The old man stood up and wiped his brow. This entire episode, he thought, is inconceivable! It can't be happening, and yet it is! How could I be carrying on a conversation with . . . with . . . a what? A leprechaun? It was staggering, and his mind was beginning to whirl. His concepts of reality and myth and credibility were all at once blurred. Suddenly he had the feeling that his sanity was being challenged.

He had been through experiences like this before, many years ago during the war, when everything going on around him appeared bizarre, even surrealistic. He realized that somehow he had to arrest his flurry of thoughts. He knew that he could do this by concentrating on a single thing, something that was recognizable and palpable: the wounded raven on the ground in front of him.

Trembling slightly, he knelt down again and examined the bird, allowing himself time to relax and collect his thoughts. The wing was broken in two places, he found. Then he saw something new, something small, the finding of which at first calmed him further because it caused his mind to focus even more fully upon something outside of himself. Slowly, as he identified what it was, it angered him. Entrapped within one of the open wounds was a small, dark object. Upon scrutinizing it closely, by changing the position of the wing slightly, he identified it as a pellet of buckshot.

The situation is real, he told himself! It must be! And his own grandson had pulled the trigger of the shotgun! He had no other explanation for what had happened and what was happening. Quickly he marshalled the facts and chronicled them in his mind one by one: the gunshot, the fallen raven, the miniature being, the pellet of buckshot . . . the whole thing must somehow be true! But then, he asked himself, if the situation is real, and is actually happening, what do we do next?

The old man stood up unsteadily and glanced briefly at Nathan. Then he looked back at Gilin and said hoarsely, "This matter seems to be our responsibility. We have caused this injury, and now we must take care of it the best way we can."

He stopped for a few moments and then he went on, his resolve building. "This raven must mean a lot to you, and from what you say I can understand why. I took care of a few birds when they were hurt—a long time ago. Once in a while people would even bring them to me. I haven't done that for many years, and I have never treated one with open wounds like this, but I can try to help it."

Kneeling down again, he said to Gilin, "In order to care for it, it'll have to be back in the lodge. I'll have to carry it there."

He removed a handkerchief from his pocket, and was applying it over the head of the injured bird, when Gilin stopped him and asked what he was doing. "Unless it's dead or deep in shock," explained the old man, "it'll bite me or claw me when I try to pick it up, or even try to handle it. Covering its head like this will only calm it down."

Gilin turned and spoke a few words to the raven in the language of curlace as the incredulous humans looked on. Then, turning back, he said to the man, "This bird will not harm you nor resist you in any way."

"Okay, we'll give it a try," said the old man, willing to accept almost anything at this point.

He gently picked up the bird. He had never seen one respond in this fashion, he thought as he did so. He had never seen anything like it! The creature, despite its wounds and its pain, made no attempt to struggle, and if anything, appeared to be trying to cooperate. Standing up, he cradled the raven in both hands, and, still astonished by the unfathomable sequence of events, he began to limp slowly toward the lodge.

Gilin, not about to allow Loana out of his sight, started immediately in pursuit of the old man, and the two astonished boys followed him with their eyes. The kirin moved with a long, loping gait, unlike anything they had ever seen before. It moved effortlessly and kept pace with their grandfather with no trouble. The delighted boys, who had been relishing the entire episode from the start, moved after them down the pathway toward the hunting lodge.

Ruggum Chamter was still deeply distressed about what was transpiring, and yet had no intention of being left behind. He knew that if he was to be of any help to the injured Loana he must go after Gilin and the human beings. Summoning the awaiting Alsinam, he boarded his ilon and took off into the air to follow.

After a short trek, this most amazing procession arrived at the front door of the lodge. Grandpa Versteeg reached out one hand to open it, supporting the raven in the other, and then disappeared inside, the screen door swinging shut behind him.

Arriving at the gigantic human structure, Gilin balked for the first time during the entire encounter. An enthusiastic participant until this moment, it suddenly dawned on him what they were doing, trafficking with human beings. Struck precipitously with doubt and apprehension, he impulsively recoiled from the door and froze.

Ruggum was circling overhead. He could easily identify where Gilin was because the two human lads stared unabashedly at him wherever he went. Intuitively the overseer sensed what was happening to Gilin below. Loath to enter a place such as this himself, to a greater degree even than Gilin, the elder was nonetheless becoming more realistic about their circumstances as time went on. He realized that the only chance they had for Loana, and consequently for themselves, was inside the giant structure. Consciously attempting to force fear and disgust for humans out of his mind, and sensing that he must be the one to act now, Ruggum flew down and landed where he thought his companion was.

"Gilin, are you here?" he called in the common kirin dialect.

The two enthralled boys took their eyes off Gilin for the first time and gaped in amazement at what appeared to be a crow speaking gibberish.

"Yes, I am here!" answered Gilin, moving toward the elder, relieved to have his friend close by again.

"Loana is inside this building!" said the elder firmly. "We also must gain entrance in order to oversee what happens to her! And hopefully, if the proper materials and environment are available, I can care for her injuries there."

Recovering his sense of reality and again thinking of Loana, Gilin recognized that Ruggum was correct. If they wanted to be with the injured ilon, they had no choice but to go inside. Summoning his courage once more, he turned to the two lads and entreated them to swing the enormous door open in order for the kirins to enter.

Christopher had been mesmerized. His eyes had darted back and forth from the raven to the tiny being as their unintelligible conversation transpired. But now he quickly stepped forward and opened the screen door. Gilin stepped hesitantly past the doorstep and into the manmade structure. He was soon followed by a strutting Alsinam, the practical-minded, yet reluctant Ruggum Chamter aboard.

Once inside, the kirins were confronted by an immense, labyrinthine interior, giant corridors jutting off to either side, and neither Gilin nor the elder knew what to do or where to go. Looking back at Christopher and Nathan, both now in the doorway, the bewildered Gilin asked where the damaged raven might be found.

"Grandpa!" called Christopher. "Where are you?"

The old man appeared in a doorway at the distant end of the cavernous space. He was still holding Loana carefully.

"At the end of the hallway in the shop room," he answered, and again he moved out of sight.

Having seen their faithful bird, the kirins started down the hallway, Gilin trotting and Ruggum upon his ilon. The captivated boys followed. The screen door slammed noisily behind them and momentarily frightened the kirins.

Arriving at the far end, the kirins looked upward through the doorway and saw the old man. He was apparently preparing to do something on a high wooden bench, but they could see no sign of Loana, and they moved inside.

Surveying the wood structure, the undaunted Gilin was certain he could scale it. Informing Ruggum what he was about to do, he strode to the nearest leg of the bench and started upward. When kirins climb sheer surfaces or difficult areas, they utilize their resourceful feet almost exclusively, their upper limbs being used only for balance and control. Finding toeholds in minute irregularities in the wood, Gilin ascended effortlessly, the boys ogling his every movement from the doorway.

The overseer dismounted. Even though he was unable to see Gilin, he knew precisely where he was by observing the young humans. Leaving Alsinam at the foot, he also moved to the leg of the structure and climbed after his companion with equal ease.

As Gilin reached the top, he pulled himself over the edge and onto the working surface, Ruggum following shortly after. Gilin touched the overseer on the shoulder. Together they stood near the edge, watching the old man, who was cleansing the open wing of their beloved Loana in a basin of sudsy water.

"Cleaning the wounds is the correct procedure," Ruggum

confided quietly to Gilin. "They must be thoroughly washed, and I can only hope that the solution the human is employing is proper. But I am also concerned about what must be done next. The wing must be properly set and splinted. I must be involved in that operation."

What a deplorable predicament, thought the disenfranchised overseer. At home, it would be I who would direct a party of our clansmen in the gathering area, the entire clan if necessary, to clean the open wounds, to set the broken bones as accurately and as painlessly as possible, and to dress and immobilize the extremity. The ilon would be observed and nurtured for weeks thereafter under my guidance and gradually allowed to increase activity. Here we are only two kirins, far from Rogalinon, far from home. We are virtually helpless and in an unprecedented situation. We are forced to rely upon human beings for everything with which to minister to Loana: both the materials for healing and the handling of the injured wing.

"I must speak with it," Ruggum said to Gilin, nodding with distaste toward the elderly man.

Gilin knew that Ruggum should be included in the upcoming procedures. But he was amazed when he thought about what was occurring. Not only had he been communicating openly with human beings, but he now found himself in the unheard of position of being an intermediary between a human and another kirin! He was the only one visible and he possessed the calamar. He must be the one to deal with them.

Gilin sucked in a deep breath, looked upward, and addressed the giant being. "My companion, here, is an elder, an overseer of our clan!"

The old man looked away from his work and glared down at Gilin. The youth took a step backward but quickly recovered his composure. "He is accomplished in the handling of injured birds and animals!" said Gilin. "He knows how to treat them, both acutely and as they are recovering!"

John Versteeg had been shaken by the unbelievable events of the day. But he had busied himself tending to the bird, knowing that concentration on a task like this would clear his thoughts, bring them into focus and perspective. As he gently lavaged the open wounds in the clean basin, he did not appreciate the arrival of the little being on the working surface nearby. It disturbed him all over again. Then the small creature spoke, and what it said took him by surprise indeed.

He cleared his throat, licked his lips, and responded. "Well, then, perhaps I can use his help," he said. But as the little creature was obviously alone, he asked, "Where might your companion be?"

Gilin realized, of course, that it was impossible for the man to see Ruggum. Yet he could think of no other alternative than to introduce him.

"My name is Gilin," he began. Then he pointed toward the elder. "And this is Ruggum Chamter," he said, as the bewildered gentleman and the two enraptured boys stared at the nothingness their tiny guest was indicating.

PART THREE

∎ ∎ ∎

C H A P T E R   1

WHAT DO YOU THINK he will give me?" asked Lindor.

"Who will give you?" answered Hut.

The two lads were striding across the floor of the cave toward the stream. They were in animated conversation, Hut now virtually recovered from the effects of the barwood tree. As he gazed about, he was amazed at the immensity and the intricacy of the space.

"The magician of your clan," replied Lindor, in a voice somehow more mellow than Hut would have expected from a child his age. "He said it would be something from his bag. I found the silver box and the vial."

"Oh, I was asleep when that happened," said Hut, glancing at the Shillitoe boy. "I know not what Speckarin had in mind for you. But if he promised something, he will fulfill it, and it will undoubtedly be worth waiting for."

All at once Hut stopped, and seeing him do so Lindor did likewise. Hut eyed the boy. "Where did you find those things, the vial and the box?" he asked. "Those were mine, you know, at least on the trip to the barwood grove."

"They were in the stream over here," replied Lindor. He

began trotting toward the water and Hut followed. "I saw them glittering at the bottom as I was swimming," he said, reaching the edge. "I dove down to get them right over there!"

He pointed out into the moving water. Hut stared intently into the shimmering stream, searching its rocky bottom.

Arriving upon the bank at almost the same moment was another Shillitoe, a youth who stopped a short distance away. He observed the other two for a while and then strode up and introduced himself to Hut.

"You would not remember me," he said. "My name is Runagar. We journeyed together upon my ilon the distance from your camp by the hemlock tree to our cave here."

Hut stared inquisitively at the newcomer. "Are you one of those who rescued me from the barwood tree?" he asked.

"Not exactly," answered Runagar. "I was with Issar on a mission for our queen when we detected the scent of barwood essence in the air. Knowing this to be an unusual and potentially hazardous occurrence, we investigated immediately. We searched the barwood grove and eventually discovered you, not by the lacerated tree, but a safe distance from it."

Hut was struck, as he had been with Lindor, by the voice of the Shillitoe kirin. It was not an especially soft one, but one spoken with a subtle quality and style somehow pleasing to his ear. For a few moments he was mesmerized by the sound.

But fascinated by the content of the story, and anxious to hear the voice again, Hut went on. "Speckarin and Diliani mentioned that I was found some distance from the tree, but they had so much to relate in such a short time that they never told me how it might have happened. My last recollection was being overcome at the foot of the tree. I could barely move! My chest felt heavy, so heavy that I could hardly heave a breath! And everything around me was blurred!"

Realizing for the first time what a terrifying predicament it had been, he stopped for a few moments. "How could I possibly have escaped from that?" he asked.

"Thank your ilon," said Runagar. "From footprints and

tracks we found about the base of the injured tree, we are virtually certain your raven helped you away, probably carrying you in its beak. She is the one who saved you from the barwood tree."

"But," responded Hut, "I have never heard of that happening, an ilon carrying a kirin in its beak!"

"Nor had we," said the Shillitoe kirin. "But your magician told us later, beside the hemlock tree, that such things are known to have occurred and have been chronicled by magicians in the archives of curlace magic. He said this instance would be recorded and remembered and told by generations of kirins to come. Inhalation of barwood essence is as intoxicating and perilous for birds as it is for kirins."

Hut turned his thoughts to the faithful Lisam. He had not possessed her for long, and she was his first bird ilon. She had not only served him well and willingly, but now he was discovering that she had saved his life! What marvelous creatures these ilon are, he thought affectionately. Especially Lisam!

All at once he desired to see his raven. "Where are the ilon being quartered?" he asked.

"Over there," replied Runagar, pointing toward one of the shafts at the base of the cave.

Hut looked in the direction indicated, but did not initially see the ravens. Instead, for the first time since he had been in the cave, he caught sight of sleek animals occupying several of the passageways. He gazed at them, intrigued by their size, their innate beauty, and their gentle yet powerful movements. These must be the beasts this tribe uses as ilon, he surmised with interest. But before asking about them, he began again to search for the ravens. This time he found them, safe in their own tunnel. But from this distance and vantage point he could not make out Lisam.

"May I go and greet them?" he asked.

"Of course," said Runagar, understanding why the Moger youth wished to do so. The three of them started off in the direction of the birds. On the way they continued their conversation.

"I do not know how to thank you for rescuing me and for bringing all of us here," said Hut. "I am told that without your help, and that of your tribe, we would still be alone in the woods."

"You are kirins," replied Runagar. "You were in trouble. You would do the same for us if we were in danger in your woods."

"Those animals," said Hut, nodding toward the contingents of gray foxes. "They are quite magnificent! Are they the ilon of your tribe?"

"They are indeed," answered Runagar proudly. "We have utilized the breed for several hundred years."

"To think that I rode all that way with you upon a beast such as that!" said Hut. "I only wish that I had known what was occurring at the time!"

"And your girl, still in the fairinin," remarked Runagar. "She rode with Issar upon his ilon."

They proceeded along the edge of the flowing stream. Hut asked questions about many aspects of the cave, and of their lives within it. Runagar responded in kind, questioning him about the Yorl and the Moger clans and their life in trees.

As they moved along Hut eyed the sheer wall of the cave and its honeycombed surfaces. "How many kirins are in your tribe?" he asked.

"I know the answer to that!" interjected Lindor, left out of the conversation for a long time. "Two hundred and thirty-nine!"

"Oh!" said a surprised Hut. "That is a total far larger than either of our two clans! Quite a number more, actually, than both of them put together! How can you possibly get to know anyone else in your tribe?"

"We know everyone," replied Runagar. "We see one another all the time. After all, we live in one place, this cave." He paused, as though in thought. "But I envy you, and all of your clansmen, for living the way you do in trees. I have always wanted to live that way, since I was very small, because . . . then I would have a chance to fly."

"Does your tribe not use birds as ilon?" asked Hut.

"No," answered Runagar. "In fact, we are taught we would not be able to trust bird ilon. Because of its hazards, flying is not to be undertaken by any member of our tribe. But I am not afraid of bird ilon. I have always desired to use one. I have always dreamed of flying, but I have never had the opportunity. The Shilliron tribe, which lives a short distance away, has a small number of bird ilon. But our tribe employs none and the elders wish to keep it that way."

Hut recalled his own dreams of flying before they became a reality. He would like to see Runagar enjoying the same thrill, he thought, as he gazed at the Shillitoe youth. After all, this kirin might have saved his life. Suddenly an idea came to him.

Hut was young and imbued with the impetuosity of youth. He had not yet experienced the need for conservatism. He had taken a risk initially in departing his own room and his tree with his cousin Gilin. He had acted somewhat rashly and unwisely in the barwood tree. And when this idea struck him, without taking the time to think it through, he simply voiced it.

"Would you like to fly upon one of our ilon?" he asked.

"I would greatly enjoy doing so!" responded Runagar, attempting to control his eagerness.

"So would I!" echoed Lindor.

"I am afraid you are too small, Lindor," said Hut. "With no formal training it would be too dangerous for you. But," he said to Runagar, "I am sure you could do it. Let me think about how we could accomplish it."

Just then they arrived at the mouth of the tunnel in which the ravens were cloistered. They look wonderful, thought Hut, glad to once again be in the company of the selfless creatures. He entered the passage, located Lisam behind Ocelam and Manay, and approached his faithful bird. Then, as the Shillitoe youths looked on with interest, he placed a gentle hand upon her neck and spoke a few carefully chosen curlace phrases, praising her and thanking her for her courage and fortitude in rescuing him.

The raven was mindful that her master had been gravely stricken. She had witnessed him succumbing to the sweet-smelling tree, and had later observed apprehensively as the foreign animal bore his limp body to this place. As with all ilon, she was outwardly almost always unemotional, seemingly unmoved by events occurring about her. But now her small master, apparently resurrected, had reappeared and was standing next to her, stroking her and speaking words of adoration.

The great bird was so relieved at his appearance and his apparent recovery that from her throat emanated a sound, a husky purring of satisfaction, a sound the surprised Hut had never before heard and was unaware she could produce. Yet he recognized what it meant, and he stood with her for a brief time longer, before turning back once again to his newly found friends.

As they departed the tunnel Hut looked back and reassured Lisam that this time he would not stay away long. The three youths again resumed their hike, discussing the matter of Runagar flying, both Runagar and Hut becoming more involved in the plan all the while. They decided that they would attempt something the following morning, but the details of their adventure were yet undeveloped.

Before returning to the guest chambers, and after the departure of Lindor, Runagar escorted Hut in a wider exploration of the cave and its environs, explaining what they were seeing as they went. Not only did they investigate the main hall of the cave, climbing up and down the pathways cut into the wall, but Runagar introduced his visitor to something new, which none of the traveling party had previously known about. Behind the circular wall and beneath the cave's floor was an elaborate series of tunnels, a veritable labyrinth of passageways. They were dark, and Hut could readily have become lost had it not been for his more experienced guide.

Finally Runagar ushered Hut to the home of his family in one of the upper corridors of the cave. The small visitor was introduced to his friend's mother, father and sister. But at Runagar's request they did not discuss their plans for the following morning because of the dislike and distrust of bird ilon among members of the Shillitoe tribe, something felt even in his own family.

It was late in the evening, according to Runagar, when the Shillitoe lad escorted Hut back to the guest chambers. Time of day meant nothing to Hut now, both because he had slept for two days and because he was inside a space where neither the brightness of daylight nor the darkness of nighttime ever made their presence known.

"How do you know it is late?" asked a curious Hut as they arrived at his room. "You have neither sunlight nor darkness here."

"We have timing instruments," answered Runagar. "I will show you one tomorrow. They inform us of the time of day outside so that we will never venture out at an inopportune time. Much of our activity occurs in the out-of-doors on errands and missions, like the one we were engaged in when we found you in the barwood grove.

"By the way," added Runagar with a chuckle, "you were a sorry sight out there! It was lucky indeed that we happened by!"

Hut could only respond by thanking his host again for rescuing him. "In return," he said with sincerity, "I will take you for a ride on one of our ilon. We will do it tomorrow morning. Come to my room when you awaken."

Runagar was stimulated by the prospect of flying, and he slept little during the night. In the morning he arose early, and without having breakfast he departed for Hut's room. He found the Yorl kirin also awake, but not quite as ready to go as he was. Hut had slept only a short while himself after such a long rest so recently, and for some time he had been wondering what to do about his offer to Runagar.

Having seen the ravens in the tunnel, Lisam among them,

he was certain that he could procure her. No one was guarding the birds and she would willingly obey her master. But several additional matters concerned him. First of all, how could he persuade one of the other ilon to go along with Runagar, and then to fly carrying him? He knew that Speckarin and Diliani would not approve of his untrained Shillitoe friend soaring aboard one of their ravens.

Having been through so much recently, and having thought about it much of the night, Hut found that he would have to agree. An inexperienced kirin ascending upon one of the ravens was something that might pose problems. In addition, Diliani had mentioned how unnerved the ravens were during their passage into the cave. She said that while the birds were undoubtedly looking forward to being outdoors again, traversing the tunnel to get there was something neither she nor the ravens would enjoy.

Uncertain how to break the news about his reservations to Runagar, Hut had initially determined he would attempt to discourage the Shillitoe youth when he appeared. He would center his arguments on the difficulty in exiting the cave.

On the other hand, Hut had thought, Runagar was instrumental in rescuing him from disaster. He had invited him to fly, and he felt an obligation to supply him the means to do so. He recalled his own words to Lindor, the boy, just the day before, about Speckarin and the fact that whatever he promised, he would most certainly fulfill.

When his newfound friend entered the room, despite feelings to the contrary, Hut went ahead with his plan to dissuade him. He expressed concern about departing the cave.

"Oh, leaving is no problem," said the Shillitoe youth. "In several locations throughout our cave are passageways to the outside, some for ventilation and some for access. A few of them are near the roof. We could fly up to one of them and depart to the outside."

Hut was astounded by what he heard, that the lad could consider such a possibility. He had no training in flying whatsoever, and yet what he proposed doing was to pilot a strange ilon off the floor of the cave and exit through a small hole in the ceiling! Hut knew that such an attempt by an unskilled flyer would be doomed to failure, and probably dangerous for both rider and bird. He began to realize how much of a neophyte he had on his hands.

"No," he said firmly. "You would have to be an expert in flying in order to accomplish a feat like that, and I cannot teach you to fly inside the cave! What other means of exit is there?"

"You have no recollection of it," responded an undaunted Runagar, "but when you entered the cave you came with me upon the fox ilon through one of our larger tunnels. Your magician, your woman Diliani, and all four of your ravens entered through another passageway with Issar. He had dismounted from his ilon and led them on foot. The path he took is a more direct and expeditious route to the outside. We could go out that way with the ravens."

Within a short while Hut had acquiesced. Runagar was an enthusiastic and convincing candidate. Reluctantly Hut agreed that if they had come in that way they could leave in the same fashion. Neither he nor Runagar, of course, had a very complete idea of how traumatic that entrance had been, especially for the four ravens.

Nonetheless, the two youths made their way down the wall to the base of the cave. They traversed the floor, and because it was early, no other Shillitoe was seen along the way. They approached the tunnel in which the birds were resting. The ravens were unguarded, as Hut had expected, and the youths entered. Lisam came immediately to attention and Hut walked up and greeted her warmly. Then he eyed the other three ravens, trying to decide which one to approach for Runagar. Ocelam, he thought, belongs to Speckarin, and Manay to Diliani. We would be in greater danger of being chastised if one of those were gone than if Faralan was missing, since Talli is still unconscious.

He went to Faralan and began to stroke the ilon gently. Attempting to ease the great bird's apprehensions, he spoke phrases in curlace, ones he had been taught by Lugor on

Rogustin, the tree of the Mogers. He also used a greeting he had grown accustomed to even earlier than that, as a child on Rogalinon.

"Orann," he said. He had learned the word when he was very young and had used it frequently with his old squirrel, Stala. Caressing the raven's neck and speaking softly, he motioned for Runagar to come closer.

Since they had entered the cave, Faralan had still not seen his mistress. The last time the ilon had seen Talli she was alarmingly limp and helpless, even unresponsive. The sable bird was deeply concerned about her, and was perhaps more pliable and easily influenced than usual. In a normal state the bird might have opposed taking on a strange master, but at this time he was not inclined to resist as Hut introduced him to the eager Runagar.

Lisam moved immediately on Hut's command. Faralan took surprisingly little urging to follow. The two ilon were led from their resting place across the floor of the cave to the tunnel they had passed through the day before. The ravens immediately recognized the entrance and the dark space within it as things they wished to avoid. But through repeated pleas and commands, and by praising and stroking the reluctant creatures, they were eventually coaxed into entering. Lisam went in after her young master. Faralan followed behind Runagar.

■ ■ ■

After a long sleep, a refreshed Diliani arose from her bed. To her surprise and delight, while she had been resting, the attendants had cleaned and folded her traveling garments and had delivered them back to her room. The travelers had washed their clothing in ponds and streams whenever possible throughout the journey. But this was the first time they had been immaculate since departure from the Moger tree. With great enjoyment she dressed in her fresh and clean garments. She found food on a silver platter, also put there by her attendants. She consumed a leisurely breakfast, alone in her comfortable chamber.

She did not realize that timepieces were available, and would not have known how to use one. Having no idea of the time of day, she took leave of her room and strolled onto the veranda overlooking the cave. She stretched and gazed about with pleasure, relishing the view of the immense and splendid interior, until her eyes happened to fall upon a raven.

It was Faralan. She was surprised to see him on the floor of the cave, some distance away and adjacent to the entrance of the tunnel.

What could he possibly be doing that far from his resting place, and apparently alone, she wondered? But before she could call out, or do anything at all, the great bird stepped into the mouth of the tunnel and disappeared into the dark opening.

C H A P T E R   2

HUT AND RUNAGAR
moved through the blackness of the tunnel with more
difficulty than either had anticipated. Hut was unconscious
when he entered the cave, strapped to the back of a fox ilon,
and he had no memory of the brief trek. Runagar was aroused
at the prospect of flying and had selected this passageway for
their departure, the one the ravens had passed through the day
before, because it was the shortest route to the outside. He
had no idea that the passage would be so difficult for the
birds. Nonetheless, they persevered.

Runagar slipped past Hut and both of the ravens so that he
could be in the lead. He had gone this way so many times
that it was second nature. Because of this, the party moved
along at about the same speed Diliani and Speckarin had the
day before, with Issar in the lead. Hut lagged slightly behind,
coaxing the birds onward. He was the only one who had
previously handled bird ilon. He quickly found, in this
gloomy and cramped space, that all of the skills he had
learned were being put to use.

Eventually a welcome slit of sunlight greeted them,
knifing through a perpendicular fissure ahead. Runagar

stopped when he saw it, as did the rest of the group. The Shillitoe youth then tilted back his head and began a chant. It was a melody consisting of four clear notes, repeated in varying sequences several times over, and it poured forth in as mellow a singing voice as Hut had ever heard.

He turned back to Hut. "Stand clear!" he said. "Keep the birds out of the way!"

Just then giant structures shuddered and began to stir. To Hut's surprise, Runagar left him and ran to the vertical aperture, where he peered outside as if attempting to find something. He was dwarfed by the magnitude of the slowly shifting things, and because they were moving, Hut feared momentarily for his friend's safety. At first, because of the darkness within and the light breaking through, it was difficult to judge what was happening, but then it became apparent that massive doors were opening. As the slash of sunlight became wider and wider, it was obvious why Runagar had instructed that they stay back. The huge structures were rumbling open in the direction of the small party.

As the wooden door to the left was swinging ponderously, the Shillitoe youth walked at its foot, a hand upon its lowest portion. Once the doors were fully open, they revealed a gaping exit to the outside world, and Runagar signaled for the others to proceed. Hut and two relieved ravens marched through the mouth of the passageway, blinking as they stepped into rays of the early morning sun. As they passed to the outside, Hut observed that the heavy doors were decorated on the exterior by a collection of earth, grass, and thick shrubbery. He suspected what the purpose of this might be, but he waited to ask about it.

Runagar followed them out, and once they were all clear of the entrance he turned and faced the tunnel. Again he chanted four notes, the same ones as before, or so it seemed to Hut, but in a different order than they were sung before. The giant doors began to swing and the party watched until they had closed completely. Hut was amazed as he stared at the area from which they had exited. He could see no sign that the entrance existed. It was camouflaged completely, disguised as a part of the hillside, unrecognizable for what it was except to a trained eye.

Hut was full of questions. "Why did you run to the doors as they began to open?" he asked. "And how did you set them off or start them operating in the first place? It was your song, of course! But why could not a kirin from another tribe, or possibly even a human being, should one chance to overhear your singing, activate the doors in your absence and gain entrance, or leave the doors open and your cave unprotected?"

"We fear no kirins in our region," responded the Shillitoe youth. "As a matter of fact, they can and they do use the entrance any time they wish. They must be acquainted with the notes to sing and the correct sequence in which to sing them. Thankfully, humans are scarce in this part of the countryside. We have encountered them infrequently over the years. They inhabit territories to the north and do not often venture into our forest.

"I approached the door," he said, "when it was open only a crack, because at least one member of a party taking leave of the tunnel must look outside before the doors are fully open. We need to see whether anything unusual or threatening is lurking at the foot of the hill. Occasionally, it is unwise or even hazardous for the entrance to be opened, or for us to venture outside. The movement of the doors can be arrested and reversed should the need arise.

"But now," he said with enthusiasm, "let us be on with our purpose for being here!"

Hut glanced about. Maple trees dominated the vicinity. He looked upward toward the overhanging limbs. The foliage was too dense in the immediate area for the safe takeoff of a novice pilot, he concluded, and he suggested that they find a more open area. Runagar walked ahead and led them on foot a considerable distance from the tunnel until they came upon a grassy clearing. It was ideal.

Hut called the ravens to him. He instructed Lisam to fly in the lead with him.

"Your mistress," he said to Faralan, "lies stricken in the cave we departed. But we hold out hope that the fluid Lisam and I collected from the barwood tree will yield a substance to resuscitate her. We will probably know whether or not it is effective later today. You may recognize this foreign kirin as one of those who rescued me in the barwood grove. I would like to repay him by granting him a wish. It is a deep desire of his, one that goes as far back into his childhood as he can remember. It is to fly into the air upon the back of a great ilon such as you. But he has not previously flown upon a bird, and your flying must therefore be gentle and the duration must be brief. We cannot risk him becoming disengaged, as your mistress did."

Next Hut gave Runagar an abbreviated course on flying. He taught him as many of the ordinary commands as he thought necessary, trying not to overburden him with details. It was obvious that the eager Runagar was learning swiftly and competently. After only a short while Hut was satisfied, assured that his friend was adequately prepared.

"We are ready for takeoff," he said. "But remember something. Deliver your instructions clearly and loudly enough for Faralan to hear. When we are moving rapidly or are headed into a breeze, and the wind is whistling past his ears, they can be difficult for him to understand. Most important of all, we must remain together at all times."

Hut helped Runagar board the raven and position himself properly on the creature's back. His legs were placed about the bird's neck, but held in a different fashion from the way one would straddle a fox, mainly because the neck of the bird is smaller. Hut situated his companion's feet so that they would stabilize him well but not grip so firmly that it would be uncomfortable for the bird or so loosely that the rider would be in jeopardy. Never having done it before, it was a little awkward for the Shillitoe youth, but he adapted nicely.

With Runagar settled and Faralan prepared for flight, Hut climbed onto Lisam. Then he instructed both ravens to depart. As Faralan stretched and flexed his great wings, inactive since the day before, Runagar was awed by the length and breadth of the sable extremities. The ravens beat their wings powerfully and lifted off the ground. They ascended gracefully between the branches of a lofty evergreen on one side and a young sugar maple on the other.

The Shillitoe youth was thrilled to be in the air for the first time in his life. When they were above the trees, Hut, who was slightly in the lead, signaled for Runagar to follow and to give Faralan the command for straight-line flight.

Hut spoke directives to Lisam, and they started off at a leisurely pace. The Yorl lad turned to the rear to observe. Runagar stated a command loudly, and Faralan obediently complied. Soon the two kirins were flying in tandem. Runagar tried to control his exhilaration, but both Hut and his protege were profoundly pleased with the excursion thus far.

The morning was quiet and cool, with only a gentle spring breeze, and they flew confidently across the countryside. Soon Hut turned toward his companion again and this time motioned for Runagar to come alongside him. The Shillitoe lad thought for a moment. Then he gave one command for greater speed and another for a mild veer to the right, both of which Faralan accomplished without hesitation. When Hut was immediately to his left, Runagar instructed steady, straight-ahead flight. Onward they coursed, the ravens' shining wings beating rhythmically for a period of time and then resting as they soared serenely through the air. These peaceful interludes would seem to the mesmerized Runagar to go on forever until once again the wings repeated their undulating movement.

During their ascent, Hut had purposefully not taken them to a great height but rather to a comfortable elevation above the treetops. As he became less concerned about Runagar and his competence as a pilot, Hut settled back to enjoy the scenery himself. He remembered what a pleasure it was to be out-of-doors and to be flying above the earth, breathing the fresh spring air. He could understand why his companion had envied kirins who lived in trees and traveled upon flying ilon.

As he glanced below, the terrain was moving quickly beneath them at this low altitude. The forest around the Shillitoe cave was brilliantly verdant this early morning and full of animal life. He identified a family of deer, not commonly seen in his home forest. They were grazing on the bark of white cedar trees. But he could observe them only briefly as they cruised by before the animals disappeared into the forest.

As Hut relaxed and gazed about, he searched for the grove of barwood trees, desirous of seeing the mysterious and intriguing trees once more. Speckarin and Diliani had told him that since his rescue the entire grove had flowered with blossoms of a golden hue, a sight Issar said was unforgettable. They also mentioned that the grove was exceedingly hazardous now because of the insidious potency of the fragrant blossoms. Hut was not anxious to go near the trees, but he was interested in seeing them in their present state. He was unable to locate the grove from this low altitude, however. And, not knowing the direction, he eventually gave up the effort.

A fleeting concern suddenly disturbed Hut. He wondered whether Runagar was acquainted with this part of the forest and knew where they were headed. Most important, did he know how to get back to the cave?

"Runagar!" he called, leaning to his right. "You know where we are, do you not?"

The Shillitoe youth had never observed this territory from anywhere but the ground. Nonetheless he answered Hut's question forthwith. "There, up ahead!" he said, pointing emphatically. "It is the pond where I swam frequently as a boy! It seemed so deep and wide at the time! Yet it looks so small from up here! And it seems so serene and peaceful! If only the otters down there knew where I was! They would destroy its tranquility in a hurry and put on a show for us!"

Hut settled back again, his fears allayed. As he observed his exhilarated cohort, he recalled the pleasure he had experienced on the first day of the quest, the day the party had departed Rogustin, the first full day of flight. Except for that part of him that wished to be home on Rogalinon, he had thoroughly delighted in the flying. He knew that Runagar had looked forward to this moment for as long as he could remember, his entire lifetime, and it was unmistakable how much he was enjoying the occasion.

All at once another thought came to Hut. Runagar and Faralan were doing so well that perhaps they could venture a little higher, where they would be able to make wide turns, not having to worry about trees, and where they could see further across the terrain, perhaps even catch a glimpse of the barwood grove. Almost simultaneously with this idea, however, came his own rebuttal: Runagar had never flown before, and he had been airborne for only a brief time. Granted, he had done well up to now, but he had certainly not been challenged. Should he be, he might in some way falter. Hut carried on the argument within himself for a while, but in the end his youthful and adventurous side won. His companion, after all, had a firm grip with his feet, just as he had been shown. He was piloting Faralan, a good raven, and he was doing so smoothly. Quite simply, Hut could see no harm in going to a higher altitude.

Hut had not been master of a bird ilon for very long himself, and was not fully aware of the depth and sensitivity of the creatures. Faralan was keenly aware of the circumstances under which Talli had been injured. No kirin had ever fallen from his back before, and the occurrence had disturbed him to the core. In addition, while in the cave, Faralan had observed that Hut, also stricken like his mistress, had suddenly reappeared to greet Lisam and seemed fully recovered. Yet his own mistress was still absent and the great bird remained deeply concerned. As an ilon, nonetheless, Faralan desired to please all kirins, especially Hut, one of the youths of the traveling party. He was conditioned and committed to anything Hut asked of him, and to doing it to the best of his ability.

Hut's control of Lisam had become skillful, more skillful than even he realized. He exercised it now almost unconsciously. The fact that he had not been master of a raven for long, however, and had flown on none other than Lisam, left him unaware of the intricacies and the subtleties of communication between kirin and bird. Each species of creature utilized as ilon has its own unique capabilities. Squirrels are able to climb with incredible agility and quickness, and to leap from branch to branch. A gray fox is capable of moving rapidly and of ascending trees adroitly, but hardly of becoming airborne. And ravens, of course, have limited capacities on the ground or even in trees, but they can climb and soar and bank through the air in a manner entirely alien to earth-bound animals. Instructions therefore must be different and more demanding from the back of a flying creature than from an earth-going one. A fox may travel either rapidly or slowly, and may alter its course to left or right. But a raven is capable not only of varying rates of speed and of turning in either direction, it may also climb or descend, adding a third dimension missing from all earthly creatures. Lifting off and landing, of course, are solely in the sphere of winged creatures.

Hut's plan had been to teach Runagar phrases in the tongue of curlace especially pertaining to birds. His intentions were virtuous, and his instructions were clear and concise. The commands he taught the Shillitoe lad were useful and appropriate. What he did not realize, as he concluded his session with Runagar and Faralan, was that neither of them was as prepared as he thought.

Faralan was eager to please and was well meaning. But deep within his heart his interest and concern remained with Talli, his fallen mistress. In addition, although he was not aware of it, one ramification of the accident was that his confidence in flying with a kirin aboard had been shaken.

Runagar had been aroused and enthusiastic, stimulated by the entire affair, eager to depart the ground. Unbeknownst to himself and to Hut, however, the commands he learned lacked sufficient complexity and depth to accomplish what they were intended to do. The combination of this and his inexperience upon a bird meant that they were heading for trouble indeed.

"Why not try going a little higher?" asked Hut of a glowing Runagar.

The Yorl lad needed to say no more. Runagar was eager to commence. Hut gave Lisam instructions to elevate the course of their flight plane slightly, and upward they went. Runagar wanted to accomplish the same thing, and paused momentarily as he considered various commands. Then he spoke the directive for descent.

Before Hut realized it, Faralan was heading for the uppermost branches of a stand of birch trees. Hut immediately circled downward, barking out the proper instructions as he approached. As soon as Runagar heard them he corrected the command, and a startled Faralan flapped his wings strongly as they skimmed the tops of the trees. They began to ascend rapidly, air streaming past the Shillitoe youth. To Hut's relief, Runagar appeared to be collecting his thoughts and recovering control of the bird.

Hut pursued Runagar upward and soon overtook him, telling him that he was climbing too quickly and that he should decrease both his speed and his altitude. Sensing that serious problems might be in the offing, he even suggested that they should turn back and return to the Shillitoe cave. The increasingly apprehensive Runagar agreed. As Hut reminded him of the correct commands, he called them out to Faralan.

But since the close call with the trees, the great bird and his kirin rider had somehow lost the interdependence, the synchronization, and the synergy that are key to kirin flight upon ilon. At the rate at which they were traveling, Faralan had recognized that they must not descend. Yet his temporary master had ordered it and the bird had responded by carrying out the instructions.

Faralan was undeniably confused. For the first time in his life he had begun to lose confidence in the kirin aboard, and he was bewildered. The unfortunate result was that Runagar's orders were greeted with hesitation. To hesitate at a kirin command is something ilon are never known to do. In a cooperative endeavor so intricate and complex as flying, even momentary inaction can prove disastrous.

As time went on, the confusion only became worse, the ilon wondering with each instruction whether this rider actually intended the movement called for. Because of the halting responses of the bird, the perplexed and frightened Runagar became himself more uncertain. Hut, for his part, was becoming frantic as he tried to steer Lisam after the erratic pair, calling out instructions all the while. But, if anything, this made matters worse for both Faralan and Runagar.

Had human observers been on the ground and gazed into the skies, they would have observed these two ravens with keen interest. They might have wondered what kind of attraction the first bird had for the second. Were they male and female in a courtship exercise, an ardent male chasing a coy female? Did the leading bird possess something, perhaps carrying it in its beak, with the trailing one attempting to snatch it away? Or was the pursuing bird angry because the other one had robbed a nest, attacked its young, or in some unseen way perturbed it? Never in their wildest imaginings, however, could they have guessed the truth, and if they were close observers of birds, they would next see maneuvers they had never before witnessed.

Hut doggedly followed the stymied Runagar. Faralan, now panicky, climbed until he was at a great height. He soared and then swerved to the left, hovered momentarily in the air with wings flapping wildly, dove steeply to the right, and veered off to the left again. Next he glided downward, spun rapidly around, and accelerated upward again. Runagar was helpless in controlling the bird, and Hut feared for the Shillitoe youth's safety.

"Hold on! You must hold on!" Hut called as loudly as he could, trying to stay somewhat near the careening pair. He wondered frantically what he could do to arrest the unpredictable flight, visions of Talli's fate running through his addled mind.

Suddenly an idea came to him: He recalled what Runagar had said, and what Diliani and Speckarin had mentioned previously, about Lisam saving him from the barwood tree. She had probably picked him up and carried him away from danger in her beak. Is it possible, he wondered excitedly, that she could perform a similar act in midair with the runaway Runagar?

Hut was conscious of how hazardous this would be. She could miss her mark and dislodge him, the two birds might collide in flight, or Runagar might somehow be disengaged after rescue and tumble earthward from her beak. But Hut could think of no other alternative. He knew of no other way to alter the terrifying predicament and he decided that an attempt must be made. Runagar had rescued him, and it was his turn to rescue Runagar.

Hut ordered Lisam to follow them even more closely. He stalked them, waiting for the right opportunity. As soon as Faralan came out of a convoluted series of turns, and the exhausted raven was drifting along slowly in a relatively undeviating line, Hut quickly directed Lisam to descend upon them. She was to concentrate all of her attention on the Shillitoe youth and to grasp him in her beak, by his garments if possible, and then to lift him off of Faralan and away from trouble.

Following his directions to the letter, Lisam dove immediately and did not level off until she was just above the other bird. There she glided momentarily and then intuitively performed an act that even Hut had not anticipated. The sable bird waited until her wings were beating in sequence with Faralan's, knowing that if they were not, the ravens might make contact, resulting in both of them losing a measure of control. As soon as they were flying in harmony, she edged her way downward. Coursing barely above the undulating body of Faralan, she focused her attention on Runagar.

All at once, to the astonishment of Hut, Lisam's wings ceased moving completely. She proceeded to soar above Faralan almost as if in a trance. She was hardly moving at all, and at first Hut was totally bewildered about what she might be doing. Suddenly he became aware of something emanating from below. It was a sound, and one that he would never forget.

Hut leaned to his right as far as he could, straining to see what was happening underneath. He could see Runagar and he could tell that an intonation, unlike anything he had ever heard, was coming from the Shillitoe youth. When he later pieced it together, he realized that it was this sound that had caused Lisam's wings to stop beating.

By the looks and demeanor of Faralan, the bird was now, quite astoundingly, under the control of Runagar. The Shillitoe lad was not calling commands, as he had been taught, and was not in fact speaking in any tongue Hut could understand. He was uttering syllables and words unintelligible to Hut. In addition to influencing Faralan, they appeared to be mesmerizing Lisam.

It was not only the language that astonished Hut: The tone and alluring quality of Runagar's voice amazed him even more. The intonation was a gentle yet penetrating monotone, deep-throated and mellow, interspersed with indecipherable phrases. Yet they were obviously meaningful to Faralan and Lisam. Both birds seemed completely under the sway of Runagar and his extraordinary voice. They were flying calmly, one above the other, Lisam moving her wings casually and in slow cadence once again.

Then, just as abruptly as it started, the voice ceased. Lisam began flapping her wings briskly and shaking her head as if awakening from a dream. Then she broke away from the other raven, swinging off to the right and flying normally again. Hut called out directions for her to remain close to Faralan, and she listened and responded in a routine fashion, maintaining contact with the other bird but flying now alongside him.

Hut called to Runagar, asking whether he was all right. The Shillitoe lad replied that he was, in his usual and natural voice. He said that he could now exercise control over the bird, a fact that Hut clearly recognized. The Yorl lad had no idea how Runagar was doing this, but it was hardly in a conventional manner.

Hut suggested that they land, and Runagar readily agreed. Hut scanned the landscape below, searching for an open area. He spied a grassy knoll only a short distance away and directed Lisam toward it. Downward they sailed, Lisam and Hut in the lead. As they neared the ground Lisam flapped her massive wings vigorously, decelerating until she was all but hovering above the turf, and then touched down.

Faralan landed next to them, and Hut leapt from the back of his ilon and ran quickly to Runagar's side. The Shillitoe youth was unharmed.

"What happened was my fault!" declared Hut. "You were not prepared for that sort of flight! But you turned things around, altering Faralan's behavior and even controlling my raven! It was the change in your voice, and both of the ilon responded to it!"

"Don't blame yourself entirely," said Runagar, looking less worse for the wear than Hut would have thought. "It was as much my fault as yours.

"I am not certain what happened after I lost control," he continued, attempting to explain what had occurred. "Just when it seemed there was nothing I could do to change the wild flight, something welled up inside of me that I did not know was there. Whatever it was altered the tone and articulation of my speech in such a way that I was capable of willing the bird to respond. Some of my words came in a tongue I have not utilized for years, in a language that is a form of curlace magic. It was taught to us by Queen Lanara when we were young, to use in influencing animals and birds other than ilon, should the need arise. It is an ancient kirin language. It goes back to the time before kirins and animals worked in concert. Kirins employed it to protect themselves from beasts in the wild. I had not used it for so long that I actually thought I had forgotten it. Yet it poured forth when I needed it most."

"I have heard of that practice from the past, the taming of animals," said Hut. "My father and grandfather have talked about it. But in our clan we were never taught such a language. I was not aware that it still existed. Perhaps our magicians know it."

"The Shillitoe tribe," explained Runagar, "has maintained a working knowledge of several old tongues, and of other magical methods relating to voice. Our magic today is performed chiefly with voices."

Runagar proceeded, but now as if he were puzzled. "I mentioned that only some of my vocalizations were in the venerable language. Something else occurred as I began to control Faralan, and this part I do not understand. More than the ancient language came forth from me. Words I have never heard, and therefore could not have learned, were intertwined with those I was taught as a child. I have no idea where they came from. I was as surprised by the whole process as you must have been, but very glad to be able to influence the raven. Upon our return home I must discuss everything with my family and our queen."

Then Runagar added a remark that Hut would never have expected. "Flying is the most enjoyable thing I have ever done! The first part of the flight was wonderful! After that it was ruined because I forgot the commands. Faralan got away from me. But that was corrected! I would love to try it again!"

"Right now would be as good a time as any!" said Hut with a chuckle. "After all, we must find our way home. For a short trip the two of us can ride upon Lisam without causing her any discomfort. Faralan will fly along with us, but without a passenger. You may have been able to control him with your voice and your old language. But I would prefer that next time you do it in a conventional fashion!"

He pointed a finger at Runagar. "If you came through that experience still desiring to fly," he laughed, "you are a born flyer! You should have seen yourself! I'm amazed you still want to do it!"

"I did not enjoy the last portion, of course," said Runagar. "But that was not the ilon's fault. Faralan is a fine raven. It was my mistake to be so eager to get into the air before digesting the instructions properly. Given another chance, I will take more time. And you are right about something. I know it and have known it all along. I was born to fly."

"I sincerely believe you were!" said Hut, shaking his head, amazed at his friend and the incredible events of the morning.

He thought about the trip back to the cave. He had done something to prepare for it. He recalled all too vividly the morning of the volodon chase, during which everyone concentrated so intensely upon the attackers that no one knew where they were when it was over. Since questioning Runagar about their whereabouts earlier, Hut had consciously recorded features of the landscape, even throughout their topsy-turvy excursion.

He described to Runagar how they would board Lisam in tandem, Hut in front. He instructed Faralan to follow them into the air, and not to tarry or wander, but to stay with them all the while, even though he would not have a kirin rider. They climbed onto Lisam and she took off without difficulty, Faralan flying behind.

Runagar, who was clinging to Hut, began to recognize the hills, ponds, and groves of trees, and together they had no trouble negotiating the way home. Along the way, having been reminded of the volodon incident, Hut cast apprehensive glances in all directions. They had been free of attack in recent days, and yet those and other terrifying creatures were doubtless lurking somewhere, near or far away, searching for Talli.

"I am anxious to be home again," said Hut turning toward Runagar, aware that the word referred to the Shillitoe cave. "I want to be with Talli again, and with Speckarin and Diliani."

He wondered about Talli and the sap that he had procured. It was possible that it had been distilled by now and administered to his fallen compatriot. Perhaps it had been successful in stirring her from her slumber. He pictured

Speckarin standing at the bedside, pensive, waiting to see whether Talli would arouse. The magician had been with him yesterday as he was shedding the effects of the barwood tree. Hut was in the picture himself, also waiting for a response from his unconscious friend.

Then he had a disturbing realization. Diliani was not there, not present in the scene at all, and yet she had been there when he had wakened. He wondered why she was not present in his mind's eye as he portrayed the vigil for Talli. He was puzzled, but he concluded that it mattered not, and he dismissed his omission of her as meaningless.

Little did he know that what he had experienced was a fleeting throwback to the ancient times of his ancestors, when kirins were able to look into the past and the future. What he had envisioned was a glimpse of an event yet to come. But not in the depths of his imagination, as he considered the absence of Diliani, could he have guessed the fate that had befallen her.

C H A P T E R   3

T HE ALARMED Diliani
knew she had no time to waste. Presuming that Speckarin
was still asleep, she did not delay her departure to waken
him. Moving immediately to the closest pathway for descent,
she climbed down the wall as rapidly as she could. Realizing
she might require a bird ilon to intercept Faralan, she ran
across the floor of the cave to the tunnel containing the
ravens. She saw, to her astonishment, that only two remained,
Manay and Ocelam.

Quickly astride a surprised Manay, she asked for speed as
the great bird stalked out into the open. To move more
quickly she commanded flight, and her ilon lifted off
somewhat uneasily and clumsily in the enclosed space of the
cave. They flew only briefly, a few strokes of the great bird's
wings, before arriving at the entrance through which Diliani
and Speckarin had come the day before. The flight was a feat,
however, that many Shillitoe kirins would have marvelled at
witnessing, since a flying kirin was a rare sight to them. But
it was early, and no one was present to observe.

Arriving in front of the dim orifice, Manay balked at the
prospect of entering, just as the other ravens had. It took

much encouragement in the way of curlace phrases and reassuring strokes before her ruffled feathers were calmed. Even then the ilon would consider re-entering the dark passageway only with Diliani on foot and in the lead.

This time, moving in the direction opposite that which they had traveled the day before, Diliani desired to hurry through the darkness. Knowing the tunnel's approximate dimensions and something about its course, they moved along as quickly as they could. Running through her mind was why Faralan, most likely accompanied by Lisam, would ever have left the cave, and especially through this tunnel, which she knew the ravens despised. At first she could think of no reason, and was nothing but perplexed. She did not tarry as she considered the problem, however, wishing to reach the outer exit and to be out-of-doors searching for the two missing birds as quickly as possible. As they moved haltingly through the blackness, she half-expected to collide with the other ravens at any moment, or to hear the low groans of their displeasure. But her passage was unimpeded.

Finally she caught sight of a slim shaft of light ahead. It was a long and narrow beam of sunlight, penetrating a perpendicular slit in an otherwise dim surface. As they came nearer she could see by the growing illumination that they were coming to the end of the tunnel and moving into a larger space. By the pale outline of the structures through which the light came, she could decipher their configuration. She was at the entrance. The light was filtering in through a crack between two giant doors. We entered the passageway here yesterday, she surmised. It is the doorway to the outside world.

"We will begin our search for Faralan and Lisam," she announced to Manay as they continued across the floor of a vast entryway. All at once she stopped, realizing that she did not know how to open the massive doors. In her hurry, and in her concern for the birds, the fact that she might have to open them had not crossed her mind. This cannot be a difficult procedure, she told herself. Shillitoe kirins must pass through here with great frequency.

She called out to any kirin who might be within earshot, who might be there to regulate the doors, or to any kirin who might perchance be in the vicinity. If anyone heard her, she asked, would they activate the doors for her and her ilon? She was searching, she explained, for two birds, two raven ilon who must have preceded her by only a few moments, and her business was urgent. But her pleas were answered only by silence. No one responded and the huge doors remained unmoving.

Undaunted, she began to stride back and forth at the base of the dusky walls, palpating their stoney surfaces for any evidence of a device that might control the doors—a lever, or a wheel, or any kind of fixture she could find. She could barely see the interior of the chamber as she moved along, light from the thin crack illuminating the area only obscurely. Nonetheless, she searched both sides of the space high and low and found nothing but cold, bare stone.

How could Faralan and Lisam have gotten out? she began to ask herself. We most certainly did not pass them in the tunnel! It was far too narrow and the ravens are too large to possibly have missed them. Perhaps they were not alone. Perhaps someone who knew how to operate the doors had accompanied them. But who? she wondered. And why? Who would possibly have wanted to remove Talli's raven and probably that of Hut, and coax them from the cave into a dark tunnel that all the ravens dreaded? For whatever reason? Finally, how did they open the doors?

There must be a way, she reasoned. After all, Faralan and Lisam are no longer here. The doors must somehow be operable from this location. She tried once more, calling out and searching the walls, but again without success. Then, moving to the base of the wooden doors, she pushed and pulled against them as powerfully as her strength would allow, but the massive structures did not budge. Eventually she discontinued her efforts, realizing they would be of no avail.

She turned and leaned against one of the doors for a rest. As she considered the situation, she became more and more convinced that someone had escorted the two ilon out of the cave and through the tunnel. Just as Manay would not, the other two ravens would never have entered the dark corridor without persistent coaxing.

We have little knowledge of these Shillitoes, she told herself. In conversation with an attendant at the fairinin the evening before, while Speckarin was investigating the condition of Hut and Talli, she had briefly discussed bird ilon. The attendant had said that Shillitoe kirins have never employed them because of the dangers in their use, typified precisely by what had happened to Talli. And yet, he said, another tribe living a short distance away did use a few bird ilon. Diliani had briefly wondered what species they might be. She did not ask, however, and the matter had not been discussed further. Could it be, she now wondered, that someone from the Shillitoe tribe had borrowed Faralan and Lisam and was taking them to show them off to the other tribe? Or even that someone from the outside could have entered the cave and abducted them?

Right now, she told herself, it does not matter. Faralan and Lisam are gone, and we can do little to recover them.

Having spent a good deal of physical and mental energy attempting to reach the outside world, but resigned that she could not do so, Diliani stepped away from the giant doors. She looked over her shoulder at the imperturbable and impenetrable structures, and walked toward the Shillitoe cave. We must return to the cave, she thought. I must alert Speckarin that the birds are missing. We will obtain aid from the Shillitoes in opening these unyielding doors.

She instructed the bewildered Manay to follow her back into the tunnel. What little illumination penetrated the doorway was soon gone entirely. As she proceeded in the direction of the cave, urging Manay to follow all the while, she was troubled by the idea that when Talli arose it was possible she would have no ilon.

"We must obtain help," she told Manay. "Then we will return and find the two ravens."

Onward they moved in total darkness, Diliani in the lead, threading her way along the passage. The tunnel undulated in its course, just as she recalled from her first encounter with it, and she spoke encouragingly to her beloved raven, knowing the trek to be far more painful and frightening for the bird than for herself.

Soon she began looking ahead for light, the circle of brightness she had seen as they approached the cave yesterday. As she peered ahead into the blackness no such light was forthcoming, but she persisted, feeling her way along the rocky walls and floor. She recalled Issar's shrill voice coming from ahead, beseeching them to follow, and explaining that the tunnel would narrow. She smiled as she remembered Speckarin's remark, after they bumped their heads, that they had doubtless discovered the portion that narrowed. Stretching arms and hands above her head, she was surprised to feel nothing.

"We must be moving more cautiously and slowly than I thought," she told Manay. "Let us try to go a bit faster."

She attempted to do so, and the bird followed faithfully behind. The tunnel fluctuated in its course and soon they found themselves scraping the walls and the ceiling.

"This is where it narrows," she said. "Be patient. It will take but a short time longer and we will see the brightness and once again be inside the cave. That, however, will be a brief respite, my friend, for we will be returning this way to look for Faralan and Lisam, just as we would for you if you were missing."

Here something occurred that took her by surprise. When she was certain that illumination from the mouth of the tunnel was around the next corner, the passage abruptly widened. She found that she was not able to touch the rocky ceiling. She did not recall this area of expansion at all, but as she mulled it over she thought of an explanation. During our trip through the tunnel yesterday, Speckarin and I were exhausted and I must simply have forgotten what the passageway was like.

They persisted along the tunnel, Diliani becoming more puzzled by the moment. Why are we not arriving at our destination, she asked herself? She strained with every step to see the welcoming glow ahead.

Suddenly she was going down a mild incline. Her right foot and then her left were becoming cold and damp, and when her right foot next stepped down it caused a splash. She stopped immediately.

This water was not here yesterday, she said to herself. And then she had a sickening realization: Nor was it, she noted with growing apprehension, when we passed by here a short time ago.

Could the water, she wondered, possibly have flowed into the passageway from an underground tributary, perhaps from the stream within the cave? It cannot have been here very long. Perhaps we can ford it, she thought. She moved forward, cautiously in the total darkness, placing one foot carefully in front of the other. But the liquid became deeper the farther she went, and when it was almost up to her knees she balked. She turned around and began to climb back out.

"Something has happened," she told Manay, who was just starting to follow her in. "This was not here before. You must change direction and go back!" She placed a hand upon the bird's neck and helped her turn around, and they both headed toward dry ground. "This water must have seeped into the tunnel from somewhere."

She stopped, wondering whether it was, in fact, water. She reached down and scooped some of the fluid into her hand and raised it to her nose. It was odorless and as it dripped from her palm and seeped through her fingers it felt like nothing other than cool water. Then they completed their ascent to the dry floor of the tunnel.

"I fear going farther into this water in such utter darkness," she told the ilon. "It might become deeper, or we might encounter something . . . unpredictable."

But now what do we do? she asked herself. If we cannot go forward we have only two other alternatives: waiting here for someone to come by, or retracing our steps and going back the way we came, back to the doors. Perhaps we should return to the entrance, to the gateway to the out-of-doors, where at least a modicum of light shines through. There, hopefully soon, we will be able to exit the tunnel and begin our search for the ravens. Someone will certainly pass by that way, either coming in or going out, and we will obtain help.

She moved again in the direction of the giant doors, Manay trailing behind. They progressed for a considerable length of time along the corridor. It bent to the left and to the right, and upward and downward, but for some reason Diliani found herself unable to recognize any of the features of the rocky walls, or the floor, or the ceiling. She became keenly aware of details of the craggy surface, the only clues she might possibly have to their whereabouts.

Once again she peered into the darkness, straining to discover the ray of light she knew was ahead, just ahead she hoped, from the slit between the doors. Nothing appeared, however, and they labored onward. In her mind they had no alternative.

All at once a disturbing thought struck Diliani. Could there be other tunnels leading to the Shillitoe cave? Could they be confluent with the one they passed through yesterday and traversed today? Could she have taken a wrong turn at some juncture in their trek? She recognized that she had no way of knowing these things, nor any means of finding out, and that all they could do was go onward. She tried not to think of anything but moving forward, and she encouraged Manay, and herself, with words of promise and success.

Now, as they felt their way along, she began at intervals to call out, asking whether anyone was able to hear, explaining who she was, that she was with a bird ilon, and that she was not certain where they were. After each such attempt she stopped to listen, quieting Manay, but she met with no response.

She and Manay soon began to fatigue, both from the physical effort to avoid collision with rough and harsh surfaces, and from mental stress. Although frustration and concern were driving her onward, Diliani eventually realized that they must rest. As they did, she again wondered where they could have gone wrong and where they might be. Could it be that a series of passageways exists, intertwining, convoluted, and interconnecting beneath the ground? Stopping here is not going to help us find the entrance, she concluded, and they resumed their progress.

After edging their way along for a considerable length of time, finding nothing but perpetual blackness and unending tunnel, they were both tired, and once again she called for a halt. They rested, this time slightly longer than before, and then moved ahead once more. They persevered for some time in this pattern, forward progress through the omnipresent darkness alternating with periods of rest. The more exhausted they became, the longer were the segments for recuperation, and the shorter the periods of exploration. Throughout they succeeded in discovering nothing more than continuing passageway, and after a while Diliani realized that she had no idea how much time had elapsed.

Finally she called for another stop. She stood still for a moment, her back against the wall. Then she slid heavily down the surface until she was seated upon the floor, her spine against cold stone. She shivered as a deep and unsolicited apprehension crept into her consciousness, one she had fought against but that she now allowed herself to recognize. For the first time since they had begun the ordeal, she admitted that she had no idea where they were. She had no notion where the tunnel entrance or the Shillitoe cave might be. The brave kirin refused to ruminate upon this disquieting recognition, knowing that to do so would be of no benefit. She reached out to touch Manay, already prostrate on the floor of the passageway, and spoke reassuringly.

"We must rest for a while and renew our energy," she said tremulously.

Harsh and strident sounds of distress were emanating from the raven's throat. With Diliani's words, however, the bird attempted to lift her troubled head and to turn toward her mistress. But uncharacteristically she gave up, unable to see anything at all, and she laid her head back on the rocky floor.

Gradually the sounds from the bird subsided as Diliani sat in the gloom. She was resigned to the fact that, at least for the moment, she knew not where they were. But she was convinced that when they resumed their search for the entrance, after another brief respite, they would eventually come across it.

Before long the spent raven was almost silent, the only noise Diliani could hear being the creature's quiet and rhythmic breathing. Even that became even more subdued as Manay instinctively calmed herself to preserve energy for the next inevitable foray into darkness.

Diliani, for her part, now forced her mind back into methods and concepts taught early in training. She utilized thought patterns and instructions designed for situations such as this, when one is lost or disoriented. Especially you children, she could almost hear her old instructor saying, remain where you are and protect yourself, for the clan will realize soon enough that you are missing. They will come for you and find you. Getting further afield will only make matters worse.

That is exactly the way it is in the forest, near the clan trees, she told herself. Unfortunately that is not the case now, she thought, a pang in her stomach, because no one here even knows I am gone. Speckarin was asleep in his chamber. Hut must have been also. During our hurried departure we did not encounter a single Shillitoe kirin. When they eventually discover that I am missing, they will have no indication where I am.

Not allowing herself to dwell on disheartening ideas, she thought of another survival technique. She mentally retraced their steps, both from the cave to the large doorway, and from the doors back toward the cave. As she searched her memory for a clue about where they might have made a wrong turn, she became drowsy. She did not combat the sensation; rather, she welcomed it as an escape from current circumstances. Shortly, she fell into a fitful sleep.

Before very long, however, she sensed something, something filtering its way into her dreams, a presence, the presence of someone or something. As she began to come back to reality, she realized that whatever it might be was within close proximity to her. Bringing herself abruptly back to life, she identified an unmistakable sound, one that Manay never made. Then, as she felt warm breath against her neck and cheek, she recognized to her great dismay that something unknown was not only close to her, but was sniffing her.

C H A P T E R   4

GRANDFATHER Versteeg eyed the kirin and squinted at the space it was pointing to. But naturally he could see nothing.

"I would very much like to meet your friend," he said to Gilin. "I could probably use his advice."

But as he could perceive nothing but Gilin, and since he was confused enough by the whole affair as it was, he turned away from the kirin's introduction almost as though it had not occurred, and went on with his lavage of the raven's injured extremity.

"My compatriot can help you," said the undaunted Gilin, clutching his calamar. "If you are not certain how to care for Loana's wounds, I know that Ruggum Chamter is."

"Who's Ruggum . . . Chamter?" asked Nathan. He and his brother were observing everything from the doorway with intense interest.

Gilin turned to face the two boys. "Ruggum Chamter," he said, "is a respected overseer of the Yorl clan, the clan of my heritage, which makes its home in a great tree many clan dominions to the west. But other kirins, beings like us, live the world over in many different lands and habitats. The two of us happen to be from a forest far away, and we cannot move onward toward our destination without Loana, the damaged bird."

Turning back toward the old man, he said, "My friend can undoubtedly help you with her."

The befuddled John Versteeg was still highly uncomfortable about conversing with a being as minuscule and anomalous as this. Wondering how he could possibly be doing so, he found himself carrying on anyway.

"Why doesn't he just step out and show himself?" he asked. "Is he hiding from us? We've seen you and we've been talking and you certainly haven't come to any harm. And I'm absolutely certain I could use his help."

"He is standing here," replied Gilin, "next to me, directly in front of you."

Then he revealed something that astounded the already shaken gentleman and delighted the two boys, something he had not mentioned in his discourse among the trees.

"He is not visible to you," said Gilin, "nor is he to any human being, nor has he ever been, nor have any of us for thousands of years, except under unusual circumstances. We have remained unknown for so long because we are invisible to humanity, to all of you, just as Ruggum Chamter is to you now. I am one of the very rare exceptions. For reasons too involved to explain, I was rendered visible to you, and as far as I know, to all humans. But our race exists, and we live the world over just as you do, and we are just as real as you are!"

"You do right work!" came the voice of an impatient Ruggum Chamter in halting English.

The humans heard it coming from somewhere in the vicinity of Gilin. The overseer had been growing increasingly uncomfortable, both by being in such close proximity to these giant beings, and by not being able to communicate with them about Loana. He had concluded that the only way anything would be accomplished for the suffering raven was for him to take charge of the situation. He had decided to speak even though he realized that in doing so he would be handicapped by three factors. First of all, he was repelled by the huge beings. Second, his command of the human dialect was lacking. And last, he was invisible.

Through the actions of the elderly human, Ruggum realized that this being must know something about taking care of birds. But it had admitted in the woods that it had not performed this kind of task for many years, and never on one with open wounds. And never, thought Ruggum to himself, on such an unusual and important bird as Loana.

Ruggum Chamter had been involved in this sort of activity for years, as had the kirin race for untold centuries. He concluded that the time had come to interject time-honored concepts of ilon healing into the proceedings. Mustering up what little of the human language he could remember, he determined that he would put his concerns aside and give it his best try. Upon seeing that the human seemed to be hearing him, perhaps even comprehending what he was saying, he went on.

"Wash much as can!" said the Yorl elder, his distaste and fears dissipating slightly as he became more involved in the process. He even took a few steps toward the basin to get a better look, and Gilin followed.

As time went on and the care of the bird proceeded, ideas and information were passed between the old kirin and the old man, Gilin acting frequently as interpreter, all of it to the amazement and great pleasure of the boys.

"I wish Pat and Mike were here!" Nathan whispered to his brother. "They wouldn't believe their eyes!"

Christopher knew his brother only too well. As they had been observing the incredible phenomenon unfolding before them, he had known this was coming.

He pulled Nathan back into the hallway by the arm. "You shouldn't tell them!" he responded in a harsh whisper. "You shouldn't tell anyone! Let's leave these little people or things alone! Let them do what they want to without anyone interfering! If someone else finds out about them, they'll all want to come out and see them!"

Christopher wanted to gain some time for the little creatures before what he envisioned would be an onslaught upon the scene, a madhouse, even a circus, all of it engendered by his brother. Nathan had never respected living beings the way he did. His brother would step on any ant or insect in his path. He would just as soon crush it as leave it alone. He might even go out of his way to do such a thing. Chris had always avoided injuring creatures if he could possibly help it, be they large or small. He realized that he and his brother were simply different. But with this little being and perhaps its invisible counterpart, he could see what was going to happen.

Over the past few weeks Chris had been in a dilemma. He had not decided how he felt about hunting wild animals and birds—mainly about shooting them. He had been swept into learning to shoot a gun on his birthday out of respect for his grandpa and his grandfather's love of hunting.

When Chris was younger, he had questioned the old man about the reasons for killing birds and other game. He had always remembered the answer.

"Chris, we all must eat," Grandpa Versteeg had replied. "I want you to listen carefully and think about what I am about to say. Is there a difference between these two alternatives? The first is this: For many thousands of years our ancestors have brought to earth wild creatures that populate the world. They have done so with their own skills and instruments to use the creatures for food. This activity is still possible in today's world in the form of hunting and fishing. Now, the second choice is this: Today one can obtain meat, sometimes the same meat that can be procured by hunting, by purchasing it in any supermarket in the land. That meat is harvested from animals sacrificed in a slaughterhouse. Now which of these choices is more noble and which is more degrading? I do not have the answer to that question myself, Chris, but I can tell you something. I am not ashamed to hunt and fish if the specimens brought home are consumed as nourishment. It is one of the unalterable realities of nature that every living creature must eat to survive. However, needless and wanton killing is never warranted, must never be approved of, and is to be condemned."

Christopher had not comprehended all the words, but he had understood the meaning of what his grandfather said. As he pondered it years later, he did not know the answer either. And he was still quite unsure whether he was suited to be a hunter.

Yet it was clear that Nathan had none of his qualms in these matters. In fact, he had shot the raven apparently on a whim. Chris knew his older brother would be impelled to tell someone about it. He knew Nathan simply couldn't keep it to himself.

Christopher's own instincts, however, told him that he should try to protect these little people, these tiny, intelligent creatures, only one of which they could see. He should try to protect them as long as he could. He realized that his grandfather was dazzled and overcome by the whole affair, and Nathan was already anxious to involve his friends. Chris recognized that he was probably alone in his feelings, and yet he was not surprised or ashamed by what he felt. These were live beings who apparently had a purpose. They should be left undisturbed in their progress toward this goal, whatever it might be, and aided by any feasible means. He resolved that he would help them.

The process of cleansing the bird's wounds was coming to an end. Ruggum described, for the most part through Gilin, the details of the next step, the dressing and splinting of the wing. John Versteeg listened intently and followed the instructions to the best of his ability. But as Ruggum explained what must happen, he became increasingly frustrated at the lack of usual materials. Eventually he stopped trying to communicate with the human and spoke to Gilin.

"In the home trees," he told his compatriot, "we would next utilize cords made of the kalas plant to bind the wing to the body. These would be covered by a coating of pitch from an evergreen tree, causing them to adhere, so that they would not slide off the raven's feathered surface. With a bird of this great size, and injuries of this magnitude, the healing time will be long and the splinting material must remain in place for much of the interval. Where are we to find cord made of kalas among these humans? They would know nothing of it! Second, when treating open wounds we apply a dressing to the open areas, a cloth imbued with liquid made from shavings of the leaves and stem of tominyeto, an herb with medicinal qualities. It is capable of reducing inflammation and of repelling the invasion of unwanted organisms, thereby preventing infection. How can we get access to a tominyeto plant here? And yet we have no time to tarry, for the untoward behavior of a wound like this begins immediately, simultaneous with the onset of the injury!"

Ruggum was silent, unable to conceive what they might do to obtain what was required for Loana.

Gilin was thoughtful for a brief time. Then he turned to Mr. Versteeg, who was waiting expectantly for the next suggestions. "We are stymied about what to do now," said Gilin. "The materials we normally employ are, we presume, not available here."

He explained what Ruggum had told him about the twine of kalas and the pine sap and about the herb called tominyeto. He discussed in detail the ways in which each would be utilized in this situation.

The old gentleman was gradually feeling less disturbed about communicating with the tiny beings. He knew that the situation was indeed real, and that their problems must be dealt with. He considered what Gilin was telling him, and then asked some questions about kalas and tominyeto. After thinking a few moments he responded.

"I know of something that might do the same job as your twine," he said, half to himself. "It would be sticky on one side. And I wonder whether one of our ointments would replace the herb on the dressing?" Turning to the two boys, he said. "Which of you will run and get the first aid kit out of the kitchen? It's in one of the lower cupboards on the right-hand side of the sink. Bring it here."

"I know where it is!" said Nathan. He turned and ran down the hallway and up the stairs. He soon returned with the packet his grandfather always kept there for emergencies. He handed it over to the old man. John Versteeg opened the kit and removed a rounded tin. Opening it, he found the end of a white tape, pulled a strip away from the reel, and tore it off. He then reached his hands down toward Gilin, demonstrating the adherence of the layer on one side, and the strength of the material by stretching it tautly between his hands. Gilin turned to look at Ruggum, who was examining the strip intently.

"I have never seen anything like it," Ruggum told Gilin. "Astonishingly enough, it appears as though it might work!" Gilin passed the overseer's tentative approval on to the human.

Next the old man fumbled through the other objects in the box, and came up with a small metallic tube. He examined the label for a few moments and then unscrewed the plastic cap. "This is what we call antibiotic ointment," he explained. "This particular kind of salve has the ability to fight infection. It's a little bit old," he said, turning the tube over in his hands. "The expiration date has passed. But it works well on humans with open sores or cuts. It might be able to replace the herb you use on your birds."

He turned his attention to the case again, and after searching through it once more he brought out some packaged dressings. He tore the wrapper off one and showed the gauze pad inside to his tiny guests. "We could apply some of the ointment to this material," he said, "and cover the open wounds in that fashion."

Ruggum was deep in thought. Never had he dreamed that he would find himself with this kind of problem in such foreign and undesirable circumstances. Yet the alternatives proposed by the human seemed viable.

"These things will have to suffice," the overseer said finally to Gilin. "What other choice do we have? Now, we must still deal with the immobilization of the wing."

Gilin expressed to the human that the supplies and

materials were adequate and could be applied to the bird. Relaying further information from Ruggum, he explained that the outer break must be splinted with unyielding struts, one on each surface of the wing, both the upper and the lower, and that they must be held in place by the white adherent strips.

The old man glanced intently about the work shop. His eyes fell upon a pile of small wooden scraps, intended to be used someday as kindling for the fireplace. He retrieved several of them and showed them to his tiny advisors. Together they selected a pair of lightweight smooth pieces. The old man trimmed them off with a small saw to the length indicated by the kirins, just long enough to span the wing from its tip to the outer joint. After dabbing ointment onto a folded dressing, he placed this over the distal wound, applied wooden splints to both aspects of the extremity, and carefully taped them into place.

"Adequate work thus far," Ruggum confided to Gilin. "Now we must immobilize the entire wing because of the more proximal injury."

He proceeded to direct, now always through Gilin, the method of accomplishing this. As he did so John Versteeg followed his instructions to the letter. First a strip of tape was wrapped about the entire body, just below the shoulder joints of the bird and underneath both wings. Another ointment-covered pad was gently tucked under the wing to cover the wound near the body joint, and a second tape was applied. This one was carefully passed around the upper portion of the injured extremity, running first along the under surface and then along the outer surface. It was joined then to the strip around the entire raven near the center of the bird's back.

"This piece will lend support to the whole wing," Ruggum explained to the old man through Gilin. "It is mandatory for breaks near the body joint, which would otherwise cause the injured wing to hang limply, the complete weight of the limb pulling downward from the damaged region. That would be both painful and disabling to the bird. Our job will be concluded," he said, feeling more and more satisfied with the results of their endeavors, "with one more strip of material. This must also be applied to the piece around the body, beginning inferior to the wing, passing over it, and then extending once more to join the body tape above." Grandpa Versteeg complied and finished the immobilization precisely as instructed.

"This latter strip," Ruggum went on, "will lend greater immobilization, necessary here because one break is near the body joint. It may be released after twelve or fourteen days to allow the wing to begin gentle movement. The other supports must be left in place for an additional period up to twice that time in a bird the size of a raven, perhaps even longer."

John Versteeg was also pleased with the results of their efforts. Whatever or whoever these little beings are, he thought, they seem to know what they are talking about regarding these procedures.

The injuries appeared to be the responsibility of Nathan, who fired the shotgun. But the old man had supplied the gun, and he was, after all, the boy's grandfather. He was happy to be able, at least in some measure, to rectify the situation and repay the miniature masters of the bird for the damages his family had inflicted.

The raven, which had been amazingly quiet and cooperative throughout, now seemed to be resting as comfortably as her wounds would allow. John Versteeg finally released his gentle grasp of the creature. He stroked it and finally stood back, satisfied that he had done everything he could.

Ruggum also stood still, recognizing that it was all over, silent for a few moments in wonderment of their accomplishments. Not long ago he had been profoundly discouraged about the prospect of this raven even surviving, and of Gilin and himself escaping unscathed. But consider what has been done, he told himself with rising exhilaration. Every procedure seems to have been performed properly, all of the splinting, immobilizing and cleansing. Now, with time, there is a reasonable chance she will heal, and we will be able to depart!

But most amazingly of all, he thought, was that every element of the execution, and the end result itself, had depended totally upon cooperation between human and kirin. He understood the significance of what had transpired, and could feel his heart thumping rapidly. He and Gilin had just witnessed, and had been a party to, the first known instance of cooperative endeavor since the time of their ancient ancestors.

By no means having gotten over the fact that Loana was assaulted, Ruggum found nonetheless that he was moved by the efforts of her attackers. He was incalculably grateful to the old human. He stared upward at Mr. Versteeg for a brief time and then glanced at Gilin, who was awaiting further instructions.

"Relay to it," began the old overseer, "that in these surroundings we could never have accomplished this without its help. I am deeply thankful . . ."

Here he halted. "Never mind," he said. "I will tell it myself."

Ruggum looked up once more into the face of the old man, knowing that he was not visible. He swallowed and took a deep breath. Then he began to speak, his English having been revitalized to some degree by the recent conversation.

"Humans and kirins . . . friends . . . long time ago," he said, starting slowly. "Kirins always want be friends again." He paused, as he carefully selected his words. "Maybe this is . . . beginning."

C H A P T E R   5

SPECKARIN AWOKE
refreshed after a long slumber and immediately arose, once
again ready to face the world. Today is the day, he thought as
he bustled about his room, when we begin to put our little
party back together and make plans to move onward. The
barwood sap must by now be distilled and prepared. How
fortunate we are that the boy Lindor discovered it at the
bottom of the stream! I only hope I will arrive at the healing
area before it has been administered. I would like to be there
for that. Soon Talli and her aris will be on the road to
recovery. I am certain it will succeed, he concluded, as he
donned his long yellow gown, freshly cleaned and pressed by
his Shillitoe hosts.

So anxious was he to be off that he took time to swallow
only a single bite of mushroom from the breakfast tray
delivered to his chamber. He strode quickly out the doorway.
Finding no attendants in the hall, he glanced briefly at
Diliani's door and hesitated. She must still be asleep, he told
himself. No reason to wake her. She has had as trying a time
as any of us and deserves to rest. I will send for her as soon
as something happens.

Turning away, he walked onto the veranda, viewed the magnificent cave for a few moments, and then departed for the fairinin. He traversed the ramps and stairways upward with vigor and enthusiasm and soon arrived at the entrance. There he stood, noting that the drone of the distillation engine had waned significantly, to the point where it was now only a low hum. He hoped this meant everything was going well within.

He stepped inside and looked down at the recumbent Talli and was immediately disappointed to detect no change in her. Just then he was greeted by one of the young attendants.

"I trust you rested well," said the Shillitoe kirin.

Speckarin acknowledged that he had slept soundly, making note of the sweet voice, a trait found in most of these new kirins. He had previously been too exhausted and preoccupied to think much about it, but it was certainly an unusual characteristic.

"Has any alteration occurred since . . . yesterday?" the old magician asked, hopeful that Talli was not worse than the day before. But he stopped because he was confused. Was it really yesterday that I was last here? he wondered. Or could it possibly have been the day before? I have lost track of time!

"How long did I sleep?" he asked inquisitively.

"Overnight and a short time into the morning," came the reply.

Speckarin glanced out into the cavernous space. The brightness within was the same as it had always been. How would this kirin know, he wondered, what time of the day or night it is? Could it be that in the vast interior of this cave the flames of illumination are somehow diminished during the night and rekindled during the day? No, it could not, he answered almost rhetorically. That idea is absurd! The torches are far too many and too scattered for that to happen. But then how do they keep track of time?

He asked and was informed that Shillitoe kirins possess an instrument that tells them the time of day or night and that he was welcome to use one if he should so desire.

"Thank you, but no," chuckled the old magician, shaking his head and thinking of the calamar. "I have enough trouble with the things I already have! I have never had use for anything like that, nor have I encountered anything like it. I think I will try to get along without it. But where is Lidor, and how is the processing of the barwood material coming along? It must be about finished by now, is it not?"

At that moment the fairinor appeared in the doorway of the small cavern. He saluted the Yorl magician. "You are looking marvelously better today," said Lidor. "And your young charge here," he said, pointing down at Talli, "is holding her own nicely, awaiting the moment when the essence of barwood is ready."

At least I have not missed the administration of it, thought Speckarin. He accepted the fairinor's invitation to once again view the distillation process. The magicians and the attendant moved to the rear of the space and stopped in front of the purring engine. There it was, percolating on the bench before them, the large door for the evacuation of noxious fumes still gaping open behind. The apparatus was working quietly now by comparison to the noise it had produced yesterday, and they stood for a time observing its operation. Low flames burned under several of the metallic fixtures.

Listening closely, Speckarin thought he could hear something new. It was a gurgling or a bubbling sound that he had not heard the day before. I could not have detected it even if it had been present, he concluded, because of the uproar this machine was putting forth. I am certainly glad now, he admitted, that we were not confronted with the task of processing raw barwood sap on our own, out in the forest.

After a short time Speckarin became anxious. No one is saying anything, he thought uncomfortably. Could that be an indication that something is wrong? He examined the heated apparatus more closely, although he had not the slightest notion what he should be looking for. Finally he turned to Lidor, who was observing the process placidly, and he spoke, trying not to reveal his concern.

"I trust the procedure is going as well as you had hoped," he said.

"Indeed it is," answered the fairinor, looking straight ahead. "But the essence is not fully prepared. It is impossible to predict precisely when it will be finished, but it appears that it will take a little longer. Unfortunately we can do nothing to hurry it up."

"But it is brewing properly and behaving as you would like, is it not?" asked an uneasy Speckarin.

"Yes, of course it is," nodded Lidor, perusing the machine.

I wish I knew what he was looking at, thought the Yorl magician, staring once again at the instrument. I can see nothing except that it is a foreign structure, warmed by flames, and making odd and confusing noises. I sincerely hope my fellow magician knows what he is doing, he thought impatiently. He gave the fairinor a sidelong glance.

"What, may I ask," said Speckarin, now pointing at the instrument, "was the last occasion upon which you enlivened this machine, and was it successful in distilling the sap?"

"It has been a long time indeed," came the reply. "Just how long I cannot recall at the moment. But it has been years since it was last in operation." The fairinor stopped there, offering no further information.

"Years?" remarked Speckarin.

"Yes," said the fairinor.

"For what reason," persisted Speckarin, "if I might be so bold as to ask, was the sap processed on that occasion?"

"It has been some time," answered the preoccupied Lidor, "since a kirin of our tribe, or of any of the neighboring ones, has been stricken sufficiently to require barwood essence. We have not had the need of the mechanism for perhaps . . ."

The Shillitoe magician paused and looked away, as though trying to recall the last episode. "I suspect it has been eight years, or perhaps as many as ten," he said. Then he stopped again and stared at the device as though his attention and concentration might serve to inject power into it.

Speckarin was frustrated at not receiving complete answers, and he asked, "Was the extract successful on that occasion?"

The fairinor responded cooly and in a mellow voice, contemplating the machine. "I think on that occasion it was not," he said without changing expression. "But as we discussed yesterday, one can never be certain of the effects of barwood essence. The results are not known until the liquor has been administered. Nonetheless," he said, now looking directly at his visitor, "what other choice have we?"

Speckarin glanced away. He knew no alternative existed. He was resigned to trusting the skills and judgment of these kirins, while knowing little about them.

He was apprehensive indeed about the prospects of the essence for Talli. There was nothing he could do about that, however, except wait. In the meantime, he decided, there is something else I can do.

"Would it be possible to have another audience with your queen?" he asked.

"I would presume so," replied Lidor.

The fairinor instructed his assistant to escort Speckarin to the dwelling of Queen Lanara, to inquire whether she was in.

Preparing to depart the healing area, the Yorl magician was saying a silent farewell to the recumbent Talli when Hut and Runagar sidled quietly through the entrance. They stood still momentarily observing Talli, and then glanced furtively at Speckarin.

"Well," said the old magician, taking notice of them. "Where have the two of you been? What have you been up to, exploring the cave or something even more interesting? You seem a bit quiet, though. Are you still feeling all right, Hut? Did you sleep well, little one, or should I say, did you sleep at all after your prolonged slumber?"

"I needed little sleep last night, sir," answered Hut. "I am fine today. How is Talli?"

"Her condition did not change overnight," replied Speckarin. "She still awaits the results of the distillation process, as yet incomplete. In the interim I will speak with

Lanara, queen of the Shillitoe tribe. You have not made her acquaintance as yet, Hut. Perhaps you should come along."

"I would be happy to join you," said the small youth. "But first, may Runagar and I have a word with you?"

"Why of course," said Speckarin. "What is it?"

"We were hoping to discuss something with you," said Hut, "in private."

"Well then," said Speckarin, curious to know what the youths might have in mind, "let us step outside."

The three of them moved out onto the terrace of the healing area. Runagar suggested they might go even a bit farther away, along one of the pathways. With Speckarin's interest building all the while, they proceeded to the entrance of another passageway, which proved to be unoccupied. There they stopped and stood for a few moments, Hut and Runagar eyeing each other while the amused magician waited.

"Well?" chuckled Speckarin after a time.

"Runagar," blurted Hut, "would like to join our quest!"

"What do you mean?" laughed the old magician. "You are jesting, of course. But our mission, my young friend, is not a matter to trifle with."

"I am perfectly serious!" replied Hut. "We have discussed it thoroughly and Runagar feels he was destined to join our party!"

The magician paused, the humor of the situation dissipating rapidly. He was astounded that the two lads seemed to be in earnest, and he allowed himself a few moments of consideration before responding. But when he did it was in unmistakable terms.

"Preposterous!" he declared. "What you are proposing is the most preposterous thing I have ever heard! Whether it was preordained or not, it is totally impossible! You have discussed this between yourselves, but have you considered it with anyone else? Have you examined what you are saying, Hutsin? How could it possibly be accomplished when no Shillitoe has ever flown upon a bird, when no Shillitoe possesses a bird ilon?"

"But he has flown upon a bird ilon," answered Hut. "In fact a raven!"

Speckarin was stunned and was silent for a few moments. Then he turned and spoke to Runagar, and his speech was in stern and measured terms. "Yesterday morning in the woods by the hemlock tree," he said, "Issar chided you for desiring to fly, and mentioned to you that there are many and varied dangers in flying. I assumed from what was said at that time, and from what I have heard since, that neither you nor any Shillitoe has flown upon a bird, and that Shillitoe kirins have no intention of flying, nor of allowing youths such as yourself to do so!"

"Yesterday morning I had not flown," said Runagar, "not in my life!"

"But Hut has just said," replied the increasingly perturbed magician, "that you have flown upon a bird ilon! And it was a raven!"

"I am afraid you will not like this, sir," interrupted Hut, "but early this morning we borrowed one of the ravens. We went outside the cave and flew, Runagar upon Talli's ilon. If you look downward now, you will see that the two ravens are still there at the base of the wall, Lisam and Faralan. We left them in the company of one of Runagar's friends instead of returning them to their den, to show you that they have been outside and used by us, and that Runagar has actually been flying."

Speckarin craned his neck and looked down over the edge. Not having noticed them before, he was amazed to see two of the ravens at the foot of the wall. For one of the first times in his life, he was speechless.

The youths cringed as the old magician turned to eye them. They waited some time in his glare before a response came. When he did respond, it was in a withering fashion, which was not unexpected, and the youths shuddered as he began.

The magician was dumbfounded, he stated, that Hut had abducted one of the precious ilon of the Moger clan. Had he not thought about the creature's untold years of training, to say nothing of its relationship with a kirin master, and its inestimable value to the traveling party? He had allowed a neophyte youth of a foreign tribe to take a frivolous ride! What about the safety of the untried youth? After all, what had happened to Talli, the experienced mistress of the very same bird? Did he not realize that the youth could fall from the bird and plummet to earth as Talli had? What then would a tribe of kirins say who were already distinctly opposed to flying?

The rebuke and harangue went on until Speckarin was spent. He finally dismissed the youths and sent them away, stating that he was thankful the Shillitoe youth had come through unscathed.

"I have changed my mind about you meeting the queen," he told Hut. "I am leaving to see her now. Go wherever you like. But you might do some good if you go to the fairinin and keep track of Talli."

Speckarin's logic and language could be pummeling, both in intensity and in effect, something Duan of the Moger clan had learned long ago. The youths had spoken little in their defense, except to say that Hut had given his companion a lesson in flying before they commenced. What was never mentioned, neither on this occasion nor at any time in the future, was that Runagar's ride had been anything but smooth. No one else would ever know how harrowing it had been, how close to catastrophe Runagar had ventured. This secret was forever kept between the two youths and served to bind them more closely together and to strengthen their friendship.

The two parties separated. Shaking his head, the disturbed Speckarin shuffled off, making his way toward the dwelling of the queen. The youths, for their part, were satisfied to go in any direction other than the magician's, and moved away toward the fairinin. Runagar stopped just long enough to signal to his friend below, indicating that the birds should be returned to their resting place. Then the two lads ambled away silently, each recovering quietly from the assault.

Finally it was Runagar who spoke. "Hut," he remarked, "did you notice something about what your magician said?"

"I noticed many things," replied his small friend, "and none of them were very pleasant. What did you have in mind?"

"After he heard that I have ridden upon a bird," said Runagar, "he did not deny my request to join your mission! In fact, he did not mention it again!"

"Does that give you cause for encouragement?" asked Hut incredulously. "In his oration and argument he became so aroused that your request to join us was the farthest thing from his mind, so out of the question that he never referred to it again!"

"But at least," said the ever-optimistic Runagar, "he did not mention it again! Perhaps something will change his mind!"

The youths continued upon their way, exchanging views on what had occurred and what might happen with the quest. As they talked, the Shillitoe youth's exuberance eventually began to rub off on Hut. Before Runagar was finished, Hut was almost believing that Speckarin would welcome the lad with open arms and be grateful for his presence on the journey. In the end Runagar convinced Hut that they should join Speckarin in his meeting with the queen to discuss their aspirations and plans.

The old magician found his way to the terrace of the queen. One of her servants informed him that she was not present. But she had given strict instructions that she wished to be called whenever one of the visiting party arrived. Speckarin was left alone for a time, which he passed in perusing the cave below from the vantage point the elderly queen enjoyed. He found the perspective to be appealing, the waterfall, the stream, and the entire landscape falling into an especially pleasant arrangement.

His musings were interrupted by the attendant, who touched him on the shoulder. Speckarin turned to see the wizened queen. She was resting upon her throne, examining him with eyes as bright and inquiring as they were the day before. What do we look and sound like to her? he found himself wondering.

He strode forward and stopped immediately before her. Feeling more familiar on their second meeting, he reached out his right foot and briefly touched hers.

"You look well today," she began in her reedy voice. "Are you rested?"

"I am feeling fine, thank you" said the magician. "Much better than yesterday. I will be even better when the barwood sap has been distilled, our youngster has recovered, and our small entourage is once again complete. Although your hospitality is unequaled, our goal is to be off as soon as possible to complete our expedition. We have a purpose. We must not be delayed any longer than necessary."

Exactly as the day before, at the magician's reference to their mission the venerable queen's eyes darkened and the color faded from her face. Yesterday he had begun to speak of gronoms and the havoc they caused among the home clans when she suddenly stopped him, visibly moved by what he was saying. But she did not explain why. By her reaction Speckarin concluded that she must be acquainted with the purpose of the quest, or with the new evil in the kirin world. She may have intimate knowledge of it, he thought. She pales at the mere mention of it. Once again his curiosity was aroused and he decided to inquire further.

"I wish not to cause you discomfort or alarm," he said. "But we are on a quest. Ours is a perilous undertaking. We are in need of any aid we can acquire, in the form of knowledge of our enemies, influence against them, or the kind of haven your clan is so generously providing. Is it possible, my good queen, that you have information, experience or insight into the problems I began to discuss yesterday? If so, it would be of the greatest help."

The wizened queen shifted uncomfortably upon her stony throne and was silent. Then, as though she was wrestling with some problem or inhibition deep within herself, she trembled, slumped back into her seat, and closed her eyes. After a few moments she opened them and spoke, and what she had to say was of profound interest to the fascinated magician.

"You need not describe the deadly creatures," she said, "nor elucidate their grievous activities. We know far too well."

She stopped again and appeared to sink into her own thoughts once more, and said nothing further. She was the first kirin Speckarin had encountered outside of the home clans who had knowledge of gronoms. Perhaps she knows something we do not, he thought, something that might be of benefit to us. He was determined to find out.

"What precisely do you know?" asked the magician earnestly.

The old queen seemed to revive somewhat, and again she spoke, but now almost as if in a trance. "My brother was a magician," she said, her voice a thin monotone. "He gained knowledge of something, something he would never reveal to me nor to any other kirin. Thereafter he was unmercifully persecuted and pursued. Finally he was slain. He lies entombed within our cave."

Slain! thought Speckarin. Slain! Both of our youths were rendered invisible by the fiends! But Olamin, he recalled, had revealed that the creatures had a number of options should they capture a victim, death certainly being among them. Why then were ours spared, only their state of visibility being altered, while her brother was killed? For this he had no answer. But he wondered whether this ancient woman might, and he anxiously persisted in his interrogation.

"Have you any information," he asked, "about the origin of these creatures or the powers behind them, what might be driving them?"

"I know nothing of those things," came the listless response. "I can only surmise that Hodorvon, my brother, was somehow too dangerous or threatening for them, perhaps too knowledgeable, to remain alive."

Is it possible, thought Speckarin, that his information was somehow different from that of our youths, and that his punishment was therefore more severe?

Without warning, the old queen was suddenly aroused and wide-eyed. "You are on a mission!" she said. "You are in search of the home of these vile creatures!"

"We are on a mission indeed," replied Speckarin. "But the exact nature of it is known only to the girl who lies in your fairinin, whose aris awaits barwood essence! She is the only one who knows where we are going and what might be required upon our arrival!"

The queen was alert indeed, sitting forward on her throne. But she was silent for a while as if in thought. "I want to help you," she said finally. "But I am not certain how."

At that moment Hut and Runagar clambered excitedly over the edge of the promontory, but stopped short as Speckarin turned to glare at them.

"You two do not belong here!" said the magician sternly. "Queen Lanara and I are discussing our quest! What we are saying is of the most profound importance! Please be respectful enough to leave us alone!"

"But," replied Hut anxiously, "we wish to talk about the expedition too!"

"You have talked enough about it already!" said the magician, now angry.

"Wait!" admonished the old queen. "What about the quest have the three of you discussed?"

"Nothing of importance," replied Speckarin.

"I would like to join the expedition!" declared Runagar.

The astonished queen looked on as the lad started an animated presentation of his desire to live outside the cave, and of his longing to fly. He described the sensation of flying, which he had done today, and he told of his lifelong desire to live in a tree. He wanted very much to go on the mission, he said, of which Hut had told him as much as he knew.

As the youth carried on, the queen was more and more involved and interested in what he was saying. Eventually she raised a wrinkled hand to stop him.

"Was it the bird of the fallen girl you rode today?" she asked. Runagar acknowledged that it was.

"And," interjected Hut without revealing the harrowing nature of their flight, "he flew so skillfully that at one point he controlled both his own ilon and mine, with a voice unlike anything I ever heard!" He went on excitedly to describe the tone, the words, and the effects of Runagar's voice upon the ravens.

The old queen came to attention. All at once she knew what she could do to help the traveling party.

Turning to the Yorl magician she spoke. "Would it be possible," she inquired, "to have Runagar take the fallen girl's place, should the barwood treatment fail?"

"I do not wish to think about that turn of events," replied Speckarin with gravity. "I wish only to think it will succeed."

"Naturally, we all do," said the old queen. "But if something untoward should result, would you consider including this Shillitoe lad?"

Speckarin's instincts told him that an additional youth would be nothing but trouble. Another youngster for me to shepherd, he thought with agitation. But he was not eager to disagree with the queen. She must, he conjectured, have good reason to even consider the possibility. I will not give an absolute refusal. And as things transpired, he was very glad he did not.

"Diliani and I would have to consider it carefully," he responded.

"Good," answered the queen.

She knew her tribe exceedingly well, and had come to recognize several things in Runagar. She had observed him as he grew up, and over the years she had seen that this lad was different from the other youths, especially in his desire to live in trees and in his longing to fly. Of her tribe, only the royal family was aware of where the Shillitoes had lived before moving into their cave. She interpreted Runagar's longings as an inward and atavistic recollection of what his ancestors once were. What he was describing were the revered customs of their ancestors, the old ways of living. She was enthralled that the ancient instincts and intuitions still shined through after all these generations. However, she kept her thoughts on this matter to herself.

Now, upon hearing that Runagar had impelled the birds to obey with a mysterious voice, using an old tongue of the Shillitoes, she realized to her satisfaction that two things had come together in him: the recollection of old times and the gift of voice.

The gift of voice was an uncommon but powerful manifestation of Shillitoe magic. Throughout the development of kirins in this region, tools and implements of magic such as calamars had become increasingly rare and now were all but lost. But they had developed other forms of magic, especially with regard to hearing and speaking. Infrequently one was especially endowed in voice. By the actions of Runagar aboard Faralan, the queen recognized that he was an occasional kind of individual, rarely born to the Shillitoe tribe, born with a gift. To outsiders all Shillitoes had unusual voices, but few could do what Runagar had done.

"If he is allowed to join you," she went on, "you will benefit from something you do not currently possess within your entourage, something he already has but that I can improve and magnify in him. This lad, young as he is, has a special power, one rarely found among us. Once it is enhanced, he will be capable of doing things that even you, a magician, cannot begin to do."

All were wide-eyed as they listened, for none of them, not even Runagar himself, knew about these capabilities. She offered no further information as she awaited Speckarin's response.

"But should Talli recover," said Speckarin, "this lad, no matter what his powers might be, will have no ilon!"

"No matter," answered the wizened queen. "That business can be taken care of easily through a neighboring tribe. They possess bird ilon. With his talents he will be able to direct one readily."

"It seems vitally important to you," declared Speckarin, "that this lad depart his home, his family, and this wonderful cave and accompany us upon a perilous quest!"

"It is," replied Lanara succinctly, "and for two compelling reasons. First, he has been endowed with an exceptional attribute, the gift of voice. And second, he is my slain brother's grandson!"

C H A P T E R   6

ANAY!" CRIED Diliani as she leapt to her feet.

In doing so she struck her head against overhanging rock, but she was so intent upon taking leave that she paid no attention to it. She instructed the raven to arise immediately and be off in the direction from which they had come.

The confused Manay struggled to her feet, turned with difficulty in the gloom, and followed her mistress down the tunnel.

Diliani scrambled away as quickly as the darkness would allow, deeply apprehensive about who or what could have been so close to her, investigating her as she awakened. She glanced back many times, but to no avail. She could see nothing because of the total blackness, and she did not tarry to listen for anything coming after them. They progressed for a considerable period of time, making their way as rapidly as they could, the alarmed kirin looking frequently over her shoulder, straining to discern what, if anything, might be trailing them.

As they moved along, something strange happened to Diliani. The length of time she had been in the darkness, the anxiety she was suffering, and her profound need to see all seemed to coalesce. Together they created a haunting desire, a yearning, but one she had never before experienced. She became aware of a hunger, a craving, for something she had not sensed for she knew not how long, for something simple, something commonplace, something totally natural: for light. Although she was unaware that it could happen, her brain was starved for light, and also for color, which goes hand-in-hand with illumination.

As they progressed onward through the gloom she began to imagine that she could create light in her mind, that she could project it backwards toward any pursuer, and that she was able to illuminate and envision whatever it might be. In her desperation she actually attempted to do so. She hoped that some deep and previously unfathomed capability from the past when kirin magic was potent would suddenly come to the fore and cause a dazzling flare within the corridor, allowing her to see her tormentor, even if momentarily. But of course she failed, and could only keep pressing forward.

The requirements for light and color still clung to her being, however, and she began to fill her mind with visions of anything that might glitter, and glisten, and sparkle. Through her memory she could bring back scenes of the pale and deep greens of a summer meadow, of the glimmerings of a wavy blue pond, and of clan gatherings by flickering yellow firelight. But her eyes perceived nothing, and this blindness, in the midst of everything else happening, was wearing deeply on her.

As they moved haltingly through the dark, she considered that her longing might be dulled by imagining something bright, and the most lustrous thing in the world was the sun. She had lost track of time. She wondered whether it was daytime or nighttime outside, whether the sun was still high in the skies or had already set beyond the western horizon, the moon now aloft. She had no way of knowing.

How she yearned, in her midnight of gloom, for the sun. She pictured the inviting glow of an early sunrise, viewed from the branch just outside her door on Rogalinon. She thought of the brilliance of the sun in a cloudless blue sky at noontime, directly overhead, illuminating every green pine needle, every bursting bud, every red berry in the forest. What a miracle it was, she thought, that something—anything—could possibly be so splendid and dazzling as to be capable of doing that. Lastly, in her mind's eye she composed a portrait of a radiant sunset, a peaceful lake in the foreground, lengthy thinning clouds brushed with hues of yellow, pink, and gray hanging above the orange disk of the sun. All was mirrored in the quiet water, the sun descending inexorably beyond the far shore.

But she found to her dismay that these images did nothing to satisfy her longings, and if anything brought them into keener awareness. She tried to force them out of her mind, to think of something else, anything else.

Her hearing was unimpaired, she told herself. When she decided that they must rest, she stood very still. She held her breath and utilized one of the senses she still had: She listened intently for any sound coming through the gloom. But she heard nothing, save the sound of the faithful raven's breathing.

Diliani was profoundly uncomfortable about her circumstances, and about the possibility that she was yet being hounded by an unknown and unfathomable pursuer. Though she had detected no evidence of such a creature throughout the trek, she urged Manay to depart once more. Off they moved for another considerable distance until she finally called for a halt. When she put a hand to her head she felt a knot where she had struck against the ceiling. But she paid no attention to it. Again she strained to listen for anything, and this time she thought that she was actually perceiving something.

Trying to quiet Manay with subdued commands and gentle caresses, she struggled to hear. She could detect an almost imperceptible sound. She wondered whether it was there or was just a figment of her imagination. Nonetheless, after listening for a while she felt that something was there, barely audible as a low, steady sound. And then, since it was the only thing she could sense, other than her companion Manay and the rough surfaces of the tunnel, she decided she should try to ascertain which way it was coming from and what its source might be.

Their progress began anew in the direction in which they had been moving. Diliani took pauses in order to listen, each time asking the raven to be as silent as possible. As the noise appeared slightly stronger each time, she became more and more curious about what it might be. Her spirits rose as she considered that it might be coming from the out-of-doors, or from the Shillitoe cave, or from some other form of local kirin activity of which she was not aware.

One time when she stopped to listen, the noise was a little fainter. She thought again that her imagination might be playing tricks on her, and she instructed Manay to go onward. But the next time the sound was perceptibly diminished, and she was momentarily perplexed. But she decided that, even if they should run directly into a pursuer by doing so, she would turn back and pass through the same section of tunnel they had just traversed, to discover whether the sound would increase. They did so, and this time she stopped more frequently to judge the volume. To her satisfaction it grew louder, but eventually it diminished. She turned around again, and investigated back and forth until she was certain they were at the point where the sound was loudest. And there she stood, leaning against the cool, rugged wall and listening.

As she attempted to characterize the noise, to describe it to herself so as to better identify it, she found it varied slightly in volume, throbbing or undulating mildly. At times it was more a low vibration than a sound, coming through the passageway or somehow through the walls. To even better assess it she moved instinctively across the corridor, in the direction from which it appeared to be emanating. But where she expected to encounter the rocky wall of the opposite surface, she met with nothing. She realized immediately that she was entering another passageway, a new one jutting off the one they had been traveling. To her delight, as she moved farther forward, a hand upon one wall, the sound grew louder. She turned back and called for Manay, asking the raven to follow, and together they ventured in this new direction.

Shortly after they started, her hand encountered something on the wall, and she stopped. She explored the object with both hands. It had an odd smell, an old one, very faint and yet pungent, and quite distinct. It was the odor of something burnt. Suddenly she recognized what it must be. Hanging on the wall of a tunnel completely devoid of light, this, she surmised, must almost certainly be something that had burned with fire, a torch of some kind, probably very old but doubtless kirinmade.

It was the first sign of kirin life Diliani had encountered since being before the massive doors to the outside world. Now she wished she had taken the time to bring her belt satchel. In it she had flint and steel for starting fires, with which she might be able to bring this ancient firebrand to life. But she had departed the terrace so hurriedly that she had left everything within her guest chamber. How she wished that she had taken those few moments to bring it with her!

She left the object hanging where she found it, and moved forward toward the noise. In her progress she encountered many more of the pieces she interpreted to be ancient torches hanging on both walls. They were once employed, she imagined, to bring brightness to this black tunnel. Her confidence was bolstered even further as she pictured the corridor as it must have been in the past, lined with blazing torches, resplendent, orange fire lapping against the walls now enclosing her.

The rumbling was ever more perceptible as they moved along. Even if it were something dangerous, she resolved, she would not deny herself the opportunity of discovering it. While she was not eager to encounter peril, she wanted to find something, anything other than cold stone and utter darkness. Onward they proceeded, and as they did so the muffled sounds increased steadily until they became a dull roar.

All at once she knew what it was. It is the sound of moving water! As they progressed ever closer, the bubbling, splashing, and surging from rapidly coursing water could be heard. But it was even more than that. It was as though water might be falling, or cascading, or merging with another body of water, but it was very difficult for her to be certain. And, as she moved even nearer, still with no light and the floor of the tunnel becoming damp, it was apparent that the source of the swelling sound was imminent. As drops of moisture splashed onto her feet, she slowed her progress appreciably and instructed Manay to do likewise, so that they would not inadvertently slip, or slide, or step into whatever body of water this might prove to be.

Very shortly she was glad she had done so. Her skin and clothing were moist, and the floor was soaking wet and treacherously slippery. Suddenly, as she was feeling her way gradually along, her right foot passed over the edge of what appeared to be a promontory, her forefoot all at once unsupported, while her heel remained upon a firm rocky surface. She stopped immediately and cautiously placed all her weight on her left foot. She was beginning to step backwards onto solid ground when her backbone suddenly encountered the head of the forward moving Manay. Diliani's shrill cry arrested the startled raven in its tracks.

Diliani wavered for a moment, trying desperately to maintain her balance. But the forward impulse was too great to overcome. Unable to right herself she toppled forward over the brink, plummeting headlong into the abyss. Descending through the air for what seemed an eternity, but was actually only a matter of moments, she struck a cold surface of water, and her momentum carried her well under.

In addition to being good climbers, kirins are exceptional swimmers. Whenever the need arises their long and sinewy feet are capable of propelling them powerfully through water. Thus it was that Diliani was able to turn herself around underwater and rise almost at once to the surface.

The water was choppy and wavy, and she found herself

being tossed about. She assumed that the water was moving, that she was being carried downstream, and judging from the resonance of the deluge around her, probably at a substantial rate of speed. And yet she could feel little if any undertow, or even current. She thought the stream might be conveying her so powerfully and smoothly that she could not actually detect it.

She swam in the direction she surmised the wall to be, and soon she located it with her hands—hard, stoney, and slick. But here, she discovered, the water was only lapping against the rock on both sides of her. The wall appeared to be stationary. It was not passing her by, as it would seem to be if she were being dragged by current. To her surprise and delight, she was not moving downstream at all! At least in this portion of the stream, or whatever this might be, there appeared to be no current.

Grateful for this bit of good fortune, she clung to the clammy wall and called upward to Manay. "I am all right!" she stated. "I have fallen into water! But I am not harmed!" Then she gave several commands. "You must remain exactly where you are! You are a brave bird, and a faithful one! But you must make no attempt to rescue me! You must not move! I must know where you are at all times! I would not be able to tell that if you should move!"

She was not certain Manay had heard her instructions over the din of the churning water. But she was deeply afraid that the great bird would try to climb down after her, or even to fly down, and she knew what perils such an attempt would entail. The effort would almost certainly fail, and in the process she might lose the ilon. I will try to work my way out of the water on my own, thought Diliani, and then climb up the wall using my own power, without any risk to the raven.

Thus she began palpating the wall with her hands, and to her dismay found it to be sheer and featureless. She moved to her right and to her left as she explored. But she did not wish to stray far afield, fearing that in the dark she would lose her orientation. She might venture too far from the precipice over which she had fallen and not be able to find her way back.

She knew Manay was waiting above, but the bird seldom uttered a sound, and in the tumult she recognized that she would not hear the raven even if the bird made a strong call. She continued to search, but could find nothing to grasp, even with her capable feet.

Kirins are adroit climbers of inclines, even steep ones. If they can find a toehold, they can ascend even vertical surfaces. And Diliani might have been able to climb this rocky face had it not been for two factors. The surface was saturated and slippery. In addition, the wall was not even perpendicular: It angled toward her as it rose. She made many concerted attempts, but was unable to scale it. Eventually she suspended her efforts and dropped back into the water.

"Manay!" she called once more, fearful that the bird would try to do something. "Stay where you are! I am all right!"

But she was not all right, and she knew it. She had run out of ideas for escaping the water—and at least temporarily out of energy. She was more concerned by the moment about her predicament. Treading water adjacent to the wall, head bobbing above the surface, Diliani tried to think of how the bird could help.

All at once she felt something touch the left side of her face. It moved, and instinctively she swept it away with her hand, having no idea what it could be. But it returned momentarily, brushing lightly against the opposite cheek, and again she batted it away. She sidled quickly to her left, hands walking along the wall, but after she stopped and waited, the thing found her again. This time she felt it on her forehead, and she shook her head violently, and swiped frantically at it. By then, having made contact with it three times, she began to develop an impression of it. It was something thin and pliable.

The next time it found her in the dark, once again upon the left cheek, she pawed at it out of frustration. Then she grasped it, with one hand first and then with both, and found that unlike anything else around her it was completely dry, and it was not slippery. As she struggled to identify it, she felt it and tugged at it and smelled it, and suddenly she thought she knew what it was. Having no idea how it came to be dangling here, what she held in the firm grasp of both hands was nothing other than a rope, coming mysteriously and miraculously from somewhere above!

C H A P T E R   7

DILIANI HELD ONTO
the cord as tightly as she could. She tested its integrity by
jerking on it several times and giving it a strong, steady
pull. It appeared to be anchored firmly above, and with that
knowledge, she hesitated not a moment longer. She began to
haul herself upwards. But before she was even partway out
of the water, she was amazed to find that, without any effort
on her part except to grip the rope, she was ascending as if
she were being drawn upward. She found herself being
hoisted out of the water, and then up the wall by someone or
something unknown. Grateful for any help she might
receive, and from whatever unseen source it might come,
she hung on tenaciously and allowed her feet to walk up the
wall, scaling the steep face of rock as she was lifted
powerfully aloft. Reaching the rim of the precipice, she
stepped over it, still clinging to the cord. As soon as she
was standing upright next to the greatly relieved Manay, the
rope slackened at the opposite end and dropped limply to
the floor in front of her.

Dripping wet, she stood for some time peering into the
utter darkness of what she knew to be the tunnel, wondering

who or what her unknown benefactor might be, but there was no communication. Eventually, as she could see nothing whatever, nor hear anything but the churning water she had left behind, she released her end of the cord, and it too fell to the moist floor.

She attempted to dry herself, but without much success. Then she turned to Manay and stroked her neck, speaking soft and comforting words into her ear, finding as much relief in them herself as the great bird did. As still no further evidence of her savior came, she finally determined that she had no alternative other than to act herself. She decided to scour the area for any chance of help or any hope of escape.

"We must investigate this dark space further," she told Manay as she turned back toward the water and the overhanging face of rock. "I will search to the right first."

She sensed that the flow was coming from that direction, but she had no idea why she thought so. Cautiously she made her way across the damp floor to the wall, where she followed it with hands and feet, outwardly toward the brink. There she noted that the upper portion of the wall came to an end, while a very low segment and the rough floor went on toward the water. With her sensitive feet, drops of moisture spraying over them constantly, she detected that in this lower extension the texture of the wall changed: It became smooth and even. As she felt further, she found that it, and the floor, ended at the edge of the promontory.

She continued to investigate this formation with her feet, following the undeviating and perpendicular surface upward. She soon discovered a second surface, contiguous with the first but at a right angle, running away from her, parallel to the floor, and this one was just as flat and smooth as the first. Beyond that her foot encountered a second vertical surface, then a new horizontal one. She found herself becoming excited, but attempted to rein in her eagerness because of the need for extreme caution. What she was feeling was something recognizable, something commonplace, something found almost everywhere within the Shillitoe cave, yet was virtually unknown to the clans at home.

These cannot be natural stone formations, she reassured herself. They must be the same as structures employed for climbing within the Shillitoe cave! They must be stairs, built or carved by kirins, and as such they signal the prior existence of our species in this location! These have been hewn out of solid rock by kirin hands and kirin tools, and they must lead somewhere, probably back into the cave! What other purpose could they serve?

She bent forward and tested the superficial features of the stone with her hands. Though they were damp, everything about them was solid and even. Next she applied her right foot to the first slab, and with her right hand upon a wall that seemed to rise with the stairs, she stepped all the way up onto it. She stood there for a moment palpating the outside edge of the plane with her left foot. It came almost immediately to the border, beyond which she could sense that there was nothing but air and spray, with tumultuous water below.

Turning back toward Manay, she said firmly, "You must remain here! You must not follow!"

Again facing the direction in which the stairs appeared to be going, she raised her left hand above her head, recalling the blow she had previously received from the ceiling, and ascended one step at a time. As she climbed she noted that despite her increasing elevation the roar of the water was constant, or perhaps even grew in intensity. The stairway became more saturated and more slippery the further she rose through the total darkness.

Because of the foam and noise she encountered no matter how high she climbed, she eventually decided that the stairway must have been constructed beside an underground waterfall. It must cascade into the pool below, she told herself, and all at once she had an explanation of why she had sensed no current in the water. I must have been near the place the waterfall enters the pool. That area would be calm, the current building elsewhere, where the water empties out of its rocky confines.

Upward she progressed step by step, so many by now that she could not begin to guess the number. She wondered where she was heading, what she might be getting herself into, and whether the ascent would ever end. The smooth slabs seemed more drenched and ever slicker the greater the elevation she achieved.

All at once, as she placed her weight on the polished surface, her left foot skidded toward the brink. Momentarily she lost her balance, as she had earlier on the precipice. But she caught herself this time and clung to the craggy wall, her heart beating rapidly.

After catching her breath she began her ascent once again. Suddenly her left hand encountered a dripping, rocky surface above. She stopped immediately, having come to, she surmised, what must be the roof of the space. She searched with both hands for evidence of a door, for any kind of latch or hinge, or any opening. But to her dismay she found nothing other than cold, perspiring stone. Crouching, she felt the remaining few steps with her hands, and found that they ended at the ceiling.

She had apparently come to a dead end. After convincing herself of this, she had no alternative other than to descend. She would try searching another area, the opposite side of the promontory. Turning carefully about upon the wet surface, she began to move downward with measured steps, wondering what kind of a staircase this could possibly be that was built to end in nothing, to lead nowhere, but she had no answer, and disconsolately continued the descent. Not having thought to count the stairs during her climb, she did so on her way down. When she finally stepped onto the rugged floor of the tunnel, and was greeted by Manay, she had descended eighty-eight stairs.

"Manay, I must look to the other side now," she said. "I found nothing useful on this one. But I did find kirin stairs, and kirins must have been here at some point in the past. I am certain now that we will find our way out."

Creeping past the raven she found the opposing wall and

again moved cautiously outward toward the precipice. Clinging to the wall with her hands, the brave kirin found its border with her feet, and discovered that on this side also the craggy wall ended before the floor. Instead of stairs, however, here she found a narrow ledge cut into the bare stone over the water, sheer wall above, and restless water below. It must be a pathway, she concluded, stirred once again by the prospect that kirin hands had hewn it out of the dense rock. It is one more piece of evidence, she told herself, that kirins have been here before!

Buoyed by this newest discovery, she turned again to her faithful raven. "Wait here, Manay!" she repeated. "Do not attempt to follow! There is no room for you on this ridge!"

The great bird obeyed and made no attempt to pursue her kirin mistress as Diliani edged her way onto the strip of rock. She began to creep deliberately in a direction opposite that of the stairs. This must lead to something, she told herself, as she felt her way slowly along the narrow shelf. She soon found that she was unable to progress while facing the wall, both hands against it. Her feet were too long to be accommodated by the slim ledge. She was obliged to advance, albeit slowly and cautiously, one foot in front of the other.

She progressed methodically, but she thought she had accomplished a substantial distance, when the pathway, as far as she could tell, began a gradual decline. As she followed the mild descent, she noticed that the sounds of the water were diminishing. Soon, however, they became louder than before, the agitated waters appearing to be nearer than ever.

"I hope your course takes us both into the Shillitoe cave," she said, addressing what she presumed to be a building and coursing stream below.

Along she went, moving ever farther from the mouth of the tunnel and from her beloved Manay. At one point, as she placed her right foot forward onto the meager shelf, the surface shifted. Then the rock began to crumble, and next to disengage, and all at once the only support she had was under her left foot. She clung grimly to the clammy wall, hoping that nothing further would yield, as she heard fragments raining into the water below. Slowly she elevated her front foot and brought it back toward the other and found what appeared to be a secure foothold. Then, carefully extending her foot beyond the defect, she tested the shelf on the far side, found it apparently stable, and placed her weight gradually on it without incident. Stepping cautiously across the gap, she continued her slow progression toward a dark and unknown destination.

She had moved considerably farther when all at once she caught sight of something ahead, something she could not believe she was seeing, something she had yearned for and had longed to discover for an interminable length of time. She blinked and momentarily turned away, but then looked back, shielding her eyes with her hand. Ahead, but how far she could not estimate, was a pinpoint of brightness, an insignificant spark of luster. It would have been overwhelmed, irrelevant, and totally lost under any other circumstances. But here, streaming through the blackness, it was almost blinding after such an endless period in the dark.

It was a single streak of light, but one that conveyed far more than illumination alone. It was not only a ray of light, but also of hope, both for herself and Manay, and she was overjoyed at its discovery. She was jubilant, and had to remind herself to be deliberate, and calm, and not to move too quickly, nor to make a false step. But she found that she could not restrain herself from such an instinctive desire as to be reunited with light, which she had never before known she required, but which this horrendous experience had taught her she truly did. The radiant beam seemed to beckon to her, and she hurried toward it.

But even as she did, she was also relieved to discover that the pathway broadened and blended with a wider area of cave flooring. As she moved toward the small ring of brightness she found herself running, and tripping over outcroppings of rock and slipping on loose pieces of stone that she still could not see. All at once she encountered a ridge and had to

clamber over it. Then she stumbled up a mild ascent, the
growing jewel of brilliance ahead of her all the while.

Finally, as she approached the diminutive circle of light,
she could discern that it penetrated the darkness through a
small gap in the rocky wall. She took the last few steps and
pressed her face against the hole, large enough to
accommodate just one eye. As she stared through it, the glare
was blinding, and she was forced to turn away because of the
sheer magnitude of it. She drew back, waiting several
moments, blinking the remnants of brightness out of her eye.
But she was starved for light, so long had she been in a world
wholly devoid of it. She looked through the opening again,
and slowly became accustomed to the brilliance.

When able to see clearly, to her profound joy she saw
what she had hoped for: Before her was a panoramic view of
the Shillitoe cave. She reveled in her vista from on high,
allowing herself to drink in every wonderful aspect and
delightful detail of the scene, even locating several Shillitoes
moving about upon the floor of the incredible space. She
thought of crying out, but she hesitated, certain that her voice
would not be heard through this tiny a hole and from this
great a height. I can always call to those below, she told
herself, if I can find no better means of communicating. But I
will search this wall for a larger opening.

She allowed her eye to find locations she was acquainted
with. She saw the fairinin, and she wondered whether Talli
still lay within, whether she had already been administered
the essence of barwood, and whether she had awakened. She
found the route leading downward from the healing area,
along which she and Speckarin had escorted the intoxicated
and erratic Hut, and she followed it all the way to the guest
chambers. She smiled as she recalled the dizzyingly
precarious trek they had experienced while accompanying
him. Next she sought out the tunnel to which she had led the
ravens in order for them to rest. She was gratified to see that
they were present, but from this great a distance she was
unable to identify the birds individually. Finally she looked

back toward the guest chambers, and recalled the breakfast that had been brought to her, the last meal she had eaten, and remembered that her clothing had been cleaned as she slept.

Now, as she took her eye from the hole and looked down at her garments, she could see them only dimly by the light filtering through. They had been saturated with water and were frayed and torn from the abrasive rock. They are a far cry, she thought, from the way they were when I put them on.

Looking again through the aperture she recalled that it was from the terrace of the guest chambers that she had spied Faralan departing the cave, she knew not how long ago. But it was that discovery that had led to this fluke, this fiasco, she thought miserably, of being trapped with Manay, so tantalizingly close to the others, and yet so exceedingly far away.

Then, to her right, she caught sight of something vast. She turned her eye in that direction to see the waterfall, tumbling gently and gracefully, or so it appeared from her vantage point, into the cave below. What she had hoped for was in fact the case: The underground water she had fallen into and had been progressing adjacent to did indeed form the cave's waterfall. She marvelled at the sight of it, shimmering and glistening as it cascaded into the cave from this great height. That water is going where I wish to go, she told herself. Just as it has, I must discover a way through this wall. It has found a pathway out of this dungeon and into the light. I will do the same.

She forced herself away from the opening, away from the light, and back into the blackness of her cave. She had business to attend to, and she scrambled away toward the stream in search of a larger opening. Skirting the craggy wall and examining each part of it in detail, she investigated every nook and cranny in its surface, but found no further light. She felt and probed, and discovered no weakness in the impervious and unyielding fortress of stone. Soon she arrived beside the surging water itself, at the termination of the stream, where it gushed wildly through the rock and descended as a waterfall into the cave.

She approached the rushing stream with caution, not desiring to make a slip and slide into the rapidly moving current. The only light was a meager rim about the upper border of the torrent as it exited her cave and entered the other. She examined the area, and it was readily apparent that not enough room existed for even a kirin to squeeze between the chute of surging water and the stoney encircling rim.

"I will find another route out of this cave and into the one below," she said to the flowing water. "If for some reason I should happen not to, I might return and join you in yours."

She departed and retreated back along the rocky bank of the stream in the direction of the pool she had fallen into. She wanted to discover a place where she could cross over, in order to search the wall on the opposite side of the water. She explored for some sort of natural bridge, or even stepping stones by which to reach the other bank. But she was unable to find either. She tried fording the stream, but the current was too swift and powerful, sweeping her feet from under her no matter how far back she traced the course of the water.

Undaunted, she retraced her steps toward the wall. Upon reaching the point at which the stream exited her gloomy cave, she stood quietly for a while, staring pensively at the water. She wondered what would happen if she should enter the stream, as she had mentioned almost casually before, and depart in concert with it. She could picture herself gushing forth from the aperture, falling peacefully through the air, splashing uneventfully into the clear pool below, and then stepping out onto the bank unscathed, to the delight and the appreciative applause of Shillitoes passing by.

At the same time she realized, of course, how foolhardy a proposition that was. It was but a reassuring dream. There was little if any chance of it succeeding. A descent such as this was not only likely to be injurious, but could be deadly. Her aris, she knew, was too fragile to tolerate such a buffeting without serious consequences. She turned away again.

She searched the surfaces of the wall a second time, retreating all the way back to the hole she had peered through and even beyond. She could locate no other defect in her prison of stone. Discouraged, she circled back to the small aperture, her only means of contact with the rest of the world. She allowed herself to gaze through it once more. She could see Shillitoe kirins far below, moving to and fro, going about their daily business, and she wondered whether they even knew she was missing. They seemed so unruffled, so unharried, strolling about their cave in such a routine fashion. Should I be fortunate enough to rejoin them, she told herself, I will find enjoyment in each moment of the day, and never again go about being bored or taking things for granted, as the kirins below seem to be doing.

Wondering how she could possibly have gotten into this predicament, she thought of the quest, and of Talli, and Hut and Speckarin, and of what they were doing without her. She wondered whether Talli had recovered, and if they were making plans to go on. She hoped that her absence had not dampened their enthusiasm to the point of jeopardizing the mission. She wondered whether a search party had been dispatched to find her. She despaired that, if one had, it had precious little chance of locating her in her lofty stronghold. And yet she had located them, and had no means of informing them of it.

Finally, deeply frustrated, she placed her mouth to the small opening and shouted at the kirins below. "I am here!" she called. "I am above all of you! Can you not hear me? I am Diliani of the Yorl clan! I have been lost, but now I have found you and your cave! But I cannot enter, and if I do not soon find a way inside I do not know what will become of me!"

Again she looked down on the kirins so far away. None of them were paying the slightest attention to her or to her pleas for help. None of them had heard her at all, as she knew they would not. She turned away and sat down dismayed, her back against cool stone, trying to think what she could possibly do next.

Eventually she got up and returned to the place where the stream exited. She examined it forlornly one more time.

About the borders of the water was the thinnest margin of light, originating from the Shillitoe cave, and she wondered whether this might prove the only means by which she could leave her dark confinement. She sat down by the raging stream, watching swell after swell surge through in its final exodus before falling toward the clear pool below, and she came to an agonizing decision. Should she exhaust all other possibilities and be unable to find an alternative, she would take her chances and join the water.

Not wishing to think any longer about her only means of escape, she arose dejectedly and was walking back toward the aperture of light when she remembered Manay. The faithful raven was doubtless awaiting her return. Should she be forced to implement her plan, she wanted to be with her ilon one more time. Changing her course, she headed in the direction of the narrow ledge. Arriving at the widened portion of the path, she moved slowly and cautiously. She came to the point where it tapered, and soon she started out onto the slender ridge. Once again sliding deliberately along it, the sound of the flowing water below, she moved uneventfully toward her destination. She anticipated the defect left when the rock loosened, feeling for it with her feet. Reaching it, she was careful to step over it, and then she continued her progress. Eventually she arrived at the mouth of the tunnel once again. Stepping onto the promontory, she was greeted by a joyous and celebrating Manay, who had been waiting patiently in the darkness all the while she had been gone.

As she stroked the bird and praised her for her diligence, the impact of the confinement of both of them suddenly came into sharp and painful focus. Diliani, all at once overwhelmed, threw her arms about the neck of the raven, and for the first time since childhood she embraced an ilon. She stroked and patted the bird until they were both at least partially relieved of tension and fear. Then, leaning back against the wall, tears of frustration burning in her eyes, the embittered kirin allowed herself to slide down to the clammy floor. There she reclined, her back against moist stone, trying to think of anything that would wrest them from their unwarranted and unnatural imprisonment, when all at once something cold grasped her by the wrist, hoisted her from the floor, and began dragging her unceremoniously down the tunnel.

C H A P T E R   8

S PECKARIN MADE his
way thoughtfully down the wall toward the fairinin. He was
anxious to relate to Diliani what he had heard from the queen
about Runagar's uncanny abilities, and to discuss with her the
feasibility of his joining their mission. He assumed she would
be awake by now and would be waiting with Talli.

Speckarin was anything but convinced that they should
take on another individual, especially another youngster, and
one of whom they had little knowledge or acquaintance. He
is, of course, a kirin, the magician told himself. But he
possesses characteristics we do not have and speaks in a
tongue foreign to us. He has a highly unusual voice, Lanara
has explained, and it might be something we could use. If this
lad can accomplish what the queen has intimated, he could
prove to be of more than a little value to us.

She referred to his voice as something special, he thought
as he neared the healing area, but one that she could enhance
even further. She could teach him to do things that even
magicians could not conceive. Through Shillitoe magic, he
would be capable of extending the range over which his
voice could be heard. Even more compelling, he would be

given the ability, through voice, to persuade and influence. But most intriguing of all to the Yorl magician was that Runagar would have the capacity of imitation and mimicry of virtually any living thing, be it bird, beast, kirin or human being. None of us knows, not even Talli, with all of Olamin's knowledge, precisely what lies ahead. All of these Shillitoes have unusual voices. But what Lanara has said about Runagar's is almost too much to believe. Yet I have no reason to disbelieve it.

But now, he told himself, taking a deep breath as he arrived at the fairinin, I must find out about Talli and the barwood sap. He stepped inside and his gaze fell immediately upon the reclining lass. She seemed hardly to have stirred. She appeared unchanged. I sincerely hope, thought Speckarin, that administration of the essence has not yet been attempted.

Glancing about the space he saw no one in attendance, and he hurried from where Talli lay to the rear of the cave. There he found Lidor and two helpers, all three bending forward and peering at something in a low portion of the distillation apparatus. None of them greeted him, nor seemed to notice him, so engrossed did they appear in their examination.

Speckarin stood silently, observing them and listening to the machine, quiet now in contrast to the cacophony of yesterday. He leaned forward and tried to determine what they were so involved in studying. But once again he was unable to fathom the intricacies of this instrument, except to be aware that it was producing a purring sound. Finally, curiosity overwhelming him, he moved closer to the others and cleared his throat.

One of the attendants turned and glanced briefly at him, a grave look upon his countenance. But he spoke not a word, and shortly turned back toward the machine.

"May I inquire," said the undaunted Speckarin, "how the distillation is progressing?"

Lidor turned toward the visitor. "It has been completed," he stated, a note of severity in his voice. "Our product has arrived. But it is . . . questionable."

His commentary was left hanging there, which was highly unsettling to Speckarin. Lidor turned back to the apparatus.

"What do you mean questionable?" asked the visitor in earnest.

"I mean," said the fairinor, in a voice that was now wearing upon the Yorl magician, "that our product appears viable in quality, but it is a scant amount. What is questionable is whether it is of sufficient quantity. We had nothing to do with that. We had so little sap to work with, so little to be distilled from your vial, that our end result was . . . might I say, slight. We wait at this moment to be certain none further will be forthcoming."

He turned to face Speckarin directly. "Our traditional mode of administering essence is through the mouth, by the induction of swallowing. I fear that in this instance we have not enough for that to be appropriate."

"Then," asked Speckarin apprehensively, "what other means do you propose? What other method do we have for delivering the product?"

"Not in memory," said the fairinor, "have we had so diminutive a supply of sap to work with. We have never, therefore, been challenged with the problem we now face. Nevertheless, we have options. I must warn you that none have been attempted in my lifetime. Procurement of further sap is impossible, now and for some time to come, because of the flowering of the barwood grove. I did not wish to discourage you about the amount, because it was simply all we had. But I must be frank with you. The quantity in the vial was minimal."

"Are you trying to tell me," said Speckarin, now profoundly concerned, "that the likelihood of saving Talli has diminished since the last time we spoke?"

"No," replied Lidor. "We needed a greater amount of raw sap from the start. But since we had no more, we went to work with what we had."

"Then I must ask," said Speckarin shakily, "what her chances are with the quantity you have? What are the possibilities, other than the mouth, through which to give the essence?"

Lidor turned back to the machine. Pointing to one of its lower lobes, he responded. "If you look closely, you will see what we have achieved—our product—within this crystal receptacle."

Speckarin moved much closer and peered anxiously through the transparent wall of the container. There he faintly saw what the fairinor was demonstrating with a single finger, a tiny gleaming droplet. It was poised quiveringly at the tip of a small glass tubule and appeared to have the viscosity of liquid. Not having enough mass to fall to the concave base of the receptacle, it clung to the tip of the small pipette. The minuscule quantity of fluid, teardrop in shape, was opaque and of a silver hue, and looked almost like a miniature jewel.

"This," said Speckarin, staring at the droplet and aghast at the paucity of the result, "is the extent of the process? This is all that has been recovered? And . . . and, the color, is it normal? Or does it reflect the fact that my silver tube was used for procurement of the barwood liquor?"

"No," replied Lidor, "to answer your second question first. The essence is inherently silver. It is a dense and weighty liquid. And to respond to your first question, yes, the droplet you see is indeed the result of our procedures."

"Can this be sufficient," asked Speckarin, "to revive Talli?"

"No one knows that," said Lidor unemotionally. "The effectiveness of barwood essence, in whatever amount, depends upon the response of the victim to whom it is administered. We have not applied the substance in the fashion I am about to discuss, and we have never had so little to utilize. But ancient teachings hold that application of essence to the lower lid of the eye, upon its interior surface, might result in absorption into the vascular system. How much good this quantity will do cannot be predicted."

"I can only hope," said the enervated Speckarin, "that its energy will be true and to the mark. When may it be administered?"

"Now," answered Lidor. "But the next procedure must be performed with utmost care, or we might lose what little we have."

Without further ado he unlatched a small portal on the transparent compartment that housed the tiny drop, the gem of hope for Talli. Almost before Speckarin knew it, working through the aperture, Lidor had maneuvered a smaller container, hemispherical in shape and of a crystalline substance, into the region of the precariously quivering droplet. Next, with the middle finger of his left hand, using a motion as deft as the Yorl magician had ever seen, the fairinor flicked the droplet off its tenuous moorings and it fell into the new receptacle.

"There," said the fairinor. "We will transport the essence to your lass."

Clasping the small flask with both hands and protecting it with utmost care, he moved methodically away from the machine, and the bench, and the shaft to the outside world, and strode to the front of the fairinin, where Talli lay.

"Draw open the lower lid of her right eye," instructed Lidor succinctly, as the others joined him. One of the helpers moved to the girl's side and did what the fairinor directed, exposing the rich vascularity of a pink, moist surface.

Talli was unmoving except for slow, rhythmic breathing. The fairinor, chief magician of the healing area, moved into position. Kneeling at the bedside, he rotated the flask, slowly and purposefully, until it was nearly upside down, at which point he gave it a slight tap. Then he stood up summarily.

"It is done!" he announced with flourish, handing the receptacle to an attendant.

Speckarin gazed down at Talli. The attendant released her eyelid and moved away.

What is done? Speckarin asked himself. If anything fell from the flask it was not visible to me! How can he be so certain, both that the imperceptible droplet is gone and that it found its way to the mark?

Speckarin stared after the attendant, who was carrying the container toward the rear of the cave. For a moment he wanted to follow and examine the flask for himself. But he realized what an affront this would be to the fairinor, and declined to do so.

I can only trust and believe it has been done correctly, the Yorl magician told himself. All we can do is wait, and hope that the diminutive amount is in the proper place and will prove effective.

But he was far from confident about what had transpired as he observed the unconscious youngster, and suddenly he craved the company and assistance and comfort of his friends.

At that moment Hut stepped through the entrance. "How is Talli?" he asked excitedly.

"I am glad you are here," said the magician, approaching the lad and forgetting his recent anger toward him. "I hope all of us are here when she awakens."

Suddenly Speckarin remembered Diliani. He realized that she was missing all of this. She would be vitally interested in what was happening. He wondered why she was absent, why she had been asleep for so long. She had been exhausted, but she had certainly had enough rest by now. I must go and wake her, he thought, and bring her here. She will want to witness the rest of this, the revitalization of Talli.

He turned and began to move toward the mouth of the cavern. But he found himself torn between his desire to remain at Talli's side and his wish to inform Diliani about what was occurring.

Whatever happens to Talli, he finally decided, will happen with or without me. I must bring Diliani. As he was stepping outside, Lidor called and asked where he was going so soon after the essence had been applied. Speckarin told him about Diliani.

"No," responded the fairinor. "You remain here. Your place is here. The fuel of aris is now in your girl. The re-ignition of her spirit might occur at any time. She might show signs of life at any moment. I will dispatch Gunvir, one of my helpers, to convey your message and to escort the visiting woman here."

Without consulting Speckarin further, he turned, apparently instructed the attendant on the errand, and the Shillitoe kirin was off.

The old magician relaxed and took the opportunity to examine Talli more closely. As he bent down he was concerned that no new response or evidence of recovery had appeared. No alteration could be seen in the face of the fallen girl, nor in the rate or manner of her breathing, in her level of consciousness, nor in any parameter he could study.

"Give her longer," remarked Lidor, aware of the foreign magician's concern. "It may take time for the process to be completed. Give her time."

But just then the upper eyelid of the lass flickered, the right eye, Speckarin noted, the one into which the distilled droplet had presumably been placed. He watched attentively, trying to curtail any excitement he felt, but imagining a joyous reunion of the four voyagers, some of whom had gone their separate ways of late, but all of whom were ultimately reunited. He allowed his imagination to play over the events that would be forthcoming when they were together again. He thought of what he would say to Talli, the light-hearted reprimands he would tender cheerfully, about not holding tightly enough onto her ilon as every kirin should, as she had been taught to do from childhood. But at the same time he knew this would never come to pass. He would never tease Talli about something that was not her fault, a calamity that had occurred when she was in such a sad state over Gilin, the gronoms, and the volodons, and their entire predicament.

Speckarin's thoughts continued in this fashion for a long time as he observed the early stirrings of Talli. At times he was optimistic and cheerful, and at others merely reflective. He was oblivious to all things surrounding him, concentrating only upon the early and reassuring movements of the youngster, which seemed more detectable and frequent as time went on.

His train of thought was interrupted, however, when he overheard words from the fairinor's aide. Gunvir had returned from the guest chambers and stood directly behind the magician delivering a report to Lidor. It was in the local dialect, and Speckarin could not understand a syllable. Soon Lidor approached him and touched him on the shoulder and told him in Ruvon that his aide had something surprising to relate. The Yorl magician listened, and what he learned jarred him to attention.

"I went to her quarters," said Gunvir, now speaking in Ruvon. "The visiting woman was not there. Thence I proceeded to the passageway housing the bird ilon, and one of them was absent. I asked about your woman and no one had seen her, not since last night, neither the attendants to the guest rooms nor anyone I encountered along the way. I asked everyone I saw."

Diliani not in her chamber, and one of the ravens missing? How can that be? Speckarin questioned. It cannot be true, he concluded uneasily. Where could either one have gone? Diliani must be about, somewhere in the cave. She has found something unique to explore, or someone interesting to talk to. What trials we have had since leaving home! What if she is missing? A veil of doubt momentarily imposed itself over his thoughts. No! he said to himself, almost laughingly. The woman has been as steady as a rock throughout all of our adventures—and misadventures! She has always been where she was supposed to be, has never failed! I must simply go and find her!

Speckarin took a last look at the marginally reviving Talli. He asked the fairinor how lengthy the process of recovery might be. He was advised that it might still be some time, but also that this was not an exact science, that no one could be certain when or whether she would awaken, and that it would be wise for him to stay.

"You remain with Talli," Speckarin instructed Hut abruptly. "I will return shortly."

The magician left immediately, descending the wall

intently and striding to the chamber he knew to be Diliani's. He entered hurriedly without announcing himself. He glanced about and found the room empty except for the accoutrements of travel. Scattered randomly were articles from her satchels and clothing and food provided by the Shillitoes.

There! he told himself emphatically. She cannot be far away! Her belongings are here! She would not have left without the important ones! And if she had, she would have straightened up the others first! But where is she?

He turned on his heel, left the room, and descended rapidly to the passageway housing the ravens.

"Manay!" he called as he entered. "Are you here? Manay!"

He counted quickly. As Gunvir had stated, only three ravens were there. He searched the area. Then he examined each of the ilon critically, and it became painfully apparent that it was Diliani's raven that was missing.

She may have gone wandering or exploring by herself, he reassured himself. Not likely, came his own rebuttal, his level of apprehension rising. It would be totally out of character for her to do so. She is missing and so is her ilon. Those are facts. The faithful Diliani is gone. But where could she have gone? As he became more convinced that she had disappeared, he realized how much this woman meant, not only to himself but to the entire traveling group. As he stood alone among the ilon, his sense of loss was profound.

What more can happen? he wondered. First we lose Gilin, one of the two with the knowledge. Next the distracted Talli falls and her aris is damaged, perhaps mortally. Hut succumbs to the barwood tree, and now my faithful counterpart, the responsible Diliani, has vanished! What else can happen?

His ruminations were interrupted by Hut, who was entering the passageway. "I could not help myself," explained the lad. "I had to follow you and see about Diliani. We must enlist the aid of the Shillitoes to find her!"

Speckarin knew he was correct. Once more they needed

help, just when it appeared they would be fine and the party would be reunited.

Speckarin turned from the three ilon. Accompanied by Hut, he ascended the wall to the domicile of the queen. He demanded an audience with her regarding a serious emergency. The ancient woman emerged shortly and asked the nature of their predicament.

"One of our party is missing!" said Speckarin. "Diliani, the woman, is inexplicably absent! May we start a search for her?"

"Of course," responded the old queen without hesitation or the slightest perturbation. "We will organize and dispatch parties immediately. She cannot have ventured far. We will locate her forthwith. How long has she been absent?"

"This we unfortunately do not know," said Speckarin. "No one appears to have seen her since last evening."

"No matter," said the old woman.

She barked out short commands in her rasping voice in the local tongue of the Shillitoes. Several of her helpers left immediately.

"We will find her, naturally!" said the queen reassuringly. "Do not worry! She can hardly have gone far!"

A realization struck the old magician. He knew it had not occurred to him before this because of his agitation. The raven Manay was obviously accompanying her. Where else could the bird possibly be? And in that case, they would almost certainly be flying. At this point they might be anywhere the raven's wings could carry them! But these Shillitoes do not fly, do not even possess bird ilon! How could they find the missing Diliani when they never so much as leave the ground?

Speckarin knew almost nothing about the animal ilon of their hosts, but he was certain they could not travel as fast as ravens. Diliani and Manay could cover as much territory in a brief time as the foxes might in a morning! The Shillitoes would be helpless in locating Diliani!

"We, Hut and myself," he said, his anxiety rising, "are the only ones with bird ilon! We must be involved in the search!"

Lanara extended a shriveled finger toward the visiting magician and glared at him. "You can be of no help in this matter!" she dictated emphatically. "You have little knowledge of our cave, and almost none of the surrounding environment, even though your lad has recently taken a ride through the countryside! You will remain here! Return to your fallen lass in the fairinin!" she said, pointing toward the healing area. "Await the results of the essence! But do not venture outside this cave!"

She turned and disappeared into the corridor behind her throne. Speckarin stared after her, alarmed at her harsh tone and demeanor. And he considered the chilling prospect that this ancient queen knew something more about the entire affair than she had chosen to reveal.

C H A P T E R   9

N HISTORIC EVENT
was taking place at the hunting lodge of John Versteeg. Two
intelligent species who had occupied the same planet since
prehistoric times, but for untold generations had been almost
totally dissociated from each other, were together, once again
working toward a single goal. As far as the kirins knew, it was
the first time their species had related openly to human beings,
exchanging information and ideas, for thousands of years.

Ruggum Chamter, Gilin, and their raven ilon were resting,
but uncomfortably so, in the gigantic shelter of the humans.
After Loana was treated, the humans had insisted she remain
there, her masters along with her, and the kirins knew they
had little choice.

The night passed painfully, not only for the injured raven
but for the two kirins as well. As Ruggum attempted,
unsuccessfully, to sleep, he estimated that they would be
sequestered here, allowing the bird's injuries to heal, for a
minimum of thirty-five days. But at least now, he thought,
she has a chance to recover.

The kirins and their birds were housed in one of the spare
bedrooms on the ground floor. Mr. Versteeg had suggested

they occupy one or both of the beds, but the kirins declined. In their natural habitat they preferred to be above ground. But they found here that they had more of an aversion to human furniture than they had to the floor. The old man provided them with cardboard boxes that he cut and fashioned for the birds to rest in. The kirins settled on a carpet near the wall farthest from the door and covered themselves with a small towel supplied by Christopher.

As he was departing, John Versteeg had asked whether they wished the overhead light to be on or off during the night. The kirins were at first undecided. They were baffled by the explanation they were given of electricity. Nonetheless, they determined that it might be best to leave it on in case they had reason to tend to Loana. Later, Ruggum decided that it was one of the reasons he could not sleep. He tossed and turned, thinking again and again about what had happened the previous day.

Christopher had stayed with them for some time. After delivering their bedding, he was joined by Nathan. The two enthralled boys posed unending questions about kirins the world over, about ilon, and magic, the clan they were from, and the purpose of their travel. The kirins, Gilin in particular, whom they could see and who could speak with them through the calamar, attempted to answer all of their queries as well and as accurately as possible.

Gilin posed a question also, one embarrassing to both boys, but especially to Nathan. He asked why a weapon had been fired in their direction. The explanation proved most difficult, both for the boys to provide and for the kirins to accept. But eventually, as they discussed it over and over, Gilin translating for Ruggum Chamter, they all began to accept what had happened as a tragic accident, an unforeseen and unpremeditated occurrence.

Ruggum at first thought it was a disastrous waste. But as he considered it further, he realized that it had, ironically, brought humans and kirins together for the first time since the very distant past.

The kirins asked about human culture and life, about families, homes, hobbies, and forms of transportation. As the evening wore on, the kirins gradually became more at ease, realizing that these giant beings did not mean them further harm—and apparently had not intended them harm in the first place.

Eventually Grandpa Versteeg appeared in the doorway. After listening to the conversation for a long while, he indicated that their small guests required rest, especially the assaulted bird. He instructed the boys to go to their bedrooms and to go to sleep, and they reluctantly agreed. After delaying as long as they could, they finally departed.

Now, as the old overseer restlessly changed position, he wondered whether Gilin was as sleepless as he, and once again he wished he could see his companion. The night seemed exceedingly long, but to his relief it was passing without incident, and ultimately he slept.

■ ■ ■

Christopher stole toward the room of the kirins very early in the morning. He pushed the door open ever so slowly, holding his breath, hoping against hope that they were still there. As he stood in the doorway a smile crossed his face, and he lingered for a while observing the sleeping Gilin and the two ravens. He was amazed all over again at their presence and at everything they had revealed the evening before. He resolved again that he would help them in any way he could. Then, satisfied that all was well, he crept back to his bedroom and into bed, thrilled that these creatures existed at all, and that two of them were actually in their midst.

■ ■ ■

Further conversation occurred between the human beings and the kirins the next morning, much of it on the deck overlooking the lake. The ravens, Loana included, were brought along to absorb the warmth of the sunlight and to be near their masters. The injured raven was allowed and even encouraged to move about and was given free access to every place she could walk or climb in the lodge.

Food and drink were provided by John Versteeg, for the kirins and the birds. For the most part, however, the old man remained aloof and apart, as he had been the evening before, not feeling nearly as comfortable as the boys with these tiny creatures. Nonetheless, as Ruggum Chamter had more opportunity to observe the old human, he became interested in the idea of communicating with him, knowing how kind he had been with Loana, and seeing that perhaps they had something in common.

The following day Mr. Versteeg announced that the three humans would be leaving in the afternoon to return to their homes in the city. He said that they would return, hopefully in five days, during which time the boys would be in school. A plentiful supply of food was left for the four strangers, and the deck door was slid far enough open for them to exit to the outside. Later that day, after locking all the other doors, the humans bade their guests goodbye and departed.

The kirins felt an unexpected void when they found themselves alone. They passed the remainder of the day exploring the close-by terrain, leaving Loana by herself for short periods of time, sharing the back of Alsinam for their excursions. That evening and night went by without incident.

The next afternoon, while sitting beside Loana, Gilin had a sudden and inexplicable feeling regarding Talli, his compatriot of the Moger clan and his companion in knowledge. He had not forgotten that several days earlier he had sensed his friend was in uncommon danger. Now he had the unmistakable feeling that something was changing, or had changed. He had no idea where the other party might be or what they were doing, but he knew something was happening to Talli. What it was he could not decipher, but he hoped that it was good.

I wish Ruggum and I would also see progress toward the end we seek, he thought. But he realized that they were awaiting Loana's recovery, and there was nothing else they could do.

I wonder whether I will ever see Talli again? he thought. Because of what lay ahead for both parties, and because they had been apart for so long, he knew that the chances were slim indeed. Unless both of them made their way back to the home forest, they might never meet again.

The kirins spent the next three days at the lodge. On the following day, as promised, the humans returned. The kirins were surprisingly happy to see them and greeted them warmly. Grandfather Versteeg immediately made his way to Loana. He examined her dressings and their supporting structures. Although nothing was seriously wrong, he said that the gauze pads should be changed because of minor drainage from the wounds. Ruggum concurred, and the entire entourage repaired to the shop room downstairs. There Ruggum and John Versteeg worked in concert again, the kirin overseeing the procedures for placing fresh dressings on the bird. But this time Ruggum relied less upon Gilin for translation, conferring directly with the elderly human, each adapting his English as well as he could so that the other could better comprehend. After their mutual task was completed, the two elders returned to the upstairs and continued their conversation.

The old man had required a few days away to come to grips with things: namely, the fact that these little creatures existed. He had not mentioned them to another soul, nor had he said a word about what was happening at the lodge. But he had taken time to think things over, and upon his return he was much more willing, even eager, to associate with them.

Throughout the next day and a half, before the humans again departed, Ruggum Chamter and John Versteeg spent most of their time together. Even though the old man could not see the overseer, they discussed the problems of kirins and humans, and of the world itself, and the wisdom of these elders of different and yet coexisting races passed freely and openly between them. Ruggum's English improved remarkably as he persevered in speaking, which allowed their dialogues, profoundly interesting to each of them, to proceed meaningfully.

Gilin, Nathan and Christopher were involved in the same kind of exchange, but on a less philosophical level, and the time went by all too swiftly for everyone concerned. But they were aware that ample opportunity would exist for discussion. Loana would require a lengthy time for recuperation, and the kirins would be going nowhere during that interlude.

The humans again took leave, returning to the city to carry on their daily lives. The kirins could do nothing but wait. They became frustrated at the seemingly endless length of time they had to live under these circumstances. But they were grateful they had sheltered surroundings for Loana.

On the fourth day after the humans' departure John Versteeg returned. But this time, surprisingly to the kirins, he was alone. When they asked about the two boys, he explained that they were not as free as an adult because of their responsibilities to school, and the kirins understood. With mild embarrassment, the old man admitted that he had simply wished to visit the kirins and their ravens, to make certain they were getting along all right. He did not express that he had become increasingly captivated by the miniature beings and everything about them: their magic, the relationship between ilon and master, and their knowledge of nature. He was fascinated by the entire idea that such a race existed, and he returned because he was unable to stay away. He explained that he would not remain overnight, for fear that he would draw suspicion among family members that something unusual was going on at the lodge. He would leave for home later in the day. Their presence, he reassured the visitors, was a secret shared only by him and his two grandsons. No other human knew about them.

Ruggum Chamter had grown fond of the elderly human over the twelve days they had been there. He was moved that the man would come this far to visit them, and realized that he was doing all he reasonably could to protect and aid them.

The two elders retired to the workroom once again to check Loana's progress. Both to the old man and to the old overseer, everything seemed to be proceeding satisfactorily. Ruggum said that she could now begin exercising her wing. The tape that bound her wing to her body, he told the man, the final one that had been applied, could be removed. John Versteeg complied, taking off the outermost stripping of adhesive tape.

"I've been able to see Gilin, of course," he said, finishing up his work. "But it's too bad I'll never see you. How do kirins look when they grow older? We humans simply become grayer and balder and plumper. What do kirins do?"

All at once Ruggum had a strange urge, one he knew other kirins had experienced before, but that he could never have dreamed he would feel himself. He was not certain what to do nor how to accomplish it. But his faith and trust in this venerable human made him desire to do it.

"I will try to show you," he said.

Standing on the wooden bench where the two of them had nursed Loana, Ruggum attempted something he could never have imagined he would. He began to will himself to be visible. Slowly, after several false starts and inconstant results, he gradually, but only for a few moments, overcame the ancient spell of no'an and was perceptible to John Versteeg.

The surprised and pleased old man stared as the kirin came into view.

"So . . . you are Ruggum Chamter!" he exclaimed. "I have wanted to meet you, or to see you, for quite a while! You have a gray beard, and your feet are the same as Gilin's! What is it that you have in your belt . . . a small axe? Well," he concluded, as the image of the overseer faded once again into nothingness, "I'm glad to have seen you . . . even for a moment!"

It was something that neither of them would ever forget. Later, when Ruggum would relate how it felt to want to be seen, and to actually be seen by a human, he found that the sensations were inexpressible. So long have the races been separated, so dependent are kirins upon the spell of no'an, and so distrustful are they of humans, that encounters between the two species are exceedingly rare.

Ruggum was aware that an occasional kirin had shed the cloak of invisibility in the past. He had discussed the matter with Gilin after their surprise meeting with the human girl by the lake. He had questioned his friend as to whether he had wanted to be seen, Gilin vehemently denying it.

Ruggum had never understood how a kirin could choose to be seen by a human being. What impulse, he wondered, could force a kirin to do something as incomprehensible as that? He had considered it virtually a betrayal of the kirin race. But now he knew how it felt, how utterly profound a desire it was. It was as though a primal urge deep inside, one he had no idea was there, welled up within and allowed him to overcome all the established customs of his race, even the spell of invisibility itself. As he later pondered what had occurred, he was certain that the longing had origins in the ancient bond between the races, in the relationship human and kirin ancestors enjoyed before recorded history. And at that moment, when he was visible to John Versteeg, something else happened to Ruggum Chamter. He had greater hope that the two races might be reunited than any other kirin upon Earth.

■ ■ ■

For the following three days, the kirins were alone again at the hunting lodge. Under Ruggum's supervision Loana began to gently move her wing and to increase its motion day by day. She seemed to do so with little discomfort. The kirins were cheered that the healing process appeared to be coming along satisfactorily and on schedule. They realized that she was far from ready to travel, but they finally believed that their long period of waiting would come to an end.

During the fourth night after John Versteeg's departure, the kirins were sound asleep on the floor of their room, the two ravens nearby. Gilin was dreaming of soaring upon a strong and mended Loana when something else insinuated itself into his fantasy. Someone or something was summoning him by name, but strangely enough the words were not in Ruggum Chamter's voice.

What an unusual dream, came the thought, and from the back of Loana he turned his head to look downward, to see who was addressing him. But below was only darkness, and he could see nothing at all. Then he was aware that he might be partially awake, and he attempted to concentrate with more determination. As he did he heard his name repeated several times over.

"Who is calling me?" he asked aloud, eyes still closed, not certain whether he was awake or asleep.

When the response came he relaxed again, satisfied that he was still dreaming, happy that this was part of his dream.

"Gilin! It's me!" came the words. And the voice was none other than Talli's.

C H A P T E R   1 0

F OLLOW ME, MANAY!"
cried Diliani as she was being drawn away.

"Can anyone hear me? Can anyone help me?" she called,
but with no response.

Something clung grimly to her right wrist, clutching it so
firmly that it was causing her pain. At first she was simply
hauled by whatever kind of thing it was. But after a while she
regained her footing and was able keep up by walking at
times and running when she had to, always trailing behind
her captor. The discomfort in her arm was eased when she
was on her feet.

On several occasions she attempted to resist and pull
herself free, but whatever was gripping her was too strong
and too unrelinquishing. As her efforts were fruitless, she
gave in and followed along helplessly through total darkness.
She could only hope that her ilon was pursuing, but she had
no way of knowing this.

She assumed that the first passageway they traversed was
the same one she and Manay had taken on their way to the
water, with ancient torches upon the walls. As they moved
steadily along she gathered her thoughts and composure and

recognized that escape from this being would not be easy. Her hand was becoming numb from the pressure, but she could do nothing to alter the situation. She also realized, to her surprise, that although they were moving more rapidly than she and Manay had ever been able to, she was not colliding with walls, or the ceiling, or the myriad rocky outcroppings that had plagued her previously. They were marching along unimpeded, as though her leader knew precisely where everything was and was capable of avoiding the impediments. Or was it possible, she began to question, that nothing was there with which to collide?

Could it be, she wondered, that we are in a new hallway, so spacious that we would encounter nothing in our way? But as they progressed ever farther she discounted this as a likelihood. No underground arena could be this large. It would dwarf even the Shillitoe cave. There must be some other explanation.

Her thoughts went back to the astounding occurrences on the promontory above the pool. Could it be, she questioned, that this abductor is the same being that lowered the cord and rescued me from the water? And then, having been too preoccupied to think about it at the time, she replayed in her mind how that had occurred. Those events had taken place in darkness, and yet her benefactor had located her, and not purely by chance, she concluded now, with only her head bobbing above water. How could anyone have found me that far down, except through incredible luck? Unless . . . is it possible . . . that it could have seen me in the dark? If it can see in the dark, she reasoned, or in some other more alien way sense things in the darkness, it might be leading me through tunnel after tunnel without striking anything along the way!

She remembered the faithful raven, and she turned as well as she could toward the rear. "Follow, Manay! Follow!" she called. But she had no way of determining whether the bird was pursuing, as she was forced to continue moving forward at a steady pace.

She was escorted unceremoniously for a very long time, and for what she estimated was a great distance, during which passage she heard nothing from her unknown companion. On several occasions she requested, both in Ruvon and in her home dialect, to learn where they were located, why she was being borne away, who might be accompanying her, and what their destination might be. But she received no response. The pull on her wrist remained intense and unyielding, and she sensed no opportunity to escape. Escape to what, she began to ask herself: into the gloom and a maze of corridors? She almost started to laugh as she considered her situation, and she noticed that she was less frantic than she would have predicted she would be under the circumstances. Because of her exhaustion, because of the trials she had been through, and because she half-suspected that this was the creature who saved her life, in a twisted way she found it a relief to be in the company of another being, even though she had no way of knowing what manner of thing it might be.

Eventually her companion slowed and then came to a complete halt, an action much appreciated by the flagging kirin. For a while nothing happened. Not a sound could be heard. Then without warning the grasp upon her wrist was released. She rubbed her wrist with her other hand until the circulation and sensation returned.

She took the opportunity to call again for Manay, but she could hear no sound from the ilon. She wondered how far away her raven was, and what fate had befallen her.

She stood for some time in solid blackness. She could see nothing, nor could she hear anything from the one who had abducted her. She became aware of a musty smell, one she could not fully identify, but that seemed to be coming from something very old. All at once came a series of low grunts and mutterings, the meaning of which, if any existed, she could not decipher. Prior to this she had presumed that only one being was present. But now, to her growing discomfort, she got the distinct impression that more than one were in proximity:

The semblance of a guttural conversation was unfolding.

She held her breath as she waited for something to happen, trying to be as quiet as she could. Soon she heard shuffling and movement nearby, and then all was quiet again. But now the smell was strong, and she could sense that something was very near. She could not judge in which direction it was, however, until she felt warm breath on her left cheek and then on her neck. To her consternation, again came the sniffing she had endured once before.

Although she cringed and shivered, this time she made no attempt to run, aware that there was no means of escape. *Something is merely investigating me*, she tried to reassure herself. But her anxiety was rising and her heart was pounding.

The sniffing was brief, however. Then the presence near her seemed to recede. Soon another exchange of low murmurings and sounds came, but this time from farther away. This conversation was followed by silence and then more shuffling. All at once both of her wrists were grasped, and she was pulled forward in the darkness.

She did her best to keep her footing and stay upright, but they were moving even faster than before. Occasionally she faltered but she never fell. She tired more and more the longer the fatiguing trek went on. *Whoever or whatever they are*, she thought, *they are anything but slow afoot and they are wasting no time.*

Suddenly they stopped, as abruptly as they had started. Both wrists were relinquished by her captors, who again appeared to move away from her. A few moments later she heard a chinking sound, as if a chisel was being tapped against rock. Then came a grating, as though stone were sliding against stone. Finally came a resounding crash that reverberated throughout the space. The brave kirin flinched and crouched at the unexpected and harsh sound, but at the same time something came that gave her relief.

In her lowest moments, Diliani had given up hope of ever seeing light again. But all at once she sensed illumination ahead of her, emitting from what source she could not discover, even as she strained to see. Nor did she very much care where it was coming from, because at least it was light. Under other circumstances this would have been the palest of light, but here she blinked and turned away from what appeared to be dazzling luminosity. Then, holding a hand up to shade her eyes, she searched her murky surroundings.

She stood erect, and could dimly see rocky walls, and she could also see what had made the reverberating noise. Lying on the floor of what appeared to be a tunnel was a sizable piece of stone, debris scattered all around. Cautiously she approached the object. Soon she could see that the light was coming through the ceiling, through a hole obviously created when the stone fell from it, dust still rising in the dim rays filtering through from above.

Again she looked around, as her eyes gradually became accustomed to illumination. She discerned that she was indeed within a cave. It had a low ceiling and passageways that entered it and became confluent with it one after another. Finally, at a distance, she saw the obscure outlines of two creatures. One of them, she assumed, was her abductor.

Suddenly she detected movement toward her. Instinctively she backed away, but she realized she had no way of escaping, and she stopped her retreat a short distance from the source of the light. At least I can see them now, she thought, whatever they are.

An idea struck her. The aperture might be allowing beams from the sun to enter, and might lead to the outside world! Moving quickly into position beneath the hole, she raised her arms upward and attempted to touch the interior edges of the orifice, but they were well out of reach. She jumped, and discovered that she could barely touch the opening. She sprang upward repeatedly, grasping and clawing at the smooth and flinty surfaces, but she could obtain no hold at all. As the two creatures continued to approach she gave up the attempt, and again backed a short distance away from the light.

Through the murky illumination she strained to see what manner of beings she was dealing with, but she could make out little more than outlines. They had arrested their progress as soon as she stopped her retreat. Neither she nor the two made a move, each party investigating the other. She could distinguish little detail regarding her antagonists, except that they were about the same height as her. She was feeling more uneasy about their intentions when one of them moved again. The creature shuffled forward and stopped directly underneath the hole, rays from above illuminating it so that she could now, for the first time, see it in its entirety.

Standing before her was something she had never before envisioned. Clad in a hooded garment of roughly woven dark red cloth was a being indeed no taller than herself. The odor, Diliani concluded, must emanate from the cloth. The being's torso and limbs were entirely covered by the cloak. Its feet did not project beyond the hem of the floor-length garment, as would those of a kirin. What she assumed to be a face was hidden from the light by an overhanging brim of the hood. It was all but indistinguishable except for a pair of prominent features: Projecting from the lower part of the opening were two short tusks or fangs, one on either side.

"Broms!" came a guttural sound from the creature as it struck its breast with one of its upper limbs. *"Broms!"* it repeated. Then, turning, it pointed an arm toward its counterpart, still waiting in the dark. *"Boros!"* it said, and the second one grunted.

The first, which remained beneath the aperture, then tilted its head upward, its face toward the light. Diliani examined the thing with morbid interest. What she assumed were the two eyes of the creature were tightly closed, as if to avoid the penetration of any light. But it appeared that they were huge, and the swarthy skin about them was deeply creased with wrinkles. Beneath them was a slight protrusion with two wide nostrils, and it was with this organ, Diliani presumed, that she had been smelled. The mouth was straight across and short in length, a tusk protruding from each corner. The creature held this position for a brief time, and for no apparent reason, thought the kirin, except to allow her to peruse it. Then it lowered its head once again.

She thought she could see it open its eyes slightly, then squint at her from beneath the hood. The being turned toward its companion and made a few sounds while motioning it forward. Diliani could see that it had an appearance similar to the other's. The two of them bent over and together grasped the huge stone plug from the ceiling, and, with an ease that startled the kirin, hoisted it off the ground. Next, the creature who had referred to itself as Broms helped shift the weighty object into the arms of the other. Then it aided its companion in raising the piece upward and overhead. Finally, to Diliani's amazement, Broms squatted down and lifted the other being off the ground, the stone still held aloft. When directly beneath the hole, the creature elevated the stone with both hands and maneuvered it skillfully into the exact position from which it had come. To the regret of the kirin—because the next action shut out all vestiges of light—the segment of stone was tamped back into place by an instrument she never had the opportunity to see.

The bewildered and disappointed kirin was returned to darkness after too brief a respite of light. Her wrists were grasped, but not with the same firmness as before, and again she was drawn forward. This time, after a short trek they stopped and she was released. She heard further shuffling and deep-throated conversation.

Suddenly a welcome sight met her eyes again: brightness. But this time it was from a low burning flame that one of the beings, the one she thought had revealed itself under the light, was bringing toward her. The diminutive fire was held out to her, the creature's vision protected from the dim light by a forearm in front of its eyes. She knew not when, nor where, nor by what method it had been ignited, but she gladly reached out and took this object whose tip emanated but a thin, pale glow. She accepted it with a grateful hand, the beings apparently knowing that light was something she required.

Wondering whether the sounds the creature uttered earlier could actually be names, with this apparent act of kindness she attempted communication anew. "Thank you, Broms," she said, first in the dialect of the home clans and then in Ruvon.

Staring at her through eyes open slightly, the being cocked its head to one side as though listening intently, as if it had heard something it recognized and was attempting to decipher.

"Will you help me?" Diliani asked, eager for the creature to comprehend, and aware that it seemed to be listening to her. She explained several times who she was, and that she desired to return to the Shillitoe cave. They gave her no response, talking instead to each other in a dialect she could not understand.

Motioning her to follow, they moved off down the tunnel; she had no choice but to pursue them. Shortly they entered an enlargement in the passageway, so large that she could not make out the interior borders of the space with her meager, flickering torch. What she could see, however, was that several more beings were present. They were protecting their eyes from her light, yet at the same time studying her, low mutterings and utterances emanating from all around.

The creature she thought to be Broms approached her again, this time carrying a glittering object. Shading its eyes, it handed her a funnel-shaped piece and indicated with grunts and gestures that it somehow belonged with the small torch she held. Diliani examined it, rotating it in her hand. It was fashioned crudely from shiny metal, and all at once she recognized what to do with it. She slid it over the flame, the open end of the funnel upward, covering the fire from the view of the creatures around her. But it allowed light to be directed toward the ceiling, which she could now see was very high. When she did this, the beings gave low-pitched groans—apparently of approval. Many more of the creatures were arriving at the scene.

Thus far they have been friendly, she reassured herself. I wish I had some way of communicating with them. The crowd of beings now surrounded her.

"Who are you, and where are we located?" she asked anxiously. She tried both Ruvon and the dialect of the home clans, but she received no response. They simply continued examining her.

All at once, Broms, the one she thought of as her friend, pushed through the crowd. It was accompanied by another being that was more wrinkled and looked older than any of the others. This one was given special respect as it passed through the throng, the crowd parting before it and deferring to it.

Not to Diliani's surprise, the wrinkled one stopped directly in front of her, and she saw that its tusks were longer than the others she had seen. Broms cuffed the older one on the shoulder, pointed to it, and said, "Silarude!"

Next, the wrinkled one spoke. It had the same guttural voice as the others, but this time, to Diliani's astonishment and relief, the words were in the ancient kirin tongue of Ruvon.

"Welcome home of Grygla," said the old one.

C H A P T E R   1 1

"**S**ILARUDE NAME! What your?" the wrinkled creature said.

"My . . . name . . . is Diliani," stammered the amazed kirin in Ruvon, hoping she was answering the question being asked. Then, encouraged that she could apparently talk to the beings in the revered tongue, and desperately needing help, she persisted. At least up to now, she told herself, they have been friendly.

"My home . . . is very far from here," she began haltingly, to the quizzical expressions of the wrinkled one. "It is a great distance to the west. I am on a long journey with friends, who are staying in the cave of the Shillitoe kirins." She paused for a moment. I can only hope they are still there, she thought uneasily.

"I wish to return to that cave," she said. "It is somewhere close by, but I have been lost for a very long time in tunnels near the cave, or what I presumed to be so. I could see nothing in the darkness. But it is important that I go back as soon as possible. Can you help me?"

Shading its face from her light, the old one looked at her with eyes only partially open. But Diliani could see that they

were huge, many times the size of kirin eyes. They must live
and see in the dark, she thought. She had never encountered
creatures such as these before, nor imagined anything like
them. She had no way of knowing what this one was
thinking, even though she was conversing with it, nor what
any of the others were thinking, nor what their intentions
toward her were. She could only hope they would remain
friendly and cooperative.

"Come," said Silarude. "Show Grygla cave."

Off the wrinkled one went, in the same fashion it had
come, barging through the crowd, a pathway forming as it
passed through the throng.

"Wait!" Diliani called after it, not knowing whether a
word of hers had been understood. The old one stopped and
looked back, protecting its eyes from the meager torch. All of
them did this whenever they glanced in her direction or
toward the dimly lit ceiling.

"I came into the tunnel with a companion," said the kirin,
"a bird, ilon we call them. I have no idea where this creature
is, but I would like to know. She was with me on the
promontory overlooking the water before I was brought here.
Do you know what has befallen her?"

Silarude stood silently, apparently turning these words
over in its mind and considering them, as if it had not heard
anything like them for a very long time. Then the wrinkled
one looked toward Broms, who was still accompanying the
old one, and spoke in throaty tones. Most of the sounds were
abrupt, coarse, and strongly emphasized. Broms responded in
kind, and a lively exchange ensued. The kirin strained to
understand, but she could fathom not a word. It was a tongue
she could not begin to comprehend.

Silarude turned back to Diliani and said gruffly, again in
Ruvon, "Bird safe. Not here. We keep."

The wrinkled creature turned on its heel and again strode
away, followed closely by Broms and several others. Diliani
was trying to comprehend what the creature meant when she
was taken by the wrist once more, by the creature she thought

to be Boros, and was escorted summarily after them. In her other hand she was permitted to carry the dim torch, and shadowy light reflected off the rugged stone roof as they moved quickly along. The small entourage pressed on ahead of her, the remainder of the crowd following haphazardly behind.

Diliani was ushered through a series of underground chambers, all devoid of light save her small flame. They varied widely in size and shape and included dark corridors, echoing caverns, and dingy lairs, all apparently occupied or somehow utilized by these unusual creatures. Some of the smaller grottos were obviously dwelling places, and a few of the larger spaces appeared to be for gatherings, much the same, Diliani presumed, as our gathering place on Rogalinon. But she had not the slightest idea what some of the areas were used for, and throughout the tour she had no opportunity to question Silarude, the only one, of whatever race this might be, she had been able to communicate with.

In several places, to her displeasure, were bare skeletons of beings of unidentified breeds or origins, strewn about on the floors of passageways, hallways and dens. Some of the remains were large and some were small. In some instances they were virtually intact and still articulated, while in others the bones were singular or thrown into heaps. Becoming more fearful by the moment for her well-being and that of Manay, Diliani examined the bones as closely as she could as she was escorted hastily by. But she was unable to recognize what species they might be of, and the other beings paraded past them as if they were not there at all. In any case, she thought apprehensively, this is most certainly a meat-eating race.

She had no way of telling how recent or how ancient these bony relics were. Could they be the remnants of birds? she wondered nervously, thinking of Manay. Or, she shuddered to think, could some of them possibly be those of kirins?

Having escorted her, so far as she could tell, throughout the entire area of their habitation, the procession eventually stopped in a large cavern. The one called Silarude positioned itself before the crowd, forty or more in number, Diliani estimated. The old one gave a speech in the explosive tongue of the creatures. When it was finished, the majority of the beings disbanded abruptly. Diliani was led away once more, now accompanied only by Silarude, Broms, Boros, and a few others who had been in the leading entourage during their excursion.

The kirin was taken to a small room with a high ceiling. Upon entering, the first thing she noticed was a penetrating smell, one she had never come across before, but that was immediately unpleasant to her. Silarude, Broms, and several others sat down on the floor around a low structure. It was circular and flat on top, and made, as far as the kirin could tell, of a rough, dark-colored metal. On its upper surface were fragments of what looked like flesh, searing and smoking, being heated by an unknown source of fuel, the odor obviously originating from them. The torch was removed from her hand, and as she watched anxiously it was positioned on the floor at the edge of the chamber. But it was not, to her relief, extinguished, shedding enough light that she could see her dim surroundings.

"Eat," directed Silarude suddenly, as Diliani was forcibly seated in front of the structure. One of the pieces was transferred to the space in front of her. She noted with her long feet that the metallic creation was warm. It appeared to be a round, low table. She surmised that they were sitting about a cooking platform, and that fuel must be burning inside the metal structure, out of the vision of these light-fearing creatures.

Diliani had not eaten for a very long time, not since the breakfast she had enjoyed in her guest room in the Shillitoe cave just before her departure with Manay. She was starving. But in her lifetime she had never tasted meat from beast or bird, nor had any kirin of her clan, so strong was their relationship with animals and birds, and so distasteful was the prospect of consuming flesh from their bodies.

Diliani reached out a hand and touched the portion of meat. It was warm. Grasping it with both hands she broke off a small fragment and brought it to her nose. The odor was stifling. Looking about, she could see that the creatures were not only devouring the material, but were watching her through large, squinting eyes. Despite her hunger, and her desire to please her captors, the famished Diliani found she was unable to place the singed flesh in her mouth, and she returned it hesitantly to the heated surface.

"You eat!" repeated the wrinkled Silarude seated opposite the beleaguered kirin.

Diliani was obliged to try eating the food of these beings, whatever it was. Again she picked up the smaller piece. She raised it up to examine it. She tried a second time to place it in her mouth, but again to no avail. As it remained below her nose she felt a wave of nausea.

Silarude turned from her and conversed briefly with Broms and then looked back and spoke to the kirin. "Not eat long time. Eat now, strong," admonished the wrinkled one.

Not wishing to offend the beings, Diliani nonetheless replaced the meat on the metal surface in front of her. Then she made an attempt to explain herself to Silarude. "I must apologize, but I have never, nor has anyone of the clan I belong to, eaten the meat of an animal or a bird, cooked or otherwise. I would like to partake of your food, but I find I cannot."

Silarude eyed her inquisitively for a few moments, and then said, "You like Shillitum. Not eat animal." The wrinkled one glanced again at Broms, and they engaged in a lively conversation, Boros and the others entering in also, until Silarude looked back at the kirin. "You differen from Shillitum," said the old one. "Smell same, but talk differen, wear differen clothes. But no eat animal. What eat?"

"I eat almost anything from the forest: honey, berries, mushrooms, legumes, and nuts," answered Diliani. "Almost anything but meat."

Silarude glanced at the others around the table, said a few words in their guttural tongue, and then looked back at Diliani. Within moments all except the wrinkled one rose, whether they were finished with their meal or not. One by one they filed out of the room without a word, each taking whatever morsels had been left in front of them. Alone with the obvious leader of this tribe, Diliani was more concerned than ever about what to expect.

"Come house, mine," said Silarude, rising and moving around the circular table to the place where Diliani sat. Helping the kirin to her feet, the old one handed her the torch. Slowly they moved out of the room and down the passageway until Silarude motioned for her to enter another room.

This new chamber was somewhat larger than the previous one. A collection of bones had been thrown unceremoniously, or so it appeared, into one corner. A few stones of low profile were positioned on the floor. Those are for sitting, presumed Diliani. On one side of the room, spread out on the floor, was an animal pelt. For sleeping, she thought.

The old one took the dwindling flame from the kirin's hand and placed it on the floor against a wall. Silarude next gestured for Diliani to sit down upon one of the stones. She did so, and the wrinkled one sat down next to her upon another.

"No your food Grygla cave," began Silarude.

How long has it been since I lost my way? wondered Diliani as she listened to the old Grygla. Part of a day? Several days?

It did not matter, because the elder's next statement gave her greater reason for optimism than she had had since beginning her wanderings.

"Take you Shillitum cave," said Silarude.

Diliani could hardly believe her ears, and yet she reveled in what she was hearing. Can it be true? she wondered. Will it finally happen? I must believe it or at least act as though I do!

"Thank you!" she said. "That is exactly what I would like to do! But I must take the raven with me! Where are you keeping the bird?"

"Bird safe," replied Silarude. "Not come this cave. Not bird or animal, unless dead, then food."

Diliani was heartened. Manay was apparently unharmed. But the gnawing suspicion remained that these meat-eating creatures might find her too tempting to resist. "When may I see the raven?" she asked earnestly.

"No see, bird safe. Not come here," the Grygla said firmly.

"May I go to the place where the bird is staying?" persisted Diliani. "This raven is my close friend, my companion. She might not be doing well without me."

"Far, not need go," said Silarude.

Diliani decided to desist in her efforts to be reunited with her ilon. For the time being I must do what it says and not irritate it, she concluded. I may have no alternative if I wish it to remain cooperative.

As they sat facing each other, Silarude revealed something that astonished the kirin. "You woman kinin," said the old one. "Broms, Boros smell, find out. I woman, too. Woman leader of Grygla."

To Diliani's surprise, Silarude gave forth a series of deep, undulating sounds that echoed through the grotto. "Not young woman like you. I old, used woman, leader of Grygla."

The amazed kirin had never thought of this creature as female or male; in fact, she had not considered these beings as having gender at all. They were simply mysterious, astounding and frightening things.

Silarude spoke in a voice not dissimilar to the others'. Broms's speech was the same, as was that of Boros. The wrinkled one, except for her aged skin, looked like and was clothed like all the rest. What were Broms and Boros, she wondered, male or female? She asked the old one.

"Broms man Grygla, Boros man Grygla," answered Silarude, and she poured forth the same reverberating sound as before. Even though the expression on her face stayed unchanged, except for her mouth opening slightly wider, Diliani suspected that what she was hearing was Grygla laughter.

Diliani asked why Silarude was the only one able to communicate with her. "How did you learn Ruvon, the kirin tongue? You live close to the kirins of the Shillitoe tribe.

Have you somehow been associated with them? Did you learn the language from them?"

Silarude had revealed she was leader of her tribe. Diliani wondered whether she had ever met Lanara, also a woman leader, and she asked about this also.

Her hostess's expression remained unaltered, but Diliani could sense that her recent questions had put an end to laughter and revelry, Grygla or otherwise. The old one stared through large unblinking eyes, open only slightly, and began a recitation that her visitor would never forget.

"Kinin no friend!" she said, to the bewilderment of the kirin. "No like kinin, no like Shillitum! Grygla remember!" She paused and looked away from Diliani as though collecting her thoughts. Suddenly she turned back, and her voice exploded. "Shillitum cave not Shillitum!" she exclaimed. Then she was silent.

Diliani was concerned why the aged Grygla was suddenly angry, and so hostile toward kirins, even though Broms, a Grygla tribesman, and possibly others as well, had saved her life. Able to see in the dark, they had rescued her after she plummeted into the water, as well as from the darkness of her stony entrapment when she had virtually given up hope. Without their help, except for a probably suicidal attempt to escape via the waterfall, she would doubtless still be imprisoned.

Unable to comprehend what Silarude meant about the cave, Diliani asked timidly again about the Shillitoe tribe and the proximity of those kirins. The old woman seemed to sift through her vocabulary, selecting her words carefully as she answered.

And gradually, as the kirin listened, an incredible story came forth haltingly and painstakingly from the teller's mouth. At first, because of the wrinkled one's broken Ruvon, and because of what she seemed to be saying, Diliani was unable to fathom what Silarude was trying to explain. Yet what ultimately came across was the picture of a struggle occurring very long ago, a struggle between rival factions, between two different races, a struggle of life and death.

One group, which Diliani assumed to be the Gryglas' ancestors, had dwelled in a home they found. They had strenuously built and improved upon it with their hands, and with their sweat, blood, and tears. There they lived contentedly for many years. But one day another group invaded their settlement and their privacy, introducing into their surroundings an element they had grown to survive completely without, and that now they could not tolerate. By this factor they were driven out of their homes, away from their peaceful habitat, and they never returned.

Silarude paused, looking at the floor for a long time, and Diliani finally asked something. "What could have displaced your people from their homes, and where did they live?"

The old woman looked back into the kirin's eyes. "Fire make Grygla go," she said. "Grygla remember."

Then she continued her tale, elaborating on what she had already told. She revealed that an unknown disaster had befallen the other race. They came looking for a new place to reside and found and invaded the peaceful space of the Gryglas. They discovered a cave, but unbeknownst to them it was the home of Grygla ancestors. They entered, bringing with them light. That very space now regarded as the Shillitoe cave had once been the haven of Gryglas.

"Grygla no like fire," said Silarude. "Go from cave, kinin stay."

Scenes of light-sensitive Gryglas, shielding giant eyes and fleeing from the blazing brilliance of kirin torches, flashed through Diliani's mind. What a tragedy, she thought painfully, and she found herself feeling guilty for something that had occurred eons ago, because she was a member of the kirin race, and it was kirins who had engendered the Gryglas' dislodgement. What kind of disaster, she wondered, could have befallen the kirins to force them to leave their previous dwelling site and invade the home of the Gryglas? And the marvelous cave! How much of that structure is the result of Grygla building, and how much owes to the efforts of the Shillitoes? As she thought of the cave now she felt quite differently about it than she had before.

Then, still uncertain how this Grygla woman could speak a kirin language, Diliani asked about it again.

"Are you the only one who speaks the kirin tongue?" she questioned, not knowing what to expect as a response.

"I say kinin word," said Silarude. "I and son Biros only Grygla say kinin word. Talk to kinin sometime. Need kinin word. I die, Biros say kinin word."

Diliani had met Boros, but not Biros, and she wondered fleetingly whether they were one and the same, the name being pronounced slightly differently. It was a matter, however, that she was not able to clarify completely.

"Then," said Diliani, questioning the old Grygla further, "when he dies, who will be able to talk to the kirins?"

"He teach son, daughter. For many family time, many . . . parent, many gen . . . genel . . . how say?" asked Silarude.

"For many generations," said Diliani.

"Many . . . genelation Grygla leader talk kinin word. Only one Grygla family talk kinin word. Leader say kinin word, teach son, daughter." And here she finally answered a question posed earlier by her guest. "When I girl, father teach," she said, striking her breast. "Go with, meet Shillitum. Kinin girl there with father. Name Lanada, never see again. We live, they live."

Then they have met after all! thought Diliani with rising excitement. These two woman leaders met when they were very young! I wonder whether it would be of benefit for them to meet again? But, in her current precarious circumstances, she made no mention of anything like that.

"How many individuals like you live elsewhere," asked Diliani, "other than those in your tribe?"

"Not know now. Many in past. Now know only Grygla," said Silarude.

"Then your ancestors remained here," said Diliani, "near the cave, instead of moving on to another place?"

The wrinkled one again made the low resounding sound Diliani interpreted to be laughter. Then she responded. "Where go? Outside cave? Outside great fire! Kinin like! Great fire blind Grygla! Build tunnel," she continued, indicating the passageways all around them, "some before, some after Shillitum come. Go them. Always hope again live Grygla cave. Not return if fire, live here. Long ago many Grygla try go cave, kinin use fire, we come back here. Wait kinin leave cave. Wait kinin go again live near great fire. Then Grygla go our old home."

Diliani was perplexed by what Silarude meant about the Shillitoes living near the great fire. But she had other questions and did not pursue this further.

"But," asked the puzzled kirin, "if you do not like kirins, why did your people save me from the water and the darkness, which I might never have been able to get out of alone?"

"You smell same," came the response, "but differen talk, differen clothes, differen kinin we not see before. Broms see you trouble, know you differen, save you, bring here."

Diliani recalled the Shillitoes' voices, so mellow, except for those of Issar and Lanara, and so enticing. Mine must indeed be different, she thought. She looked down at her tattered traveling outfit, one of the Yorl clan's, and marvelled that these creatures could tell the difference between her garments and those of Shillitoes in complete darkness. She realized they would never have seen kirin clothing of such a nature before. And, of course, she remembered being sniffed.

"But," asked Diliani, "if your people and the Shillitoes are such enemies, why do you not attack them when they are in the dark passages? They cannot see you at all."

"Not kill Shillitum," was the response. "If do, they come with fire."

"Then," questioned Diliani, "why do the Shillitoes not illuminate all of the tunnels with torches, like the one Broms gave to me, but much brighter?"

"Kinin try in past," said the old one. "Grygla wait, kill all fire in tunnel when kinin go." Here the Grygla stopped, and looked down for a moment before concluding. "But cannot kill all fire in cave."

And there it was, suddenly and sadly, plain for Diliani to see. Here were two factions, a tribe of kirins and one of Gryglas, which for hundreds, perhaps even thousands of years, had lived adjacent to each other, hardly communicating. They maintained an unwritten truce, but an uneasy one, the Gryglas not allowing their tunnels to be lighted, the Shillitoes not tolerating the assault of their tribesmen. The Gryglas, perhaps a dying race, were helpless in the light of day and found the black corridors and caverns an acceptable substitute for their cave. They patiently awaited the day when its brightness might be extinguished and it could be theirs once more. And the Shillitoes, for their part, had lived as cave-dwellers for so long that they had probably lost their skills and their appetite for living in the out-of-doors. They were now not inclined to move. All of the pieces of the puzzle were in place, save one. What had caused the Shillitoe kirins to seek an alternative shelter in the first place, and thus to invade the cave? But Diliani did not ask about this. She had extracted as much information from the wrinkled Grygla as she felt comfortable doing.

What an innocent and sylvan existence we lived—she caught herself employing the past tense, and did not bother to correct it—in the woods of Rogalinon and Rogustin, among all the plants and trees of the home forest. Why should it take a trek like the one we have made to tell us how fortunate we were? While we were there we knew it not.

"You hungry," said the old one. "Need kinin food. Need rest. Take you cave."

Silarude struggled to her feet and moved to the entrance of the chamber. She boomed out a single command and then returned to her previous position.

Shortly Broms appeared in the entryway, and a brief conversation ensued. Silarude then turned to Diliani and motioned her toward Broms. "Go," she said simply.

Recognizing the uneasy predicament these creatures were locked into with the Shillitoes, and knowing that they had saved her life, Diliani found that she was moved at the prospect of leaving them, especially this woman. Yet at the same time she was profoundly anxious to return to the Shillitoe cave, and, if they had not already departed, to her clansmen.

"Thank you for everything you have done for me," said Diliani.

She rose and began to move across the room. As she did so she realized how exhausted she was from lack of sleep, lack of food, and worry.

She passed behind the seated old woman and touched the rough cloth covering her wrinkled head. "I will think of you," said Diliani. "I will never forget you."

She picked up her meager torch and walked toward Broms. Then she disappeared through the doorway and was gone.

As they moved together down the dusky passageway, Diliani knew that her fate was once again in the hands of the Grygla accompanying her. Before allowing herself only optimistic thoughts, she shivered, and wondered whether she was finally being led toward Manay, and toward the brightness of the Shillitoe cave, and to freedom at last, or into some other unpredictable and hazardous misadventure.

C H A P T E R   1 2

W E MUST BE ALLOWED
to join the hunt!" Speckarin had demanded. "She is our
compatriot, and we possess the only means of finding her,
our bird ilon!"

"Your place is here!" repeated the ancient Lanara, equally
resolute that they not depart.

They were within the fairinin near Talli's bed, waiting not
only for her to awaken, if such was to be the result of
treatment, but also for news of Diliani. Present were
Speckarin and Hut, the old queen, and personnel of the
healing area. All other able-bodied Shillitoes had been
dispatched in the search.

Her arguments are sound, Speckarin was forced to admit.
The visiting kirins had almost no acquaintance with the
territories outside the main cave. They had no way of knowing
where to look. As the queen pointed out, their efforts might
confound all of the searchers, both themselves and the
Shillitoes, and might even lead them into a worse predicament.
They might end up looking for us, he confided to himself.

Nonetheless, the wait was interminable for the old
magician. He had grown agitated enough to ask again,

wanting to be able to do something, to do anything, to help locate Diliani. He wished he knew how long she had been gone. Time is impossible to estimate inside this infernal place, he thought unhappily. All of the cave's charms had dissipated for him with the startling disappearance of Diliani.

Lanara was mired in her own troubled thoughts. She recognized that these two visitors might be the only ones capable of finding the missing woman because of their bird ilon, should the foreign female be outside of the cave. But the old queen was hardly certain that Diliani was far from where they were right now. Lanara had not mentioned, nor had she any intention of doing so, that a series of passageways existed around the cave. These were too numerous and complex for the visitors to possibly explore. She had not even ordered her tribesmen to investigate the more far-reaching of them.

Shillitoe kirins were, as a rule, not acquainted with the labyrinth of underground passages, even though they were adjacent to the cave. They were not in the slightest aware of the history and capabilities of beings that dwelt within them. Rumor had it that tribesmen in the past, who had ventured too far, had met with untoward circumstances, but the details were never fully explained. What was known was that they were to remain, as they entered and departed the cave, only within tunnels commonly used. In these they would encounter no trouble. To wander further afield might lead to unspecified danger. And that is exactly the way we want to keep it, thought Lanara, her unequivocal gaze trained on the supine Talli.

Deep within her heart she was afraid the foreign kirin had lost her way in attempting to exit to the outside and was lost in that dark, secret, subterranean wasteland. Her tribesmen had been instructed to seek the kirin woman and her bird, but in the out-of-doors, beyond the confines of the cave and its tunnels, and also in the well-known passageways. As she rested in the fairinin, alone with her dark thoughts, the Shillitoe queen determined that if the lost one were not found in those areas, her tribe would be obligated to search the hidden and unknown tunnels they had never entered.

All consideration of Runagar joining the quest had been abandoned. The Shillitoe lad had been one of those departing in the hunt.

Many of the search parties had left after Speckarin made his way to the fairinin. The old magician had gone to the entrance of the small cave and had wistfully observed them departing in force with fox ilon through the same archway he and Diliani had passed through only the day before. Or was it the day before that? he wondered apprehensively. Time meant nothing to him now, and at this point it seemed far longer than one or two days.

"Attend to your fallen lass," Lanara admonished now, speaking to the Yorl magician and sounding almost reassuring. "My tribesmen, my kinsmen, will make as thorough a search as possible." Speckarin recognized that he could do no more than she suggested, and he returned to Talli's side.

Hut had waited by his comatose friend. He recalled with curiosity and wonder the uncanny vision he had had on the journey back to the Shillitoe cave, while riding with Runagar, both aboard Lisam. Unfortunately it has come to pass, he told himself. It is happening indeed. The vigil for Talli goes on in the absence of Diliani. I envisioned this. I knew it would happen long before it did.

But he had no idea how he could have done so, and yet it was obvious that he had, and he pondered it over and over again as he gazed blankly at his unconscious companion.

As nothing seemed to be changing with Talli, and as no information on Diliani was forthcoming, Speckarin divided his time between two activities. He watched over the girl, of course, and periodically moved to the mouth of the fairinin to look toward the entrance of the main cave. On occasion when he left Talli's side to cast his glance toward the floor of the space, he would think, in his anxiety and exhaustion, that he envisioned Diliani and Manay re-entering. For an instant he would be glad that two more of their entourage had returned to be among them. But each time he was disappointed, finding that the vision was but a fond hope, a product of his activated imagination, and he would return disconsolately to the reclining youngster.

There, as he observed, on more than one occasion he thought the girl was moving an arm or a leg, or a foot, more meaningfully than before, or that an altered breathing pattern had ensued. He was encouraged momentarily, until he realized that nothing was changing. The watch for the old magician continued in this grievous and discomforting manner as he moved from one point of observation to the other, his hopes rising repeatedly and then falling precipitously again.

All at once, to the surprise of Speckarin, who calculated that he had all the points of entry within his watch, a lieutenant of the queen stepped abruptly into the mouth of the healing area. He moved without hesitation toward the ancient kirin woman, stopping in front of her. She is the unquestioned leader of this tribe, thought Speckarin.

The queen turned her gaze upon the newly arrived aide, who then spoke rapidly in the local dialect.

Lanara turned calmly toward Speckarin and translated the information into Ruvon. "No evidence has been found of the missing party," she said. And to the magician's further disappointment she went on with more news. "They concentrated their efforts outside the cave, looking there first because your compatriot is probably in the company of her raven. They have also searched the customarily used tunnels. They have found no sign of the missing woman and her ilon. We may be forced to begin looking in areas more difficult to . . . reach and to cover."

The queen was silent for a few moments, apparently turning the alternatives over in her mind. "We will continue to hunt," she said.

She looked toward her aide and gave a new series of instructions. The lieutenant gazed at her as if trying to be certain he had heard correctly. Then he turned on his heel and departed as quickly as he had arrived.

Lanara made no mention to the visitors what new directives had been given. Speckarin began to wonder what her orders could possibly have been, where else the searchers could be dispatched, if they had already looked everywhere she had stated.

The vigil continued for Speckarin and Hut, but there was no demonstrable change in Talli. They knew not how long they waited, except that it was a very long time.

The old queen remained with them throughout. Eventually she suggested that they were tired, and that, as long as no further alteration had occurred in the girl, they might retire to their chambers for a rest. She said they would be summoned immediately should anything change, should any discovery be made regarding the lass in the fairinin or the absent woman.

The magician reluctantly agreed that they did require a respite. They took leave of the healing area and descended the wall to the guest rooms. There they entered, and this time Hut remained with Speckarin in the magician's chamber, neither of them wishing to be parted from the other. The youth fell asleep in a chair, while the old magician reclined restlessly upon the bed. Eventually he slipped into a fitful slumber.

He awoke with a start, unsure how long he had been sleeping. It is impossible to tell the time of day in this atmosphere, he grumbled, as he swung his long feet over the edge of the bed and stood up. He quickly woke Hut and they departed, ascending the wall once more toward the fairinin. As they made their entry they observed, to their disappointment, that everything seemed the same with Talli. They greeted the ancient queen, who appeared not to have moved a muscle since their departure.

"Nothing has changed here," she confirmed, "and no word has been received of the woman."

But almost before she finished her words, the same lieutenant who had taken her commands hurried through the entrance once again. He approached the queen and made a long awaited report. At its conclusion she translated again for the anxiously awaiting visitors.

"We have no word of your Diliani," she said. Then, after a brief pause, she went on unemotionally. She delivered the next message in her reedy voice without hesitation, doubt or equivocation. "I have made a difficult decision. With the exception of sentries in the tunnels we are acquainted with, I must bring my tribesmen home." Then she turned and apparently gave new instructions to her aide.

The drooping Speckarin found that he could not argue. But he knew what it meant. The indication for her action was clear and her message was apparent. The Shillitoes could do no more to find the missing Diliani. No one, including himself, had any recourse now other than to simply wait, and to hope for her reappearance.

The old queen had informed him sometime earlier that a series of underground passages existed around the cave. But he had no knowledge of their vastness and complexity, and no mention had been made that anything living might inhabit them. Little did he know that because of these beings, and the fact that the tunnels were indeed so occupied, the queen's judgment was being affected. The magician was deeply disappointed, but he understood that nothing further could be done, and he reluctantly began to accept the predicament as it was.

"Look!" exclaimed Hut. Speckarin turned toward him and he was pointing at Talli.

The magician quickly knelt down beside the girl. He concentrated his attentions upon her, and was soon amply rewarded. He began to detect movements that had not been present since she was laid upon this bed.

The old magician and Hut stayed at her side, now and throughout the remainder of her ordeal and long-awaited recovery. They spoke to her in hushed tones, reassuring her that she was safe and in good hands, their enjoyment and their amazement at seeing her coming back to life tempered only by their ongoing concern for Diliani.

Talli was definitely stirring, more so than ever since her fall. She was shifting in posture, and seemed to be struggling. After a lengthy period of restlessness, twitching, and haphazard movement of arms and legs, she eventually became quiet again. All at once she opened her eyes and began to blink. Then, to the delight of all who were surrounding and observing anxiously, she appeared to be casting random glances about the enclosure, as if attempting to discover where she might be. Ultimately her gaze fell upon the old magician, whom she knew so well. She reached out a hand and touched his arm. Next she placed the hand over her right eye, and massaged it gently. Finally, to the interest of all, she began to speak.

"I have been exceedingly far away," she said. She had a blank look in her eyes, but she was unquestionably looking at Speckarin. "I have been somewhere in the greatly distant past. At first I knew that something grave and traumatic had happened to me, but I knew not what it was. I found myself in a place I had never been before, and I sensed that I was almost assuredly doomed, even destined to remain there forever. I thought for a long while that I was alone, and at the beginning I was cold and lonely. But gradually I began to realize that I was among others, among other kirins, and somehow I knew that they were our ancestors. But for a very long time I could not see their faces, as they seemed to be avoiding me wherever I turned. I wandered, alone, through what seemed a dim twilight, and I knew I was lost. But I became resigned to that, and my wanderings continued through shadows, and shrouded images, and darkness, and occasional flashes of brilliant light.

"I attempted," continued the blond-haired girl, blinking and looking only at Speckarin, "to communicate with the dimly outlined kirins about me, but always without success. And then, after a time, they all seemed to be milling and congregating around something, around some attraction, but I knew not what it was. I could feel that I was weakening, that my aris was failing, and that I most urgently required help or

I would die. But they ignored me as if I were not present at all. Yet I could sense that they knew I might soon join them, and that they would welcome me graciously in that event.

"For an eternity," she said, "I wandered about the place where many of them were gathering, as if waiting for something to happen. But I received no help or information whatsoever, until in my solitude and resignation one of the ancestral beings turned toward me, and for the first time I could see a face. It was kind, and pleading, and without saying a word the ancestor motioned me toward him, as if requesting that I come nearer, and I did so. Then he turned away again, and blended in with the others, but I continued to move forward. As I did, the crowd, which had been arranging itself as if in rows about a central attraction, parted before me and made a pathway. I progressed for what seemed a great distance through the multitude, through a sea of ancient kirins, none of whom looked at me or even in my direction, nor acknowledged me in any way. I proceeded on ahead, toward a destination that all of them appeared to be facing, toward a point that they were somehow indicating I must achieve.

"And finally," she said, somewhat more animatedly, "I could see something at the center of this gathering and throng of kirins. I slowly approached it, since all of them seemed to be looking at it, and as I did so I could begin to make out what it was. It was a pedestal, dark of hue, perhaps black in color, and upon its flat upper surface burned a diminutive fire. But it barely flickered, and gave off so little light that it illuminated even the closest of the ancestral kirins only meagerly.

"Suddenly, a jarring realization came to me about what I was seeing. I was observing my aris, my very own aris, in its final dwindlings, and its waning was being observed by a multitude of our ancestors, perhaps all of our ancestors. I had been summoned to witness its demise myself, and therefore in fact to witness my own death. But without the ancestors saying a word or moving a muscle, I was made aware by them, by the multitude gathered in that place, of something very important. I would be welcomed into their company, I would not be lonely or distressed, my transformation from living kirin into one who could join them would be painless and smooth, and I would merely be absorbed cordially and comfortably into their midst.

"We stood, for a long time, watching and waiting. The only thing that changed was the flame, which continued to diminish and was eventually barely visible. Finally, the last vestiges of fire went out. Only a glowing cinder remained, thin smoke trailing upward from it. Even the glint from this became ever fainter and weaker. I knew it would soon be extinguished entirely, and that my life would then be over. I thought of you, and of all of my friends at home, and of my family. I dearly wished to see everyone one more time before I died and joined these ancestors."

Talli reached up and once again touched her right eye.

"And then, as quickly as a flash, something occurred that changed everything, both within me and around me," she said. "I suddenly sensed an irritation, a burning within my eye, and at precisely the same moment the cinder, whose glow had become barely perceptible, burst into a vivid flame of a golden color. It was small at first but it grew in magnitude, slowly but visibly. When I turned to observe the reaction of the others, the ancestors, to my astonishment they were gone, every one of the vast multitude having disappeared! I was standing alone by the enlivening blaze!

"All at once I sensed something new. I felt myself being drawn upward by some unknown and unseen force, and I was lofted above and away from the fire. I watched it from on high even as it burgeoned, and scintillated, and flourished. But it receded ever further into the distance as I went upward, until finally it disappeared as a distant flash. I had moved so far away that it was now gone from vision, and I was in total darkness. But then, gradually, I sensed light around me again, as if I were in a dim haze or a faintly illuminated cloud, and it grew even brighter as I ascended. I heard sounds, the sounds, I thought, of voices, and I was glad. I wondered whether I was going home, or becoming alive once more. I remembered happily that my aris was burning, strongly and brightly, somewhere far below, now totally out of my sight. I barely made out the outlines of an interior space, this space, and realized that I was nearing home or my previous life once again. And," she said, struggling for the first time to raise her head off the pillow, "it seems that I have returned!"

"You have indeed!" responded a most moved and joyful Speckarin, celebrating the remarkable revival of the girl and the astounding chronicle of her journey. "You have come back from something few kirins ever have, from a witnessing of your own aris, and of our ancestors, and we are exceedingly glad you have! You have been to the ancestral fields, and you have returned. You have seen something of the ways of kirin life and death. We carry on what is termed life as long as our aris burns, but when the flame of living fails, we are united with our predecessors, our forerunners, in a process neither unpleasant to us nor overburdening to them. We are taken in, absorbed, and nurtured as a part of the whole, as we know all other and future kirins will be. But we are extraordinarily happy that for the present time you will remain close to us, to the living. We have missed you profoundly," he concluded, "and have anticipated your safe return!"

Speckarin glanced about the fairinin, at the beaming faces surrounding the revitalized Talli. It is a joyous occasion indeed, he thought.

But his pleasure was all at once blunted, and he frowned, because again he remembered that Diliani was still not among them.

C H A P T E R   1 3

THE exhausted Diliani
entered the dazzlingly illuminated space. As she did so her
only thought was to make her way to the fairinin, to discover
whether Talli had recovered. She had no concept of what her
appearance might be like to the few astonished Shillitoes who
were near the entrance of the cave.

She dropped her fading torch to the ground. She
commanded Manay to return to her place of shelter with the
other ravens, and the great bird obeyed.

Only moments earlier Diliani had experienced an
exhilarating reunion with an elated Manay near the interior
entrance to the Shillitoe cave. She and the raven had been
escorted, through different corridors and by varying routes, to
the same destination. They were next led to the mouth of the
cave, where she bade farewell to Broms and another unnamed
Grygla, and she and Manay stepped into the glaring brightness.

Now, hands shielding her eyes from the blinding light,
brighter to her at this moment than an unclouded sun at
midday, she staggered across the floor of the cave and found
her way to the central bridge and then to the far wall. I
know, she thought, what the Grygla people must have felt

those many years ago when kirins invaded their privacy and their beloved home with blazing and defiling fire. I am now part Grygla myself, unable to see because of the brilliance, and yet able to comprehend what one living thing can do to another.

As she had moved through the dim passageways with Broms on the way to the joyful meeting with Manay, Diliani had thought of Silarude, as she had promised to do. She knew she had been changed by her experience in the dark and with these underground people. Later she attempted to explain to Speckarin and to others what had befallen her, what her saviors had been like, and how she felt about them. But no one could seem to fully fathom what she meant, nor what indelible impressions had been made upon her. And yet from that time onward, when she looked at Shillitoe kirins she saw them in a different light. In fact, she felt differently about all kirins, wondering what they were made of, deep down inside, and what they might be capable of doing if truly provoked by unusual or untoward circumstances. But she kept all these feelings to herself, never mentioning them to another kirin for the rest of her lifetime. And from that day forward she thought many times of Silarude and the Grygla people, having forever been altered by them and by what they had done for her.

Sometimes later in life, as she was going to sleep at night, she would see Silarude, her face crinkled into a strange smile, and would hear her speak. "Grygla people always live underground," she would say. "Like dark, not like fire. Live good in dark. Grygla eyes never need flame."

How dissimilar those beings are from us, Diliani would think, shunning light and not tolerating the sun whatsoever, while those things are such necessities for us. And yet I owe everything to them, for without them I would still be in the dark myself.

Now disdaining the help offered by kirins nearby, for reasons they could not begin to understand, Diliani found the stairway leading upward from the base of the wall. She began a halting climb up the vertical surface, moving laboriously but as industriously as her flagging strength would allow. Followed closely by two kirins whose aid she had refused, she found her way eventually to the location of the healing area. Arriving at the promontory of the small cave, she arrested her progress and turned unsteadily around. She looked toward the waterfall emerging from the wall of stone that had been her profound restraint and her prison. She searched briefly but vainly for the minuscule aperture which had been her only window to this world. It was so far away that she could discern nothing but solid rock. Then she cast her glance downward, toward the floor of the cave, a sight she had last seen through the tiny opening in the wall, how long ago she did not know. She was too haggard, she found, to appreciate even a sense relief at viewing the scene from this new and more friendly vantage point.

Swaying from hunger and lack of strength, and barely able to remain standing, she turned toward the entrance of the fairinin. Through sheer resolve she forced herself forward and stumbled inside, searching for Talli as she did. For the first time in days a look of satisfaction crossed Diliani's careworn face. She caught sight of the blond girl, sitting up and blinking at her in amazement, before she collapsed heavily at the foot of the bed.

■ ■ ■

Speckarin might have been depleted to the point of exhaustion by now. But everything was changed by the startling reappearance of Diliani and the long-awaited rebirth of Talli. The old magician divided his time and attentions cheerfully between the two of them, moving between their resting places within the fairinin. He inspected them and ordered nutriment and drink, oblivious to the fact that he was but a guest himself. He cared little about anything except that at long last the four of the traveling group, Hut, Diliani, Talli, and himself, were back together again.

■ ■ ■

Some time had elapsed since Diliani's entrance into the fairinin. The crowd of Shillitoes that gathered upon word of her arrival had long since dispersed, and only Lidor, his attendants, and Speckarin's party remained. Those within the healing area settled into a pattern of caring for Diliani and Talli. The old magician was ecstatic, as was everyone else, Shillitoe and visitor alike. They celebrated that Diliani had found her way back and that, except for being exhausted, she seemed unharmed.

In the days to follow, the energy of the Shillitoe tribe was concentrated upon the visitors. Their ministrations were gracious and appropriate, and were gratefully received. A consistent recovery was seen in both patients. The Yorl woman grew stronger more quickly than the girl, her only needs being rest and, as Silarude had suggested, "kinin food," both of which were amply granted. Talli's recuperation was steady also, however, and heart-warming to her compatriots and the entire Shillitoe tribe, which relished the response of their visitors. The girl's return to strength simply took longer, so near had her aris been to extinction, so close had she been to death itself.

When Diliani was capable of speaking, Speckarin questioned her about where she had been and what she had encountered, having been gone for so long a time. She responded slowly and superficially, determined that before revealing the entire history, even to her magician, she would speak privately with Lanara.

■ ■ ■

"This will be a mission of far greater hazard, but also of more profound significance, than either you or your son can imagine," counseled Speckarin.

"We know little of what is involved," replied Bynaran, the father of Runagar, "except what our queen has said. It is an expedition of vital and far-reaching importance to all kirins, not just those of our tribe, and our son is deeply desirous of joining it."

"We are proud of everything we have learned of our son," added Rana, Runagar's mother, "beyond what we already knew."

Speckarin was reminded of a different gathering, also one of great importance, on the eve of their departing Rogalinon. The parents of young Hutsin had agreed to the mission, and had attested to his desire to go. I wonder, thought the old magician, whether Hut was quite as eager to go as this Shillitoe lad appears to be.

The gathering currently under way was momentous in its own right, a meeting of individuals seated about the throne of Queen Lanara. The purpose was to discuss the quest of the visiting kirins, and to decide about the proposed participation of young Runagar.

Twelve days had elapsed since the awakening of Talli and the re-entry of Diliani into the cave. Both had made steady advances in recovery. Diliani was nearly back to normal, but Talli was not. She was not as confident in her flying capabilities as Speckarin and Diliani felt that she should be—that she must be—in order to participate in the endeavor they would face upon departure. The girl had been working with Diliani every day, attempting to improve.

In addition to Runagar and his parents, present at the conclave were all the kirins of the traveling party, selected elders of the host tribe, and Loos, the chief practitioner of curlace magic of a neighboring tribe.

"Loos and Diliani have informed me," said Speckarin to the parents of the Shillitoe lad, "that Runagar has made great progress, unbelievable progress in fact, with the newly borrowed ilon. His enthusiasm and intensity with this bird, and the magic of his voice, have me thinking he might be a member of value in our party. But I must again caution you about the mission. As I look at you, his parents, I am not fully assured that you or he, as brave a lad as he appears to be, are wholly aware of the nature of our quest. For that reason I asked your queen to convene this meeting tonight."

That bird is an unusual creature, thought Speckarin, reminded of the new ilon. What a huge thing it is by comparison to our ravens, themselves among the largest birds in the home territories. He stifled a chuckle as he contemplated the strange bird and its habits, thinking of its head, and of how it slept.

The neighboring Shilliron tribe had been approached for the purpose of obtaining an ilon for Runagar. It had to be a flying one, of course. The Shillitoes possessed none and were opposed to employing them. But the Shillirons were told everything about the trek and the intentions of the traveling entourage, and the gigantic creature was loaned. What a sacrifice it must be, thought Speckarin. That tribe has only a few of these birds, great and awkward as they are. But after an appeal from Queen Lanara herself, who traveled from her cave for the first time in many years to make it, they were convinced that Runagar might make a serious contribution to the mission. After consideration they acceded and granted the use of Glinivar, the most prized among their birds, to join the quest as Runagar's vehicle.

"The Shillirons are aware," said Lanara in her rasping voice, "of the occurrences prompting our decision to join this mission. I think most tribes are by now. Many have been touched and troubled by the same evil that befouled the Yorl and Moger clans, and our tribe. More and more kirins are willing to involve themselves in support of activities like the expedition of our brave friends." She nodded in the direction of the visitors. "Thus the Shillirons parted with their esteemed ilon, signifying their dedication toward the purpose of this quest. I am not surprised they did. The evil has become too rampant for us to ignore it, even though many of us did for a very long time."

My sentiments exactly, thought Speckarin. It was that way with Duan, my companion magician of the Moger clan. He was reminded of countless debates he had conducted with his friend on the same subject. He wondered how his old confrere was holding up all this time they had been away. He allowed himself a moment to reflect upon the home clans, and upon Rogalinon and Rogustin. How far away they seemed. He thought about a statement he had made at the final gathering on Rogalinon, that it might be more taxing and perilous to remain at home than to go on the quest. He wondered whether this had proven to be true. He suddenly felt compassion for all those at home, and a profound desire to be among them. He wanted to greet them, to find out for himself that they were all right, if indeed they were. But he knew that the only way he could return to them would be to concentrate his efforts here, to continue planning, and to carry out the expedition. He forced his attentions back to the meeting at hand, and to Lanara, who was addressing him with a question at that very moment.

"When would you like to make your departure?" she asked, as the old magician brought himself back to reality.

"As soon as feasible, of course," was his response. "Runagar has already been approved for the trek, only five days into training with his ilon. We await Talli's fitness for flying and concerted travel."

"When do you expect," asked the queen, turning to Diliani, "that Talli will be prepared?"

Diliani had been strangely silent throughout the proceedings. The old queen had taken note of this, and directed this inquiry toward her purposefully, in order to involve her in the conversation. As with Speckarin, Diliani's thoughts had not been totally upon matters at hand. But when called upon she stood up and responded.

"She will not be ready to depart," she said cooly, "for several more days, perhaps as many as four or five. Having fallen from her bird, and then having come so close to death's door, she still requires time. We must not hurry her." But after answering the question posed to her, she did not stop.

Several days earlier Diliani had requested an audience with the queen. The two of them were alone. She had attempted to uncover information regarding several situations and problems that had been plaguing her. To her disappointment and chagrin, however, she had been entirely rebuffed. Her questions had been dismissed, no answers given at all. This evening, however, as she sat among the others at this gathering, she determined to try once more. In the company of the others, and in the framework of a formal session, the old queen might be forced out of embarrassment or pressure to respond to her questions. Diliani felt she had nothing to lose. After all, she is not my queen, the Yorl woman told herself.

Instead of facing the queen, however, she looked at the others of the assemblage as she spoke. "All of you are aware," she said, "that I was lost with my brave raven, Manay. We were in the tunnels around this great central cave. What many of you do not know is by what means I was able to escape, and to return to this place."

Before she could say another word, the aged queen interrupted. "I have considered all your questions thoroughly," she said, "and I will answer them. But it must be in a private meeting, not here."

After her previous experience with the queen, Diliani was hardly satisfied with this response. I might receive the same treatment the next time I am alone with her, she thought. She had resolved that she would have her say, on this occasion and at this conclave. But now she sat down and said no more, deciding to bide her time, to wait for the proper opportunity.

Talk returned to the purpose of the mission and the unusual ilon recruited for Runagar. The bird was being maintained outside the main cave because of its great size.

Issar stood up and looked at Speckarin. "Glinivar could not be escorted through any of the tunnels to our cave," he said in his thin, shrill voice. "We have no experience with bird ilon in our tribe. When I led you into our cave those many days ago with your black ilon, I underestimated their magnitude. I have not told you this before. But I thought your ravens could make it with ease through the tunnel. I had no idea how much trouble you were encountering behind me until I talked with you later. Then I realized how small a space and how tight a squeeze it must have been! I wondered what was taking you so long! I knew you were exhausted, and I led you in by the most direct route to the cave. At the same time, Runagar was leading our fox ilon and your fallen youngsters through a larger tunnel, the customary one for animals. But even that is not large enough for the great bird outside. I must add something here to indulge my prejudices once more, and then I will stop. Shillitoe kirins should stay away from bird ilon! We were not meant to cling to the backs of flying creatures, nor are kirins of any background! That practice can only lead to trouble!" Thus, ending his speech abruptly, he sat down.

His commentary about bird ilon was nearly too much for Diliani. She was preparing a response when Runagar chimed in, almost literally, in his unusually musical voice. "I made the same miscalculation," he said, "about the size of the ravens. When Hut and I left the cave for me to fly, for the sake of expediency I led the birds through the tunnel with the shortest course to the outside, the same one Issar used. Naturally we had similar trouble. But," he said, looking at Issar, "I must differ with you with regarding one point. Some of us were born to fly."

"Indeed you were!" interjected Diliani, who had been chafing. She was again on her feet, having made up her mind to speak. "Your queen has said that you are one of those destined and intended to do so! But you are not alone! You are not the only one of your tribesmen born to fly!" Here she eyed Issar directly and went on with emphasis. "It is my speculation that all Shillitoe kirins were born to fly!"

Expressions of wonder were upon the faces of all present,

except that of Lanara. She merely looked down at the floor and was silent.

"Earlier I mentioned my imprisonment in the stone corridors and caverns that surround this cave," said Diliani. She was warming to the task, but took her time, choosing her words judiciously. Because of the complexities of the matters she was about to address, she had not mentioned them to anyone but the old queen, not even to Speckarin.

"I was irretrievably lost," she said, "except for a time when I could see the bright cave. It was through a tiny opening in the otherwise impenetrable wall adjacent to the waterfall. I did not find my way out alone, as all of you have assumed. I believe it would have been impossible for me to do so."

"Then," asked a bewildered Hut, "how did you return to the cave?"

Diliani cast her gaze upon the queen, who had still not looked up. "I was delivered from the blackness, from the perpetual midnight of the passageways," said the Yorl woman, "by members of a race of beings . . ."

"No!" interrupted the old queen, now glaring at Diliani, her reedy voice as piercing as anyone had ever heard it. "You may say nothing further!"

Diliani had been suppressed long enough, and was not going to be denied. She is not, she reassured herself once more, my queen! To the astonishment of Speckarin, and all the others in attendance, she persisted.

"By members of a race of beings," she repeated undauntedly, "who designed and built the very cave you live in!" She turned and pointed outward into the cave behind her, the giant illuminated space they were all so accustomed to.

"They occupied this space," she declared, "for hundreds of years! But they were displaced by a tribe of kirins . . . with the name of Shillitoe!"

Looks of disbelief and wonder were on the faces of all present, with the exception of the queen. Lanara simply drooped even further than was natural for her ancient body.

It is finally out, the old queen told herself. It is known.

Then she noted a queer sensation within herself. Deep down in her heart, among all of her other feelings about it, she sensed that something new was there. Perhaps it is good that it has been revealed, she found herself thinking. Perhaps it has taken a foreign kirin, coming into our midst from the outside, one not involved in the predicament, someone such as this woman kirin, to bring into the open the unholy and unsettling arrangement we have had these many years. The old queen said nothing further until Diliani's story was told.

To the amazement of all, except of course Lanara, Diliani related everything. She told of the Gryglas' past and present existence, and of them rescuing her and escorting her to what is now regarded as the Shillitoe cave. She talked about Silarude and the unresolved affairs of this underground race. Lastly, she mentioned something else, hoping to plant a seed that would someday grow into reconciliation and peace. She spoke of a moment long ago when Lanara, venerable leader of the Shillitoes, had met the veteran leader of the Gryglas, when both were children. She wondered whether somehow they could make contact once again.

When she was through all were silent. Eventually Bynaran spoke. "At first I found it most difficult to conceive that what you were saying was true," he said. "It seems impossible that a race of beings can have lived so close to us all of these years without our realizing it! And yet, considering everything we have heard about the tunnels, and the many experiences we have had, I think it may well be true!"

"It has been an uneasy truce," said Diliani. She went on to explain that for a long time, too long for any living Shillitoe to remember otherwise, the Gryglas and the Shillitoes had coexisted without conflict. But it had not always been that way.

"Long ago," she said, "Gryglas assaulted Shillitoes who were going through the passageways, moving to and from the outside world. But in doing so they provoked retaliatory attacks by the kirins, with a dreaded weapon: fire. When the kirins attempted to illuminate the corridors with torches, the Gryglas would find ways to extinguish them. But they were unable to eliminate all the flames and brightness in the central cave, the one they created but kirins usurped. Thus a stalemate developed many centuries ago, and this silent subterranean race has been all but forgotten by you. But of one thing you can be certain," she concluded. "The Gryglas have not forgotten you."

"We have always known," said Bynaran, "that we were not free to enter the outer and unfamiliar passages, especially alone, and never without a torch. We seldom do so even under those circumstances. We have always heard that danger exists there, that harm could come to us should we venture into the unknown. Such harm has come to kirins who have disregarded the warnings. Therefore we stay away from them. None of my generation has ever been assaulted, nor have we had any trouble at all. When I was young a childhood friend told me that some kind of animal or reptile lived in the outer tunnels, and that they were to be feared. I have never forgotten that. Never would I have thought that they might be what you describe, a race of rational and speaking beings!"

After a long silence Issar got slowly to his feet and posed a question to Diliani. "What, may I ask," he said, in a much more subdued manner than before, "did you mean about all Shillitoe kirins being born to fly?"

For days the Yorl woman had been pondering what Silarude had told her. While recovering in the fairinin, she had dissected every detail of the old Grygla's words over and over again. What puzzled her at first were Silarude's references to the great fire, and the fact that Shillitoe kirins might someday go back to live by it. All at once the meaning had come to her, and she made sense of it. Before they moved into the cave, the Shillitoes had lived in trees, a location that would have seemed as close to the great fire, the sun, as the land-bound and light-fearing Gryglas could imagine.

But instead of Diliani responding, it was the ancient queen who struggled to her feet and spoke. "It is true," she

412 K I R I N S

rasped. "Everything she told you is true." She turned to Speckarin. "The presence of this race in the tunnels was the reason I did not allow you to search for Diliani. All along I suspected, especially when we could not locate her out-of-doors, that she had lost her way in the labyrinthine passages. You were barely acquainted with our environment, and I feared you might become lost in the same corridors. I was also uncertain how Gryglas would react to foreign kirins. But the answer to that is now clear.

"The reason our tribe originally entered this cave," the queen continued, "is unknown today. The event took place too long ago. What is known, by a few of us, is that we were ourselves displaced from our natural homes and habitat, probably by some unremembered disaster, possibly a flood or a fire in the forest."

"If I might ask," interjected Issar, "what did you mean by something you just said, known by a few of us?"

"What is remembered of our past," said the queen, "and of the Grygla people, has been passed down from generation to generation through the reigning family of our tribe, from one member, one king or queen, to the next. For many years, in fact for centuries, it has been the custom of the ruling family to keep this information to themselves, as they attempted to work out a solution to the Grygla problem. But as time went on we became mired and entrenched ever more deeply in our circumstances. After a while, simply remaining in the cave became too easy and too comfortable for us. Over this long period we Shillitoes have lost something: our natural proclivity for living in the out-of-doors, and, believe it or not, for inhabiting trees. All of our skills in tree architecture have been lost through attrition. We would be virtually helpless in the forest we once occupied. But especially dormant is our desire for flying upon bird ilon."

Issar and the others were astounded. "It is my belief," said Lanara, "that good reasons exist why Runagar has longed for flight since he was a small boy, and why he has uncanny ability in controlling the birds he has had the chance to pilot!

First it was Faralan, once he found his magical voice, and now Glinivar, whom he commands skillfully after such a short time! Runagar goes back, through ancestry and genes, to the old times, when Shillitoes dwelled in trees and soared upon bird ilon!"

All but Diliani were astonished, and words of disbelief were quietly exchanged between those of Shillitoe heritage. Runagar's parents were not as shocked as some. From early childhood their unusual son had expressed a profound desire to do these things.

"Because of this," said Lanara, "and because of his voice, unique even among Shillitoes, I am convinced that Runagar would make a worthy addition to the questing party. From the moment of his grandfather's death, at the hands of the same beasts that attacked the clans of our visitors, I have searched for a way in which our tribe could fight back! They struck down Hodorvon, who was my brother, Bynaran's father, and Runagar's grandfather! Fortunately such an opportunity has arisen! These kirins have come from afar with just such a purpose! It is my desire that Runagar carry the title, the reputation, and the honor of the Shillitoe tribe into battle, to be our representative in vanquishing an unspeakable foe!

"I have worked with this lad," said the queen, "with regard to voice. He is prepared. He has the ability to persuade, to imitate, and to be perceived over a great distance. Runagar now embodies the deepest magic of the Shillitoe tribe. His participation in this quest is all our tribe can do to perpetuate your mission and contribute to its cause. If you are willing to accept him," she said, staring at the Yorl magician, "he is prepared to go."

Speckarin had known for some time that this moment would arrive. But he had not known how he would respond. A dialogue about this matter had been carried on in his mind for days. He had also discussed it with Diliani, but he knew that the final decision would be his.

Speckarin had come to admire the enthusiasm and tenacity of young Runagar. From Lanara he had learned about the attributes of the lad's voice. He realized that Shillitoe magic had become concentrated in this kind of ability, and that objects such as calamars were not found among them. He also recognized that, with all of his accoutrements of magic, he could not accomplish things it appeared this boy could. In this regard he might indeed prove useful.

On the other hand, he was a foreign lad, and his ilon was strange indeed. No one could predict how either would react in the emergency situations they were bound to encounter. If one of them should act wrongly, it might endanger the entire expedition.

Speckarin cleared his throat and took a step toward Runagar. Then he made a pronouncement. "If you are prepared to go, as your queen has indicated, may I be the first to welcome you as the newest member of our traveling entourage."

PART FOUR

■ ■ ■

C H A P T E R   1

I WILL MEET WITH
Silarude, leader of the Grygla people," Lanara assured Diliani.

The ancient queen and the Yorl woman stood in the beaming sunlight of morning. They were at the foot of the hill outside the disguised passageway to the main cave. All members of the traveling group were there, as well as every individual of the Shillitoe tribe. The giant camouflaged doors stood open. Departure of the expedition was imminent.

"I recall our coming together well," said the queen. "We were both but children. A rare assemblage was secretly called between the leaders of our tribe and theirs. It was because of a disagreement, the substance of which I cannot remember. My grandfather was king. My father was next in line, and I, as the eldest grandchild, accompanied them through tunnels I had never seen before. We were led by one of the Gryglas. Then, in a dimly lit cavern, we met with Grygla leaders, and somehow a conflict was resolved, whatever it might have been. I remember Silarude well. I have never forgotten her. We were the only children present. She stared at me through the inquisitive eyes of a child, but huge and penetrating ones. Nor have I forgotten how I felt about those creatures, having been told before we departed about the history of the Gryglas, and of our unhealthy relationship with them. The guilt of the Shillitoe tribe for these many years, and my guilt personally, will now be addressed. No easy answers will be forthcoming, but one thing I will promise: We shall meet, and we will make a beginning."

"I do not know whether what I am about to suggest is possible," responded Diliani, "because I know not our destiny. But I will try to return to this place, if it is at all feasible to do so, to visit both you and the Grygla people. I will never forget you, nor will I forget Silarude."

As she spoke, Diliani was reminded of something that had happened just a short while before, as she was traversing the dark tunnel with the others on their way to this entrance. In the beginning a fleeting suspicion had entered her mind, and then an impression, and finally she had the sensation that something, a presence, was somewhere nearby. How she was receiving this information she could not understand. But she realized that, after all the time she had spent in the black corridors, she had developed an alternate means of perceiving things, especially in the dark. She began to recognize that the image was emanating from an adjoining tunnel, and all at once she knew what it was. It was Silarude. Somehow she had known that Diliani and her party were departing. She had left her dingy abode to come to bid her respects and her goodbye to the strange kirin woman from a faraway land.

Diliani had turned toward the place where the presence seemed to be, and at first wanted to go to the old Grygla. But she realized what a spectacle and display and even confrontation it might cause for her to take leave of Manay and the slowly moving train, to separate herself from the entourage and go to a Grygla. She resisted the temptation to do so. She nodded her head in the direction of the old woman. Then she said, to the surprise of Shillitoes nearby, "I will miss everyone who has helped us here. But most especially I will miss those who have helped us the most."

Diliani had looked forward once more, and had moved on. But as she did so she pictured the response of the grizzled old Grygla, a slight smile creasing her wrinkled face, and in the privacy of her own mind Diliani bade her farewell.

The party was now outside, breathing the fresh early morning air, ready for departure. We have spent fourteen days with this tribe, thought Diliani. For two and one-half of those I was lost. Much of my time thereafter was spent in the air nearby, training Runagar and his fascinating new ilon. How remindful this is of the morning we departed Rogustin, and now, with the acquisition of the Shillitoe lad, we are back to our original number of five.

It was early summer. The morning was warm and misty, the grass covered with sparkling dew. The travelers-to-be cast long glances toward the sky. It was to be the sphere of their existence, their realm, for unnumbered days to come. Yellowish-white clouds intermingled with a hazy blue background on this mild morning. A warm breeze filtered through leaves and branches above. It looked to the explorers like a good day for flying.

Speckarin had taken a position next to the Shillitoe queen. While waiting for all to assemble, he noted that the grass they stood upon was intermingled with exquisite tiny blue flowers, the likes of which he had never before seen. He wondered what new flora they might encounter tomorrow, and the day following that, and where they might be in five days, and in ten, and how much progress they would then have made toward their unknown destination.

Soon he called for silence in as loud a voice as he could. He had never spoken to such a large audience before. All conversations ceased and all eyes were upon him.

"At long last, my good friends," he began, "the time has arrived for departure. Our purpose and mission have been incalculably strengthened by you, through your generosity and kindness. When we entered your midst, we were a sorry and beaten crew. But now we are replenished and revived because of you, and are even to be accompanied by one of your courageous fellows. No words or means exist for us to demonstrate our appreciation and gratitude for what you have done, except to be upon our way in pursuit of our goal. We intend to rid the world of this new menace! It has affected you as well as us, and doubtless many others throughout the expanse of kirin civilization! You rescued us when we were at our lowest! You nurtured us, and we are prepared to begin our quest anew!

"One of you, however," he said, lowering his voice, "must be recognized individually, and be given recognition of a special kind. This lad was instrumental in saving Talli, and many days ago was promised something in return for that which he gave up. Would Lindor be somewhere in the crowd?"

The youngster marched eagerly out of the throng and moved quickly toward Speckarin and the queen. He had parted with two treasures he retrieved from the bottom of the stream, a vial and a silver box. He had been anticipating something in return.

As soon as he arrived before Speckarin, the magician opened his bag and began searching through it. "I promised you something from here," he said, "and you will have it . . . if I can find it. Ah, there," he said, bringing out a small object. "This is one of the less consequential products of kirin magic in my possession. I am not certain how it made its way in here. But I ran across it recently and I thought of you. It is a ball, but a unique one indeed, and you are to be its master. When you bounce this ball it will continue to rebound, perpetually, and to the same height it did on the first bounce, until either you snatch it from the air or someone else intercepts it. But if anyone else attempts to do the same, it will react only as any other ball would. Upon my bequeathing this to you, it will respond in this special way for you alone."

Speckarin uttered a few words of incantation under his breath, and then handed the small sphere to the lad. "It is only a plaything," he said, "a toy. But I think you might enjoy it."

Taking his prize in hand, Lindor examined it with pleasure, and then thanked the magician. "I thought maybe you had forgotten me," he said. Then he turned away and walked slowly back to his parents in the crowd, fingering the ball all the while, his progress followed closely by the stares of all Shillitoes present. Articles of magic were almost unknown within their tribe, and this gift made the boy happy indeed.

Speckarin turned toward the wizened queen beside him, and with his right foot he touched hers. "We will think of you throughout our travels," he said. "We will remember you and your tribe as long as we live—long and peaceful lives at home, I hope—after the accomplishment of our mission. No matter what our fate is, however, rest assured that you have succeeded in placing our depleted troupe back in order and once again upon our way."

The magician faced the crowd of Shillitoes. "Your compatriot, Runagar, will be treated as one of us, as a valued and respected member of our entourage. We will bring him home, unscathed and unharmed if possible, should any of our party be capable of doing so."

Without further ado the old magician strode to Ocelam's side and mounted his raven companion. The other visitors followed suit, climbing aboard their ilon. At Runagar's command his massive bird bent her knees and lowered herself toward the ground. When she was close enough he climbed upon her back. He gave further instructions and she stood up to full height once again.

"We will return," called Speckarin, all of the travelers standing ready, "when, and only when, our world is cleansed of evil!"

At the magician's bidding Ocelam lifted off the ground. He was followed closely by the other three ravens, and lastly by Runagar aboard his unique and gigantic bird. Once airborne each traveler glanced to the rear, to see for a last time the Shillitoe tribe below. Within a few moments the entrance to the tunnel and all of their friends on the ground were out of sight.

The party initiated its customary course to the east, toward the sun, which was well above the horizon by this

time of the morning. Through a prearranged plan, Speckarin
assumed the lead position of the flying formation. Talli, the
only one in the company with the knowledge of Olamin,
came behind and to his right. Back of him and to his left flew
Runagar, upon what Speckarin considered such an ungainly
and interesting bird. Diliani trailed them. To the rear of Talli
came Hut, thus filling out the "V" formation they had started
with so long ago when departing Rogustin.

Speckarin found that he could not keep his mind off the
unconventional bird bearing the Shillitoe youth, and
something bothered him about it. The new bird was so unlike
the ravens that its presence in their flying pattern would draw
attention, be it from other birds or animals, from gronoms or
volodons, or even from human beings. Nonetheless, he
resolved that nothing could be done about it. He had
approved of Runagar and Glinivar, and he forced himself to
cease worrying about it.

But he found, as they cruised along, that he turned his
head at frequent intervals to observe the giant bird, at times
doing so almost involuntarily. The creature was huge, even
by the standards of ravens, and appeared awkward and
strange in the flying formation. By comparison to any bird of
the home forest, its legs and its neck were extraordinarily
long. Standing on the ground the bird was three to four times
as tall as an adult raven, and in the air its wing span seemed
to be almost twice that of the largest raven he had ever
known. Its beak was long and narrow and its body was
mostly of a grayish-rust color. But of more interest to the old
magician than anything else was the smooth, feathered crown
at the top of its head of a coloration entirely red. How
amazing, he remarked inwardly, that all the pieces of this
unusual creation fit together! What strange and unique things
are found in nature!

The creature appears to be a strong flyer, Speckarin
thought, for the moment unable to think of anything else.
Birds of this species are reported by the Shillirons to be
durable long-distance flyers, perhaps even more so than

ravens. Maybe in the long run it will outdistance us. What was it, he wondered, that Loos and the other Shillirons called it? Its name is Glinivar, of course, but what was the name of the breed or species? They intimated that it is a relatively common bird throughout the western reaches of the land, but it certainly is not seen in our home forest. I believe "crane" is the name of its kind, he concluded.

Glancing backward once more, Speckarin observed Runagar riding comfortably upon the massive ilon. The lad does well on the back of this creature, he commented to himself. And he made note of something else, the unusual flight characteristics of the bird. It does more beating and flapping of its lengthy wings than do our ravens, probably to keep itself aloft because of its great size and weight. But it also glides part of the time, in a manner similar to the ravens. In contrast to our ilon, however, this bird has a quick upstroke of its wing just above body level, and its elongated neck is held fully extended as it flies.

What a vehicle for young Runagar, he thought, aiming his glance forward once again. It appears, as its reputation would have us believe, that the bird is a powerful flyer. I only hope it is as capable as we have been told. It will be tested before we are through.

The day was warm, and Speckarin attempted to keep his mind on where they were headed and what they might next encounter. He glanced apprehensively about the skies for signs of volodons, which he knew might appear from anywhere and be upon them in moments. But the vistas were clear in every direction, and he settled back to enjoy the flight as best he could, not wishing to ask for trouble that was not apparent.

The company progressed throughout the day without incident, and as evening drew near they searched for a place to stop. When an appealing spot appeared, mature trees beside a body of water, in this instance a fairly sizable lake, they cruised in for a landing. They found suitable places to sleep in two adjacent trees. Dry, inhabitable holes were occupied, and Runagar spent his first night ever sleeping the way he had always dreamed, in a tree. After finding sustenance, the ravens took their places in the branches above the kirins, while the curious bird of Runagar, unaccustomed to being in trees in any fashion, spent the night on the ground.

After they settled in, Talli was restless. She was fully cognizant that she was the only one in the party with the special knowledge. Gronoms, volodons, and possibly even unknown creatures of evil were homing in upon her at that very moment, from a great distance or from nearby. The sheltering qualities of the Shillitoe cave and the tribe inhabiting it, all of which she had grown accustomed to since regaining consciousness, were gone. She felt more vulnerable in the wild, in their small party of five, than she ever had in the cave, even though all those surrounding her now were friends.

Nervously she reclined in her tree hole, and did something she had not done since before her confinement. She began to toy with her ring, still positioned upon the third toe of her right foot. Eventually she slid it off and examined it closely. It was silver and smooth, with no markings at all.

Olamin told me some things about the ring, she reminded herself. But I still don't know why I was capable of contacting Gilin the night of our separation, after the gronom seized Reydel, and have never been able to do so since. By now Gilin has probably arrived home, and is safe and sound. Perhaps he is too far away to be found by the ring.

Then, half-seriously and half-playfully, she held the ring up and aimed it toward the sky, as she had on many previous occasions, always recalling that the moon had been a key influence in her success.

The evening was soft and warm. The heavens were clear and dotted with glimmering stars. But the night was young, and the moon had not yet arisen. After a brief time she found that she was becoming sleepy. She replaced the ring on her toe, closed her eyes, and drifted off into slumber.

She was awakened by the screech of an owl. Her eyes were closing again, and she was about to drift off once more when she noted that the moon was high in the sky. She brought herself back to a state of wakefulness. Removing the ring again from her toe, she gripped it in both hands. As she had always done before, she looked through it directly at the moon and concentrated all of her thoughts upon Gilin.

But nothing happened. As she had on all those nights prior to her fall, she wondered what she could possibly be doing wrong that would prevent her from making contact with her friend. But she knew that little chance of actually finding Gilin existed, and she was only mildly disappointed as she slipped the ring back onto her toe.

She began to drift off again, and as she did she profoundly hoped that the reason she was unable to locate him was not that something untoward had befallen him. Gilin is safe, she reassured herself, and then she slept.

C H A P T E R   2

THE FOLLOWING DAY
was again uneventful as the party moved eastward, widening
the distance between themselves and their last haven, the
Shillitoe cave. In the evening they located another place to
pass the night. They spread out into trees which were close to
one another.

Talli had lost none of her uneasiness and was not sleepy.
She found herself again desirous of trying the toe ring to find
Gilin, while at the same time she knew how dismal she would
feel when she failed. For a long time she was restless, but held
off, not allowing herself to touch or look at the ring, even
though she stayed awake, and even though the moon had
arisen in a clear and cloudless sky. It is huge, she thought,
turning her head to stare at it as she reclined in her snug hole.

It was white, and plump, and shining, and a sudden
realization jarred her. The moon was full, and round, and
inviting, and was the first full moon since the night she had
contacted Gilin! The first full moon, she repeated! She sat up,
aroused, and to her amazement saw that something else was
happening that had not occurred since that fateful night. The
toe ring was aglow!

It is glowing again, she told herself, for the first time since it worked! Dimly glowing, but nonetheless alive! Could it be, she wondered, as she fumbled to retrieve the ring from her toe, that it functions only when the moon is full? Her hands would not work fast enough as she glanced from the luminous orb above to the glowing ring on her toe, and back again to the moon, and she almost dropped the precious thing after finally detaching it. She stood up and stepped quickly onto the branch outside of the hole. She gripped the ring enthusiastically in both hands and held it skyward, sighting the moon through it. She watched with growing zeal as the radiance of the ring intensified immediately.

To her astonishment and joy, for the first time since she had seen Gilin within the magic ring, a mist began to fill the illuminated circle. It clouded her view of the moon until she could no longer see it at all.

It is working again, she thought with exhilaration! I must concentrate all of my energies upon what I wish to see! Without a moment's hesitation she thought of her lost friend. As it had done before, the cloudiness within the ring began to clear, and a vague outline gradually became visible. The picture was at first blurred, but then it clarified itself, and finally it was clear. Hardly able to believe her eyes, the overjoyed Talli was seeing the unmistakable likeness of Gilin.

"Gilin!" came the involuntary cry from her mouth. Her friend was lying down and appeared asleep.

"Gilin!" she called several times. The reclining youth finally stirred, and turned his head sleepily to the side. His eyes were closed, but to Talli's amazement he actually responded.

"Who is calling my name?" he said.

"Gilin! It's me!" cried his old companion. "It is Talli! I have found you once again, and it was through Olamin's magic toe ring! I am seeing you right now!"

Gilin raised his head and blinked his eyes. He glanced anxiously about. "Talli?" he questioned. He sat up, still staring about, attempting to ascertain where the voice could

possibly be emanating from. "It is not a dream after all?" he
said. "Is it truly you? Have you found me?"

"Yes!" shouted the ecstatic Talli. "I have finally
discovered how to activate the ring! As Olamin once
suggested, it must be in communication with your calamar!"

Gilin reached for the belt satchel he had taken off for
sleeping. He removed the calamar.

"It is warming just as before!" exclaimed the astounded
lad. "The two objects must be working together as they did
the first time!"

"Gilin! Are you all right?" asked Talli.

"I am fine!" replied the lad. "Unfortunately Loana has
met with a frightful accident! She is gradually healing, and
Ruggum Chamter is aiding in her recovery. Talli! I have so
much to tell you, and to ask . . ."

His image and voice began to fail, and the mist to return
to the space within the ring. Talli looked up quickly to see a
bank of clouds edging its way across the circle of the moon.

"Gilin!" cried Talli. "Can you still hear me?"

No answer came.

The moon was shrouded only partially at first, but the
advance continued inexorably until it was covered
completely from view, and by then Gilin was gone.

The distraught Talli tried over and over to reestablish
contact, but it was to no avail, and she knew why. The full
moon was no longer visible.

"Speckarin!" she shouted into the trees, not knowing
where the old magician had found a place to rest.
"Speckarin!" she repeated at the top of her voice. "I found
Gilin! I have spoken with him!"

From a tree nearby came a sleepy voice out of the
darkness. "I thought I heard something about Gilin, but I
decided I must have been dreaming," said Speckarin. "You
were dreaming also, and talking in your sleep!"

"No!" said Talli defiantly. "I saw him!" And then a
startling realization came to her. "I saw him," she repeated
blankly. "Speckarin! He was not invisible! His invisibility

was gone! It must have disappeared! How wonderful for him! And he looked good, and said that he was all right! But he also revealed that Loana had suffered injuries, and that Ruggum Chamter was treating her! Speckarin! That means Gilin did go home after all, and that he is safe, as we have all so deeply hoped!"

By now Diliani, Runagar, and Hut had also appeared upon branches outside of holes they had been sleeping in. They began asking what was happening.

"I suspect Talli has been dreaming," answered the old magician. "But perhaps not. She says she has envisioned and communicated with Gilin, and that he is not only alive and well but is visible, and at home with the clan! I wish I could believe it to be true! What a relief it would be to know it were so! If it is true, I wonder whether the fact that his condition has been altered will have an impact upon our quest! Perhaps something has changed in the kirin world that we are unaware of!"

"I can make contact as soon as the moon comes out again!" declared Talli. "I am certain I can! It was not a dream! It happened in the same fashion it did when there was last a full moon, when I found Gilin deep in the forest with Hut!"

Speckarin and the others were quiet for a few moments. "Let us meet at the foot of Talli's tree," came the old magician's voice.

They climbed down to the floor of the wooded area and gathered in the darkness at the appointed location.

"It is the moon that activates it!" explained Talli, holding the toe ring out for all to see. To the surprise of the others the ring gave off a pale glow. "But I discovered tonight," said the lass, "that the moon must be full, and must be completely visible in order for it to work!"

Speckarin looked skyward. They were situated under the boughs of a tree and did not have an unencumbered view of the sky. "Let us move," he said, "to an open area."

They found a clearing nearby where they could view the full expanse of the upper atmosphere, but not the moon because it remained obscured by clouds. They could see, however, that the opaque mass of vapor was moving at a fairly rapid pace, and at the magician's suggestion they sat down upon the ground to wait.

Before long the clouds parted enough for them to see the edge of a spectacularly radiant moon. Talli got to her feet quickly and aimed the ring skyward, the others looking on with keen interest. As soon as the entire circle of the orb was visible, the glow of the ring grew in intensity and a haze appeared within its confines. Talli closed her eyes so as not to be distracted by anything, including the presence of the other kirins around her. She concentrated her attentions solely upon Gilin. The mist in the ring began to dissipate, and a form once again took shape within its space.

"Gilin!" called Talli, and as he had before, her startled friend glanced intently about. This time, however, he had not been asleep. He was seated upon what appeared to be a hard floor.

All of the others, in wonderment and somewhat in disbelief, stood up hurriedly and crowded around Talli as she held the illuminated ring high. To their astonishment they also saw the image of their long lost friend, and when he spoke they could hear his voice clearly.

"What happened to you?" asked Gilin. "A short while ago we were talking, or so I thought! But suddenly you stopped responding, and I wondered whether it was actually a dream! But here you are again! Talli, how far away are you? What is your location?"

"We are still on the expedition!" said Talli. "Many things have happened to us, as I am certain they have to you! But we are all safe now! We are deeply relieved that you have arrived home, and that you appear unharmed!"

Gilin seemed puzzled. "I am on the trek also," he replied. "I am far from home, just as you must be if you are still moving eastward. But I cannot go on because of the damage to Loana."

"But you mentioned earlier," said Talli, "that Ruggum

Chamter was caring for your ilon! You must then be at home!"

"Ruggum is with me on the mission!" said Gilin. "You could not have known this, but he trailed us from the time we left Rogustin! When I was separated from the rest of you during the rainstorm, he followed me instead of you! And thankfully so, because he has accompanied me ever since!"

Just then a sleepy Ruggum Chamter wandered into the picture. "What's happening?" he was heard to ask. "Who are you talking with?"

Why, the outrageous old scoundrel! thought Speckarin. He simply could not stay at home! He had to follow us! And the two of them have persisted in carrying out the mission on their own! What courage that must have taken! I find all of it hard to believe!

"Talli!" said the magician, crowding closer to the girl and her upheld ring. "Is it possible for me to have a word with them?"

"I do not know whether that will work," said the lass. "But you may try!"

"You keep holding the instrument!" instructed Speckarin. "I feel certain it will function only through you! But I would like to communicate with them if I can!"

He moved underneath the ring so that he could clearly see the two kirins encompassed within its circle. Then he began to speak. "This is Speckarin!" he called. "Can you hear me?"

"Yes, we can," said a surprised Gilin, again glancing about as if to discover the source of the voices. "Where are all of you, and are you all right?"

"We are indeed!" said the old magician. "And much the better now for seeing you, and knowing that you are unharmed! Gilin! How wonderful that you have lost your invisibility!"

Both Gilin and Ruggum appeared bewildered, but neither of them spoke. After a pause it was the overseer who answered. "I have no idea how you are observing us or communicating with us," he said. "But Gilin has hardly shed his invisibility!"

"But," said Speckarin, "he is perfectly clear to our vision, to all five of us, I believe." He glanced about at the others, who all nodded in agreement.

At once Speckarin realized what was happening. It was the ring. The magic piece was capable of penetrating the shroud of invisibility, and to those utilizing it Gilin could be seen. Without it, as was the case for Ruggum, the lad remained invisible. The magician's heart sank.

"It is the ring," said the magician dejectedly, both to his party and to the perplexed Gilin and Ruggum. "The ring casts aside the spell of the gronom, and to us Gilin is as plain as Ruggum! Gilin, we have not seen you for a very long time! You look good to us!"

The old magician was deeply disappointed, however, that nothing had changed after all.

Gilin had been searching for the source of their voices, and had again extracted the warm calamar from his satchel. As Speckarin was speaking, he made a discovery. "They are coming through the calamar!" he said to Ruggum. "Their voices are emanating from the device!"

Just then Talli noticed a massive grouping of clouds moving in from the west. She quickly pointed them out to Speckarin.

"If the moon is blotted out again," she exclaimed, "we will lose our channel of contact, as I did earlier! Unless the sky clears later tonight, we might not be able to reestablish it until the next full moon!"

"We must hurry!" said the magician firmly, noting the clouds himself. "Where are you?" he asked of the party of two. "Do you have any idea where you are with relation to us?"

"We had been traveling to the east," said the overseer, sensing the urgency in Speckarin's voice, "for six days before Loana's injury!"

"Can you give us any other indications where you are?" asked the magician.

"We are . . . with humans," said Ruggum.

This remark so astonished, so dumbfounded each of Speckarin's party that for a time none of them could respond.

It was the old magician who eventually spoke. "I must not have heard you correctly," he said shakily. "It sounded as though you said you were with . . . humans." He laughed nervously.

"That is what I said," replied the overseer. "In my wildest imaginings I would not have dreamed it possible before leaving home. But in fact we are residing, during the healing period for Loana, within a human structure."

Gasps of amazement and horror escaped every one of the group of five, and no one could say a word.

Talli, however, had noted with increasing trepidation that the cloud mass was moving ever nearer to the moon, and she again pointed it out to Speckarin.

"How long will it take for Loana to heal?" questioned the agitated magician. "We must hurry!"

"It has been fifteen days," said Ruggum, "since her injuries were incurred. She will require at least twenty more before she is ready to attempt . . ."

And here, to the consternation of all, the transmission ended. The cloud bank spread inexorably over the moon, and the haze within the ring reestablished itself.

"It is no use to try communicating now," said Talli. "But as soon as the moon is out again, we will make contact once more!"

The five of them, astounded at this most unpredicted turn of events, milled about in the darkness. They discussed the meaning of everything Ruggum and Gilin had said, especially the parts about human beings, and damage to Loana, and the fact that Ruggum had followed them. They wondered what they should say during their next period of communication, should it indeed come to pass.

"We must at all costs try to join them!" declared Hut. "We cannot allow them to go on alone, just the two of them! It would be too dangerous! It must have been terrible thus far!"

The conversations went on, all of them bewildered and

shaken, but relieved that Gilin was alive and well, and by the fact that Ruggum Chamter accompanied him.

After a time Speckarin called Diliani aside. "They had been traveling eastward for six days before Loana was injured! How many days have we been journeying since losing track of Gilin?"

Diliani knew the answer immediately. "The day after the rainstorm was the one on which the volodons attacked," she said. "We went south after that searching for the campsite and for Gilin. We began making our way eastward the following day, and had traveled five days before Talli's accident. We departed the Shillitoe cave yesterday morning. Therefore we have been moving eastward, without Gilin, for a total of seven days."

"Then," suggested a heartened Speckarin, "we may be as little as one day's flight apart! I sympathize with Hut! I think we should try to find them!"

"But," said the practical and realistic Diliani, "even if we should locate them, would it be wise for all of us to wait twenty days for Loana to heal before continuing our mission? We would never leave Gilin alone, nor could he depart without Loana."

Speckarin did not answer. It would hardly be prudent for them to wait that length of time. His group had been delayed long enough by its own troubles. She was right on all counts. And yet he was drawn to the prospect of uniting the traveling parties—so deeply, in fact, that he moved away from Diliani and the others to sequester himself, and to think.

He sat down upon the ground, his head in his hands. He began to ponder all the possibilities, his mind at work with more intensity and rapidity than it had ever been before.

What an amazing turn of events! he marvelled. Gilin and Ruggum Chamter are together, and still on the quest, and perhaps no more than a day's flight away! We must find a means not only of locating them, but of allowing them to come with us! There is no other way! But how? How can we possibly do it?

An idea struck him. Through Talli's ring and Gilin's calamar! With the help of a clearing sky, we can speak to them again and then locate them! Talli was drawn to Gilin in the forest at home! The same thing can happen again! But the great and perplexing problem is Loana! She must have been damaged severely indeed!

He racked his brain for a solution to the incredible and frustrating predicament. He considered all of his objects of magic, and the diminutive supply of healing substances he carried within his bag. But all of those things are here, he thought forlornly, not where Loana is! And he was not convinced that any of them would help her anyway.

Suddenly he remembered something. It was a function of ancient kirin magic he had not thought of for many years, and he stopped to consider it. He had not been involved with anything like it in his lifetime, and he was hardly certain it would work. There had never been a need for it in the home woods. His greatest concern, however, was that a lengthy communication might attract the attention of gronoms or other evil beasts. I could send the others away to protect them from of assault, he thought, as I did the last time I employed my calamar. But at the moment we do not have that kind of time, and if we attempt it I will need their help!

It might work, he reassured himself, and he could come up with no other alternative. We must attempt it, he decided finally, whatever the consequences!

He leapt to his feet and paced quickly to where the others stood. They were again observing the sky. Talli indicated that the gloom above appeared to be breaking up, and that they soon might be viewing the moon again.

"We will need the moon!" announced Speckarin. "I have a plan! I will require the expertise of Diliani in curlace magic, and the support and help of all of you! We might also need more than a little good fortune! But should we be able to make contact, I have an idea about how to help them!"

The vapors began to clear from the face of the moon and its border shined radiantly through. As soon as it showed fully, Talli raised the glowing ring. The circumference became intensely illuminated and a haze formed within the circle. Talli concentrated her thoughts on Gilin, and once again the magical instrument did not fail. The image of Gilin, sitting with calamar in hand, gradually reappeared.

"Gilin!" called Speckarin, wasting no time. "Where is Loana? Is she in your vicinity? Can you go to her immediately?"

The startled lad responded quickly. "She is in the same space with me! Certainly I can go to her! Do you wish to see her?"

The magician ignored his questions. "Go to her!" he instructed. "Do so immediately!"

Gilin arose and walked several steps, his image remaining in the center of the ring. Ruggum Chamter was seen to follow. The lad stopped in front of the reclining raven.

"What damage has she received?" asked Speckarin intently.

"Open fractures of two areas of the right wing," said the youth, indicating the dressings and supports in place over the wounded extremity.

"Place your calamar directly against one of the wounds!" commanded the magician. "Awaken the bird if she sleeps, for she must be a part of what we are about to do!" He glanced furtively at the clouds above, which were moving continually across the heavens. "Do so immediately! We might not have much time!"

Gilin complied, even though he understood nothing of the purpose. Loana was already awake, and he applied the instrument of magic to the more proximal wound, near the body joint.

Speckarin called Diliani to his side.

"I will need your help," he said hurriedly. "I do not know the words in curlace that apply to specific parts of the bird!"

Without further explanation he closed his eyes. For the first time any of his companions had seen anything like it, he appeared to be placing himself into a trance.

"Lan lonilin dulowan, robasilam gralo, tay ilon, Loana!" he intoned, in a voice unlike his natural one. It was deeper, as if coming from a distance, and the others listened and looked on in amazement.

Then from the magician issued forth a series of incantations, none of which the observers had before heard, or could comprehend, neither the group around him nor the two far away. But through the toe ring Loana could be seen to stir, and at that moment Speckarin brought himself out of his state of concentration. He asked Diliani for the curlace names of several anatomical parts of the bird's wing. Then he lapsed back into his trance, and unintelligible words and phrases once again poured from him.

Finally the magician brought himself back to consciousness and instructed Gilin to reposition the calamar over the second wound. Gilin complied. The old magician sank again into his state of abstraction and delivered the same manner of incantation.

Talli watched the skies apprehensively throughout. Although clouds and haze persisted in moving across the heavens, nothing blocked the moon, and eventually Speckarin's words came to an end.

The old magician drooped as soon as he finished, as if physically and mentally drained. Runagar and Hut helped him to sit down. "It is done," he said quietly. "Tell Gilin and Ruggum, if you still have time, that I have transmitted a spell to Loana, an ancient one. If all went well it should aid in the healing of her injuries. But we must put an end to this communication. I fear it is being listened to, or intercepted, by those we would least want to hear it." Exhausted, he said no more.

Diliani passed Speckarin's information on to the two distant kirins. "I have never heard of such a spell!" Ruggum was heard to say.

"We seldom have use for this magic now," responded the old magician in so subdued a voice that only those close by could hear it. "It is virtually never utilized in the home woods."

"What should we do next?" asked Talli, turning her head slightly, trying not to take her eyes away from the moon and the glowing ring.

"Tell them we will try to find them," said the enervated Speckarin. "We will depart in the morning. We will rely upon the powers of your ring and Gilin's calamar to locate them."

Talli relayed the magician's statements. Gilin and Ruggum appeared visibly relieved by the news.

"We will soon see you, Gilin," declared Talli, "in the flesh!" But she stopped abruptly, remembering her friend's persisting condition, and rephrased her remark. "We will be together as soon as we can cover the distance between us!"

"How far apart do you think we are?" asked Ruggum.

Diliani was beginning to answer when the edge of the moon was blemished by a cloud. It proceeded slowly across the face until the orb was once again gone. The mist returned momentarily to the ring as Talli lowered it, but then it too was gone, and the space within the circle was normal once more.

"Just as well that it ended there," said Speckarin, recalling the deadly confrontation with the gronom he had experienced while communicating through his calamar. "We came out of that transmission unscathed. We must rest for what is left of the night. Tomorrow we begin an entirely new adventure."

The magician got to his feet and found his way slowly back to his tree hole. Now human beings, he thought disquietingly, as he settled down within it, trying to become comfortable enough to sleep. I am utterly astounded! Why are they with human beings? As if we do not have enough trouble with gronoms, and volodons, and everything else that has befallen us upon our way!

I can only hope, he told himself, as he finally began to doze off, that these humans will not intrude upon us or our friends and will place no obstacles in our pathway toward reunion.

C H A P T E R   3

I'LL BE two hundred
dollars richer when we get there!" declared Nathan
confidently. He was lounging in the back seat of a white
sedan. His two friends were in front.

"I'm sure!" responded Michael sarcastically from the
right front seat, turning his head to look back. "I'm sure
we're going to see a little man one foot tall!"

"And with feet a foot long!" laughed Patrick, the driver.

"Foot-long hot dogs!" chortled Mike.

"I never said they were a foot long!" said Nathan. "They're
only about . . . this long." He demonstrated a length of four or
five inches between his hands as both boys glanced back.

"Why don't you just give us the hundred bucks now,"
joked Mike. "We'll turn around and go home!"

"Yeah, but where's he gonna get it?" asked Pat. "How's
he gonna come up with that kind of money?"

"I don't know," said Mike. "But it's a bet, and he's gotta
pay off!"

They were on their way to John Versteeg's hunting lodge
to settle their wager. Patrick Bradley was sixteen years of age,
just old enough to drive, and Michael Tomlin was fifteen.

Christopher had beseeched Nathan not to reveal to anyone what was happening at the lodge. We must allow them to be free to do whatever they want, he had implored. In the beginning Nathan had agreed and had complied. For more than two weeks he had not breathed a word of it. But he thought about it constantly, and one day, while in routine conversation with his friends, temptation finally overcame him and he blurted it out. He stated that he and his brother were taking care of someone special at his grandfather's hunting lodge, a tiny person who could speak English. He described the dimensions of Gilin's stature, even his feet.

The two boys agreed that their friend Nathan, who was fourteen, had exaggerated things in the past. But this was too much. They didn't believe a word of it.

Naturally, questions, remarks, and insults issued from his friends, a fact that only made Nathan more insistent that it was true. At first Nathan had no intention of escorting them to the lodge and allowing them to see the kirin, but in the end he wanted to prove that he was right. When he added that two ravens were present also, which the little man and an invisible partner flew on, his friends challenged him. After considerable discussion they made a wager. Each of his companions bet a hundred dollars that he could show them nothing of the sort, and they would drive to the lodge to settle the issue.

"Tomorrow is the only day I can go," said Patrick. "I start working my summer job Monday."

The following day, Chris and Grandpa Versteeg were about to leave for the hunting lodge when Nathan informed them that he had other obligations that day, lawns he had contracted to mow. He couldn't go with them, but he would see the kirins the next weekend, or perhaps during the week now that school was over. His grandfather and brother went on without him. He did have lawns to mow, and he did them hurriedly. Then he met his friends and they departed.

"This was a long way to come, even for a hundred bucks," remarked Pat as they finally arrived at the parking area. He pulled the car in next to that of old Mr. Versteeg.

They climbed out and, led by Nathan, headed through the woods toward the lodge.

As they moved along the pathway, Nathan was hoping against hope that his grandfather and his brother would be somewhere else when they got there, somewhere outside, perhaps out in the boat. Otherwise his grandfather would question how he had gotten there, and why he had not come with them, to say nothing of what he would say when he saw the other boys. Right now all Nathan could think about was what an exceedingly bad idea it had been to come today.

Upon reaching the clearing adjacent to the building, Nathan asked the other boys to wait where they were, and they did so reluctantly. Nathan covered the remaining distance alone, approaching the lodge cautiously and expectantly. He entered the door on the ground floor and took a few steps inside. Then he listened. As luck would have it he heard no sound. He could detect no evidence that anyone else was in the building. Moving quickly to the bedroom occupied by the kirins, he pushed open the door. He looked down and there was Gilin, sitting next to Loana on the floor. The kirin glanced up, startled at the sudden appearance of the boy he had been told would not be there that day.

"Good afternoon, Nathan," said Gilin, getting to his feet, calamar in hand. "I'm very glad to see you after all. Your grandfather said you had other things to do today."

Without saying a word Nathan bolted from the room, burst through the door of the lodge, and ran as hard as he could toward his friends.

"Come on!" he whispered hoarsely as he neared them.

"For what?" replied Mike in a loud voice. "The little man? Just fork over the money and we'll go home!"

"Quiet! Just come on!" repeated Nathan. "Hurry it up!"

The three of them trotted across the grass, Pat and Mike guffawing and prancing all the while and Nathan imploring them to be quiet. They entered the door and Nathan led them down the hallway. When they reached the doorway to the bedroom he stopped.

"There," he said, pointing down at Gilin.

The boys looked into the room and were greeted with the greatest surprise of their young lives. Before them was a being with an appearance just as Nathan had described. It had long feet, dark and penetrating eyes, and it was no more than a foot tall. Next to it was a huge black bird with taping and struts upon it. The dumbfounded boys stared down at them incredulously.

"What did I tell you?" asserted Nathan in a whisper. "Now, let's get out of here!"

He was profoundly afraid someone would discover them. And at this moment, in the very act of exposing Gilin, he felt guilty about the entire escapade.

"Can it talk like you said?" asked an amazed Pat Bradley. "You said something about it speaking English! Can it say something?"

"Not now!" responded Nathan, more desperate by the moment. "You've seen him! Now let's go!"

Gilin was shocked, astounded at the sight of foreign humans at such close range. His immediate desire was to escape. But he was trapped. He had nowhere to go. They were blocking the doorway with their huge bulk, the windows above him were closed, and there was no other exit. He was deeply relieved when, shortly thereafter, at Nathan's insistence, the two strangers backed through the doorway, still ogling him as they did, and then moved off down the hallway. He could eventually hear the exterior door close behind them.

Once outside Nathan goaded the other boys into running toward the trees where the pathway began. There, sheltered by the foliage, they stopped for a minute to discuss what they had seen.

"It's the most unreal thing I've ever seen!" exclaimed Mike. "I can't believe it! Where did it come from?"

"Man!" said Pat. "That thing just stood there watching us, and it looked like it understood! That's unbelievably weird!"

Mike had an idea. "Can you imagine it on *Good Morning*

America or *Saturday Night Live*?" he suggested excitedly. "That would be a blast! I'd like to see that!"

"I'd like to sell the rights for that thing to some agent!" said Pat.

"Why don't we catch it?" asked Mike. "We could make a mint off it!"

"No! You're going too far! You can't do anything like that!" said Nathan.

"Why not?" replied Pat, grinning. "Do you own it?"

"No!" said Nathan. "Nobody owns him! He's a free person or being just like us! You've seen him! That's all we came for! Never mind the money! You don't have to pay me! Let's just get out of here!"

"What's the big hurry?" asked Mike.

The debate went on for several minutes at the edge of the clearing, and eventually the two older boys prevailed, or at least convinced themselves that they should attempt to capture this unearthly creature. They started back toward the lodge, the frightened Nathan staying where he was. They opened the door and tiptoed down the hallway. When they arrived at the bedroom, however, they found no sign of Gilin or his raven.

Unbeknownst to the older boys, during their argument Christopher had come along the pathway returning from a hike in the woods. Overhearing voices, he had stopped abruptly to listen. He soon realized what the boys had seen, what they were discussing, and what their intentions were. While they were still talking he quietly but quickly skirted their location. Stepping out from the trees at a point behind the building and not visible from their position, he hurried to Gilin's room. But he found it empty. He called the kirin's name several times, saying that it was Christopher. Eventually Gilin and the raven crawled out from underneath a bed. Chris reluctantly informed the kirin what was happening. Gilin and Loana departed for the door as rapidly as the bird could move, and Chris followed.

"I know a hiding place!" said the frightened Gilin once

they were outside. "When Ruggum returns, tell him I am with Loana in the same place we were after first being shot down!"

Off they moved, Loana struggling along as best she could. Chris ducked around the side of the building, and they were all just out of sight when the older boys returned to the basement.

"It's gone!" exclaimed Mike, returning to Nathan's location. "Where do you think it would have gone?"

"I have no idea," replied a greatly relieved Nathan. "Now, may we please go home? We'll never find him! He can fly! You saw the bird with him!"

"I'm not so sure!" said Pat. "We saw a crow! But it was all bandaged up, and it didn't look to me like it could fly! I think we should look around outside!"

The two boys began to canvas the surrounding territory, Nathan praying all the while that they would find nothing and that his grandfather would not return. Christopher remained by the lodge and at the periphery of the clearing so as not to be detected.

Soon Ruggum Chamter and Alsinam returned with John Versteeg. They had been in the boat, on an excursion of the placid lake. As the old man and his new friends climbed up the hillside toward the lodge, Christopher burst from his hiding place and ran to them.

"Two other boys have been here!" he exclaimed as he approached. "They have seen Gilin! They are looking for him now! But he left with Loana!" He paused, glancing about to make certain he was not being overheard. "He told me to tell Ruggum," he continued in a low voice, "that he would be waiting in the same place they had hidden before!"

Ruggum and Grandpa Versteeg were astounded at this unpredicted turn of events. All had been quiet and peaceful when they departed, and in fact had been for more than two weeks.

"I know exactly where they are!" declared Ruggum urgently. "I will go to them! The humans cannot see me!" He climbed upon Alsinam immediately. They lifted off and were gone.

"Who are these two boys?" demanded John Versteeg. "Where are they?"

"I don't know where they are!" was the answer. "They went off to look for Gilin! They are friends of Nathan, Pat Bradley and Mike Tomlin." Then he revealed something that incensed his grandfather further. "Nathan must have brought them here."

John Versteeg had grown very close to the kirins during their stay at his lodge, and especially to Ruggum Chamter. He had gotten to know them well—almost as well as any human had gotten to know kirins for many millennia. He had developed a deep respect for their knowledge, their lore, and their bravery. He was infuriated that two strange boys had arrived upon the scene to endanger them once again, when things were going so well.

His knee had begun bothering him again, and he felt helpless. He could not chase after the boys and search for them high and low as he would like. Instead, after thinking things over he elected to wait. He retired to the lodge while Chris went off into the woods to see what he could do for his friends.

Soon Mike and Pat tired of looking for the little creature by themselves. But they had seen something unbelievable, a tiny being unlike anything they had ever before seen, and they had no intention of giving up on finding it. They decided to go for reinforcements. Avoiding the clearing around the lodge for fear of being detected, they picked their way along the edge the woods and then dashed for the car.

They drove to the nearest village, where they telephoned several of their friends in the city and told them eagerly about their amazing discovery. They discussed animatedly what it could mean to capture this little thing, to go on talk shows, sell rights to Disney, and get rich. Their friends did not believe them, of course, and wondered what they were thinking about. But on a warm Sunday in early summer a few of them had nothing better to do. A ride into the country on a wild goose chase might be fun. Before long a carload of youths, mostly Mike's and Pat's acquaintances, were on their way to the secluded lodge.

It was early evening when they arrived, and if it weren't for daylight-saving time, darkness would soon have been upon them. They were met on the road near the parking area by the two excited boys. From there they descended upon John Versteeg's property in search of a minuscule thing that, they had been told, might even have come from outer space.

Reaching the vicinity of the lodge they moved noisily into the clearing, being anything but stealthy, deriving a sense of safety in numbers. They were soon confronted, however, by an angry Mr. Versteeg. He had heard them coming along the pathway and had exited the lodge immediately. He demanded that they go no further, that they leave at once or he would call the police. But the youths had not come all this way to be turned back so easily by an old man. Some of them began to filter around him as he lectured, and soon they all followed and scattered into the woods in search of the whimsical creature Patrick and Michael claimed to have seen.

John Versteeg knew that the lodge had no telephone, and as the group dispersed he was torn between going to his car to drive for help, and remaining on the property to observe what happened. He decided to return to the lodge, where he went out onto the deck to watch and listen. What next occurred both surprised and saddened the old man, and remained fresh in his memory for the rest of his life.

Christopher wandered through the woods alone. He knew where Gilin and the ravens had originally been found. He wondered whether he should go there, to be certain they were all right and to discuss what should be done next, or whether he should stay away and not attract the attention of the searchers. But eventually, glancing around all the while to be certain he was not being observed, he made his way to the glade of trees where Nathan had originally discovered Gilin. There, instead of finding the kirins or their ilon, he was surprised to find his brother.

Nathan had been angry and disgusted with himself for doing such an ill-advised thing, bringing Patrick and Mike to see Gilin. Having no precise idea where the kirins might be, he had done basically the same as his younger brother: He had gravitated toward the place where the first contact was made, in hopes that he could now be of aid to them.

"What are you doing here?" questioned Christopher angrily.

"Probably the same thing you are," said his brother. "I'm trying to find them, to see if I can help them."

"You could have helped them by not telling anyone!" admonished Chris.

"I know, but it's too late now," said Nathan unhappily. "I was stupid! All I want to do now is try to help them! They'll have to be here for another two or three weeks, and we'll have to protect them! I'll never do anything that stupid again!"

Ruggum, Gilin, and the two ravens were in the same hollow log they had occupied immediately after Loana was wounded. The kirins had taken turns peering out of the hole to the outside world, to see and hear what was occurring. Ruggum had been doing so more frequently than Gilin because he was invisible to humans. It so happened, however, that Ruggum was tending to Loana, and Gilin was at the watch, when Nathan arrived and was followed shortly by Christopher.

Gilin was not able to see them, but he overheard their conversation and he recognized who they were. The kirins had been hiding for quite a while by now, and Gilin was keenly interested in discovering what was happening and what they should do next. He knew they could not remain where they were forever. He took it upon himself to initiate communication with the boys. Calamar in hand, he stepped out of the hiding place and moved stealthily into the open.

"Come back!" he heard Ruggum saying behind him. But he was too anxious to talk with the boys to heed the elder's advice.

"Nathan! Christopher!" called Gilin softly. The youths immediately turned toward him. "Are the other humans gone?"

"No!" whispered Chris, glad to see his little friend, but anxious for his safety. "They've called others to help hunt for you! They're all around here! Hide again, right now! We'll let you know when it's safe to come out!"

A cry rang out from behind Nathan and Christopher. "It's here! Everyone! Over here! It looks just the way Mike said it would, and it's speaking English! Over here!"

Ruggum was out of the hole immediately and assaying the treacherous situation. He commanded that the two ravens come out of the log also. Then he called to Christopher. "Quickly!" he said. "Remove the wrappings from Loana!"

Without thinking whether he was doing something wise or unwise, in the confusion of the moment Christopher simply reacted. He knelt down and unwound the strips. He released the bird from all its bindings and left them lying upon the ground.

"We have no choice!" said Ruggum to a bewildered Gilin, Nathan and Christopher looking on apprehensively. "We must hope the spell of Speckarin has already succeeded! We must escape! Board Loana before it is too late!"

The circle of hunters was closing in. But only the one who had first seen Gilin, and who continued to shout directions about where they were, was near enough to see them.

"We have no time for good-byes!" said Ruggum hurriedly, the kirins astride their ilon. "You have aided us immeasurably! We will not forget you! Gilin! Command flight!"

Gilin leaned forward and spoke phrases in curlace. Loana stretched her right wing as close to full extent as she could. It was obviously stiff and uncomfortable, but she gamely attempted to follow directions. After more words of instruction and encouragement, she spread her sable wings for the first time in sixteen days. Then she began fluttering and finally gently flapping both wings.

At that moment several of the excited youths crashed through the brush, arriving upon the scene. They stopped abruptly upon seeing the two giant birds. One of the ravens was lifting off the ground. It flew upward into the air gracefully and effortlessly.

"There they go!" cried the one who had found them. He had been observing since Gilin had stepped out of the hollow log, but had not dared to approach them himself. "Stop them, somebody! The little guy is on that bird, the one still on the ground!"

The raven he referred to appeared to be experiencing difficulty, beating its wings unsteadily and incongruously, as if trying to take off but being unsuccessful in doing so. Suddenly the other bird, the one ascending, wheeled in midair and altered its course downward. Then it flew directly toward the humans on one side, veering away only when immediately above their heads, the youths dodging and hurriedly backing away. This action was repeated several times over in various directions, the creature pausing briefly between forays as if deciding which course to take next. The searchers fell backwards with every charge, and even took cover after a while, having no inclination to advance now.

The aroused Ruggum, ascending upon Alsinam, had looked back at Loana. He saw that she was not able to raise herself off the ground. Not knowing whether this might be temporary, or whether she was simply not well enough to fly, he determined that he must protect her and her master. He instructed his ilon to descend, and to take the aggressive action, flying at the human beings and swerving away at the last moment.

Soon the hunters noted something new. The second bird, still upon the ground, seemed to be coordinating its efforts more efficiently, its wings beating more strongly and synchronously. All at once it began to lift itself into the air. At the same time the other bird desisted from its assaults and flew upward once more, almost as if to allow the second one more space in which to maneuver. At first, as the faltering bird struggled into the air, its course appeared alarmingly random, which concerned the human beings surrounding it. This curtailed any interest they might still have had in deterring or capturing it. But the creature seemed to gather strength and control as it gained altitude, and within moments the two birds were climbing through the air side by side.

John Versteeg had been observing from the deck of his lodge. As soon as he perceived the commotion in the woods, he turned, descended the stairs, and headed for its location as rapidly as his troublesome leg would carry him. He arrived in time to see the ravens achieve the height of the tree tops. He saw them level off in their ascent and turn toward the east. He was amazed that both ravens were able to fly, and he had no idea how it could have happened. He raised a hand to wave, but it was too late. The birds and their riders were gone.

"Go, Gilin! Go, Ruggum!" came Nathan's cry to the heavens. "Don't stop for anything!"

■ ■ ■

Some of the humans present never did see the little person described by Patrick and Michael. He was seen only briefly by a few of the others. Those who had not witnessed the being remained highly skeptical. As their lives went on, they soon lost interest in the matter and it was forgotten. The ones who had seen Gilin tried to explain what they had perceived. But after a while, when no one believed them, they also stopped talking about it. The subject soon became less and less important to them, and eventually it was no more than a vague recollection.

But John Versteeg and his grandsons never forgot the affair, nor did the memory fade. They treasured their experiences with the kirins and their ilon and remembered them for the remainder of their lives. They talked about them on numerous occasions when they were alone. The humans had expected the kirins to stay until Loana was healed, and regretted that they had not had more time to spend with their visitors. Even though Ruggum had mentioned that they were contacted by their compatriots and that a spell had been transmitted to Loana, they were never able to understand how the bird's wounds mended so rapidly. As humans in today's world, the concept was completely beyond their comprehension.

What an incredible race, John Versteeg concluded later. We would have had much more to learn from them. They told us that human beings used to practice a magic similar to theirs, long, long ago. I would dearly like to learn more about that, and about many other things they know. I can only hope these friends will return, or that others of their kind will reveal themselves to us. And not just to Nathan, or Christopher or me, but to the entire human race so that we may once again be together in peace and in harmony.

The uncivilized group that approached the kirins so suddenly and harshly and with such apparent hostility did nothing to resolve the differences between the two races. An even greater disappointment was that he had not had the opportunity of completing his discourse with Ruggum Chamter, for whom he felt respect and affection as long as he lived.

John Versteeg was in the latter part of his life, and he ruminated upon these things often. I would have had so much more to say to them, he thought, had circumstances only worked out differently. He was particularly sad that it had not been possible to bid the kirins farewell.

But he lived the remainder of his days confident of one thing: With the exception of Nathan's youthful mistake, his family's behavior toward these unique beings would someday benefit the reconciliation between the races.

What he and his grandsons would never know, however, was what impact this historical contact with two wayfaring kirins would have on the entire future of human-kirin relationships.

C H A P T E R 4

S THE SHOCK of their narrow escape began to dissipate, Ruggum Chamter and Gilin were silent. They were flying away from the setting sun, almost absent-mindedly and instinctively selecting their course, even though they had not been in the air for so long a time.

As they contemplated what had transpired with the human beings, the kirins were sad about the way things had ended. They mourned the fact that in their hurry, scant opportunity had been available to wish Christopher and his grandfather farewell and to thank them for everything they had done. They were confused and profoundly disappointed by the behavior of Nathan, realizing that he had been responsible for shooting Loana and calling in other humans. They were disturbed by the actions of the gathering of humans at the end, the occurrence of a skirmish while Loana was trying to lift off, and the dire necessity of a forced departure.

It could have been disastrous in two ways, thought Ruggum. We might not have escaped at all, and Loana's healing wing might have been damaged by employing it too early. Is the human race truly ready for association with our kind, as I thought so recently, or is it still too early for any kind of reconciliation? He especially deplored the fact that he had not been able to say good-bye to the elder human, whom he had grown to enjoy and respect.

Gilin, for his part, was becoming involved in Loana's flying. She was maneuvering her previously lame extremity with the same power and grace as her opposite wing, almost as though she had never been injured. She appeared exhilarated, overjoyed in fact, at being free to fly again after the horrifying experience of being brought down by gunfire and incurring devastating wounds. Gilin lamented what had happened with the humans, but he and Loana were so glad to be in the air that they were relishing the occasion immensely.

Ruggum knew that they had precious little time for reflection, the sun having nearly gone down. He forced himself to think about where they were headed and what they would do next. He realized that their rapid evacuation might undermine their plans for reunion with Speckarin. They were dislodged from the place they were expected to be. He did not know whether that would be detrimental to the other party's finding them, and he asked Gilin about it.

"I know not," replied the youth. "I hope it will not matter, that Talli's ring will be attracted to my calamar wherever we are."

As darkness fell they located a campsite for the night. But as they attempted to relax they found that the events of their recent days with human beings turned over in their minds. Wouldn't it be wonderful, thought Gilin as he accompanied Loana on a short walk, if this were our last night alone?

■ ■ ■

"The pull of the ring is diminishing rapidly," reported a disheartened Talli to Speckarin. "It has been decreasing for some time, but now it is so weak that it is barely distinguishable."

"Why do you think that is occurring?" asked the old magician. He had been concerned for some time that they were losing their capability for homing in upon Gilin and Ruggum Chamter.

"The ring's power may be fading," answered Talli, glancing at the magician, "because the full moon has been gone from the skies for a long time. But in honesty I do not know what the problem is."

The party of five was in flight, and had been moving southward as steadily and speedily as the ravens and the crane would tolerate. At daybreak they had departed the site from which they had corresponded with their two compatriots, having slept little after seeing them. Their great desire was to be reunited with Gilin, and to see the overseer for the first time since they had left Rogalinon. Runagar was unacquainted with either of those two kirins, but he could sense the excitement radiating from his companions, and was eager to find them himself.

Talli had not slept at all, both because of her stimulation over their communication, and because her ring had begun its pull as soon as the moon went down. It was as if the ring were being drawn away from her, as it was when she located Gilin in the forest, and she knew that it was again being attracted to Gilin's calamar. At first she expended significant effort in simply restraining the object, afraid to put it down or let go of it for fear it might float away. Finally, however, she replaced it on her toe, where she continued to feel its traction but where at least it proved to be secure.

As they flew onward all of them could observe the difficulties Talli was experiencing with the ring now, late in the afternoon. She was flying in the lead, her ring held straight out in front. The magic piece had lent strong direction to the party in the early going, Talli at times seeming hardly capable of holding on to it, but its power was obviously waning. Apprehension had been aroused in all of them, even before she mentioned anything to Speckarin, by the way she angled the ring about, from side to side and upward and downward, as if trying to obtain a sense of traction but receiving less all the time. Finally, with the light of day diminishing, the discouraged Talli placed the ring in front of her, still holding it with both hands but allowing it to rest upon the neck of her raven. All the others, save Speckarin, wondered what they could do to find Gilin and Ruggum.

Earlier in the afternoon, as the magician began to suspect Talli's difficulties, he had searched his mind for another method of locating their friends. Any method, he had told himself, other than what he had employed in his previous attempt. He wondered whether Runagar's voice might help. He knew that the voice of the Shillitoe youth could be heard over great distances. But he decided it would be of no benefit under the present circumstances, because the others would not be able to send information back as to their whereabouts. In the end, as he gripped Ocelam ever more grimly, he considered again the possibility of employing his calamar. It was a prospect which filled him with dread.

"Speckarin, what about your calamar?" came the innocent query from Hut. But the magician was so deep in thought he did not bother to answer.

It was almost sunset when Speckarin finally instructed them to land. They did so within a grove of formidable oaks. At the old magician's direction they dismounted, and he spoke to them gravely.

"There is another way of communicating with our friends as Hut suggested. It is, of course, the calamar," he said.

"You must not use that again!" declared Diliani adamantly. She knew something had gone terribly wrong with his first attempt.

"I have not discussed it with any of you," said Speckarin, "but severe difficulties may exist with this method. I must be alone for a while to think it over carefully."

He would say no more, to the dissatisfaction of the remainder of the party, who wanted answers about what they would be doing. The old magician kept to himself throughout the evening and the long night, but he slept not a single wink.

The others had never known what a colossal battle had been waged between Speckarin and the gronom. Never in his life, however, would he forget the invasion of the fiend into his brain. The loss of control of his mind, and the very sharing of it with so noxious a creature, had been abominable. The idea of it happening again caused him to tremble and to breathe shallowly and rapidly as he thought about it during the chilly night.

I must remain calm, he admonished himself, as he struggled to retain control of his emotions and his reason. *If we have no other way, I simply must attempt it again! Our only other choice would be to abandon Gilin and Ruggum! I have no intention of doing that, whatever the cost to myself! Besides,* he assured himself, *we have not encountered a gronom or a volodon, nor any other such heinous thing, since before we entered the Shillitoe cave! Perhaps we are out of their range or their territory!*

The magician aroused the others early in the morning and they gathered at the foot of a tree. The toe ring was still inert and would obviously be of no use for the time being.

"We have only one additional method to locate our friends," said Speckarin, trying to control the tremor in his voice. "By the utilization of my calamar. You all, or all but Runagar, recall the results of my previous endeavor. I did make contact initially, but communication was . . . unsuccessful."

"Must you attempt it again?" asked Diliani, deeply concerned. "Is there no other way?"

"No, there is nothing else!" responded Speckarin vigorously. "We have no other means! I have thought of everything. I can come up with nothing else that would work. It is our only hope, and it must be done if we wish to find our friends. Now, just as you did when I attempted this before, I want all of you to board your ilon and depart. Go somewhere! I do not wish to know where! I must not know! All of you, go!"

The magician thrust an arm upward. He pointed a finger toward heavens, which were brightening with the light of early day. "Do not return," he said, "until the sun is high in the sky!"

The others offered no argument. But most of them did not understand why he did not want to know where they were going. Nonetheless, without further ado they mounted their birds and lifted off. They moved away with Diliani at the lead, Speckarin purposefully not observing the direction in which they went. They might home in upon me again, he told himself, but they will not find my companions.

When he was certain they were gone he sat down upon a small log. With trepidation he reached into his pack and felt for the calamar. He found it and pulled it out. He dropped the sack to the ground, staring at the gleaming, opaque instrument he held tightly in his hands.

He wasted no time. *"Tabaylan vay norsulo,"* he intoned, gazing into the heart of the calamar. Instantly it began to warm. He wanted to see his lost companions, and he concentrated all of his thoughts upon Gilin. The opacity cleared almost immediately, and vague masses and images began to flicker before him within the confines of the magical circle, none of them focused or recognizable. But all at once the continual succession of blurred pictures ceased, and a single outline remained centered within the calamar. As the likeness sharpened, Speckarin was overjoyed. He identified Loana prowling along the bank of a stream, searching for something to eat. The wrappings that had bound her wing just a brief time ago were gone. He celebrated within himself.

"I have found you!" cried the magician almost involuntarily. "Loana, I have found you! Where is your master?"

"Who calls for me?" came the response, as the startled bird stopped in her tracks and peered into the semi-darkness of early day.

Speckarin was momentarily baffled, for the speech seemed to be emanating from the raven. But the voice came again. "Who calls for me? Who is it?"

The voice was that of Gilin. The old magician was relieved, thankful he would not have to deal with some new phenomenon, some unheard-of transformation, such as an ilon that could talk.

He called out. "Gilin! Are you there? Can you hear me?"

"Yes!" came the reply. "It sounds like Speckarin! Are you contacting me through Talli's ring?"

"No!" said the magician. "This time through my calamar!" And then, wondering why he was seeing only Loana, he went on. "Gilin! I cannot see you now, as I could through the ring! Has anything . . . changed?"

"Nothing has changed," came the answer.

The calamar, concluded Speckarin, must not be capable of cutting through the cloud of invisibility as the ring could. No matter. We must carry on the way we are.

"We must hurry," said the old magician, "for reasons that I will explain to you later when we are together! Tell me where you are! The power of the toe ring to locate you diminished a short time ago and then ceased altogether! We know not how to revitalize it until the next full moon! You and I must somehow stimulate our calamars to locate each other!"

"I have no idea how to do that!" said the puzzled youth. He removed the calamar from his belt satchel and noticed that it was warm, realizing that this transmission also must be coming through the device.

"I do not know either," answered Speckarin. "I have used my calamar little over the past few years . . ."

"Speckarin!" said Gilin. "I have an idea! My calamar has bearing finding capabilities, but I have no idea about yours! I have employed this aspect of my device only once, when Hut and I escaped the gronom upon squirrels! It told me just how far and in what direction the home trees were!"

"How did it tell you?" asked the magician intently.

"Olamin instructed me to speak in Ruvon whenever addressing the calamar," said the lad. "He mentioned that it had the ability to sense my location in relation to another place. On that occasion I simply posed the question: Where are we in relation to home? As I gazed into the device the answer came in the form of symbols, the ones we were taught to use in the forest, the written form of Ruvon, which you yourself used in leaving a message for me at your campsite.

When I asked for this information it was at night, and the figures were alight within the calamar. They told me exactly where we were! Olamin said we were to utilize my calamar to find the final destination of our quest, but not until we reached the great water. Therefore I have not used it during our trek."

A question suddenly came to Speckarin, and it bothered him enough that he asked it, despite his desire to keep the communication as brief as possible. "If the traveling party was to use your calamar to find the ultimate destination, what were we supposed to employ after your separation from us?"

"I do not know," answered Gilin. "Perhaps Olamin instructed Talli to use her toe ring for that purpose."

"I seriously doubt that," replied the magician, shaking his head, "after witnessing all of those days and nights when she tried unsuccessfully to activate it! But we have no time to talk of that! What you have just revealed makes it all the more imperative that we be reunited!"

"I will ask my calamar to tell to me what your location is," said Gilin.

He spoke several words of the ancient tongue, holding the instrument in his grasp. He gazed into it expectantly. But nothing happened.

"I see nothing," said Gilin, disappointed. "Perhaps it had grown used to where my home was, and could readily supply me information about that. Here it may be as lost as we are."

"I sincerely hope not!" said the magician. "We must try something else and we must hurry! One thing I have learned along the way is that these instruments come from ancient kirin magic, and that they are all somehow interrelated. Ask your device where the calamar of the magician Speckarin might be."

Gilin did so. Immediately a series of symbols appeared within his warming instrument, and his response was spirited. "You are nine hundred and eighty-seven clan dominions to the north of our position!"

"Is Ruggum Chamter near you?" asked Speckarin quickly.

"Yes!" answered Gilin. "He is a short distance away!"

"The two of you must remain where you are," said the magician. "Now that we have some idea of your location we will come to you. I wish to take no chances! Should we both begin to move, I fear that somehow we might pass each other by. We have a full day of daylight ahead. We should be able to cover that distance before nightfall."

But little did Speckarin know that his last series of instructions were never received by his compatriot. The transmission had finally been detected by one of the creatures he most feared. His words were being intercepted and deciphered by a gronom. The creature's procedure involved interrupting the communication and then capturing it, which resulted in the message not reaching its destination. If anything in the transmission proved attractive, the position of the sender would be traced.

The beast's unmistakable outline was taking shape in front of Speckarin's astonished eyes, as it had one unforgettable time in the past. He threw the calamar summarily to the ground, and contact was severed before the fiend could seize upon the opportunity to attack.

Just what I dreaded most! thought the shaken magician. It happened again! The thing may know where we are! We must move quickly! He glanced about and searched the skies, hoping to see his companions returning. But he had impressed upon them so profoundly that they should go and stay away that he found himself alone with Ocelam for some time. He had retrieved the calamar and was fully ready for departure by the time the party flew in for a landing. They jumped off their ilon and ran to him to make certain he was all right.

"I am fine," he said impatiently. "We must depart immediately! I was able to make contact with Gilin! We are currently nine hundred and eighty-seven clan dominions to the north of them! If we hasten we might find them before nightfall!" Just as when he previously saw a gronom in his calamar, the magician made no mention of it. He was unwilling to agitate anyone, especially Talli, at the prospect of something assaulting them again.

They took off and adopted a southerly course, and onward they flew into the late afternoon. Speckarin was hesitant to use his calamar for any purpose now, but he needed to know what progress they were making. Finally, even as they traveled, he removed it from his pack. He asked in Ruvon for the location of Gilin's calamar, but to his disappointment and dismay, nothing appeared within the device. He wondered whether his piece did not embody the same functions as Gilin's, whether his instructions were faulty, or whether the interference of the gronom had anything to do with his lack of success. In any case, he told himself ruefully, once again we have no precise knowledge of where Gilin and Ruggum are.

"My friends!" he called out. "We must land! I must think about what to do next! I cannot determine Gilin's location! I thought I could!"

They descended rapidly to earth, where they all dismounted. "I was not able to receive a reading on my calamar about the whereabouts of Gilin and Ruggum," he said. "They cannot be far away, but we must know exactly where they are in order to find them. For the moment, however, we could all use a respite."

Speckarin sat down, his head in his hands, uncertain what to do next. He was loath to employ the calamar any more than he had to. At first the others milled about, anxious to be off again, but eventually they found places to rest. Finally the magician took out the shiny instrument. He asked about the location of Gilin's calamar once more, but he met with the same negative result. Irritated, he replaced the object in his bag, and tried to lie down to rest. But the apparent proximity of their lost friends gnawed at him, and after a while he had the calamar out once again and he asked the same question. This time, to his surprise, he obtained a reading. As Gilin had described, figures within the device were alight and were indicating the distance of his friend's calamar. To his dismay, however, it was not anything like what he had expected it to be. It showed Gilin's calamar to be eleven hundred and fifty-six clan dominions away! A preposterous figure! he thought. We have covered eight or nine hundred clan dominions today! But then he noted the direction of his compatriot's calamar, and was dumbfounded. According to the symbols, Gilin's calamar was indeed that distance away, but it was to the north of his party!

"How can it be?" questioned Speckarin aloud. The others turned to look at him inquiringly. "How can they be farther than before? But worse than that, they are now to the north of us! Something is wrong, fearfully wrong!"

None of the others could help the old magician in his quandary. Exhausted after his long night and the trek today, he paced back and forth, talking to himself, trying to understand what could possibly have gone awry. "Can the estimations of these calamars be incorrect?" he asked. "If so, we are in profound trouble! If not, we have no explanation as to why we are still so far apart!"

Finally he stopped and stood still. "I must risk another communication," he said evenly. "And I will do so right away. Again, all of you! Leave me once more! But this time be back in a short while!"

They obeyed his orders, and soon he was alone with Ocelam and his calamar. He spoke the charmed words, concentrated upon Gilin, and within moments the image of Loana was clearly visible in the heart of the magical instrument for the second time that day.

"Gilin!" he cried. "Are you there? It is Speckarin again!"

"I am here!" called Gilin. "But I just tried my calamar, and it registers you as being more than eleven hundred clan dominions to the south! I cannot understand why! I received no reading at all while we were in the air, but now that we are on the ground the symbols are as definitive as ever! Maybe the device will work only if it is stationary! If it is in motion, the distance to be calculated would constantly be changing! It might not be able to do that! It might register nothing at all while it is moving!"

"Then you have been flying?" queried the magician intently.

"We have indeed!" replied the lad. "As fast as possible!"

"Gilin!" said the magician. "Why did you not heed the instructions I gave when I last talked to you? I told you to remain where you were! I suspected that otherwise something untoward was going to happen, as it apparently has!"

"No instructions like that came through!" said a bewildered Gilin. "Our communication ended abruptly, but I received no such message! We were so pleased to learn we were close to you that we decided to start northward, toward you, confident we would be able to locate you at any time through the calamar! But once we were airborne we received no response from the device! Thinking that we might be missing you, we stopped a while back! We must have nearly crossed paths at some point today!"

"My interpretation exactly!" said the disappointed Speckarin. "We must terminate this transmission quickly! Now, remain precisely where you are! It is too late for travel today, but at daybreak we will depart! I suspect you are correct about the calamar having to be stationary to give direction and distance! In fact, both devices might have to be so in order to function together in this capacity! That may be why mine did not work recently, even while I was on the ground! We will find you by stopping along the way to gain our bearings! We will make our way to you! I will end this message now! Stay where you are!"

With that, Speckarin placed the warm instrument upon the ground. Its opacity returned and the contact was broken. No interference, nor interruption, nor attack from anything that time! he told himself defiantly. Perhaps our luck is changing after all!

One more night apart was the only thought on the mind of every member of both parties as they attempted to rest. In the early morning Speckarin's group flew off to the north. They knew that concerted travel would be necessary in order to cover more than eleven hundred clan dominions in one day, but they were committed to doing so. At various points along the way they landed and checked their progress, closing in upon their friends with each successive leg of the journey. On their first stop they were eight hundred clan dominions away, and then five hundred, and three hundred, and one hundred. They maintained their pace and their diligence throughout the long day, gaining optimism every step of the way. Light of day was waning, however, when they were still forty clan dominions from their goal.

"We are now but three clan dominions to the southeast of them!" announced Speckarin triumphantly, staring into his calamar upon their most recent touchdown.

"We could walk that distance!" shouted Hut.

"Indeed we could!" said Speckarin. "But it will much be faster to fly!"

"I presume they will have some kind of signal for us!" said Diliani once they were in the air again. "Something for us to recognize from above!"

Just then a thin trail of smoke came into view ahead, rising from a fire, they surmised, still not visible from their vantage point. They approached its origin with great anticipation, and upon nearing it soared over a final ridge of maple trees and were immediately above a clearing. In the center was a fire tended by a kirin whom all but Runagar recognized immediately. Descending, they could see two ravens nearby, and as they sailed in for a landing the startled kirin leapt to his feet.

"Ruggum!" cried Speckarin as he jumped off Ocelam and ran to greet his old friend. Their right feet embraced. "You simply could not stay at home, could you? I am very happy, and all of us are deeply grateful, that you could not! You have taken good care of Gilin! But where is the youth?" he asked, glancing about apprehensively.

"I am here!" came a response from the vicinity of Talli, as Gilin touched the blond girl's foot with his own.

And Speckarin's heart sang. Finally, he realized with unbridled joy, they were reunited! All of his charges were safe! Until Talli had contacted Gilin three days earlier, he had never dared to dream this might happen!

And the reunion among this small conclave of kirins, all but one of them dislocated far from home, was a grand one indeed. First Runagar and his unusual ilon were introduced to Gilin and Ruggum Chamter. The two kirins eyed the giant bird with curiosity and admiration. Then they, who had themselves been out of touch for so long, mirthfully welcomed the Shillitoe youth and his crane into the traveling entourage of the Yorl and Moger clans.

Darkness was falling, and the fire was rejuvenated. During the day Gilin and Ruggum had found food, plentiful in this region of the land. They all sat down and ate, and as they did so they conversed and became acquainted with one another all over again. Even the ravens seemed gratified to be united once more with old friends, and although Loana and Alsinam at first gazed circumspectly and curiously upon Glinivar, the crane eventually appeared to be acceptable to them.

With the fire blazing brightly, the kirins sat in a circle around it. As if around the gathering fire at home, the ravens took positions beyond their masters to observe what was happening. The crane, which had never seen an assemblage such as this, remained well in the background, surveying the gathering.

It was Speckarin who first got to his feet. He used official salutations to greet his two compatriots who had been missing so long. Then he asked each individual to share with the others what they had done and seen, what they had been through since the traveling party was broken asunder. They did so one by one, standing in the fire's flickering light, relating what incredible things had happened along the way, what unimaginable experiences they had encountered.

Gilin and Ruggum were fascinated as Hut told of the bark, and the sap, and the elusive and enigmatic powers of the barwood tree, which had not only felled him but had revitalized the compromised Talli. They were spellbound as Diliani portrayed her period of exile in the black tunnels about the Shillitoe cave, told of her eventual rescue by the unique beings of the Grygla tribe, and discussed the peculiar and tragic history of that people. And they were stimulated by Runagar's description of the Shillitoe tribe, of its customs and use of magic, and of the vast and illuminated cave in which it dwells. Finally, they were moved at Talli's account of her journey to and from the forum of kirin ancestors, and the witnessing of both the demise and rekindling of her own aris.

Then Ruggum and Gilin stood together and chronicled what the rest considered the most astounding event of all: the unprecedented kinsmanship that had developed between them and human beings. Gilin began, however, with the rainstorm in which he had been lost, and Ruggum discussed why he had come along after all, and his ideas of his role in the mission. Then, to the amazement of the listeners, they depicted their first encounter with human beings, where a youthful girl appeared to see Gilin. They progressed to Loana's devastating assault in the air, and to the growth of their acquaintanceship with a human family. They ended, finally, with their harrowing escape from an unruly crowd.

Lastly, Speckarin came again to the fire to summarize his feelings about the kirins around him, about their uncommon bravery and fortitude, and their great faithfulness to one another. He spoke of how proud he was to shepherd this flock of kirins, of the thrills he had enjoyed at their successes, and the agony he had suffered over their difficulties. All of the others were profoundly touched. In the end he imparted his thoughts about the continuing quest. Now that they were a united team of seven, he expressed confidence and optimism that their perseverance would lead to success.

"If any of us were given a choice of being here or at home," concluded the old magician, "the decision would not be difficult to make. But we are here, and too far from family and clan to think about them comfortably. We have no such choice. We were all, in a sense, chosen for this mission. As we move forward we must act as best we can, considering all of the circumstances surrounding us. Problems and struggles will ensue as we progress toward our destiny. But we are better prepared for this task, and for confrontation with the enemy, than we ever were before. I cannot conceive of a group with whom I would rather be traveling toward this goal, nor one more likely to succeed, than that before me! I admire all of you," he said, looking into the eyes of each kirin one by one. "I salute you, every one!"

It was late before any of them thought about retiring. They lingered by the fire and conversed with one another well into the night. But finally the gathering of exhausted and grateful kirins began to disband, and each of them found a place to rest in the trees nearby. The ravens positioned themselves in the trees also, in boughs above their masters, to keep watch and to wait. Only Glinivar remained upon the ground, in her customary location, where she stood alertly and expectantly throughout the night.

This party of kirins was finally at rest, thankfully and confidently. For the first time in twenty-seven nights, they were together.

■ ■ ■

T hus ends the first chronicle of the struggle within the invisible world of kirins. The second volume, *KIRINS: The Flight of the Ain*, tells of the continuation of Speckarin's party through peril and adventure, and of their efforts to achieve the ultimate destination.

ABOUT THE AUTHOR

James D. Priest, M.D., is an orthopaedic surgeon practicing in Minneapolis. He majored in English at Carleton College and received a Doctor of Medicine degree from the University of Minnesota. He spent three years in Japan as a physician in the U.S. Army caring for casualties from Viet Nam, and four years in orthopaedic surgery at Stanford University. He has two sons of college age, David and Eric. He and his wife, Ilka, live by a lake in Shorewood, Minnesota.